MW00488200

DRAGONRIDER ACADEMY

SEASON

ONE

USA TODAY BESTSELLING AUTHOR
A.J. FLOWERS

BONUS PROLOGUE

Thank you for your purchase of the full first season of Dragonrider Academy!

As a thank you, please enjoy this exclusive prologue of an adventure between Vivi and Solstice before their true adventures began not available anywhere else...

*S*quealing, I pattered onto the beach, my toes squishing into the sand damp from the morning rain.

I didn't care that it had rained. I'd be in the water soon enough.

"Last one to the water is a rotten egg!" I shouted, my voice squeaky, even for a six-year-old.

Almost seven, if anybody was counting.

"Or a *corrupted* egg," my father added with a wry tone I didn't understand, earning a scolding from my mother for his choice of words.

The sun glimmered down through the clouds, the rays catching the wind and making me smile. I always imagined I could fly into them, rolling in the clouds and laughing with my best friend.

Although, I didn't have a best friend—yet! In my dreams, I had tons of friends, and if I was being honest, a dragon, too.

Because it was my dream, right?

I reached the shore and stomped in the sea foam, because I wasn't allowed to go down past the shallow part, while my parents tossed out one of those gigantic towels that my dad liked to wrap me up in after a day at the beach. I made a face when he leaned in and kissed my mother.

"Gross!" I shouted.

He winked at me and assured me I'd understand one day. Affection was nothing to be shy about.

When I blankly stared at him, he produced the cooler and I ran to them as he laughed, tugging at his swim shorts. "Daddy, can I have a popsicle?"

"Of course," he said, pulling out two. "Orange or strawberry?"

He always gave me two choices.

And I always took both.

"Pick one," my mother said with a stern look as I snatched them both up.

He did that gross thing with his mouth on hers again, but it distracted her long enough that I could tear them both open with my teeth.

I popped the two popsicles in my mouth and

grinned at her when she looked at me again, giving me a sigh.

When those were gone, I took in the waves while my parents talked about stuff I didn't care about. They liked to argue about my future, when that wasn't important right now. We were at the *beach.*

Even if they never let me actually swim, there were places on the beach where I could find the coolest seashells, and sometimes I'd spot illusions past the dunes when the sun hit the water just right.

"Can I go down to the dunes?" I asked my mother.

She gave my father a worried look, but he would have my back, I was sure of it. He liked my sense of adventure, as he put it.

"Is she old enough?" my mother wondered, the concern in her voice making me bristle.

Of course I was old enough! I could ride a bike, whistle, and blow a huge bubble of bubble gum. That meant I was practically an adult, right?

"Let her go," he said, his eyes soft with a sadness there I didn't understand. "She's going to have a rough future ahead of her, if your dreams are to be believed."

My heart twisted, but I didn't know why.

Her dreams?

Why would Mama's dreams say I was going to be unhappy?

Her eyes glimmered under the sun. I couldn't tell if it was a trick of the light... or if she was crying.

"You're right," she said, pulling something from her

pocket. "But only if you wear this, honey. It'll protect you."

I pattered over to her and my eyes went wide when she slipped a necklace over my head.

"It's not the real thing," she said, her fingers pinching the egg-shaped amulet. "You're not ready for that, but..." She leaned in and blew on the stone, making a tingling sensation slip through my body. She grinned at me and pinched my cheek. "I have a little magic, too, just like you, my sweet baby girl."

"*Mooom*," I whined. "I'm not a baby!"

My dad chuckled and kissed me on the crown of my head. "Of course you aren't, sweetie. Now go and play! Don't come back until you have an adventure to tell us about!"

Squealing, I pattered down the sands and spread my arms, catching the wind with my palms as I imagined soaring off into the air.

A golden glimmer of feathers joined me shortly after, my only friend in all the world.

"Race you!" I shouted at Solstice, the golden finch that seemed to appear when no one was around to see it.

Mama said I just had an active imagination, but I knew better. Solstice was *real* and I'd prove it to everyone someday how special we both were.

Solstice chirped, flinging through the air, flapping wildly to keep up speed as I screeched with joy.

The dunes crested the horizon and I dug my feet into the sands, launching up into the air.

The necklace on my chest hummed with my energy, and my feet lifted, making me fly just for a minute, soaring high enough to see the wild waves spanning out on the sunset side of the shore.

Maybe my imagination did go a little wild, I thought, but it felt so *real*.

At least I could enjoy it.

A distant glow caught my attention and I seemingly floated, watching it as dragons soared through it, screeching toward the skies.

Solstice keened back at them, as if she wanted to join their flight.

One day, she seemed to say.

One day... we will be one of them.

When I landed softly on the shore, I gasped for breath, my eyes scanning the horizon, but everything was gone.

My necklace had gone cold, the little glimmer of magic Mama had put into it already gone, and so did the necklace as it dissipated into ash through my fingers.

"Mama!" I screeched, ecstatic as I ran back the way I'd come.

"Mama! I saw them! I saw the dragons!"

I pounded across the sands, delight stretching a smile across my face as I found her staring at the sea.

Something was wrong.

My father waded into the waters, shouting my name.

My blood ran cold when he slipped under.

I ran after him, dunking under the water as Solstice chirped a final warning.

The dragons I'd seen before swarmed underneath the waves, and one of them had my father hostage.

"Daddy!" I screamed, going under... and under... before everything went dark.

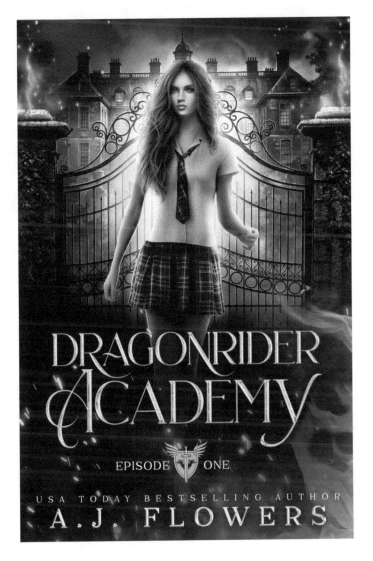

DRAGONRIDER ACADEMY

EPISODE ONE

USA TODAY BESTSELLING AUTHOR

A.J. FLOWERS

THE INVITATION

Nine Years Later...

Curled up in my favorite dark corner of the library, I chewed on the end of a Slim Jim like it was a cigar. My routine of getting lost in my favorite fantasy novels was interrupted by Oakland High's hottest track star staring me down.

I blinked up at Max Green, wondering what on Earth he was doing in the library in the first place. "I didn't know you could read," I said, spitting out the first defensive comment that came to mind.

Instead of showing he was offended, he offered me a charming grin usually reserved for the sleazy cheerleaders as he leaned against one of the heavy shelves. He ran his fingers over the book spines, making my eyes drop to the slow, deliberate movement.

"I thought I might find you here," he said, as if I

hadn't just been incredibly rude—but it was called for. All the Resorties—the sons and daughters of all the rich families who owned the Lake Resort down the street— rarely were nice to me and it was best if I lashed out first.

Plus, his dad was my mom's boss and lately had been a total jerkwad.

"Your dad shouldn't send his son to do his dirty work," I said, showing him that I knew all about why he was here. "My mom said that she'll have his documents next week, okay? She's only a few days late and it's not even her fault."

My mom had been so super stressed about the whole thing. As an accountant to the infamously over-priced Silver Lake Resort, she got to enjoy far too much responsibility with unrealistic deadlines.

Max chuckled again, his striking blue eyes threatening to make my defenses weaken. "Relax, will ya? I don't care about my dad's tax returns. I'm here to invite you to my party." He slipped his backpack off his shoulder and pulled out a paper with cartoon waves and tacky letters in graffiti font that said:

Bust out a wave! Bonfire tonight - Silver Lake Resort Crash Party, delinquents only!

I took the paper and turned it sideways as I examined it. "Delinquents only?"

Max rubbed the back of his neck, the motion showing off his toned arms, evidence of how much swimming he did at the lake. "Yeah, Henry thought the invitations would be funny. He's no graphic artist, but I promised him he could make whatever he wanted." He shrugged, casting his striking blue gaze down so that I could breathe again. "I just thought you might like to come."

"Why?" I asked, skeptical that *Max Green* actually wanted me, the lonely "odd bird" who had no friends, to show up to his cool-kids party.

Never mind the fact that I had a massive crush on him ever since elementary school, but that was a secret that I'd take to my grave.

He surprised me by kneeling. It was the first time any of the Resorties had gotten on my level, figuratively or literally. He picked up one of the books and began to thumb through it. I bit the inside of my cheek, because he'd picked up a dragon-rider novel which was probably totally nerdy to him. I loved reading about any story with dragons, especially the ones where humans and dragons became close friends. It just seemed... natural. I always understood animals better than I did anyone at school, so I found it much more relatable.

"It's an apology, I guess," he said, not commenting on the book as he set it down. "I overheard my dad on the phone with your mom."

I flinched. Yeah, that had been pretty rough. A couple of days ago the IRS had been on the resort's case about some tax inquiry that didn't sound good. They wanted to pin it all on my mom and she was putting up one heck of a fight, but she wouldn't tell me the details. "I don't know if it's such a good idea," I admitted. "Your dad will be mad if he finds out I was at the resort snooping around." The last thing I wanted to do was to cost Mom her job, and as my stomach sank, I wondered if that was Max's plan.

Although, out of everyone at school Max had always been decent to me. I wouldn't say he went out of his way to be nice, but we had an understanding.

"It'll be on the beach, so it's not even technically on resort property," Max said as that charming smile came back again. "That area is public, no matter how hard my father's tried to buy it from the city, they haven't given it up yet. Just think about it, okay?" He got up and gave me a wink that made my insides do backflips. "See you at lunch."

I stared at him as he walked off, waiting until he turned a corner before I let out a breath. Seriously, see you at lunch? I hadn't eaten lunch with another human being in probably, well... ever.

"See you at lunch," I mimicked, copying his sultry tones that made my body and mind go to war. I knew that I should never get involved with any of the Resorties, but the butterflies in my stomach hadn't gotten the memo.

Deciding to put it out of my mind for now, I shoved the invitation into my backpack and gently placed my books into neat piles. I didn't expect this section of the library to be disturbed and it would be just like I found it when I came back again. The librarian, Miss Jenny, liked to call the fantasy section my own personal "nest" because of how I liked to surround myself with books.

I waved goodbye to the elderly woman on my way out. As usual she had her gray curls pinned back into a messy bun that frayed with her wiry hair. She didn't hold back on her smile, crinkling her face into further wrinkles as she waved me off and told me to behave for my teachers and not read too much. After all, I'd already read most of the books in the library three times over—the ones of interest, anyway.

The bustle of students surrounded me as I made my way to class, and I often felt like an invisible visitor inside my own body. No one seemed to notice me, some of the bulkier guys slamming into me if I didn't dodge out of the way in time. The girls only sneered if I got too close, like I had some kind of lethal infection I wasn't aware of that would be passed on by touch.

Today, though, none of it bothered me.

Max Green had invited me to his party and even if that should have sent up a hundred red flags, I didn't care. The invitation was solid proof in my backpack and when I sat down at my desk in my second class of the day, I found myself slipping it out just to feel it between my fingers.

This was real. And even as petty or ridiculous as it might be, even if there were some other reason he'd invited me, it was proof that someone in this school knew I existed, and for once, it felt good.

"Miss Reid," the teacher scolded, making me shoot my gaze up to find the entire class staring at me.

"Y-yes, Mrs. Jhones?"

She narrowed her eyes to my hands underneath my desk. "No phones in class, please, or I'll have to confiscate it."

I realized that I'd been holding onto the invitation in my bag and it probably looked like I was texting. I nodded and shoved my backpack under my chair as Mrs. Jhones resumed her lesson on a math equation I'd solved in my head over twenty minutes ago.

This was precisely why I didn't have any friends at this school. Academics came easily to me, and I much preferred reading or working out problems in my head—which looked like daydreaming to other people —than listening to a teacher drone on about things I already knew. My mother had tried to move me ahead in my classes, but it was my father who had expressed concerns about my social development in that regard. Ever since his death, I think both my mom and I tried to warp our lives to match his wishes as much as possible, but I knew this wasn't the life he would have envisioned for me. He'd seen how hard it was for me to develop friendships even before I could remember. It wasn't my grade level that was the problem.

It was me.

When the bell rang, I hurried to my next class. Not because it was far away, but because the jungle of Oakland High's halls was a place I was more likely to get trampled than anything else. It was better to hide in the library or get to my next desk where I could pull out a book and get in a few extra minutes of reading before class started again.

As I dodged one of the giants on the football team who would squash me like an ant, I couldn't help but wonder what my dad would think about Max's party invitation.

He would want me to go.

He would say it didn't matter the reasoning or even if the invitation had a secondary agenda, this was a party with real people my age in an environment that took out the very thing that made me different.

There were no test scores on a beach, or teachers who subtly influenced on a student's social standing. This would be a place where I could blend in a little bit better, have some fun, or...

Or, I could use it as an opportunity to see what my mom's employer was really up to.

It was a good thing that I could ace my classes with my eyes closed, because I couldn't focus on anything for the rest of the day. Would there be a way I could get into the resort? What would I even be looking for? Maybe my dad's old office had something useful. I remembered where it was because I'd never forget the way my mom described it.

"An office that could overlook the ocean for miles."

I doubted there were many offices that fit that description. I could get in, get out, and no one would be the wiser.

Because to everyone else, I was just invisible, right?

I didn't even try to hurry to lunch this time to get in

line before everyone else. I waited my turn, spotting Max taking a tray outside with his friends.

I liked to eat outside, too, and I shifted my backpack as I took my tray of sloppy pizza and chocolate pudding out to my usual spot. The yard included benches that the students squeezed onto like sardines, which was why I preferred a giant oak tree out by the campus border.

I settled down onto the ground in the shade and watched the other students talk and laugh. The interactions always fascinated me in how the other girls obsessed over each other's outfits, and the guys made stupid jokes I never found that funny.

A small chirp got my attention just as I'd taken the first bite of my pizza. I set it down and wiped the grease from my hand. "Hey, Solstice, what're you doing here?"

The tiny yellow finch flapped his wings and perched on my extended finger, flicking his head left and right as he looked up at me with intelligent eyes.

I knew animals were smarter than people gave them credit for. It was kind of like babies. Just because something can't talk doesn't make it stupid.

People often made that mistake about me, too.

The little bird had been my one and only friend ever since I could remember, which I realized was odd. According to the research I'd found, finches only lived four to seven years, twelve max, and being sixteen-years-old myself, I couldn't remember a time when the little fluff-ball wasn't in my life. That made him at least thirteen-years-old. My mom was convinced that Solstice was really one of many of the little finches that loved to call Oakland their home, but I usually only saw the wild birds out in spring. Solstice stayed with me all year, even in winter.

He chirped at me again, as if saying that he just wanted to say hi.

I carefully scratched the top of his head with my pinky as I smiled. Maybe I didn't know how to get along with my own kind, but it didn't matter when I had friends like Solstice.

The sound of someone clearing their throat got my attention and I looked up to see Julie Emmerson staring down at me. She crossed her arms, pushing up her cleavage with the motion. "So, I hear Max invited you to the party. You're not going to show up, are you? It's just a gimmick to see if you'll really go." She leaned in and lowered her voice. "We all know your dad died out there and you're terrified of the water."

"Excuse me?" I snapped, rage filtering my vision red as Solstice flew off, leaving me to fend for myself.

Didn't blame the bird. I would fly from Julie Emmerson too if I could.

She narrowed her overly shadowed eyes that positively dripped with eyeliner. "What's with the bird? Are you Snow White, or something?" She smirked. "You couldn't be. Your feet are way too big." She kicked the bottom of my boot.

"That's Cinderella," I replied. At least the dimwit could get her fairytales straight.

She frowned. "Look. I like you. You know your place and keep out of everyone else's business. You don't belong here and at least you know it, but if you show up tonight, that's way out of line, so don't even think about it."

Know my place?

I stood up and gave her my best death glare. She flinched, clearly not expecting me to literally stand up for myself. "Listen," I snapped. "I know my family isn't rich and I was allowed to attend this school out of courtesy to my father, but it doesn't change anything. The scholarship that *your* families opened up in my father's name says that if I can keep my grades up, I can attend Oakland High." And by *keep my grades up*, they meant I had to keep a perfect 4.0 GPA, which I knew none of them expected me to be able to do. "That has nothing to do with my 'place,' so go back to your hyena friends whose favorite topics are your waist sizes and leave me alone. I didn't ask you to come bother me."

She stared at me, mouth agape, as a group within earshot openly stared.

"Daaaaaang," one of the girls whispered, only to have one of her friends elbow her hard in the ribs.

Julie scoffed and leaned in. "Listen, *odd bird,* I won't have anyone of your class talking to me like that. This is your final warning. You show up tonight? You're *dead.*" She turned on her heel and kicked up my food tray on her way, ignoring me as my pizza and chocolate pudding went flying into the grass.

The entire yard lit up with excitement over the "cat-fight," including Max Green who watched with those intense blue eyes that dared me to defy those "better than me."

Well hold onto your jockstrap, Max Green, because this girl is about to show what happens when an odd bird decides to fly.

A WARNING

The rest of my school day dragged on and I was more than ready to jump on my bike and ride home. I didn't care that it was almost ninety degrees during a sweltering Michigan summer. The dry breeze as I pedaled as fast as I could made it feel like I could just push a little harder and soar right on into the sky and leave everything behind.

Turning onto my street reminded me just how different life would have been if my dad were still alive. As Vice President of Silver Lake Resort, my childhood had been one of lavish events, all the stuffed animals I could want for my tea parties, as well as a house big enough to hold at least four of the shack my mom and I lived in now.

Although now, I had come to realize that I didn't care about any of it. As I pedaled past the dwindling mansions that led to the single blue-collar neighborhood in Oakland for all of the resort's employees, I knew that none of that really mattered. Not the events, not the luxuries, and certainly not the snobbish people who only cared about the numbers in their bank account.

All I wanted was to see my dad again—a wish that would never be granted.

None of these brats knew how lucky they were. None of them had lost their father to the lake, drowned trying to save me when I'd gotten caught in an undertow.

My mom said that it was a blessing that I was too young to remember. Nobody needed to relive something like that and she often showed me pictures of my dad holding me as a baby just to remind me how much I've always been loved.

I knew that, but it didn't change that it still felt like my life was in limbo waiting for something that would never happen.

It was time to change that. I made up my mind to stop being afraid, to stop being isolated as I rolled into my driveway.

Parking my bike against the rusty garage, I didn't bother locking it because the neighborhood kids wouldn't want to steal a bike that could barely keep its chain on. The Resorties had much better rides they often left outside and were too lazy to report if one or two went missing.

Still, I patted my trusty steed goodbye before heading on inside.

"Hey Mom," I said, immediately taking note that she

was in the exact same position that I'd left her in this morning. She hunched over her desk that doubled as our dining table, surrounded by papers strewn about. She gave me an absent wave that showed off ink blots all over her fingers.

"Hey, Vivi," she said without looking up. "Have a nice day?"

"Mhmm," I murmured as I went to the fridge and began pulling out the groceries I'd bought yesterday. I placed chicken and some vegetables onto the counter before I dipped under the sink to scoop out a cup of rice. If I didn't cook dinner, my mom would go without eating for days, and I couldn't live on Slim Jims forever.

I whistled an old tune while I worked, chopping up the chicken and throwing it in a bowl to mix with some spices.

My mother finally looked up from her work and narrowed her eyes with suspicion. "You sound happy. Something go on at school today?"

My whimsical mood cut short as I realized I had no idea how I was going to tell my mom about the party. She wasn't like other moms. She wouldn't care about it, and she'd probably be happy for me.

But the lake?

That would be a big fat "no."

"Uh, yeah, actually," I said, folding the chicken over on itself with the spices. "I was invited to a party and I was thinking about going, if that's okay."

Her eyebrows shot up. "A party?"

"Yeah," I said, trying to keep my voice steady. I

turned on the burner and coated the pan with coconut oil—my key secret ingredient. "It's across town," I lied.

She thumbed her pen, popping the cap on and off. Telling her about the party was a risk if she knew there would be a bonfire next to the Resort, which if she ever went into the office she would likely be aware of. One glance at our kitchen table with papers strewn about and yesterday's coffee mug assured me she hadn't left the house for days, which was no surprise, given she preferred to work from home. She didn't like to go into the office, given Silver Lake Resort was so close to where we lost my father.

"Well what are you doing cooking me dinner, then?" she asked, making my shoulders relax as she smiled. She brushed her hands on her pants and joined me, taking the spatula out of my hand. "Go on. Pick out something to wear and take your time for once. I'll finish up here."

The party wasn't for another couple of hours, but I liked the quirky smile on my mom's face. I pinched her cheek. "That looks good on you," I said.

She smirked. "What? You mean two-day-old makeup?"

"A smile," I remarked on a laugh. After the daily crap life dealt us, smiling was something too far and few between around here.

She turned over my chicken even though it hadn't cooked enough yet, but I didn't comment on it. "Well, seeing my little girl happy puts a smile on my face." She grinned. "Will there be boys there? What am I saying, of course there will be. Do you have your eye on any of them?"

"Mom!" I gasped. "I so do not want to talk about this with you."

She sucked in a breath as if she was twenty years younger and we were two besties talking it up. "There *is* a boy!"

I waved her off as I turned to escape upstairs. "I'm not talking about this with y-ou!" I reiterated in a singsong voice.

Her laughter followed me up the stairs as I ran into my room, but I had a smile on my face. I closed the door and leaned against it, taking a deep breath to steady myself. Maybe I was really blowing this all out of proportion and he just wanted to see me. Even if giving me attention was just to make his ex jealous, I didn't care. I would enjoy it no matter how long it lasted, because I wanted to indulge in this new life where I didn't have to hide in my invisible bubble anymore. A life where Max Green invited me to a party and wanted to talk with me, laugh with me, maybe even kiss me.

My cheeks turned red and I covered my face. I didn't want to become some lovesick teenager, and maybe Max had an ulterior agenda and I shouldn't be getting so worked up about it in the first place.

A gentle peck at the window brought me out of my hormone-induced dilemma. I scampered to the end of the room and popped open the glass, letting the humid breeze come in, along with a flittering golden-speckled finch that chittered at me in greeting.

"Hey, Solstice," I said, not able to get the goofy grin off my face. "Are you going to help me pick out something to wear?"

He landed on the raised end of my bedpost and quirked his head at me, looking at me with his beady black eyes.

I frowned. "Don't look so judgmental. It's just a party."

I didn't know if birds could have preferences when it came to people, but Solstice seemed like he didn't like Max. He chirped again when I opened the closet in a low, disapproving pitch.

Ignoring his protests, I rummaged through my clothes and wondered what on Earth I was going to wear. I ran my fingers over the same wardrobe I'd had for the last couple of years, since I'd finally stopped really growing. I didn't care what I wore. Who did I have to impress?

Tossing out items onto the bed, I started to feel deflated until I came across a cute tank with sequins that my mom had bought me for my birthday. I didn't know where she thought I'd wear it. Maybe she had hoped this day would come where I'd finally take the leap into the socialized world.

Pulling it out, I drew in a deep breath and held it up to my chest. "What do you think?" I asked Solstice, only to find him perched on my dresser glaring at me.

Solstice bounced on the edge, chittering at me with

warning.

"Come on, Solstice," I complained, propping one hand on my hip. "What's your problem?"

He chirped again, and this time it sounded exactly like *Stay*.

"I'm not staying," I enforced, tossing my shirt onto the bed over the pile of clothes before stalking up to the tiny creature. "I'm going to this party, okay? And if you're not going to be supportive then you can just flutter right on out of here." I pointed at the window. "What's it going to be?"

Solstice bounced a few times, chittered his discontent, and then flew out of the window, crushing my spirits as the room seemed to darken without his presence.

Trying to ignore the sting of rejection, I snatched open the dresser and rummaged for one of my good bras. I found one with the tag still on and I snipped off the overpriced number with my teeth. My mom was definitely not like other moms.

"He's just a bird," I grumbled to myself, but even I knew that wasn't entirely true. Solstice had been with me all my life, at least what I could remember of it. I liked to pretend that my father had sent him to me, a well-meaning spirit to watch over me since he couldn't be here anymore.

If Solstice didn't want me to go to the place where my father died, perhaps that was a warning I should have listened to.

But I didn't.

PARTY ON THE BEACH

*W*ind rushed around my ears and swept my hair from my face as I sped down the dark streets on my bike.

Today, I didn't care I didn't have an expensive ride, because I was on my way to a party that Max Green himself had invited me to. Nobody could say I wasn't welcome, because this was his party, near his father's place, and even if I wasn't naive enough to think he didn't have a secondary agenda, I was going to enjoy myself—and indulge in a secondary agenda of my own. Because if I found myself in my dad's old office at the resort by the end of the night and uncovered secrets the resort was trying to hide, oopsie, my mistake.

Streetlights glimmered around a sharp curve of the road where I normally turned back. The scent of lake-front fresh air gave the breeze a welcoming component and I found myself indulging in a rare smile of my own as I increased my speed.

Going far too fast to stop, there was nothing I could do but brace myself when I heard a wild revving of a Corvette that was only growing in my side mirror. I'd recognize that engine anywhere. It didn't matter that I had reflectors and lights strapped all over my bike and my body. All my safeguards managed to do were to give Julie a target.

I glanced over my shoulder just in time to see the convertible swerving toward me, but not to hit me. Julie and her friends cackled, their laughter swept away on the wind, as a massive wall of black mud shot up into the air.

Crap.

I swerved and nearly lost my balance as the wave hit, drenching me with cold, wet grime as the corvette screeched off, Julie waving and blowing me a kiss on her way to the lake.

Managing to stop my bike, I shuddered in a breath and tossed my bike down. I flung my fingers and splattered mud to my feet. I looked down to see that my sequin top was impossibly ruined and mud quickly matted in my hair.

Tears threatened to come, but I pushed them down with ruthless determination.

"You aren't winning this one today," I vowed, and ripped off my shirt and my ruined shorts.

I'd worn a bathing suit underneath my outfit and it clung to my curves, luckily not touched by the grime, and instead glimmering with moisture that added a pleasant shine.

What to do about my hair, though, I wondered. I turned my shirt inside out and scrubbed my head as best I could, then tugged up the loose strands into a messy ponytail as I pulled over a hair-tie I kept permanently wrapped around my wrist.

Yanking up my side mirror from my bike, I appraised my appearance, tucking away a few more loose strands of hair.

Satisfied, I wrangled my bike and began walking, my rage too raw to be able to trust myself on any sort of vehicle right now.

The rest of the fifteen-minute walk gave me enough time to cool down and I stowed my bike in the trees before I stepped out onto the beach.

I spotted Julie in the distance pawing at Max, although he didn't seem very interested. He nursed a beer as he leaned against a table. The roaring flames reflected pleasant gold and copper tones across the sharp angles of his face and I found myself mesmerized as I took my time with my approach.

He must have felt me studying him, because he glanced my way, then did a double-take.

I noticed that everyone else was fully clothed. I'd entirely forgotten that it would get chilly today, even though we were in summer the coast could sometimes get cold bursts. Although being the freak that I was, I never got cold, no matter what. It was a problem, really, and my mom constantly had to remind me to wear a jacket so I didn't get sick—even though I couldn't remember a time I was sick, either.

Yeah, a whole bunch of things were wrong with me, which made it clear why I didn't get along very well with other people. I was too much of a freak and normally, I was invisible to them as I roamed through crowds without anyone noticing me.

Tonight, I definitely didn't have that problem. I locked my knees to keep from allowing them to buckle when so many eyes landed on me at once. There I was, practically naked in front of half of my school bundled up in sweaters and scarves.

"Now it's a party!" one of Max's dude buddies shouted, whooping as he ripped off his shirt. "I need to catch up to where she is! Bring on the beers and let's get this party started!"

The crowd cheered and Julie glared so hard I thought she might just melt a hole in my chest.

Max grabbed one of the red party cups and filled it from a keg. He marched over to me and handed me the drink. "Well, you sure know how to make an entrance."

My mouth bobbed open on a silent sound, something in-between "thanks" and "oh my God I'm going to die of humiliation."

Luckily, Max couldn't decipher my meaning and chuckled as he wrapped an arm around my shoulders. He surveyed the crowd who had started chugging beers and taking off articles of clothing. "I knew you'd liven up the party. I was bummed a cold front was coming through tonight."

"Yeah," I managed to chuckle against my dry throat. "Weather can be unpredictable out on the lake." I glanced out at the dark waters on reflex, my heart skipping a beat as I thought of my father.

"You going to drink that?" Max asked, cutting into my thoughts. He bumped my drink with his. "It'll loosen you up."

I gave him a raised brow. "How can you tell I'm not, uh, loose?"

He chuckled and lowered so that his lips brushed my ear, making goosebumps shoot across my skin. "You might have everyone here fooled, but I know you're about to bolt. Take the edge off, Viv, and relax. This is a party, after all."

I gave him a nervous chuckle as I considered the drink again. It probably wouldn't affect me, given how weirdly I reacted—or rather, didn't react—to things. So I took a long gulp to satisfy him before I gave the dark silhouette of Silver Lake Resort a glance. If I got everybody drunk, then maybe I could slip away undetected, since clearly I was not invisible tonight.

"That's my girl," he said then whooped to his friends before knocking back his drink. "Turn up the music!"

The party ramped up from there, music pumping and everybody having fun. Of course Julie and her friends continued to stalk me and glare holes in the back of my head. Max didn't take his arm off me the entire time, keeping me pinned to his side, and it felt kind of nice to be wrapped in a jock sweater for the night.

"What's this, a tattoo?" he asked, running his fingers over the white swirl on my left shoulder.

I could almost feel Julie seething as he touched me, but I kind of liked it. "It's nothing," I said on a nervous laugh as I buried my face in my drink again.

"It's strange for a tattoo," he continued as if he hadn't heard me, still running his fingers over the elaborate swirls. "I don't think I've ever seen a white tattoo before, not with ink, but it's too intricate to be a birthmark."

"There are so white tattoos," I said, the lie my mother had taught me rolling right off my tongue. It was actually a birthmark, but who would believe that? "They just require more aftercare."

He hummed thoughtfully, his fingers tracing the mark again. "Well, it's beautiful." He smiled, leaning in to press a light kiss against my hairline. "Just like you."

I held my breath and was almost grateful when Max's friends interrupted us and started swapping stories. And by swapping stories, I mean I sipped my latest drink while the guys talked about how awesome they all were and who was the fastest track runner.

Julie must have seen the kiss, though, because she stalked up to us a few minutes later.

"So you're a slut now?" Julie snapped as she crossed her arms, plumping up her breasts to show off her cleavage. She had taken off her sweater and now had jeans and her bra as a top, but the pebbles across her skin betrayed that she had to be freezing.

"Exluse... uh, I mean, excuse me? You're one to talk," I said, surprised by the slur in my voice. Well, maybe alcohol did affect me a little bit.

She smirked at my clear inebriation. "Maybe I should tell your daddy that you're underage drinking," she said, then covered her mouth. "Oh, that's right, I can't. He's dead."

Every muscle in my body went stiff as I resisted the urge to punch her in the face. A few more beers in and I just might have let go of my control.

"Julie," Max said with a warning tone. "That's enough."

She tapped her chin. "Didn't he drown, oh I don't know, right over there?"

My vision went red and somebody screamed. I didn't realize it was me until I had dived onto Julie and clawed my fingers into her hair as I slammed her head against the ground.

Luckily we were on a beach and the sand wasn't too packed in this area, or I might have actually hurt her, but in the moment, I didn't care if I hurt her or not, I just wanted her to stop.

Strong arms ripped me off of the girl as I snarled, turning wild. It was something I hadn't had to deal with in a long time. As a child, I would go into my "primal fits" as my mom called them, a sort of steroid-level temper tantrum when I felt out of control. It only happened when I felt justice needed to be served, or that I'd been deeply wronged. At least, that's how I had tried to explain it to her, but she'd just said I was a horrible child to raise and she didn't know how she would have done it without my father to keep me in line.

Now, there was nobody to keep me in line, which was one of the many reasons it was best I stayed away from people in general. I bit down on a hand that strayed too close to my mouth, only to hear a male growl as I was dragged away.

"You don't have to bite," one of Max's buddies complained as he shook his hand.

Max chuckled as he steered me away from the fire and toward the water. "I told you not to grab her like that." He rested a light touch on my shoulder, making me flinch. "Hey, you okay? I'm sorry about her. She's just mad I won't take her back after I caught her cheating on me... and she can get nasty when she's told no."

I gulped in fresh air, regaining my senses as I looked back to see Julie being restrained by her friends. She shook them off and seethed at me as sand-matted hair hung about her face, but she didn't move to follow us.

I turned on Max. "Is that why you invited me? You wanted to use me to make her jealous?"

"It's not like that," Max insisted.

"Yeah, he could have used any of Julie's friends if he just wanted to make her jealous," the tallest of his buddies said with a wry smile. "The cheerleaders are all over you, man."

His buddies chuckled and it bothered me that they were still walking with us down to the coastline. Silver Lake Resort was one of the few landmarks next to the coveted public beaches that dotted Silver Lake. They were part natural phenomenon and part man-made, with trucks full of fresh sand brought in every year to replenish the coastlines.

My toes dug into the sand as we reached the water, leaving behind glimmering residue in my footprints. The real sand from Silver Lake had natural minerals that glimmered and was part of the tourist attraction around here.

Max's buddies waded into the water, their larger footprints leaving behind more of the shimmering grains. Max rarely went anywhere without half of the track team to worship his every move. The tall one was Henry, and the twins with wild blonde hair and gorgeous blue eyes were Michael and Kevin, although I wasn't ever able to tell which one was which.

"Then why *did* you invite me?" I insisted. "Henry's right. You could have used any of those girls."

"But none of them would have pissed her off like you can," he said, his voice low.

I glanced at him, sensing truth in his words, but he was still hiding something. "I see." I balled up my fists and turned to leave. "Well, thanks but no thanks. I'll be leaving now."

He grabbed my wrist, making me freeze. "Viv, look, I'm sorry. I do like you, okay? Let's just... let's just go for a swim and cool off, yeah?"

I glanced back at his buddies splashing in the water as they tackled each other, having a good time. I knew the water was probably cold, or at least it would feel cold to them, and a part of me longed to slip into the dark satin lake and never come out.

Despite losing my father here, I loved the water. I always had.

"Only if you make me a promise," I shot back, looking him directly in his striking blue eyes.

"Anything you want," he said with a smile as he loosened his grip.

"I want to see my dad's old office."

He went still as darkness swept over his face. He schooled his features a moment later, making me wonder if I'd imagined it. "Yeah, I could arrange that. Just take a swim with me."

He let go of me and offered his hand, giving me the choice to take it.

Going against my better judgment, I slipped my fingers into his.

That was the biggest mistake of my life.

GOING FOR A SWIM

*S*uppressing a shiver, I slipped into the cool embrace of the waters and tried to enjoy the moment. It felt good to be back, even though I couldn't really remember the last time I'd been fully immersed in the lake. A small part of me rang a warning bell in my head, reminding me that Max couldn't be trusted, and even if I was pretending that everything was okay, I had suffered a great trauma here, one that Julie had just ruthlessly reminded me of.

I don't know if it was the alcohol, or just my own fatigue with myself, but I pushed all of those feelings aside and twined my fingers through Max's, going deeper and deeper into the waters until I couldn't touch the bottom anymore. I let him slip his hands around my waist and hold me close as we lingered behind his buddies who were now seeing who could swim out the farthest.

"Do you think that's safe?" I asked, noting that it

was hard to keep aloft in the water, but Max could still touch the bottom so I wrapped my legs around his waist and held on.

He took my movements to mean something else, apparently, because his fingers ran up my lower back as he hovered his lips over mine. "They can get themselves killed, for all I care. You have me rethinking all of my plans right now."

"Plans?" I whispered as he drew in nearer, his lips threatening to close the distance between us.

"Hey!" one of the twins shouted. "No kissing the enemy!"

Max chuckled and secured me against him, his hand running low across the curve of my bottom. "You let her wrap her legs around you and you'll change your mind too, Kevin."

"Change your mind about what?" I asked, lucidity coming back to me as the cold waves splashed in my face. I tried to untangle myself from the track star who had brought me into some sort of hormone-induced lull, but his hard grip wouldn't let me go anywhere.

"You're going to tell us what your mom has on the resort," Kevin's twin snapped, his blue eyes rivaling Max's with their brilliance.

I froze. "What?"

He released a long sigh. "You're such a downer, you know that, Michael?"

Henry waded over and grabbed me on the arm, threatening to rip me off of the track star but fear made me dig my ankles in.

Max chuckled. "See? She has the hots for me, and hey, if I had realized what kind of body she had under those layers, I would have tapped her sooner." He grabbed me hard and pulled me in close, slamming his mouth over mine as I attempted a scream.

No. This wasn't right. This couldn't be right. Every alarm bell in my head went off all at once and my heart pounded in my chest.

I managed to shove Max off of me and I kicked hard, launching away from him and into the water.

The one problem with having avoided the lake all my life meant I was a poor swimmer. I immediately went under and water closed over my ears, engulfing me in an aquatic roar of sound that blocked out my ability to form a single thought. Instead, my panicked senses rolled over me all at once.

Is Max going to hurt me?

They want information on my mother?

What's this all about?

Am I going to drown?

The last fear struck a chord and I began to kick, but strong arms hauled me out of the water. I coughed and sputtered and tried to call for help, but I was dunked again.

Just when my lungs started to burn, I was pulled up and met Max face-to-face. Gone was the whimsical guy who seemed to have an understanding with me and kept his distance. Alcohol and my stupid signals had turned him into an evil creature with no kindness left in his glassy blue eyes that had somehow turned dark with the night.

"You don't want me? Fine. I'm not going to force myself on you, but you *are* going to tell me what your mother has on the resort. She's trying to pin ten years in prison on my dad and I'm not going to tolerate this sort of attack on my family all for a pathetic jab at revenge."

"I don't know what you're talking about," I seethed, only to be dunked underwater again. When Max pulled me back up, black spots sprinkled my vision.

"Hey, Max, I think she's had enough," Kevin said.

"No," Max growled, throttling me by the throat. "If we don't get what we need out of her, my family is ruined, and I didn't work this hard just to watch my whole future be destroyed."

I saw the fear in his dark eyes and I realized what he meant. If his father went to prison, his family's business would pass on to someone else and the disgrace would force him to leave Oakland High. He'd lose everything. His friends, his standing, and his scholarship for when he graduated.

"I told you I don't know anything," I snarled, not having the energy or patience for this.

"Then why did you want me to take you to your dad's old office, hmm?" he growled as he pulled me in close. He hand shot under the water and secured me by my hip, making me freeze as he dug his fingers into my flesh. "You aren't wearing much, so you were trying to distract me from your real goal, was that it? Well, maybe Julie was right and you want to play the slut now." He slipped his fingers through my bikini strap. "Let's see if she's right."

Cold fear ripped through me when I realized that Max had just crossed a line, one that would have a terrible end I didn't even want to imagine.

I screamed and clawed at his face, making him cry out when I caught his eye. He roared and dove over me, plunging me underwater.

Kicking, I managed to get away from him and I went in the only direction I could go.

Down.

IT DIDN'T OCCUR to me that diving into the lake's depths might be a bad idea, but all I could think about was getting away from Max and his friends, the latter who were just standing by watching the whole thing unfold. Kevin had looked like he wanted to stop him, but he didn't, and the other two? Well, they looked like they were on board with whatever Max had planned and were hoping for seconds.

Gross.

I wasn't a bone to be chewed on and discarded, and I decided in that moment that I would rather die than be treated that way.

I kept swimming, going deeper and deeper until my lungs started to burn and a little voice inside my head started to panic.

What am I doing? Am I really going to drown just to get away from a creep?

I couldn't face the reality of what was happening. Max had murder in his eyes, among other things, and whatever was wrong with him he was going to take it out on me. I had to get away, somehow.

I looked up to see if I could return to the surface, although I wasn't sure how far out I had really swum. It all looked black, though, and I started to feel disoriented about which way was up. I went still, despite my burning lungs that gave me the urge to suck in a breath even if that breath would fill my lungs up with water. My body floated as I tried to regain my sense of direction, but it didn't work.

Choosing a direction at random, I spread my arms and propelled myself and a part of me worried I was only going deeper.

This was it. My mother was going to get the news when my body washed ashore that I'd died just like my father. Lost in the dark depths of Silver Lake with those gritty little pieces of sand sparkling in my hair.

A white light flashed, startling me, and I jerked when a woman in fluttering robes approached through the water. The current swept her long, gorgeous hair from her face and an elegant sword hung loosely at her hip, glimmering from beneath her clothes as she moved through the water as if propelled by an invisible force.

Her eyes had a pleading look to them as she offered me her hand. The motion felt reminiscent of Max offering me his hand to step into the water, and I'd given him a measure of trust I never should have.

But this time, I was dying and I had nothing to lose, so I took the woman's hand and closed my eyes as I gave in to the urge to breathe.

CHAPTER 5

WELCOME TO
DRAGONRIDER ACADEMY

I sputtered and spat out sand, wincing as pain lanced through my temple. I coddled my head and squinted at my surroundings while I tried to figure out where I was. The sun blazed down and the air brought in a pleasant humid breeze that suggested it was early morning.

Had I passed out? What happened?

I blinked the water from my eyes and a blurry world came into focus. The beach didn't look at all like I remembered it. No bonfire. No resort. No forest at the edge leading into a road that would take me home.

The sands spanned out as far as my eyes could see and the horizon wavered as if the world might catch on fire.

Struggling to my feet, I tugged at my wet, matted hair while I spun in a small circle. Waves lapped up on the shore, but a flash of my tongue over my lips told me I'd just emerged from saltwater.

Somehow... I wasn't at Silver Lake anymore.

Rubbing my head, I tried to think if the lake somehow spilled out into the ocean, but that didn't make sense. Michigan's lakes were pretty self-contained, minus some levies that controlled ships in and out of the major inlets.

Another option sprang to mind.

I could be... dead.

The uninviting span of endless sand did little to convince me that this was Heaven, although it felt hot enough to be Hell.

Walking, I ignored the burn across my feet as the last events I could remember spilled over in my mind. Max had tried to... no, couldn't go there. I was getting away from him, and that's when I got lost underwater. There'd been a woman, which could be an angel to take my spirit on or just my vivid hallucinations that came when I gave in to the urge to breathe.

I took in a deep lungful of air to test out my body. Spreading my fingers over my chest, I met my damp bathing suit that I still wore. The warm breeze washed over my skin like velvet. My nostrils flared as I sensed distant embers, burning wood, and the humid weight of an ocean with salt and sunlight drifting off of it.

If I was really dead, then why did I feel so alive?

The answer to my question came as a hard wall straight against my face. I ran into it, grunting as I spilled onto the ground and grabbed my head. I'd been looking down at my feet, not expecting to run into anything out on this endless desert by the shore.

Looking up, I matched gazes with a male who owned the most striking whitewashed eyes. Perhaps they'd once been blue, but the sun had bleached them long ago, along with his hair that brushed over his face in soft tufts that invited me to just run my fingers through them.

"There you are," he chided, a velvety sensual voice came from this creature and invaded my body, making a shiver work its way up my spine as I struggled to remember how to breathe. "I've been looking for you all morning. I'm late for class, you know." He shot his arm down and wrapped strong fingers around my wrist, pulling me up to lean against the hard wall of muscle that I'd just run into a moment before.

"Huh?" I asked, the long breath of sound the only response I could offer right now.

Maybe I was dead, or delusional. Either was a distinct possibility right now. Maybe I was passed out on the shore somewhere, baking in the sun after I'd washed up from the night's events. I was lucky to be alive, if that was the case, and I had probably worried my mother sick. I shook my head and pinched my arm, trying to get myself to wake up.

A strange squeak caught my attention, making me look up again only to spot a lizard-like creature poking its head through the male's hair. What I had thought was a strange collar was actually a small animal that had itself wrapped around his neck, its tail drifting down his chest while it poked its snout through his hair just under the male's ear, as if attempting to get a better look at me.

"What… is that?" I asked, stumbling back a step.

Before I could fall again, the male grabbed me and yanked against something on his wrist. I looked down to see the impossible, a vivid blue line of… what was that? A cord? But how was it coming from his skin? Brilliant, elaborate tattoos that were patterned over his muscular forearms began to glow and the cord came out of his wrist, growing brighter as he tugged at it and wrapped it around mine. A cold snap of energy jolted my spine straight and a sense of restraint made my knees lock.

"You'll get all your questions answered at orientation," he explained casually as if he hadn't just performed actual magic in front of me, all while a strange creature hung around his neck. The beautiful male glanced at me, taking in my shock to which he offered a smile in return. It wasn't a kind smile, or even a patient one. Just a grin with a mischievous edge that said this wasn't going to end well for me. "I can't have you running off, not after I've finally found you. Getting you here in the first place took a lot of favors, and you're going to get me enough extra credit that I can coast right on to graduation." He tested the magical cord that bound us together, one end wrapping securely around my wrist while the other disappeared under the layer of tattoos still glowing on his left arm. "That should hold for a little while."

I pulled against the restraint as instinct came over me with the urge to run. When I couldn't break free, my vision wavered and adrenaline shot through my body, but I forced down the panic and went over the options in my mind.

No need to complicate this. Ignore the magic. Ignore the snake thing with legs on the hot guy's neck. You have been restrained against your will and you want to go home. Vocalize your demands and gauge your attacker's response before making the next step.

The thought process was a gift from my mother. She seemed overly paranoid when it came to strangers, but I didn't blame her based on the articles I read online. Far too many weirdos would pull something like this, and maybe the fantastical side of what I was seeing was just a response to nearly drowning. Hallucinations could be due to a lack of oxygen.

At least, that's what I told myself.

"You're going to release me right now," I demanded, refocusing on my mission as I snapped my gaze up at my oppressor while I worked my jaw into a determined edge. "If this is some sort of sick joke, it's not funny. I'm going to sue you so fast your children's children are going to be owing my family money."

He burst out laughing—which was not the reaction I was going for. "Oh, gorgeous, this is no joke, and while I am flattered you're already talking about children, let's take it one step at a time, shall we?" He waved to the expanse behind him and the air shimmered until a massive series of gothic towers came into view. My stomach dropped when I spotted more of the serpent things winding lazy circles around the spires.

The word came to me now, a word that I had only seen repeated in my favorite fantasy novels that I read in my corner of the library back at Oakland High.

Dragons.

"You are at Dragonrider Academy, and I am your mentor and partner." He grinned when I blinked at him, again with that cocky smile that said he knew how ridiculous he sounded yet he was going to go on with it anyway. "What you see behind me is the campus, as well as some of your fellow students and their wyverns, or dragons, if you prefer, although the breed of dragons we bond with are technically wyverns." He tapped his chin, sending the blue cord between us to go taut as my arm yanked up with him. "I guess Wyvernrider Academy just didn't have the same ring to it, you know? 'Dragon' sounds so much cooler." The creature wrapped around his neck gave another screech. This time the male patted his head and then ran his finger along the ridge between the creature's nostrils and eyes. "You're right, Topaz. I haven't introduced myself yet." I flinched when he knelt down to meet me at eye-level. "My name is Killian." He tapped my nose as if I was just another pet for him to play with. "And you're Vivienne, right?"

"Vivi," I corrected him, then frowned. "How do you know my name?"

He chuckled as he casually wrapped an arm around my neck and forced me toward the campus. "I know a lot about you, Vivienne. I know that you're from the goddess tribe of lost enchantresses of Avalon." He tapped the birthmark at my shoulder and I winced as if he'd touched a bruise. "It's probably reacting to the realm shift you just went through. How are you feeling? Nauseous? Hungry?"

I felt both of those things, but I wasn't going to voice them to this jerkwad. "I'm fine," I snapped. "I just want to go home."

It was getting harder to tell myself that all of this was a massive hallucination and that I was still asleep on the beach. The sun blared down and the sounds of distant dragons rumbled through the air. Killian's warm arm around my shoulder felt very real, as did the magical cord that still linked us together and strapped around my wrist, cutting off the blood flow every time I tried to pull against him.

And yet, even though every fiber of my being told me that I should be terrified, another part of me was listening. Contemplating.

Accepting.

If this was real, then it explained so much about me. Why I couldn't make friends. Possibly what had really happened to my father.

Why I was such a freak.

"Who was the woman under the water?" I asked softly, granting the male at my side this brief moment of compliance as I worked to match his longer gait. It was only so that he would feel comfortable enough to exchange information, and then I'd work on my next objective—to get out of here.

"You don't know your own relatives?" he teased. His hand casually toyed with a curl of my hair, but the motion felt friendly, natural. He'd said that we were partners and even though I'd just met him, even though he'd restrained me against my will, there was definitely this strange sense of belonging I had with him that I'd never experienced with anyone else. A part of me wanted to trust him, wanted to lean on him for support and let him explain this strange new world to me.

Luckily, that insane part of my brain was small enough to tie up into a neat little package to be shoved aside.

"You're a descendant of a race of women who have goddess blood. Not much, mind you," he said, tapping me on the nose again. "But enough to travel realms. Enough to be recruited to Dragonrider Academy by yours truly," he grinned as if he'd just done me a great service. "You'll like it here. I promise."

Was he for real right now? Even if I could wrap my mind around everything he was telling me, he was suggesting that I leave my human life behind and pursue... what, exactly? "Why am I here?" I asked, determined to find the true answer to my question. "What is... *here*? What is a dragonrider?" I flinched away, forcing him to stop. "And why would anyone want *me*?" Goddess blood or not, I wasn't a prize. I was the girl in the library who escaped to places like this in my imaginative mind, but I'd always been able to leave.

He leveled his gaze on me with those whitewashed eyes that threatened to drown me all over again. "I know it's a lot to take in, Viv, but you're just going to have to have a little faith here. You're needed. Dragonriders protect the realms from evil." He leaned in closer. "Like the evil that took your father. Do you really think he just randomly drowned? No. The Lady of the Lake isn't the only thing in those waters. There are creatures that want you dead, Viv, and the best way to defend yourself, to defend the people you love, to keep everything the way it is supposed to be, is to become a defender of life. Dragonriders do that, Viv. We protect people. We keep people safe." He glanced back the way we'd come, his gaze turning wistful as the wyvern around his neck ruffled small wings and settled closer into the groove of Killian's collarbone. "And we avenge those we've lost."

Huh, maybe there was more to this guy than I'd realized.

"That's nice and all, but I need to get home, *Killian,*" I said, using his name for emphasis. He wanted to pretend that we already knew each other, that we were going to be fast friends and I'd just go with this craziness like I wasn't about to have a psychotic break. "My mom is going to think I drowned. I need to get back and—"

"She knows exactly where you are," he clarified. He tugged out a piece of paper from his uniform shirt's pocket. I hadn't noticed before, but he wore one of those school uniforms like he belonged in some Ivy

League school, except he kept the upper two buttons undone to complement his rebellious look. He handed me the slip of paper and waited for me to unfold it.

I blinked a few times at my mother's handwriting.

My dearest daughter,

If you're reading this, then you've been recruited to Dragonrider Academy and I've officially failed to protect you like your father and I wanted. I know it seems crazy, but this is a part of your heritage that we tried to shield you from. I'm writing this letter as I am pregnant with you, while the Dean herself waits for me to finish. She's going to make sure this letter gets to you if you're recruited—which is a day I hope never comes.

Your father didn't want children, because he knew this would be a possibility. I'm not entirely human, Vivienne, and neither are you. We come from an ancient line of women that go by many names. Human history and fiction books refer to them as Druids, Seers, Enchantresses, Witches, and many other names that attempt to describe what mortals can't understand. You and I have the blood of the goddess in our veins. With that comes the potential to move between realms, among other things. It makes you uniquely qualified to be recruited by those who protect the realms, an unseen force that keeps so many lives safe.

I'm grateful. Your father was a dragonrider and rescued me at the cost of his dragon's life. I escaped Avalon as a child and we will never go near the water again, no matter what happens, no matter if I am called back, I will ignore it. I'll be honest with you because I have to tell myself that you'll never read this letter.

If I'm being honest, and you are reading this letter, then I will say I know you are capable of anything. I feel your strength as you kick inside my stomach and I can't wait to meet you, to name you and to spend my life making yours better.

Be strong, my daughter, and know that you've been brought to a powerful place where you'll be tested over and over again—but you will survive, this I promise you.

And I will make sure you will never be alone, because my heart is with you.

Love, Mom.

My entire body trembled by the time I finished reading. My mother had said those exact words to me as part of the lyrics to a little bedtime song.

You will never be alone, because my heart is with you.

No matter what, I will find you. I will cross oceans and worlds to be by your side again.

You will never be alone.

She'd sung that to me because she knew I might one day read this letter and I would need to know that she would come for me.

My knees buckled as the realization of everything came over me all at once and I found myself caught in Killian's arms. He held me with ease and his wyvern shifted open one eye to check out the disturbance. A brilliantly blue iris with a sliced lizard-like pupil examined me for a moment before it closed again.

"It's a lot to take in, I know," Killian said, his low velvety voice calm and soothing. "But you're here now, so let's get you on campus and to orientation and… oh."

He looked down at my lack of attire and chuckled. "Well, to the dorms first, then. You're going to give half of the student body a nosebleed dressed like that. What part of Earth do you come from, anyway? I seriously need to visit this culture where the dress code is so... sparse."

Shivering, I wrapped my arms around myself and took a deliberate step away from the warm male who made my insides do backflips. I'd nearly forgotten I was only wearing my bathing suit and how inappropriate that might be in this situation. "Yeah, clothes sound like a good idea," I admitted.

I wasn't getting back home like this. Even with a wistful look back at the retreating ocean, I knew that I couldn't go the same way I'd come. Somehow, I'd traveled to a different realm, an entirely different world where dragons were real and so was the danger that had killed my father.

He hadn't drowned from being trapped by an undercurrent.

He'd been murdered.

A cold chill swept through me as I rewrote all of my memories. Even if my father hadn't wanted children, he'd loved me fiercely. I couldn't remember much, but I knew that without a doubt. Something had brought me and my mother to the water when I was a child and he'd died to protect us—to protect me.

I turned back to face the impossible scene spanning out before me like a painting. The dragons I'd spotted earlier were larger now, and one in particular had broken off from the winding herd until I noticed the elegant rider atop its back.

My heart pounded in my chest when the emerald dragon began its descent. Large, glimmering scales swept over its entire body and made it sparkle like it held green fire in its belly. Smoke drifted from its nostrils, suggesting that the illusion wasn't an illusion at all and I was in serious danger of being burned alive.

Killian didn't seem too concerned, though, and casually draped his arm around my hips, bringing me in closer to him. The only hint that he'd tensed was how he briefly dug his fingers into my skin before relaxing them again.

The dragon landed and the ground jolted underneath my feet, making me want to scream or run or do anything other than stare at this creature from my position of weakness. Killian stood his ground and forced me to remain still, so I followed his lead. He'd expressed that I was of some value to him, so I held to that fact to keep me safe—for now. He wouldn't let anything happen to me or he wouldn't get what he wanted.

A female rider jumped from the dragon's back, sauntering over to us as she glowered. She wore a feminine version of Killian's uniform, except an emerald pin glistened at her left shoulder where he had a bronze one.

She turned her glare on me as she propped her hands on her hips, taking a moment for her gaze to dip where she noted Killian's hand on me. "So, you finally found yourself a recruit," she said with a sneer. "Where did you drag this one in from? One of the fae worlds? She looks so small." She leaned in closer and her nostrils flared. "She smells like one, too. Like sunlight and stench. You really think she's going to last two days here?"

"She's human," Killian said as he ran his hand up and over my shoulder as he covered my birthmark. I glanced up at him, wondering why he'd lie. My mother's words came back to me.

I'm not entirely human, Vivienne, and neither are you.

The female's eyes went wide, revealing striking emerald irises that rivaled her dragon's colors. The beast folded its legs under it, thundering the ground again as it settled into a comfortable position. By the way it lazily narrowed its eyes and ticked back its ears, the beast thought it was going to be here a while.

"Human?" the female shrieked. "Are you insane?"

"It's not your call, Jasmine," Killian said, his tone flat. He sounded different when he spoke to someone else, as if his voice lost that sensual bite it had to it when directed at me. Maybe he wanted to mesmerize me, somehow, or control me through compulsion. If humans weren't customary here, it meant he wasn't human either, and I immediately started searching for clues to figure out what race he might be.

What was fiction? What was real? Could he be a vampire? I leaned in to get a look at his teeth while he talked. They looked perfect to me, so not that. Unless he was like the vampires in the books where the fangs could pop out like switchblades. Or maybe he didn't have fangs at all.

Or maybe he was a shifter of some kind. He had that dreamy look to him that would make all the cheerleaders at my school go bonkers.

My thoughts were interrupted when Jasmine started shouting again, this time while she grabbed me and yanked me out of his embrace. "You need to send her back, you moron. Are you trying to open up a rogue tunnel by bringing her here? Earth is a hotspot with wild dragons gaining territory every day. What kind of damage is her presence doing right now? Did you even think about that?" She jostled me again as she glared, looking into my eyes. I wasn't sure what she saw there, but she didn't like it. She faced Killian again as she shook me. "Are you just lonely? Is that it? You're tired of me rejecting you, so you think you're going to make me jealous with this little twig of a female?"

Killian snapped his fingers and a jolt of energy traveled through the cord that bound us, making Jasmine shriek and jerk away as she released me. Her dragon shot its head up and its nostrils flared while a strange rumbling sound built in its belly.

"Tell Emerald to chill out," he said, his words stern but gentle. "If she burns up the new recruit, you're going to be on tunnel duty for eternity."

Jasmine ground her teeth while she glared. My stomach dropped and I finally found my voice enough to protest. "What the heck is wrong with you people?" I shrieked, yanking against the magical bind between myself and my captor. Killian didn't budge. "You're talking about me as if I'm not even here." Maybe I was used to that back at my high school, but this place was supposed to be different.

I definitely wasn't the only freak here.

"It doesn't matter because Killian is going to send you back and reset your memory," Jasmine insisted, taking out a dagger from a leather strap at her side. I stiffened, but didn't move as she swiped down, severing the magical bond. Killian allowed it as he watched the exchange. "If you're smart, you'll run right back in that ocean and go back home," Jasmine said, pointing at the distant waves.

"She's not going home," Killian insisted, his intoxicating gaze falling back to me as his voice changed again, growing sultry and kind. "Because you want to be here, don't you?"

He wanted me to make my decision. He'd given me my mother's letter, even knowing what it said.

But he said that he knew me, which meant he knew that I had nothing waiting for me back home. No friends other than a stray bird. No real family other than my mother—and if I had read her signals correctly, she'd come find me eventually.

What I had if I stayed was a real chance at figuring out what happened to my father... and maybe finding out more about myself and what was wrong with me before my mother arrived and got me out of here.

And maybe, what I'd find what I'd been missing all along. I'd find meaning for my life, hope, and purpose.

I looked back to the campus with the drifting dragons, the magical shimmer in the air and the sense of wonder that felt like I'd falling head-first into one of my favorite fantasy novels.

"I'm staying," I said with finality.

Because whatever craziness I'd gotten myself into, running wasn't the answer. I'd been running all my life.

It was time to take a stand.

Jasmine's jaw flexed while she considered her response. "Well, then, I guess we're going to have to do this the hard way." She offered her hand for me to shake. "Welcome to Dragonrider Academy."

When I went to take her hand, she retracted it and tapped her dagger, causing it to shimmer as it extended into a long elegant weapon. She crouched into a fighting position and raised the blade.

"I hope you brought a sword, because I challenge you to a duel."

"Jasmine," Killian complained as he rolled his eyes.

"No, you said she's not leaving, so we're going to play by Academy rules. I challenge her to a duel."

He frowned. "Then I volunteer to fight on her behalf."

"No," I snapped, making them both to turn and look at me. "Nobody fights my battles," I said, and I crouched and curled my fingers into fists.

I probably looked ridiculous as I bent my skinny legs and faced off with a legitimate female knight in my bathing suit, but I still had my pride.

Sort of.

Killian smirked, seeming pleased as he took his dagger from his belt and pelted it into the sand. "Very well, recruit. Let's see what you've got."

I took up the blade and shrieked as Jasmine launched in to attack, her massive dragon lazily watching the exchange as it rested its maw on its legs.

What had I gotten myself into now?

CHAPTER 6

A DUEL

I'd never fought a day in my life, but I'd read plenty of fight scenes in my favorite fantasy novels and that counted for something.

And coming here... it had changed something in me.

Adrenaline made my heart thunder in my chest as I dove out of the way and blindly swiped with my blade, but my movement felt guided by an external force that thrummed through my veins. I knew I wasn't going to hit my target that way, but that guiding instinct told me this was how I'd get her off guard. I regrouped as I did a somersault roll to get in closer to the female. Daggers were short-range weapons, but the last thing I needed was to be out of her reach where she could use her superior skill to jump in and hit me with a well-aimed strike that I wasn't trained for.

I needed to make the first move.

Jasmine kept her eye on the blade, just as the strange guiding force had predicted, all while I moved in close. I didn't need to stab her. I just needed to make a point, and I had a feeling that this was my first test, one of many at Dragonrider Academy. I needed to prove that I wasn't going to be scared off by the first challenge that came along.

As predicted, she blocked my blade with hers, keeping it a safe distance from her vital organs.

That was exactly what the energy inside of me wanted and a small surge of warm approval spread throughout my body.

The world went still for a moment as a gentle hum filtered through my ears and the mark on my shoulder grew hot. I'd traveled worlds, and perhaps that was a trigger for the goddess lineage in my blood to come out.

Whatever the cause, I was able to work my fingers into a solid fist and I crouched, putting all my weight into my legs as I launched my punch upward, catching her chin while she kept her focus on my blade.

She grunted as her head snapped back and she fell to the ground in an undignified heap as time resumed its regular pace. Her dragon shot up and flared its wings, but Killian hissed at it, making the creature shrink back.

Huh, so Killian had some authority over another rider's dragon; that was good to know.

Both of our daggers had fallen to the ground and Killian bent down to pick them up. "Well, I think that was the shortest duel I've ever seen in my life." He grinned at me, the wicked gleam in his eyes irritating me, because I had pleased him—and I liked that I had pleased him. A part of me already sought his approval as my mentor and my partner at Dragonrider Academy. Something unspoken sealed between us in that moment as he gathered both daggers into one hand so that his fingers could brush mine, leaving an unspoken message that this was the first of many moments to come where I would be tested and he would be by my side to witness my victory.

"You lose, Jas," he said smugly, "which means you owe Vivienne here servitude for the rest of the day." He put away his dagger and then handed Jasmine hers. "I'm going to guide her to the dorm and you can wait outside like a good little girl and show her around while I attend to my errands, sound good?"

She groaned as she adjusted her jaw, a click sounding as if she had to snap it back in place.

How hard had I hit her?

She stumbled to her feet and brushed the sand off of her uniform. "Yes, fine," she growled, not looking me in the eye this time as she turned and mounted her dragon again. "Meet you there."

Her dragon spread its wings and she sailed off into the distance like a flying emerald gem that glittered with retribution. She glanced back just once. She should have been too far away for me to read her expression, but something in my eyes burned for just a moment as my vision shifted and brought her face into focus. I spotted a glimmer of a smile that said I'd impressed her before she turned around and crouched into her dragon as they flew higher.

I had a feeling that I'd made my first enemy—and maybe my first friend.

CHAPTER 7

FIRST DAY OF SCHOOL

*T*opaz—Killian's dragon—swept off his neck the moment we entered the dorm room. He flapped his thin, translucent wings that were still developing until he reached a rounded nest next to Killian's bed. He squawked at me, then snapped his jaw at Killian.

"Yeah, yeah," my mentor said as he popped open a fridge and brought out some chilled slices of raw meat. He tossed one at the wyvern who caught it in midair, throwing it back to gulp it down his gullet like I'd seen birds do. "There's your snack," Killian said, his tone stern, "now take a nap before you get cranky on me and chew up my pillow again."

The wyvern chirped at him before turning in a circle and wrapping his long tail over his nose to cover his eyes. Soon the creature drew in deep, steady breaths and Killian draped a blanket over him.

He winked at me when he caught me staring, making me blush. "They're kind of like birds. They like to be covered up when they sleep."

"Mmhmm," I said, trying to keep the human part of me from totally freaking out right now. It was odd, as if I had two versions of myself that took all of this in with completely different reactions. One side of me felt like I had come home, that this was an inevitable conclusion to my life that I was meant to endure all along.

I guessed that was the goddess part of me, and that blew my mind.

I have goddess blood... what does that even mean?

"Are you feeling okay?" Killian asked, his touch gentle as he reached out and ran his fingers up my arm. He roamed the birthmark on my shoulder, sending tingling jolts of electricity to surge through my body. "Your mark is reacting pretty strongly. It could be disorienting."

He was right. I wavered on my feet and clutched my arms around my chest, feeling suddenly cold. Killian reacted instantly, taking off his uniform blazer to wrap around my body.

His warmth and scent overwhelmed me, making me feel even dizzier than a moment before and I backed up to the secondary bed to sit down. I pulled the fabric around me anyway, feeling desperate for something to hold onto.

"It's the rider bond sealing into place," he explained as he sat next to me and draped his arm protectively around my shoulders. He leaned in and rested his forehead against me, closing his eyes as he drew in a long breath through his nose. "I feel it too," he said, his voice lowering as if we shared a deep secret.

"What does that mean?" I asked, the human part of me feeling terrified, overwhelmed, and panicked. This was all too much, too fast, and the rational part of me said that all of this was impossible.

But when Killian drew away from me and tucked my hair behind my ear, I knew this was real. I felt something that tugged me toward him, that made me want to get to know him, to trust him, and to listen to him.

The human part of me? Yeah, she wasn't having it.

He leaned in and brushed his lips across my cheek, making the battle surging in my chest explode.

I shoved him, my mind reeling back to the memory of Max forcing himself on me. "Get off me!" I screamed.

The wyvern under his nest flinched, poking his tail out to pull up the blanket a moment to look at me. Killian waved him away, so the beast snorted and draped the cloth over himself again, falling quickly back to sleep.

"Sorry," Killian said, giving me space as he leaned away. "I thought you felt it too. The rider bond is a romantic one and you called me to you, but I forget your situation is unique." He stood up and turned from me, the muscles along his back shimmering with the blueish-white tattoo that I'd seen before on his arms. Without his coat, he just wore a simple white t-shirt—

which he pulled off as he walked away and my jaw dropped open.

Scars lined his back where the tattoos disappeared, making me wonder who exactly it was I was dealing with.

"What do you mean… romantic?" I asked, stunned by that revelation. "Is this some kind of arranged marriage thing or something?" Everything about this place was a bit medieval, so maybe I had inadvertently found myself betrothed to this guy.

I mean, he wasn't hard on the eyes, that was for sure, but if he thought I would be his dragonrider bride when we barely knew each other, he didn't know me very well—which was exactly my point. How could a relationship work on a foundation like this?

He opened up his closet and rummaged through his clothes, pulling out a chainmail shirt. He glanced back at me and I blushed, realizing I'd been staring at him this entire time. He smirked. "You need me to define what romance is to you?" he asked, his smirk growing. "It would be much easier to demonstrate."

My face enflamed until I was sure that I'd turned beet red. "No. No demonstration is needed," I insisted as I tugged his coat around me, making sure none of my skin between my knees and my neck would be on display. "I just mean… why did you try to kiss me?"

"Because we're bound together," he said matter-of-factly as he approached me again. I tried not to stare at the incredible hard lines of his body and I desperately wished he'd put his shirt on so my brain would unscramble, but I had a feeling he was doing this on purpose. He knelt and offered me his hand. He waited until I took it before he spoke again, all the while brushing his fingers over mine to give me the warmth my cold body craved. "Dragons require parents—two of them, to be exact. Male and female. Both offer different benefits to the dragon and I've been raising Topaz on my own for nearly a year. He's been getting sick." He glanced back at the nest before looking back to me. "I've been waiting for you, but I couldn't risk it any longer. I received help from the Lady of the Lake and put events into motion to bring you here—a place you belonged already."

"It's your fault I'm here?" I said, my voice rising in pitch as I yanked my fingers away from his. That irritating cold seeped into my body without his contact, but his coat seemed to provide enough warmth to keep me from shivering. It was an odd feeling, because I'd never gotten cold before, not even on a snow day.

"Yes," he admitted, his eyes almost as translucent as his wyvern's wings keeping his gaze locked on me. "And if you wish to break the bond, my wyvern will die and yours will never hatch, but I will never force you to do something you do not want to do." He leaned back and twisted his shirt over his head, giving me some reprieve from his otherworldly beauty. "Our relationship doesn't have to be physical to be close. We'll get to know each other, for now, and we can exchange energies that our wyverns need by simply holding hands."

"What kind of energies?" I asked, even though my body already recognized what he was talking about. A strange force surged through me every time we touched and I craved to put my hand on his again. I curled my fingers into fists, digging my nails into my palm to resist the urge. "Never mind that," I whispered, realizing he'd referred to us *both* having wyverns. "I get a dragon, too?"

He grinned, that familiar mischievous glee in his eyes making my stomach do backflips. "Yes, if you seal the rider bond with me, I will take you to orientation where you will meet your dragon."

I swallowed the lump in my throat. The human part of my mind tried to rationalize what was going on— and the choice I had to make. If this was a dream, what was the harm in playing along?

And if this was real... hadn't I always imagined riding a dragon of my own? Hadn't I wished that my fantasy novels were real and I could live a life of adventure and magic? I wouldn't have to live as the invisible wallflower at my school anymore. I could discover the truth about my father. Whatever evil had done this was still out there... and a sinking sense of dread in my gut said it was going to hurt a whole lot more if I turned away and did nothing.

There was really no choice at all. I couldn't leave. I couldn't give this up.

"What do I have to do?" I asked, my voice trembling.

His smirk turned into an all-out grin. "You have to kiss me."

"You're making that up!" I shrieked.

He laughed and threw up his hands. "I'm not, Viv, I'm really not." He crossed his arms and leaned against the wall with an expectant look on his face. "You're going to have to come to me." He flashed his teeth with a wicked grin. "I promise I don't bite." He gave me a wink. "At least not this time."

I rolled my eyes and shot to my feet, determined to make this as chaste as possible. "Fine, I can do that." I marched over to him and looked up, realizing that this would prove difficult with my arms wrapped around myself with his blazer. I frowned.

He chuckled. "Giving up? I can take you home, if that's what you really want." He joked when he said that, but I caught the flash of desperation in his voice and the panic that crossed his beautiful eyes. He wasn't lying. I had to do this of my own free will or else his wyvern would die.

I opened my fingers before I had a chance to think twice about my decision. His coat fell from my shoulders in a puddle around my feet and his eyebrows shot up. I was still only wearing my bathing suit and my dried hair curled around my face. I ran my fingers up his arms and he uncrossed them for me as I moved in closer. I had to lean against him and stand on my tiptoes to reach him. I had intended the kiss to be quick, but the second my lips met his, everything changed.

Heat and fire shot through me and I found my arms wrapping around his neck as I sucked in a breath through my nose. Embers and an ocean breeze invaded my senses as I leaned against him, the chainmail cold against my skin but his breath scalding on my face. He deepened the kiss and I reveled in it, feeling a connection between us surging to new heights as the room boiled and threatened to catch fire.

When I finally managed to pull away to catch my breath, he smiled, his eyes now filled with golden energy that I had exchanged with him.

"Welcome to Dragonrider Academy," he said before he pulled me into a kiss again.

DRAGONRIDER ACADEMY

EPISODE TWO

USA TODAY BESTSELLING AUTHOR

A.J. FLOWERS

A KISS TO REMEMBER

*T*he kiss told me more about Killian than a lifetime of experience ever could.

In that instant, I knew that this was real, that I belonged here, and that Killian was my mate.

It felt as if I grew wings and I soared to new heights with Killian at my side. He'd lived a hard life, but he wasn't much older than me at just eighteen. He grew up knowing what he was, that he would one day attend Dragonrider Academy and would be tied to the rider bond with a female he barely knew. His race was the most common one from which knights and dragonriders were chosen. They were called Nephilim, a hybrid between human and angel which made them the perfect protectors. They were strong, nearly immortal, and had enough humanity to be compatible with the rider bond.

Being what he was, though, he didn't have a lifetime among the humans he was meant to protect. He envied that of me, that I had gotten to feel normal, but just like I explored his mind he explored mine. He understood that "normal" wasn't how my life had been at all. I'd in fact been lonely, confused, and distant and it would have been better if I could have grown up with my own kind.

My race was all but dying out, however, the women of Avalon. I saw the mystical city through his memories of the stories of what it had once been. It was an island covered in fog filled with beautiful women who wore crystalline headdresses and spoke prophecies given by the goddess. Knights protected Avalon—but they had failed a hundred years ago. Wild dragons had destroyed it and the image in my mind changed the beautiful city growing dark as it flooded with water, all light and fires snuffing out as the crashing waves overtook the city filled with screams. It kept going, the dragons swarming in the distance until there was only muted silence underwater.

Those who escaped fled to other realms, and my ancestor was the only one who went to Earth.

A tear sizzled down my cheek as the thoughts and memories flashed through my mind, all the while I was still locked in a debilitating kiss with the beautiful Nephilim and dragonrider named Killian.

Still, I sensed something he tried to hide from me. Instinct made me seek it out as I searched through his mind. We were bonded, now, and there would be no secrets between us.

I found it and a jolt of cold washed over me. What

surprised me was that this was my own secret. I had indeed called Killian, although I hadn't been aware of it. He'd been met with a golden finch throughout his life, a spirit of wellbeing that he thought had been from Heaven. It had guided him to the Academy and promised him the perfect mate, one who would make him stronger and wiser and help his dragon thrive.

That had all been a lie. I had too much humanity in me. I needed him to help me bring my father's murderer to justice, but that's all I had ever cared about. I couldn't keep his wyvern alive. I probably couldn't even bring mine into the world. But if I bonded to Killian, I would inherit his power as a Nephilim and it would be enough for me to discover who had killed my father and to do something about it.

I'd never cared about saving the world. I'd never thought what it would do to Killian or his wyvern to use him like that. I'd only been a distraught girl who'd lost everything and wanted to make it right.

When I had created the golden finch I'd named Solstice, it had taken all my memories of that intent with it. Any innate knowledge that I'd had about my destiny had vanished because it took all of my strength to create that spirit that would fool Killian into doing exactly what I wanted.

I'd won.

And now he knew.

Now we both knew.

Killian jerked away from the kiss, shocking me when rage crossed his features. He grabbed my shoulders hard and pushed me away, making me stumble back to the bed as he shook his head, seemingly trying to clear it of some vile thought I'd put in there.

He snapped his fingers and ordered his wyvern to stay as he hurried to the doorway and didn't look back.

"Killian," I said, my voice trembling now from the shock of losing his warmth. "You know I was just a child when I did that…"

He thrust up one hand to silence me and I bit my lip. His body stiffened as if he was restraining himself from turning and strangling me. Finally, he relaxed his hand to his side.

"I have to go," he said, his once velvety sensual voice turned hard as stone. "Jasmine will be here to collect you soon. Don't go anywhere and don't touch anything." He shoved through the exit and slammed the door behind him.

I rushed to follow him, but heard a latch click and his heavy footsteps marched away. "Killian?" I shouted as I hit the door. It didn't budge against my efforts. I fiddled with the handle, but it had been locked into place. "Killian!"

I looked back to the nest as my chest heaved, my lungs sucking in air like I was drowning. My skin burned from the energies we'd exchanged and I ran my fingers over my birthmark, finding it scalding hot, sending waves of power through my body enough that made me dizzy.

What had I done?

The wyvern was still sleeping through all of the excitement and I lifted the blanket to check on it.

Its once translucent wings were now a brilliant gold. It opened one eye to regard me, chirped in welcome, and then closed his eye again to go back to sleep.

To my relief, the bond didn't seem to harm it. If anything, it had grown stronger.

I draped the blanket over him again and blinked a few times as guilty tears threatened to flow. I went to the window and spotted a multitude of students on the campus grounds, all of them spanning out like a broken wave as Killian stormed through them.

Golden waves of energy emanated from his footsteps and I had a feeling that whatever the consequences of this bond... I was going to pay the price for them very soon.

Welcome to Dragonrider Academy indeed.

SERVITUDE

J stared up at the ceiling as I slumped onto Killian's bed, completely stunned by the revelations we'd both witnessed.

I'd done this to myself?

How had I even known that Dragonrider Academy had existed?

A small part of my soul must have always known. It was the goddess blood in my veins doing its best to protect me... but this wasn't what I wanted. This was a mistake and I wanted to just curl up in a ball and let this whole nightmare pass over me until I woke up.

Pulling the bedsheets over my head, I enveloped myself in Killian's scent. We were bonded now and my heart ached to be apart from him, not to be able to learn more about him and why we were meant to be together... why I had called him to me in the first place.

There was so much more to this. I could feel it

underneath the surface. So many secrets just waiting to be resolved.

I'd been so alone all my life. Just me, my mom, and Solstice, when in all reality I'd had a whole line of strong and powerful women behind me.

Something about that made me feel better. Unfortunately, I had a feeling none of my ancestors were going to help me out right now. My only ally at Dragonrider Academy was furious with me, and I didn't blame him. If something had manipulated me like that, I would have been out for blood. I could only hope that there was more to this, that our bond was real and he could grow to understand... to forgive me.

More so... that I could forgive myself.

A soft snore brought me out of my self-pity. I pulled down the sheet to peek at Topaz, Killian's wyvern. The breathing didn't sound quite right. Whatever boon from the initial wave of power was gone, and now he struggled again. I wished more than anything that I could help the poor creature regain his strength, but therein was the true problem, the reason I didn't deserve Killian's consideration or forgiveness.

I was too human. Useless on my own.

My heart twisted, boring a hole in my chest as I realized I'd let Killian and his wyvern down.

The one thing that he couldn't deny is that there had been an almost otherworldly connection between us the moment our hands had touched. I might be more human than goddess, but there was a magical part of me that responded to Killian—and if I could connect with that, maybe I could fix the mess I'd made.

The door slammed open and I squeaked. A female stood in the entryway and curled her lip back on a sneer.

"Oh. Hi, Jasmine," I said, trying to quell the tremor in my voice. Sure, she was epically terrifying, but whatever punishment she had ready for me, I deserved it.

She glowered at me with brilliant eyes the color of jade. I wasn't sure if she was more upset that I'd beaten her in a duel—one she'd started—or if she knew what had just gone on with Killian. How close were those two, anyway?

"What'd you do to Killian?" she snapped, the protectiveness in her voice surprising me.

"I don't know what you're talking about," I lied. If Killian didn't tell her, then I certainly wasn't going to be picking at that wound. She'd probably use me for target practice if she knew the whole truth, and even though I'd won a duel once, I didn't want to try my luck a second time.

Then I remembered what Killian had said the moment I'd won the duel... she owed me servitude, whatever that meant.

I glanced up at the look on her face, wondering if this was her idea of being my servant. "So, are you here to help me? Because of the duel... and all."

Her eyes narrowed and I swear the temperature in the room dropped a few degrees. "Beginner's luck," she snapped, then she rummaged through the dresser and plucked out some clothes. She threw them at my face. "Put those on," she growled. "Unless you want to run around in your bikini all day, that is, and distract more of our knights from their classes."

Ignoring her, I pulled on the outfit over my bathing suit. It was dry already and I wasn't interested in asking Jasmine if she had any underwear for me.

She waited until I pulled on the polo shirt and smoothed the pleated skirt. It felt like it was missing something until Jasmine shoved an Academy pin at me. I took it, but managed to prick my finger in the process. "Ouch!" I said with a wince. Jasmine rolled her eyes.

I stared at the bead of dark-red blood that welled up from my skin. It stung—which meant that this wasn't a nightmare.

This was real, and I needed to get my act together.

Sticking my thumb in my mouth, I fumbled with the pin until she impatiently yanked it from me and jabbed it through my collar.

"Seriously, are you scared of a little blood?" Jasmine scoffed. "What kind of dragonrider did Killian think you'd be?"

It wasn't fair, I knew that. Killian had been manipulated into thinking that I was going to be the perfect dragonrider for the Academy, that everything was going to work out and I don't know, we'd fly off into the sunset or something.

Instead... he'd gotten me, the freak-show with just enough goddess blood in her veins to get her into trouble.

As Jasmine rambled on to herself every reason she could think of I didn't deserve to be here, I couldn't help but agree with her. Everything weighed on me like a ton of bricks and a ringing began echoing in my ears. The room rushed in on me... becoming too small and too stale.

I needed to get out. I needed some fresh air.

No, not just fresh air, I needed to get out of this place. Everything felt wrong. I hadn't noticed it before how the ground slightly vibrated and something felt... off.

A thought occurred to me. Perhaps if I left the Academy it would be enough to break the riderbond before it was too late. Maybe there was a chance to undo the mess I'd made. My father's killer might still be out there, but Killian didn't deserve this. I couldn't trade his future and his wyvern's life for my own self-ishness.

If I could fix this... I should.

The second Jasmine turned, I rushed past her and she shouted after me, but I kept going.

My feet slapped against the stone floor as I bolted, not taking the time to find shoes to wear. I didn't wait to see if Jasmine was rushing after me.

I ran.

I stumbled past the students who shouted after me,

as if they knew I was a fraud. They didn't want me here. Nobody wanted me here.

I kept going until I hit the burning sand and I didn't look back.

FIGHT OR FLIGHT

My lungs burned and I gulped in hot air until I reached the Academy's ornate wrought-iron gate that ran around the far edge of the campus. One glance over my shoulder made me dizzy as I took in the swirling dragons… but Jasmine and her massive wyvern weren't among them. Surely I wasn't fast enough to outrun her. Maybe she'd let me go.

Of course she'd let me go. She didn't want me here.

Determined, I turned back to the gate and gave it a light shake.

Locked, okay. No big deal.

Goddess blood or not, I didn't have super strength. It'd come in handy when I'd fought Jasmine, though, so maybe there was some way I could activate it again.

I backed up a few steps and evaluated my target.

Okay, you got this. Just think of Superman… draw your strength from the ground… and… go!

I launched, hurling myself at the gate and slammed into it with all my weight.

Then fell onto the ground with an undignified *thump*.

"Ouch," I murmured as I rubbed my shoulder that had collided with the immovable bars.

Groaning, I got to my feet and chewed my lip. So, I wasn't going to pummel down the gate like a super-hero. Maybe I was looking at this the wrong way. I shook my hands and glanced up at the top of the gate. It had to tower at least twenty feet, but if I wasn't entirely human, maybe I could jump over it?

"Worth a shot," I mumbled, and backed up a few steps before I launched myself, this time upward instead of forward.

While it was a pretty good jump, I still didn't get farther than a few feet off the ground and I clipped my chin on the bars as I slammed into them.

Hitting the ground again, I rubbed the knot forming under my skin. At this rate I was going nowhere fast.

A *whoosh* of air rushed all around me, sending sand and dust particles clogging my nose. I coughed and sputtered as a voice came from behind me.

"What in the realms are you doing?" Jasmine asked.

I turned just in time to see her dragon crouching, eyeing me with a mischievous gleam. I realized that this time Killian wasn't here to keep me from being a snack.

"I'm trying to leave," I said, as if that wasn't obvious. "Nobody wants me here."

Her hand fell to the scabbard at her hip, her fingers flexing over the hilt of her blade. "You're right about that much, and coming out here with no witnesses was a stupid mistake."

Fear washed over me, sending that buzz in my ears on overdrive. The mark on my shoulder burned and I released a sharp breath as the pain made my vision blur.

I got up and faced the gate again. This time I didn't consider it as an obstacle. It wasn't the gate that was keeping me from going home, it was my own reservations about my worthiness to face my mother empty-handed, to go back home a failure with no lead on how to seek justice for my father—but I couldn't stay here. Killian deserved better than me and if I could fix one thing in my life, I was going to do it.

Coiling my legs, I sprang and caught the top of the gate and hung there for a moment worried I was going to fall.

Dangling, I glanced back at a gaping Jasmine.

Smiling, I hauled myself over and landed on the other side.

I hit the ground running and bolted for the ocean.

"Seriously?" Jasmine growled as if this newfound sense of strength inconvenienced her. "What kind of human *are* you?"

A thunder of wings told me that she'd mounted her wyvern and had launched into the air to follow me from above, but I didn't have any qualms about who and what I really was now. I ran faster than I ever had as a human, burning the divine energy in my blood that would always help me match my innermost desires.

I couldn't just want for something to happen—I had to wish for it on a primal level with no hesitation. That's why instinct worked best, why I'd won the duel and why I was able to jump the Academy's gate when Jasmine had found me. Fear surged my fight or flight instincts—literally.

When the ocean crested the horizon and I liked salt from the moisture in the air, I wondered how I was going to convince the Lady of the Lake to take me back home.

As if summoned by my own desires, a massive black vortex formed over the waves. "New girl!" Jasmine shouted with fresh panic in her voice. "Don't you dare go anywhere near the Tunnel!"

"It's Vivi," I grumbled back even though she couldn't hear me.

If Jasmine didn't want me to enter this "Tunnel," then it had to be my ticket home.

The second I reached the water I dove headfirst and swung my arms over my head, propelling myself forward with the strongest breaststroke I could manage.

The temperature changed when I grew closer to my target. I snuck in gulps of air as I continued my broad strokes, catching glimpses of a multitude of other vortexes spotting the horizon. Dragons with riders atop them dove into the breaks in time and space.

Perhaps this wasn't taking me home... but somewhere else.

Whether or not that was the case, I couldn't stop now. This was clearly a transit between realms and I would figure it out. If Jasmine managed to get her hands on me, she'd drag me back kicking and screaming just so she could score some points with Killian and I'd never get the chance to run again.

The stream of dragons the multitude of vortexes diminished the closer I reached my target. I realized that when someone entered a "Tunnel," it would close after them, so that would be my one chance to get Jasmine off my tail. A strange rush filled my limbs and my birthmark burned as if it'd set on fire. It was the same feeling when I'd dueled with Jasmine, and when I'd found the resolve to jump over the gate. This... this was my goddess blood.

My speed increased as I zoomed through the water. This was the last vortex now and Jasmine hurled herself from her dragon, determined to enter into it before I did.

My heart thundered in my chest and the roar of the ocean engulfed me as I went under and propelled myself with one final kick.

A rush of ice swept over my body and immediately all my weight came crashing down onto a hard surface. I coughed up salt water and pinched the sting in my nose.

For better or for worse... I was through the portal.

THIS NEW REALM didn't feel like a solid place. The air shifted as if I was still underwater and the ringing in my ears wouldn't go away. I strained to see something in the darkness, but I could only pick up screams, the clash of metal on stone, and the roar of dragons.

No... not stone, scales.

Biting my lip, I went toward the noise. Flashes of light caught my eye as knights slashed with their swords. Most zoomed in and out of my vision, flying atop their dragons, although some rushed on foot fighting... something dark.

Wild dragons.

The term came as a rush of emotion that reminded me of my short time with Killian. These were the creatures that had taken my home, that attacked Earth and brought destruction down onto the realms.

My stomach sank when I realized I'd been spotted. A massive dragon, much larger than anything I'd seen on campus, locked onto me with pitch-black eyes. Dark, slimy scales covered in seaweed and rot twisted as it took a step closer to me, using his tail to swipe away a group of knights. Another dragonrider came at the creature from above. The wild dragon reared its head and released a plume of blue fire that engulfed the attacker.

I froze, unable to assist or to do anything but stare at the death and destruction all around me.

The dragon took another step closer, only to pause and shift his stare to the darkness behind me.

I didn't even want to know what would frighten a wild dragon, but some sick curiosity made me turn anyway.

Black humanoid shadows twisted, warping the darkness around them as tiny glimmers of light flickered from their dead eyes. One *whooshed* past me, sending a wave of frost to cover my body as I choked on a scream.

A hand grabbed around my mouth and pulled me down as another dark shadow flashed by, streaking the air with red embers as it drew a dark sword.

Instead of terror, instant relief flooded my senses as I recognized the energy that sparked in my body, reacting to the skin that touched mine.

Killian.

"You shouldn't be here," he spat as he released me, flashing his sword to attack one of the shadows that turned on us. Water dripped from his white-blonde hair and his eyes glittered with a determined gleam.

He fought with all the fury and pride of a nephilim, the human-angel hybrid race that my goddess blood saw only as a source of power to be used. His entire body surged with the divine magic that far out rivaled my own, arcing with white light as he took down the shadow, splintering its dark bits into the abyss.

The sounds of battle seemed distant now as the

knights herded the wild dragons down the Tunnel. I took a hesitant step forward, wondering if Killian needed my help, or if I'd caused enough trouble already.

This definitely wasn't my ride home. I'd made a terrible mistake.

Killian's roar brought me out of my stupor as the wild dragon that had been approaching me unleashed a wave of blue fire, catching Killian on his arm before he had a chance to bring up his shield.

"Killian!" I shouted, running toward him as fast as my feet would carry me. The wild dragon whirled, readying another attack as his massive tail swiped sideways, sending Killian launching into the air.

Relying on instinct that fueled my goddess blood, I didn't stop to think about how stupid it was to face-off against the powerful creature. Instead I barreled ahead without any weapons, without a shield, without even a dragon of my own.

It didn't matter. Killian was my mate and in this situation because of me. If I died protecting him, then at least I wouldn't have failed him completely.

The massive creature flared his wings and opened his maw as a low rumble built in his throat. He reared back, readying another wave of fire.

As if it could protect me, I threw my hands up. "Stop!"

It didn't listen to me, instead a wave of roaring heat came crashing down on me. The once black Tunnel lit up like a beacon as the air all around me burned.

I kept my hands up, reaching deep within myself to fuel my desires. I wanted to live. I wanted Killian to live. I had to fix this.

The heat deflected, rearing back and launching straight into the dragon's face. It roared as it struggled to turn from the attack. Its massive wings beat as it swung itself sideways and tumbled into the darkness.

I fell to my knees and stared in utter disbelief. It felt too silent now, but I couldn't see the knights anymore. I decided that they must have herded the other dragons down into the deeper part of the Tunnel.

The dark shadows were gone, too, as if burned up by the brilliant fire that had consumed everything. My eyes went wide when I realized Killian had been behind me and I whirled to find a streak of blacked lines arching out from where I'd somehow deflected the worst of the blast. In the cradle of devastation rested Killian, limp with half of his silver armor burned and black. Blood trickled down the arm cuff where the dragon's tail must have cut through him.

"No," I bit off the word as I rushed to his side. I might have lied to him, manipulated him, but he'd gotten into this fight because of me. I'd made him emotional and angry. This was my fault."Don't you dare die," I said as I hovered my hands over him before pushing him onto his side.

He groaned and I sucked in a breath. The damage was much worse than I'd thought and the dragon must have released a talon into his shoulder when he'd struck. Blood tinged Killian's mouth as he coughed. His eyes opened, only to narrow again. "Get away from me."

"No," I said without missing a beat. "You're not going to die just because you're too stubborn to accept my help," I snapped as I wrapped my fingers around the spike embedded into his shoulder. "Bite down onto something," I warned him and he growled at me. "Fine, have it your way," I said as I yanked hard.

Killian roared with pain and I rushed to cover the wound, but blood ran through my fingers, making me dizzy.

That ringing burned in my ears again and this time I embraced the rush that came next. Golden power ran through my veins and gathered at my fingertips, sending a glow of energy into Killian's body to knit his muscles and skin back together again.

He released a sharp breath as the burns receded and the shine in his hair came back. "What..." The word drifted off as he stared at me, no longer angry with me, but mesmerized.

Instinct nudged me to push onto Killian's chest. The superficial work had been done but he was still internally bleeding. I pressed onto him and he groaned.

We sat there for a long time until I was satisfied and I sat back onto my heels. We stared at each other until Killian struggled to his feet. He wobbled, but I caught him, earning the glare again. He shook me off and stumbled back into the darkness.

"Killian," I said, his name a desperate whisper on my tongue.

"You don't deserve the gift," he snapped, his words harsh. "You're channeling power that doesn't belong to you."

What did that even mean?

"Uh, you're welcome?" I said as anger fluttered in my chest. "I'm pretty sure that I just saved your life."

He whirled on me, those white-blue eyes of his burning as hot as a wild dragon's fire. Energy sizzled between us, kindled by the immature riderbond that I didn't fully understand. "You don't even know what you are, do you?" he asked, as if irritated he had to explain something so basic to me.

"Human," I said, "with a side of goddess, apparently."

He shook his head. "You're a conduit, Vivienne. It's not just the blood. You're channeling the goddess herself, taking more of the power than you're supposed to." He sniffed. "You're good at that, aren't you? Taking what doesn't belong to you."

That stung, but I sensed the untamed rage in him. He didn't like being manipulated, much less saved by the very person who'd messed up his life.

"I didn't ask for this, okay?" I snapped.

"Neither did I," he said dismissively as he turned, leaving me with nowhere to go but to follow him. I certainly didn't want to venture further into the blackness to see where the knights had herded the wild dragons.

Sighing, I trailed after him. If I'd had a tail, it would have been between my legs.

No matter what I said, he wasn't going to listen to me. I'd just saved his life. Who cares how I'd done it? Wasn't it the deed that mattered?

Maybe Killian would never forgive me and that was just something I was going to have to live with. Still, as I watched him walk, I remembered our kiss and my tongue flashed out to capture the warmth of the memory. I wanted to feel that strange energy that awakened something inside of me, something powerful and new.

I had a feeling that I'd never get to experience the sensation ever again.

TIME OUT

*J*asmine glowered at us from shore as we waded our way onto the sand. She gave Killian a raised brow.

"Don't ask," he growled as he shoved past her, ignoring when Jasmine's dragon hissed.

"Relax, Jade," she said, soothing the beast as she rubbed two fingers down the long snout. It startled me to discover a sensitive side to her, but I had a feeling only her wyvern got to see it.

"I can babysit Vivienne. You're off the hook, Jas," Killian said, rubbing the torn armor at his shoulder. He wouldn't meet my gaze even though I frowned at him.

Jasmine sighed. "I'd love that, but the Dean is not happy with your antics." She glanced at me. "She wants to see both of you in her office, now."

"The Dean?" I asked as Killian scowled and began the long trek back to the Academy. Jasmine kept pace with us as her wyvern lifted off and headed back home through the sky. "How does he even know where we are?" I wondered. We couldn't have been gone that long.

"She," Jasmine corrected me. "Dean Brynhilde doesn't miss a thing, so don't think you can get away with the crap you pulled back there." She flicked a lock of hair over her shoulder. "Plus, time works differently in the Tunnels," Jasmine explained while Killian ignored us. "I've been staking the place out for days for you guys to return."

"Oh," I said, wilting as I fell into step behind Killian. Did that mean my mother already knew I was gone? She must be totally freaking out.

Then it hit me the absurdity of my situation. The last thing I expected when we returned to Dragonrider Academy was that I'd get called into the Dean's office. I mean, seriously, I'd never gotten in trouble before back at Oakland High. Not even detention.

I guess there was a first for everything.

Jasmine and Killian bickered about what I could only guess was dragonrider stuff while my head spun. The walk back to campus seemed to draw on forever, probably because the adrenaline had worn off by now —or maybe I'd just run out of goddess ju-ju to keep me going. Killian walked with a slight limp, revealing that I hadn't completely healed him, and Jasmine pretended like everything was fine, but the way she flexed her jaw betrayed that she didn't like this one bit.

When we got to the gates, they were wide open, of

course. No trouble getting into this place, just forget about getting out.

When we stepped onto the campus grounds, the gate swung shut behind me with a sharp *clang*, making me jump.

"It's enchanted," Jasmine explained with a cruel smile. "Any student bonded to a wyvern can enter and leave at will."

"I see," I said, not missing the smug note that Jasmine was letting me know I *didn't* have a wyvern of my own.

Students murmured as we walked past. Killian went straight for the massive dark cathedral tower at the center of the smaller spires, seemingly immune to the shrieks and groans of dragons that flapped above us. I would never get used to this place.

Jasmine and Killian took a sharp left into the building, then head up a set of stairs. I followed as best I could, but found myself wheezing for breath after only a few twisting flights of the tortuously long climb. Jasmine gave me a smirk, sending my face flushing. It seemed like no matter what I did, I couldn't hide that I didn't belong here. It wasn't like Oakland High trained me for massive spire-of-doom hiking.

When we finally reached the top, I was pretty sure I was going to pass out as I clung to the wall for support. Killian rolled his eyes while Jasmine knocked on the door.

"Enter," came a low feminine voice.

I wasn't sure what I expected from someone named

"Brynhilde," but I wasn't disappointed. A woman leaned on a wide desk, her long legs framed by an attractive pantsuit that would have been classy aside from the spread of tribal tattoos over her face and arms. I made out a sea serpent, a constellation of a dragon, and possibly a cat. She ran her fingers down one long braid as she appraised me with amber eyes.

Finding myself unable to meet her scrutiny while my chest heaved to catch my breath after the ridiculous staircase, I looked away and appreciated the leather-bound books along the wall, as well as the paintings above the bookcase that featured various dragons of all shapes, sizes, and colors. The room felt relatively cozy, minus the golden sword that hung above her leather chair. I tried not to wonder if the stains on it were real.

"So, you're Vivienne," she said with a slight accent to her tone I couldn't quite place. She gave me a raised brow and motioned for me to sit. Her lips pursed when I didn't respond.

"Want me to take her back?" Killian asked as if bored with this conversation. I envied that he wasn't winded at all.

The Dean glowered at him. "Excuse me?"

"Take her back," he repeated as if the Dean hadn't heard him. He glanced at the golden sword above her desk. "You can undo the bond. It's still immature."

My stomach dropped when the Dean shifted her weight as if considering the idea. Then she slapped the desk, making Jasmine and I flinch. "The riderbond is sacred, Killian. I don't need to remind you of that. If you didn't like your mate you should have come to me sooner. You know the rules. I break the bond only in dire cases, of which yours is not." She cocked her head. "Where is this behavior coming from, Killian? And why in all the realms would you go on a Tunnel Raid?"

Killian straightened, then glanced at Jasmine.

Jasmine sighed. "I told him that freshmen and sophomores were allowed."

The Dean frowned. "And you didn't care to inform me of that earlier? He could have died. That was a Class 5 Tunnel disturbance." Killian stiffened, but didn't look at me. He *had* almost died, but he clearly didn't want the Dean to know that.

Jasmine ran her thumb over the hilt of the blade at her side. It wasn't a threatening motion, but I took note of it all the same. "I didn't want you to send someone else to bring them in," she admitted. "I had to tell him he could go order to get him off of Vivi's trail. She was trying to escape, and honestly, I was going to let her." She rubbed her temple as if she was about to get a headache. "I didn't realize she'd run straight into a vortex like an idiot."

The Dean considered Jasmine's admission for a moment. "And why did you wait to reveal this to me now?"

Jasmine surprised me by grabbing my arm, making me squeak. "Because you had to see this for yourself. If I had told you earlier, I'd be grounded and I won't let you play favorites with Killian or his chosen mate." She yanked my sleeve up, revealing my burning birthmark.

"You know what that is, right? You can't tell me that you're okay with Killian bringing someone like her here. Not after all we've been through." The accusation was fierce, but it held a note of disgust to it as if Jasmine suspected the Dean was already well aware of my lineage.

I struggled to get out of Jasmine's grasp, but the chick had the strength to fight Max Green on steroids. "Get off me!" I screeched.

"That's enough," the Dean snapped. She pointed at Jasmine and Killian. "You both have stall duty for a month."

"But I—" Jasmine began, only to be cut off by the Dean.

"Out," she said, the word so final that it made my jaw snap shut.

Jasmine glowered at the Dean before flouncing around and stomping out the door. Killian continued to ignore me as he gave the golden sword a longing look, then turned to follow her. The door shut behind them, making me flinch.

The Dean visibly relaxed and gave me what I imagined was supposed to be a friendly smile. "You'll have to excuse them. They have a lot of responsibility on their shoulders. And Jasmine, well, I hope she'll tell you her story one day."

"What did she mean?" I asked, not able to hold the questions in as I rubbed the exposed mark on my arm. "Is it a bad thing… being what I am?"

The Dean gestured to one of the seats and waited

until I sat down before speaking. "That's a difficult question to answer, Vivienne, but I'll do my best. You have the mark of the goddess and that can come as either a blessing... or a curse."

I chewed the inside of my lip. There was definitely truth to that. On the one hand, my goddess blood had ruined Killian's life when I made Solstice and manipulated him into becoming my mate—even if it had all been subconscious on my part. But then today in the Tunnel... I'd saved his life, too. "That sounds complicated." I glanced up at the Dean, seeing my own pleading reflection in her eyes. "What does Jasmine know about me? What's she so afraid of?" My guess was she had a thing for Killian and I was totally ruining it, but he hated me, so aside from the riderbond and all... there was no reason why I should stand in her way.

My stomach twisted as I thought of the innocuous idea of giving up what didn't belong to me in the first place. I shoved my fingers under my legs to keep from picking at my nails.

The Dean sighed. "Perhaps she'll tell you her side of the story one day, but you must understand that she lost her entire family at the destruction of wild dragon attacks."

I gasped. "What? Really?" As horrible as that was, I certainly couldn't be blamed for it. "What does that have to do with me?"

She stood and went to the bookshelf, running her fingers over the spines until she reached a leather-bound tome. She pulled it out and spread open the pages on her desk, pointing at a map with an island in the middle and tiny threads connecting to smaller circles. "This is Avalon, a place where those like you used to live. It's the hub connecting all the realms together." She ran her finger around the various threads as she smiled at me. "It's a great honor, Vivienne, and it's why I have high hopes for you. But those like Jasmine who have been personally hurt by the wild dragons blame those who were supposed to protect this hub. When we lost Avalon, many worlds were invaded and Jasmine's was one of them."

I chewed my lip again, ignoring the forming blister. I didn't know what kind of supernatural Jasmine might be, but if I had to guess, it was something much more impressive than the failed protectors of Avalon. "So she blames my family?" I asked.

"She blames the goddess, I think," she said as she straightened and propped her hands on her hips. She studied the map as if she could find secrets that would solve all of our problems. "She has a lot of hatred, Vivienne, and you're going to meet others with this same pain and rage. You will only remind them of what they have lost, but it doesn't change that you have power within you that is capable of changing things in ways we've never been able to do. It's why I have such high hopes for you." She glanced back at the door. "I just hope Killian comes to see the bigger picture."

I touched my birthmark, feeling drawn in by the grandeur and aspirations the Dean had for me, but really, was this my fight? I didn't ask for this power. "What if I don't want to be here?" I whispered as shame tinged my cheeks red. "What if this is all a giant mistake? Killian didn't get a chance to tell you what I did..." It wasn't something I really wanted to get into with someone like the Dean, but she deserved to know that I wasn't the savior she was hoping for.

"I don't care what you did," she stated flatly. "I need to show you something." She cupped her hands and a dull glow flashed between her fingertips. I gasped as she drew the disturbance out, opening her arms until a massive projection filled the room. A distant dragon's roar rolled through the air like thunder, hitting my chest as an array of dragons sped through rushing Tunnels. They traveled between realms that flashed, civilizations rising and falling as their victims' cries pierced my ears. I held my breath as futuristic skyscrapers made of glass shattered; golden domes melted off of a cascade of hills.

I watched in horror as the wild dragons rained down destruction. The Dean interrupted the horror with an upraised finger as she pointed at a blue dragon that dripped with water pouring down its snout. "These are the water dragons that have claimed Avalon." Her finger shifted as she continued to point out the variances in the infected dragons. They all had a sense of madness in their eyes, scars down their backs and other signs of disease or poor health. The red dragons hailed from Vyorin, a place of fire that flashed briefly through the hologram. She sped through the different races and their home realms, showing me the contrasting difference between the friendly origins and their diseased counterparts.

If I hadn't been terrified before, I certainly was now. "I need to get back," I said, my voice straining on a tremor. "My mother…"

As if echoing my fears, the image changed to the dragons Tunneling toward Earth. They broke through the vortex and circled dark clouds.

I leaned closer, my heart in my throat. The setting looked familiar… then it struck me. This was in the past. "That's Mattsfield High," I murmured. I'd seen it on the news, but without the dragons. There had been a gas explosion, hadn't there?

"You're correct," the Dean said solemnly as the dragons released their fire all at once at the gym, instantly killing everyone… except two figures in the center. I leaned closer despite the horror.

"That's Lily," the Dean said with a small smile. She snapped her fingers and the display vanished in a glimmer of power. "You can come in now," she said, raising her voice.

I whirled as the door opened and a gorgeous girl stepped into the office. "Hi, Vivi, is it?" she asked with a light smile as if I hadn't just witnessed the destruction and death of lives all over the realms.

Numbly, I nodded as the Dean guided me to a seat. I gratefully slumped into it and braced myself on the armrests.

Lily took the seat adjacent to mine. "I know this is

probably overwhelming, but I want to say how happy I am to have you here. You have no idea what it's been like." Her eyes flashed for a moment, turning her pupils into reptilian slits before she shook her head.

I squeaked and leaned back. "What...?"

The Dean remained sentinel at my side, conveniently blocking the door. "There are many different types of dragons, Vivienne. Some are good, like Lily, some are our partners, like the wyverns who have bonded to the students, and some have lost their way." She smiled, resting her hand on my shoulder as her thumb grazed my birthmark. "Any power comes as a blessing... or a curse."

And there it was, the point that the Dean was trying to drill into my head. I was able to do something about the destruction. I came from a lineage of power that had once protected the realms and kept order in place.

There was more to this than my problems, more to this than my father's revenge. Earth was in danger. All the realms were in danger and I could be a force for good, or I could run and hide and fail them all.

I curled my fingers, digging my nails into the wood. "What do I have to do?"

Lily and the Dean exchanged a smile.

For now... I wasn't going anywhere.

REKINDLED

With the meeting concluded, I stumbled outside feeling dazed.

Dragons had already attacked my world… what was to stop them from attacking again?

I realized with a sinking sense of dread that the Dean wanted me to ask that question. The answer was simple.

I was meant to stop them.

I finally understood the importance of Dragonrider Academy. They needed me and if I could help them in any way, I had a duty to do so.

Maybe that was my goddess blood talking, being an ancient protector of the realms and all, but it felt right.

The Dean must have trusted my resolve, because nobody waited for me outside. I took a moment to watch the dragons soaring above, mixing in with the churning clouds that constantly rolled over the spires. Students on the ground hurried to their classes and despite the horror that I'd just come to realize they all faced, they seemed happy. They laughed and joked, chasing each other and feigning strikes with their swords. My high school principal would have had a hernia, but I guess when a Viking was in charge, things were run a little differently.

"I like it here," Lily said, making me flinch as she joined me to survey the streets. "It's not what I expected, but in a good way."

I swallowed hard, trying not to pay too much attention to the fact that this girl was actually a dragon. She ran her fingers through silky hair that draped over her shoulders. A pleated skirt ran short on her long legs and she was one of the few students who didn't have a sword.

With a sinking sense of dread I realized that was because she didn't need a weapon… she *was* a weapon.

Lily chuckled as I stared. "I guess I'm not what you were expecting, either, huh?"

Forcing myself to speak, I released a nervous laugh. "Uh, yeah. You could say that." I tilted my head, looking her over. "You look pretty human." But I'd seen her eyes change… she definitely was anything but human.

She shrugged. "I didn't know I was a dragon until recently, actually." She began walking, so I followed her, keeping pace. "I have a bond with one of the other students, James." She frowned as if this irritated her. "He's a Knight of the Silver Order. Human, but infused with knightly magic from his lineage that goes back to the days of Merlin and King Arthur, if you can believe it. Did you know he was initially supposed to kill me? The Silver Order has a different take on dragons. He brought me here because he thought I could be a weapon against the wild dragons—well, all dragons, if I'm being honest." She drew in a deep breath, held it, then released it through her mouth. A trickle of smoke licked across her tongue. "The Dean has been a good influence, though. She's helped him grow—and she's helped me accept who and what I am." She surprised me by taking my hand and giving me a squeeze. "She'll help you too, if you let her."

I didn't feel so terrified of Lily anymore and I managed to give her a weak smile. We walked silently minus a few pleasantries. She was heading back to the dorms and was voluntarily accompanying me. She explained with a small laugh that "stall duty" would put Killian in a worse mood than he was already in.

"Does 'stall duty' mean what I think it means?" I asked, not able to hide my wry smile. After how much of a jerk Killian had been—even if I kind of did deserve it—it felt like a decent punishment.

"Oh yes," she said with a grave nod. "The larger wyverns move out of the dorms and into their own stalls. They eat a lot and, well, it's got to come out and go somewhere."

We chuckled, the laughter loosening my shoulders and coming as a reprieve after the kind of day I'd had.

She squeezed my hand again when we entered the dorm. The humid air flushed into the cooler atmosphere inside the stone building. "Killian will be back soon. Until then, just take some time. Absorb what you've learned today and know that you can come talk to me about anything." She pointed upward. "I'm on the top floor, far room on the west side if you ever need me."

"Sure, thanks," I said as Lily waved goodbye and took the stairs.

I sighed. Did they really have no elevators in this realm?

After building up my confidence, I took the stairs as well and wandered through the corridors. When I reached the door, I smirked because my feet had taken me straight back to Killian's place, even though I hadn't exactly remembered the way.

I'd followed my heart… because we were mates.

Opening the door, I spotted Killian's wyvern keening in his nest, fighting some nightmare that plagued him. My stomach twisted, because my rider-bond worked both with Killian and his wyvern. It tore me up to see Topaz like this. Jasmine had said that time passed differently in the Tunnels, so however long I'd been gone was enough for what healing I'd done to the wyvern to completely wear off.

"Poor baby," I said as I entered the room. I approached him and hovered my hands over his faded scales, but the power wouldn't come to me. "I must have used up all my goddess gifts on Killian earlier," I murmured, disappointed that I wasn't some all-powerful supernatural that the Dean made me out to be. I had limits, limits that I was going to have to get used to.

Unable to be magically useful, I spent my time tidying up the room. Killian seemed to be relatively clean, but we'd been gone a while and his wyvern had been on his own. Somebody must have come in to help care for him, though, because I found the refrigerator still stocked with both human food and raw meats. I tossed one of the slivers of steak over to the wyvern and he gobbled it up, satisfied as he reshuffled himself in his nest. I found chewed up shoes and dangled them from my fingers. "Are you a dragon or a dog?" I quietly asked him. He preened, then tucked his snout under his wing as he fell back asleep.

I cleaned the windows, reorganized Killian's closet, and then I found my own closet and dresser had been stocked with various things. I put on some shoes after washing my feet. The room was finally starting to look presentable when Killian burst into the room.

We stared off at each other for a moment as I took in his appearance—very shirtless, hair wet, and blue eyes blazing with agitation.

"Uh, hi," I said as I forced my gaze away.

He glowered at me. "I had hoped the Dean would have sent you home," he said, his voice gruff. He stepped inside and slammed the door behind him. "I can't even take a shower without you staring at me."

"You're the one half-naked," I pointed out as I took an immense interest in the window.

"You're one to talk," he grumbled, making me smirk.

So, perhaps I had affected him just as much as he was affecting me now.

Topaz trilled at Killian, earning an affectionate scratch under the chin from the knight. "It's okay, boy. Are you hungry?"

"I fed him," I said.

Killian seethed, his eyes flashing with rage, then it passed. "Thanks," he bit out as he rummaged through his dresser. He frowned at my job of folding his clothes, but he didn't say anything. Instead he flipped over items until he found a shirt he wanted at the bottom, ruining my work, before he put it on.

Topaz whined, shifting as if something was hurting. "Is he okay?" I asked, realizing it was a stupid question the moment it came out of my mouth.

"What do you think?" Killian bit out as he slumped onto the edge of his bed. He gathered the wyvern onto his lap and carefully ran his thumb over the creature's snout like I'd seen Jasmine do with Jade.

I flinched at the harsh tone of his comment. "Is there anything we can do? I tried healing him... like I did before, but, I guess it didn't work."

Killian didn't look up at me, but his shoulders relaxed. "It's because our bond is weak and your magic needs time to rebuild. You aren't strong enough, as we have both learned by now." He glanced up at me with an accusatory stare. "Dragons need community, love, and most of all, magic to survive. Without all of those things, they don't make it... or turn wild."

Irritation made me bristle. He was putting far too

much blame on me. "Isn't this place full of magic? What about the Dean?" After the show she'd given me today, nobody could tell me she didn't have some extra magic to spare.

Killian shook his head. "The riderbond is what fuels the dragon, and even if I wanted to supplement with surrogate magic, the Academy doesn't have enough. It's been running low on everything for a while now. We have fewer students, fewer eggs hatching, and so many dragons…" His voice faltered, turning thick before he continued. "So many of them get sick and die before they can mature, no matter if they are bonded to a rider or not."

Neither of us matched gazes as silence ate away at my insides. Killian truly cared, as if Topaz was his entire world. It was such a different side of him than the violent killing machine I'd seen in the Tunnels.

"Topaz is strong," I said, turning back to him with determination. "He can get through this." I wanted so badly for that to be true. I wanted for *us* to be able to get through this.

Killian gave me a bitter laugh. "I forget how nauseously optimistic you humans are."

"Hey," I said, sitting next to him and jabbing his rib with a finger. "You're part human too, you know."

Killian shrugged as if he couldn't refute that. I reached out to pet Topaz who trilled happily in response. Killian allowed it, so I stroked down the creature's snout like I'd seen him do. He nuzzled my hand, making me giggle.

"I'm the one who isn't strong enough," Killian said, his voice so quiet I could barely hear him. "I can't harvest enough magic to keep Topaz healthy, and now I am afraid it's just a losing battle. When I found you, that was supposed to be it... That was—" He went silent as his jaw flexed, making my heart melt.

I reached out to him, unable to watch him suffer like this. The moment my fingers grazed his arms, energy surged between us and Topaz fluttered his wings. Strength made my skin heat up as if Killian and I were two parts of a wire that would ignite the room in flames.

His blue eyes met mine and I knew that he felt it too. Our bond was stronger than he gave it credit for and something else was there... something that refueled that emptiness in my chest until I breathed in and out, releasing steam from the superheated air.

"Don't," Killian weakly pleaded, but it was too late, we were both enraptured by the moment. I rested a hand on Topaz's back before our lips met.

Just like before, my world turned inside out and a roar of power flooded my ears.

Killian didn't crush his lips to mine like he had before, his touch was gentle and hesitant, as if afraid to push this too far, but he couldn't pull away. This bond between us was real, tangible, and made me feel things I had never felt before.

Power surged through me, filling my core and warming my extremities until I was sure I would burst into flames. I took some of the energy for myself, then redirected a portion of it down my fingertips and into the dragon who keened up at us, so trusting in the lap of his rider.

The sensation of fullness told me when I was done. I pulled away from Killian, even though my body tingled and the desire to get lost in him forever was undeniably tempting.

His hard blue eyes had taken on a softer glow and I was rewarded with the glimmer of a smile before he cleared his throat and turned away.

We both stared down at Topaz who shivered off a layer of golden dust. Killian brushed away the substance, revealing healthy blue scales underneath that reflected the light. The creature flapped his wings and chirped before releasing a small puff of fire. Killian laughed. "Whoa, boy, don't burn down the dorm or you're going to get me stall duty again."

Relief made me smile, but a wave of dizziness swept over me and I grabbed my head.

Killian surprised me by steadying me as he held my arm. "Hey, are you okay?" His anger was temporarily gone, the bitterness overwhelmed by his gratitude that his wyvern could still be saved. "You shouldn't have done that." The chiding comment came out flat. He disapproved of my magic, but he couldn't argue with the results.

"Why?" I asked as I waited for the spell to pass. "This is why I'm here, isn't it?" The Dean had an image of me that I meant to uphold. I would be a force for good, not a curse on those who deserved my help.

"You're a conduit," he said as if I should know what that meant. "When the goddess power in you runs dry, you can channel more of it from your ancestors... and from other realms." His throat bobbed as he swallowed. "I'm a Nephilim, and channeling the power from my realm can be dangerous. If they found out, they'd come after you."

"Oh," I said, feeling weary. "That sounds... complicated."

He chuckled. "Yeah, you could say that." He got to his feet and Topaz chirped before wrapping around his neck. "Well, from what I know about conduits, there are other ways you can refuel." He waggled his eyebrows.

"Uh," I began, then he choked on a laugh.

"Food, Vivi. Get your mind out of the gutter."

I frowned. "Right, food."

His eyes sparked with mischief. I wasn't sure how long this spell would last, but I would enjoy this side of Killian until I did something to remind him how *wrong* I was for him again. "You're in for a treat. Dragonrider Academy food is, let's say, magically enhanced. It'll taste like your favorite dish." He offered me his hand. I studied the lines on his palm before taking it.

I wasn't sure if this counted as a date, but my stomach rumbled in agreement that food was a spectacular idea.

DRAGON'S BLOOD

The cafeteria was conveniently placed on the ground floor of what I could only describe as a castle. "Do you people not understand subtlety?" I asked as Killian guided me to the long line.

I almost expected him to cut in front, being all posh and arrogant as he was, but he took his place at the end and waited patiently as he scratched Topaz who nibbled on his ear. After a minute of me staring at him, he shrugged. "I'm an honorable knight. That means we wait." He smirked and unlatched Topaz from his earlobe. "Even if that means my wyvern tries to take a bite out of me."

My tongue watered as the aroma of tender meats and mac and cheese met my nose, but none of the plates matched the description of the dishes my brain tried to process. I recalled that Killian said that the food was magical here, and I watched as students who filled the long tables stuffed spoonfuls of white mush into their mouths. It glowed, taking on different forms of sandwiches, meat entrees, and even soups. "I thought you said that the Academy was low on magic," I marveled.

"We have a couple of dwarves who serve the meals," Killian said, pointing at the bobbing heads I'd missed behind the long wall of the buffet table that seemed to miraculously refill itself. "Their magic isn't good for much other than smithing armor and making some awesome food."

"Uh... huh," I said, deciding that I wasn't going to process anymore bizarre magical facts about this place for the day.

After what felt like millennia, we sat down to eat and I spotted Jasmine glowered at us from across the room. She waited until Killian acknowledged her and she widened her eyes as if to say, *What the heck are you doing?*

He shrugged before turning to his food and digging in, making sure to slip Topaz a few bites. I wanted to ask him the same questions Jasmine had on her face, although with a lesser sense of animosity. Where did we stand? Were we a thing now? Had he forgiven me?

"Eat your food," he commanded as if he could hear my thoughts.

When I took a bite, I no longer cared about the questions swirling around in my head. "Oh my God," I murmured, then cocked my head. "I guess I should say 'Oh my Goddess?'"

Killian chuckled. "Oh, don't let any of the other

students hear you say that. We have a theology class about deities and there are those who think the goddess of the realms is just an overpowered supernatural. Just because she protects the realms doesn't mean she created them."

"Hmm," I said as I took another bite of what looked like white mush, but tasted like the best mac and cheese on steak I'd ever had. The combination had come about when I'd run out of things to cook with my mother and it had been a joke, only to turn into my signature dish. While I was glad I didn't have to necessarily give up my Catholic upbringing, I reminded myself I wasn't going to process any weird facts today.

After we ate, Killian stormed down the halls with Topaz clinging to his neck, his nose in the air as if he enjoyed every moment of feeling healthy again. Central Hall housed the majority of the classrooms, according to Killian, as well as other significant rooms that needed protecting—like the Egg Sanctuary.

"Are you ready for orientation?" he asked. "It can be intense."

"More intense than what I've already been through?"

He chuckled, opened his mouth to say something then threw his arm over me, blocking me from taking another step.

"Ow!" I bit out as his powerful blow knocked the wind out of me.

"Sorry," he said as he released me. "It's enchanted. I forgot you aren't attuned until you bond to a wyvern."

He glanced down at the pink mist that rose out from the step beneath us. I didn't want to know what would have happened if I'd run into it. He waved his hand over it and sparks flew across the ground as it was dispelled.

"Why are there booby traps inside the campus?" I wheezed as I rubbed my stomach. "Are there any other surprises that I should be aware of?"

"It's a necessity, and yes, you should always be on your guard," he said as if that were obvious. "Dragon eggs are powerful objects on their own, even unhatched. They could be a source of great evil in the wrong hands."

I bit the inside of my lip, then winced and ran over the groove with my tongue. I really needed to stop that bad habit.

It reminded me once again of the duality that the Dean had tried to describe to me.

It can be a blessing or a curse.

I followed Killian down more steps, trying not to complain once again about the lack of elevators. Several more enchantments glimmered to life as we descended. Bulbless lamps burst with magical flames and lit our way, followed by a waterfall that framed a small entrance. Killian stepped through without hesitation, so I followed. Neither of us came out wet on the other side, although a slightly sour stench clung to my uniform.

"That was the Waterfall of Intention," Killian explained, his shoulders relaxing as he appraised me.

"Another one of the dwarves' inventions. If either of us had ill will toward the Egg Sanctuary, it would have attempted to block us."

"Cool," I said, once again clinging to my decision not to think too hard about magical revelations that I didn't understand. "Sounds high-tech."

He raised a brow. "High... tech?"

I smirked. "You know, technology? Phones? Computers? Elevators?" I couldn't help but adding the last one.

A line formed as he furrowed his brows. "I haven't heard of those things."

Right. I kept forgetting Killian and I were literally raised in different worlds. "I'm getting total revenge when you come back to Earth with me," I said, bopping his nose with my finger.

He frowned and backed away as the energy from the brief contact sizzled through the air. "Don't count on it," he murmured before turning to a closed door and knocking.

I didn't have time to ask if he meant we wouldn't be going to Earth together, or if he was so arrogant to believe he was beyond culture shock. A fumbling noise sounded, followed by the eye-slot yanking open. A pair of green eyes peered at us as a grumpy male voice barked, "Who is it?"

"Orientation student for you," Killian said. "You know the rules, Finn. Don't make me wait out here all day." He wrinkled his nose. "Plus, I think your Intention Waterfall is accumulating mold."

Cursing ensued as the eye-slit slammed shut. More fumbling sounded before the door creaked open. Killian pushed his way inside while the dwarf scowled at us. He dragged along a step-ladder while he grumbled something about good-for-nothing knights.

"Vivi, meet Finn," Killian said with a wry smile. "He's delighted to meet a new student, I'm sure."

"Waste of time!" Finn grumbled as he waddled into the massive room filled with shelves of colorful, ovular objects poking out of perfectly spherical nests.

I scanned the otherworldly display, taking in the ruby reds, emerald greens, and even a few diamond and pearl shells inside the nests.

"Stop gawking," Finn barked as he shuffled over to a bucket. He yanked his ladder into place. "Make yerself useful." He shoved a brush into my hand that dripped with shimmering goop.

I gave Killian a pleading glance, but the dwarf had given him a brush too and he dutifully coated one of the eggs on the higher shelves Finn had trouble reaching.

"May I ask what this stuff is?" I asked as I found an egg of my own to coat.

"No questions!" Finn insisted. "More coating!"

If this was my orientation, I wasn't impressed.

Killian seemed unperturbed by the dwarf's demands and moved onto the next egg as Topaz settled around his neck for a nap, securing himself in place with his talons. Killian didn't seem to mind. "It's a mixture of enchanted oils and dragon blood," he said.

I paused my brushstrokes and inspected the glimmering moisture that sank into the egg I was working on. "Blood?"

Finn snorted. "Don't act surprised. What else would nourish dragon eggs but the lifeforce of their own?" He slapped another layer of the goop onto the shell. "It's not like I'm covering the eggs to fry them."

Killian smirked at me. "Don't mind Finn, he's just grumpy because he's been working overtime to keep the eggs alive." There was a note of humor in his voice, but I didn't miss the melancholy note to it.

There's not much magic left.

"I can hear you," Finn snapped. He jumped down his ladder to recoat his brush when ash began to trickle to the floor.

Blood rushed in my ears and my birthmark began to burn, but Killian rested a light touch on my arm, calming me as energy swarmed between us. "It's the egg sorting through the corrupted components of the wild dragon blood and the usable magic, keeping the clean parts and discarding the rest. It knows what it's doing, don't worry."

"Huh," I murmured as Finn absently swept the ash into a dustpan, ignoring my amazement.

"We helped you with your chores," Killian complained, raising his voice. "Can we get on with orientation now? We do have actual things to do, Finn."

The dwarf gave Killian the stink-eye. "Don't expect me to stop workin' just because a Knight and a wannabe Valkyrie shows up." He dipped his brush again.

"Ain't nobody else have the magic finesse to keep these eggs alive."

"Aren't there others who can help you?" I asked, honestly concerned about the overworked dwarf.

"Nope," he said, going back to his work. "I'm the last of the healers. My pops wanted me to become a Smithy, but I always did have a soft spot for the old ways." He ran his thumb over a crack in one of the eggs, smoothing the liquid into the seam until it healed. "Not many care about the dragons these days, not after the destruction they've caused. But there is good in them, the young an' innocent, if raised the right way." He glanced at me, then at the mark on my shoulder. "Gah, fine." He shoved his brush into the bucket and stormed up to me, taking my hands. He turned them over, inspecting them until he was satisfied. "I can't read what realm you should ally with."

"Water?" Killian suggested, his humor disappearing into a grim scowl. "She comes from Avalon ties."

The dwarf shook his head. "That's not how the magic works, boy, you know that. It's about the heart." He thumped Killian in the chest.

"So, what then?" I asked, looking at my hands again. "How do I tell which kind of dragon I'm supposed to bond with?" Jasmine had an Emerald dragon, from what I remembered of the Dean's display it was a realm of warriors and life. That reflected her personality well. Killian, his was a water dragon, which surprised me. Avalon's origins reflected peace, serenity, and the ability to adapt to new situations. Maybe that did fit him, after he'd gone from hating me to accepting our bond. The anger was still there; I felt it underneath the surface, but there was hope that we could come to some sort of understanding.

"Does she know nothing?" the dwarf spat as if disgusted with me.

"I'm new to all of this," I said, trying not to sound too defensive.

"That much is clear," he said, snorting.

"Here," Killian said, taking my hand gently in his own as he brought my fingers to one of the warm shells. Energy swarmed between us and he pulled away, allowing me to focus on the sensation of the rough shell. "Do you feel anything?"

"Am I supposed to?" I asked. I wasn't sure if I was supposed to feel an epiphany, or a surge of magic like I had with the riderbond with Killian. Other than the warmth and the faint thump of a heartbeat inside, I couldn't feel anything else.

"Try the next one," Killian offered, and so began the long process of checking each egg for some mystical connection that I was starting to believe didn't exist.

When we reached the final egg, Finn had completed his task of coating the shells and tapped his foot impatiently while he crossed his arms. I brushed away sweat from my forehead with the back of my hand before I pressed my fingertips to the shell.

Nothing.

"Well," Finn said with a sense of resign, "it seems you've brought us a dud, Killian."

Killian furrowed his brows. "This can't be right." He glanced at me, his thumb running across my birthmark. Energy surged between us instantly, making my toes curl. "I've seen the magic you can do. There has to be a dragon who is attuned with your aura..." He glanced at Finn. "Are there any others?"

The dwarf rubbed his hands on a dirty cloth. "Not any that are still alive, no, there's... hey!"

Finn shouted after me as I stepped into the darkness, drawn by a tingling down my spine that intensified with every step. I passed between a set of two bookshelves shoved closely together, reaching around to find a door that had a rusty knob. I turned it, but found it locked. A humming sounded in my ears, followed by a sensation of warmth and the need to protect... something.

"I need in here," I snapped with certainty.

"There's nothing for you in there, lass," the dwarf said, but he pulled a chain of keys from his buckle anyway. He worked at the lock and creaked the door open, snapping his fingers to send more of the magical lanterns sputtering to life. I stepped inside the room that made a strange sensation crawl across my skin. Eggs lined the shelves of the dimly lit room, except these had no color and no life. Cracks lined the shells, giving them the appearance of being left out in the sun for too long.

My nose wrinkled as the aroma hit me. Killian noticed it too. The faint stench we'd come across at the entry waterfall wasn't mold...

It was death.

"Vivi," Killian said with a sense of urgency. "Are you… drawn to one of these?"

My fingers reached out as if my soul sought for something. I shuffled forward until I happened upon an egg that had no life in it, but called me all the same. A strange pulse came from inside it, like an echo of a heartbeat that had long been lost. Tears I couldn't explain swelled in my eyes and slipped down my cheeks.

"Yes," I whispered, my voice hoarse.

But how could that be? This egg was clearly dead.

"We need to talk to the Dean," Killian said, his tone cut with steel. He reached out to grab my arm, but pulled his fingers back at the last second as if he was afraid to touch me. "It's very dangerous to connect with a dead dragon. This egg is just a husk, Viv. There's no soul inside. You could die if you tried to retrieve it from the afterlife."

"Is that even possible?" I whispered, thinking of my father and how he seemed so beyond my reach. If I could bring something of him back… anything, I'd do it in a heartbeat.

"I don't know," Killian said honestly. "You have the goddess's blood inside of you. I don't know what you're capable of."

I tugged the egg free of its prison, bringing it into my chest.

I knew I'd never let it go.

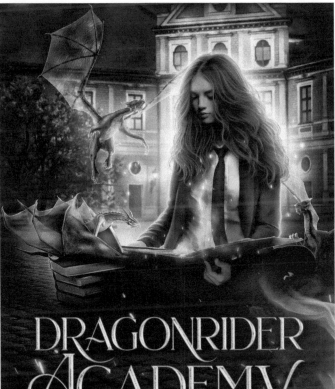

DRAGONRIDER ACADEMY

EPISODE THREE

USA TODAY BESTSELLING AUTHOR

A.J. FLOWERS

CHAPTER 1

SILENCE & SUNLIGHT

"*P*lease..." I silently begged. This was my nightly mantra, my prayer.

Nothing else mattered. My world had narrowed down to just me and my dragon's egg.

More like a husk, really. Killian wouldn't call it that, but I knew he was thinking it.

I didn't care. Somewhere in the back of my mind my other priorities screamed for my attention and I'd just shut that little voice off and go back to my mumbling. Yes, I still wanted to reunite with my mother and let her know that I was okay... but I wasn't okay, was I? Not like this. Not until I hatched my dragon.

The mystery surrounding my father's death took a backseat as well, at least for now. This was all connected to him, somehow, and if I could solve this mystery, the rest would fall into place. I just knew it.

It was all connected.

This was my answer to everything.

Killian watched over me as I devolved into despair. Maybe he enjoyed seeing me suffer like this, although I suspected he suffered with me, too. I'd called him to become my mate just so I could use him for his powers as a Nephilim, and because of our bond, he cared about me. Or maybe despite that, he cared for me because he understood my reasoning.

Even if he had forgiven me for such a heinous thing, he shouldn't.

Because I couldn't forgive myself.

Despite my failures, he watched me in the darkness of our dorm room, always the silent sentinel while I muttered to myself over my dead egg. I couldn't see him, but I could feel his eyes on me as my lips moved of their own accord, chanting my mantra over and over again.

Our dorm had become a safe haven that I rarely left. I wasn't sure how much time had passed since I'd found the egg, or rather, since it had found me.

Days?

Weeks?

... Longer?

It didn't really matter. Day and night ran together and if it weren't for Killian going on runs to the cafeteria, I probably would have died from starvation.

He'd tried to get the Dean involved, at first. She respected my choice, no matter the consequences. It didn't really matter if she approved or not—I wasn't going to give up. That wasn't possible anymore. The bond strengthened every day and my desperation ramped up with it.

When I'd stopped eating, that's when he'd tried to get me to talk to Lily or someone who might be able to "talk some sense into me."

It didn't matter what anyone else thought, though. I wasn't going to give up on trying to bring back the lost spirit tied to this egg. I clutched it to my chest with sheer determination that I wouldn't fail, no matter how hopeless it seemed.

That only seemed to frustrate Killian. In the end, we had nothing left to say to one another and silence was all that remained between us.

Despite all of that, he still stayed by my side. Even though he was mad, even though he wanted to stop me from making what he believed to be a massive mistake, he wouldn't abandon me.

He could have left. *Should* have left. My degradation only brought him down with me because of our bond.

He could have stolen the sword in the Dean's office and used it on me to break our bond. A bond that only grew stronger as I drew power from him every time he touched me. I couldn't heal him or Topaz anymore, not when I was like this. Any strength I found went straight into the egg that I desperately wanted to save.

This one-way path of power won't be sustained by our rider bond forever. While I fueled a hopeless cause, he became weaker. Topaz slept while releasing struggling wheezes. Killian shifted, new aches appearing all throughout his body that made it impossible for him to rest. He wouldn't admit how bad it was, but I could see the sores on him when he got dressed in the morning. My influence was eating away at his immortality and it was only a matter of time before I drained him too far for him to come back.

Still... he didn't leave. He stayed, and his gaze watched me throughout the night while I struggled to revive my egg.

Sunlight crested the windowsill, unusual in its obnoxious cheeriness. Dragonrider Academy had a sandy sort of allure to it, a dimness in the morning dawn that made the waking dragons look like they were coming out of a dream.

I watched them now, their scales glittering in the rare burst of sunlight. It made this place feel even more magical and my standard melancholy found itself dampened. The dragonriders lifting off, starting their rounds for the day had a mesmerizing effect. I'd been jealous of them at first, yes, but now I held onto a sense of absurd hope that I would join them, eventually.

"Look at that," I whispered to my egg, pointing to one of the younger dragons flapping awkwardly into the sky with lurches and jolts. "That's Cyprus," I said, a small smile cresting my face. "He just learned to fly." The adorable dragon gained enough height to hit a current, then tumbled through the air, eager to show off for his rider.

I'd watched Cyprus take his first few struggling leaps and now I realized why today was so special.

Even the sun had come out to spotlight such a special event. A dragon learning to take to the skies felt right... This was a good omen.

The excited chirps of the other dragons filtered in through the open window and a small smile spread over my face as I stroked the cold shell of my egg.

"Well, I should get to class," Killian said, his voice hard and scratchy, a harsh contrast against the uplifting scene outside. He hadn't slept at all, and his fatigue only reminded me how exhausted I was as well.

When I didn't respond, he rested a hand on my shoulder. The jolt of electricity made me curl my shoulders and grit my teeth. "You shouldn't touch me," I warned as sputtering golden light rippled over my skin only to sink into the thin shell pressing against my chest. "I can't control it."

"I know," he said, his voice uncharacteristically kind. "It doesn't matter."

I glanced up at him, annoyed by his tone. "Of course it matters."

He smirked and he grazed my cheek with his knuckles, leaving sparks along my skin. "Your... persistence, has expanded your impact on the bond between us." He stepped back to demonstrate. My eyes went wide when I spotted little flickers of gold in the air drifting from his heart to mine. He ran his fingers through it, disturbing the slowly drifting light. "You see? It doesn't matter because you're draining me now even if I don't touch you."

He said that so matter-of-factly, as if I wasn't slowly killing him.

I looked down at my egg that hadn't changed at all, despite all my efforts. My skin had paled and I felt sick.

This was killing us both.

"Hey, it's okay," he said with such assurance, making me glance up at him. His beautiful eyes were haunting in this light, boring into me with such intensity that I couldn't look away. "Sulking isn't getting you anywhere," he added with a smirk, "and if you're going to kill me slowly with this silent torture, the least I can do is speed it up."

"Why is this happening?" I asked, trying to prevent the sting in my eyes from evolving into tears.

He leaned down, invading my personal space as the air around us hummed to life with a soft golden hue. My heart twisted and my stomach flipped as I matched his gaze. I couldn't deny the attraction between us and his obnoxiously perfect looks weren't helping matters, either.

"You don't even realize you're doing it, do you?" he asked, genuinely curious as he twisted his gorgeous mouth into a grin. "A natural Conduit. The women of Avalon would have had a fit over you." He glanced down and his smile dimmed. "Now it's too late, I'm afraid. You've fully bonded to a lost cause."

I wasn't sure if he meant my dragon egg... or himself.

He'd grown quiet over the past few days, or weeks,

or however long it had been since this nightmare had started. I'd taken that as anger at me.

Maybe he was just angry with himself.

I looked down at the egg wrapped in my arms as I tried not to let Killian's mood get to me. The shell hadn't changed at all since I had taken it into my care. Dull specks ran in an abstract pattern around the top, filtering into lines like an illness toward the bottom. I'd memorized the pattern long ago and I ran a finger over one of the raised cracks.

The echo of a heartbeat still lingered underneath the surface. No matter what Killian thought, there was still an essence clinging to this shell... and I refused to give up.

With a sigh I looked out the window again, trying to ignore Killian's pressure on my skin as his touch ran lightly over my shoulder. I knew if I faced him I'd have to combat that pleading in his eyes and I wasn't sure if I had the strength.

There was one thing he was right about, though. Sulking in this room day in and day out was getting me nowhere.

"I'll go with you," I decided. Maybe there was something different about today. Maybe I'd find an answer that would fix the mess I'd made of everything.

"You'll... go with me?" Killian echoed with surprise. His wyvern chirped with delight, flapping awkwardly from his nest to land on his shoulder with a rare bout of energy.

I chuckled when Topaz scrambled down Killian's

arm to lick my cheek. "Yeah, yeah," I said, waving the wild creature off. "You're glad I'm leaving this room for once, huh?"

Topaz trilled, his voice gaining nuanced tones over the past few weeks of my sulking, despite the general condition of malaise that plagued him and his master. He still had a lot of growing to do and my heart broke at the mere thought of losing him.

I couldn't imagine what Killian was going through. All the more reason I had to find a solution to this mess.

"Well, I guess I owe Lily five coins," Killian said as he retreated. "Good thing she brought by one of these." The golden dust in the room kicked up as he ventured to his closet and rummaged through his belongings. He produced a pouch and handed it to me. I took the offering with one hand and turned it over.

"It's kind of big for a purse," I mused.

He chuckled. "It's for your egg, Viv." He took the straps and wound them around my waist, stringing the longer end up and over my shoulder to clasp it. I tried not to notice how close his touch ran to the sensitive parts of my body as I shyly looked away. He cleared his throat as he gave it a tug. "There. All set."

Gingerly, I tucked the egg into the pouch and stood up, finding that the design held the shell tightly against my body, providing it with warmth.

The sensation made me acutely aware that the egg held no life inside of it. The chilled exterior was just a husk with nothing but an echo of what could have been.

Swallowing past the lump in my throat, I adjusted the strap so that I could wrap one arm around the base. I didn't fully trust it to hold up the egg's weight, even if it did seem secure.

"Thanks," I said after Killian held the door open.

We walked at a steady pace down the corridor with only Topaz's light trills to announce our passage to the other students.

Outside of our dorms, nothing seemed to have changed and at the same time I felt like an entire decade had passed with nothing to show for it. I'd missed so many classes that I'd probably never catch up, but it didn't much matter if I couldn't hatch my dragon. Why the Dean hadn't forced me to pick one of Finn's other eggs, I couldn't be sure.

Did that mean that the Dean had faith in me that I'd eventually succeed? Or did she know I was already a hopeless cause and had left me to my fate?

Sunlight hit my face the moment we left the building and I jerked one hand up to protect my eyes.

Killian chuckled. "If you'd stayed in there much longer you would have turned into a vampire."

I let my hand fall and stubbornly squinted at him, ignoring how the sun made him even more beautiful in all of his Nephilim glory. Any girl could appreciate his eyes as clear as glass that matched his otherworldly white hair. His uniform molded against strong muscles that betrayed he wasn't entirely human. The only evidence of the impact my drain had on him was the way he favored one leg and a slight shadow swept underneath his otherwise striking eyes. The flaws couldn't detract from the overall picture, though, especially when he maintained his cocky attitude as Topaz slept wrapped around his neck like an ornament. It was hard not to stare at him sometimes, he was so uniquely beautiful.

"There's no such thing as vampires," I insisted, only to be met with a noncommittal shrug from my fated mate.

"If you say so," was all he said before sauntering down the street.

I frowned, hoisted my egg a fraction closer to my body, and followed him. I hated when he teased me, but I knew better than to ask what he meant by that. If there really were vampires, I didn't want to find out right now and add more madness to my life.

Killian guided me to class without remarking on the students who pointed at me or outright stared. It was easy to forget that these weren't regular students. They could sense the death that I carried around in my egg pouch. Their gazes fell to the empty husk slung across my chest, pity streaking their expression before Killian barked at them to carry on.

He cleared his throat when we arrived at my class. "Meditation is the first class on the agenda for today," he said, opening the door and waved me in. "You first."

I glanced up at him, for the first time feeling

nervous. "You're joining?" I asked. "I thought you were in the sophomore class."

He smirked. "Meditation is a mandatory class throughout all the levels." He leaned in to open the door and his other hand went to the small of my back, ushering me inside.

His absent touch made me dizzy. The motion felt natural, as if we'd grown closer over the stretch of time I'd agonized over my egg, rather than further apart.

Too dazed to think, I numbly ventured into the classroom.

Once I regained my senses, I found that everyone turned to stare at me. I didn't have time to worry about them as my gaze locked onto the professor.

Slight fangs poked from her mouth and her skin glinted with a strange layer of sparkle to it. When she shifted, I realized that a fine layer of scales overlaid her cheeks.

"Well, if it isn't the new student," she said, a light rumble to her voice. "Vivienne, is it? I'm glad you've finally decided to join the ranks of the living." Her gaze fell to my egg. She frowned, as if just realizing her poor choice of words. The students murmured until she clapped her hands. "Right, well, you two take the back. Looks like you finally get a partner today, Killian."

Killian glanced at me, smirking, before taking his seat at the back of the room. I hurried after him.

Jasmine waved hello, surprising me. She'd been nicer to me lately, coming to visit and even bringing edible offerings. Killian told me that was the equivalent of best friend category when it came to the Junior Dragonrider.

She smiled, although the gesture was a sinister one. I think she was enjoying my shellshocked reaction to class.

She leaned in and whispered something into a male's ear that sat on her bench. His dark eyes glanced up at me, calculating.

"That's Vern," Killian informed me, referring to Jasmine's seductive companion who somehow managed to look dangerous in the same uniform everyone else wore. "Her third attempt at a rider bond match, I'm afraid." Killian tilted his head, appraising the new match. "This one might stick," he decided.

Yeah, I thought, looking at how Jasmine flipped a knife over her knuckles. Those two were made for each other.

Vern leaned back against the wall, otherwise ignoring the rest of us as Jasmine held his attention. A buzzcut hairstyle paired with his bulky massive arms crossed over one another made him look like the silent, terrifying type, and not someone I'd want to cross.

"Great, like Jasmine needs a bodyguard," I lamented.

"More like an assassin," Killian said, chuckling.

I glanced at him, trying to decide if he was serious just before two dragons swooped past the window, making Jasmine giggle.

Ah, well at least their dragons got along.

Professor Emhart passed out a tray holding vials of some sloshy looking liquid. I took note of Lily and

Damian a bench down from us and I waved at them, although Lily seemed distracted while she chewed on her lip. They were an odd pair, to be sure.

Damian, a Dragonslayer Knight of the Silver Order stood out from the group with his tribal tattoos rippling over his biceps that he pointedly didn't try to hide. Lily also had a shimmering glamor about her that I recognized now as her innate primal power as a dragon shifter. I wasn't sure what to make of them, and neither did the rest of the classroom apparently, because all of the benches around them aside from Killian's and mine were empty.

I scooted down, just as much to get some distance from Vern as to approach Lily. I made sure to keep my egg from bumping the table and nudged Lily. "Hey, are you okay?" I whispered.

She startled as if she hadn't noticed me. She glanced down at my egg, then locked her eyes up to mine. "That's sweet of you to ask," she said, giving me a genuine smile. "I'm fine. What about you? Any... luck yet?" she asked gently, indicating the contraption on my chest with a wave of her hand.

I shook my head and looked back at Professor Emhart who was glaring at us now. "I just, I don't know. I'm looking for something, but I haven't found it yet."

She hummed in acknowledgment as if that made perfect sense. "Well, I'm not sure if you'll find it in this class." She accepted Professor Emhart's vial with a grimace as she set it onto the table and coddled it with both hands.

Now that I could see it up close, I recognized the substance as the same liquid that Finn had been swiping off of the eggs...

Corruption.

Now I understood what had Lily so nervous.

"We're not supposed to... drink that, are we?" I asked.

She was quiet for a long moment before she replied. "Nobody knows the corruption better than I do." She glanced up at me, her glassy eyes changing into a reptilian slit, startling me. "Part of the corruption comes from a dragon's obsession with power. They can devour their own emotions..." She bit her lip when James rested a hand on her shoulder.

"What kind of emotions?" I asked, leaning in.

"Strong ones, such as love," James replied, his tone gruff. His hand squeezed Lily's shoulder as she glanced away. "They become true beasts who transform what once made them empathetic into raw strength and magic."

Now I understood why the Academy wanted someone like James. The wild dragons had lost themselves to the corruption and there'd be no saving them.

Only surviving them.

"Enough chatter," Professor Emhart instructed as she set down her empty tray and clapped her hands. "It's time to pair off with your partners." She waited until I scooted back to Killian—who smirked at me—

before she continued. "You're going to reach into your wyvern's dreams to better connect with them in this exercise. You can pick which wyvern you wish to focus on, either yours or your mate's."

The professor made that sound so easy, as if we had a choice.

Killian watched me I bit my lip, his wry smirk putting me on edge.

"I suppose we'll try connecting to Topaz?" I asked, stroking his snout he presented with affection.

Killian hummed, but his gaze fell to my egg.

He picked up his vial and waited for me to take mine. "Cheers," he said with a wink before knocking it back.

I watched him, waiting until he set his empty vial down before I popped the cork and sniffed. A pungent smell infiltrated my lungs, making me lurch away as I tried not to gag. "Oh, that is horrendous!"

Killian chuckled. "Just pretend it's a shot of whiskey," he offered.

"I've never had whiskey."

He shrugged. "Orange juice that has gone bad, then."

I glared at him, not enjoying his smug expression, so I threw back my vial and drank down the disgusting liquid.

My heart skipped a beat and a jolt of pain went through my temple, followed by stillness.

Killian offered his hands palm up. "Let's get started then, shall we?"

Giving him a raised brow, I placed my hands on his and waited.

Nothing happened at first, aside from the current of electricity that always spun through our bodies when we touched. I grazed my fingers over his, noting the warmth, the harshness of his callouses from sword fighting, and how he responded to me by leaning in.

We sat like that for a while, stroking each other's fingers. Staring into each other's eyes until the room slowly began to melt away.

The sensation felt right, almost natural, somehow. A pinging rattled around inside of my head and the world felt heavy, almost like I was falling into a deep sleep, until Killian's hands slipped away.

Loneliness hit me hard, followed by a sense of separation I couldn't describe.

"Killian!" I shouted, but the sense of sudden isolation wrapped around me as I fell into the abyss.

CHAPTER 2

LOST

I floated in a world of in-between, lost, confused.

Alone.

My hand drifted to my chest, finding nothing.

My egg. Where's my egg?

"Killian!" I shouted again as a roar built on the horizon, building until it rolled over me like a tidal wave, sending me spinning.

I tossed under the violent onslaught until I hit the ground. I strung my fingers through the deep roots in the ground and curled myself into a tight ball. Chaos stormed all around me like a violent tempest, throwing my hair over my face and sending stinging rain to pelt my cheeks.

"Killian," I begged, his name a plea now.

Where was he?

Why had he left me all alone?

A sheet of cold washed over me, followed by a new roar as I screamed, losing my grip as the world around me disintegrated and sent me falling. A dark chasm opened up beneath me, sparkling like waves and I shut my eyes as I hit.

Saltwater rushed up my nose as I went under, making me sputter and cough, but when I tried to take in a breath I drew water into my lungs.

I knew this place...

This nightmare had plagued me throughout my childhood after my father's drowning. This was that night that I couldn't remember.

Except in my dreams.

Dad!

My plea changed now, recalling that my father was out there in this darkness, dragged under because he'd come after me.

Dad, no!

There, a silhouette in the deep, thrashed against an ethereal spirit that brought him down as it turned and twisted. I kicked and swam to him, even though my lungs protested. When I reached out, something knocked me away, hitting me hard in my chest as I went flying through the water.

Water dragons.

I hadn't known what they were at the time, but I recognized them now with their deep blue gleam and how the water heated around them as they rushed by. They moved so fluidly, blurring across my vision as they distorted the deep.

And blocked me from the fight going on below.

Let him go!

My mental command came with a crack that shot out of me in a shockwave, forming a fissure along the ocean floor.

This was when my goddess blood had activated.

The water heated, bubbles forming as the dragons shrieked and responded to my magic.

Another hit pushed me away from the danger—and away from my father who'd gone still.

Fury filled me, building inside of me like a bomb about to explode. I surfaced as something pushed me up, washing a cold breeze over me as I gasped in fresh air. I sputtered out the water I'd brought into my lungs, coughing it up onto the shore.

Gold hummed all around me, growing with intensity as my mother screamed at me to stop. She must have known what was happening, that I had lost myself to my goddess blood in that moment.

She slapped me, hard, and my face jerked. She sobbed and cried my name, begging me to come back to her.

What was she so afraid of?

I couldn't listen to her, instead my eyes locked on the horizon. Everything was too calm, too quiet as the dark waves lapped over one another, oblivious to the life they had swallowed.

The hum in my ears burned as I formed fists. This wasn't how it was supposed to be. This was not how my father died, saving me from a future I had never asked for.

I closed my eyes, giving myself over to my rage.

The cold dissipated, leaving me with a floating sensation of heat and that incessant hum of power. My rage melted away as soft lips met mine.

Killian.

His warmth brought me back to the present as his lips met mine again. He breathed into me, expanding my lungs that I realized had stopped working.

His hands went to my chest, pushing down with gentle force as I drew in a sharp breath.

His lips met mine, but I didn't need to breathe anymore, I just needed his kiss. I enveloped him mouth with mine, fluttering my eyelids with bliss as energy exchanged between us. His mouth parted, giving me free rein to explore. So I did, relishing his taste, his feel, everything that brought me back to the world of the living where I wanted to stay.

Someone cleared their throat, banishing the moment.

My eyes flashed open as Killian leaned away, a slight smirk on his swollen lips. "So, you're alive," he remarked.

My fingers went to my lips, realizing what I'd just done.

Uh...

"Were you giving me mouth-to-mouth?" I asked, not sure what else to say. I glanced around, feeling the eyes of our entire classroom staring at us. We were mates, so mouth-to-mouth wouldn't be that unusual, even if I'd gotten carried away. However, it was my reaction to the corruption is what I guessed had them all so concerned.

A moment of panic hit me as I realized I didn't have my egg on me anymore. I jerked upright.

As if he knew what had me so panic-stricken, Killian handed me the wrapped egg he'd placed off to the side and I cocooned it into my arms.

Killian cleared his throat, then stood and marched over to the professor. "Why did that happen?" he demanded. "She wasn't breathing."

Professor Emhart frowned, but didn't reprimand him for his tone. "I'm not sure," she said after a moment. Her eyes flicked into reptilian slits as she studied me. "I'll have to discuss this matter with the Dean."

I sat up with Lily's help, her fingers surprisingly soft despite the fine layer of scales over her skin. She seemed to become more dragon-like during moments of stress, and apparently I'd just freaked everybody out.

I smiled, wanting to lighten the mood. "Well, I'm definitely not shooting more corruption anytime soon."

She grinned, revealing slightly pointed teeth. "Definitely," she agreed.

CHAPTER 3

LOVE BY DESIGN

*K*illian and I walked back to our dorm in silence as I stroked the egg still in my arms. The straps hung loosely around my sides. I wasn't going to let go of it, so it didn't matter about reattaching them.

The tension between Killian and I mounted with every step. My mouth opened, then closed when I couldn't think of anything to say.

My fingers went to my lower lip again.

Thanks for saving my life?

No. That was too cold.

Hey, so, how about that kiss?

No, definitely not.

When we reached our room, I still hadn't thought of anything to say and my heart jumped into my throat when he slammed his hand on the door, but didn't push it open. His uniform's sleeve ran up, revealing his blue tattoo spiraling over his arm. It had started to turn white, as if all the color was being leeched from it with Killian's weakened state.

What if he was angry with me? What if I'd embarrassed him?

"I need to say something," he said, keeping his back to me.

"Finally, somebody is saying something," I muttered. I lifted my chin as I stared at his back. "Are you going to turn around?"

"No," he replied, curling his fingers against the door, scratching his nails along the wood as if something inside him caused him pain. Topaz shifted in his sleep over Killian's neck, releasing a small sound of complaint.

I frowned and stroked my egg out of habit. It remained cold against my touch. "Okay, fine. Whatever. What is it?"

Killian went silent again and I waited, growing more irritated every second that passed by. "I'm torn," he admitted. "You're my mate. When you…" He paused, then cleared his throat again. "When you reacted like that to the corruption, it terrified me. I care about you." He finally turned, his whitewashed eyes sparking with defiance. "That's by design, isn't it? I'm programmed to care about you."

I pursed my lips. We'd been through this. "If you want to break the bond, just say the word." I was tired of his threats and his resentment.

He glowered at me, his rage building, but I had

more important things to worry about than his flip-flopping emotions.

My dragon.

His gaze dropped and the rage seeped out of him. "Come on. Let's get some rest." He shoved the door open and stormed inside.

I couldn't decide if he was furious with me, or himself, or both.

He settled Topaz into the nest by his bed, carefully tucking the wyvern's tail over his nose before he laid down on his bed—completely clothed.

"So, you're just going to sleep in your uniform?" I asked. He was reading way too much into our kiss. I'd been half-dead and he was already kind of kissing me. Give a girl a break.

He closed his eyes and ignored me, making a point to tuck his hands behind his head that he wasn't going anywhere.

Releasing a growl, I stormed out of the room and slammed the door.

"We don't have to deal with his crap," I told my egg as I hugged it tightly against my chest.

My body protested, more accustomed to the hibernation type of sleep that Killian and I had fallen into these past few days, or weeks, or however long it had been. I struggled to keep my eyes open though as I made my way to the cafeteria.

I spotted Lily in line and marched up to her, not caring about the glares I got from other students as I cut in line.

Lily didn't comment on it and gave me a nod of welcome. After the morning I'd had, nobody better mess with me.

"What'd he do?" she asked, her tone conspiratorial as we picked up our trays. "Did he try to make a move on you?"

I snorted. More like I was the one who'd made a move on him—and he'd made it clear he wasn't interested. "That jerk doesn't know what he wants," I said, snatching up the first thing I saw. The cafeteria didn't have the magical white mush today and instead had layers of vegetables, slabs of meat, and some type of diced potatoes.

Lily sighed. "I can relate." She picked up a conservative portion of meat and nothing else. "James has some brainwashing issues with that sword of his—and it seriously doesn't like me." She shrugged. "Dragon problems, right?"

I stared at her, numbly picking up something cold and putting it onto my plate. "His sword... doesn't like you?" Was that some kind of euphemism?

She chuckled. "Yeah. He's from a royal line of Knights, so he has a sword splintered from Excalibur itself. It's *the* weapon for killing dragons, so our relationship can be... strained, at times."

And I thought *I* had guy issues.

"Well, that sucks," I said as we found seats next to her mate. James smirked at me when we sat down.

"That was quite the show today," he said before taking a bite of his sandwich. He glanced down at the egg strapped to my chest. "You're an odd one, that's for sure."

"James," Lily chided. "Don't be rude."

He shrugged. "She's intriguing. That's all I'm saying."

She rolled her eyes. "Well, stop creeping her out. We're already isolated enough as it is."

He snorted and went back to his food.

Lily turned to me, all smiles as I pushed food around my plate. I'd tried eating some of the meat, but it tasted like rubber to me. "So, are you up for more classes today?" she asked, delicately taking one of her pieces of meat and nibbling on it. "We have lance fighting next." She glanced at her mate. "It's one of my favorites, because I always win."

James winked at her. "We'll see how you do today, beautiful."

I scrunched my nose. "Lance fighting?" I asked, not looking forward to using more energy when my eyelids were so heavy.

I took another bite of the mystery meat and felt a fresh surge of energy.

Hmm, that's interesting.

James smirked. "Looks like you're not the only one who enjoys mutton," he said to his mate. "Dragons always do."

"I'm not a dragon," I said around the mouthful, which was starting to taste pretty good now.

Lily leaned in and glanced at my egg. "No, but

you're the mother to one, so you need to keep up your strength."

I smiled, deciding that I liked Lily. She didn't judge me for picking an egg with no soul inside, didn't tell me that it was a hopeless cause. She believed in me.

Unlike Killian.

"Makes sense," I agreed, working on my food as my strength fluttered to life.

Maybe I *could* do this.

My mind drifted as I considered the possibilities if I succeeded, indulging in the daydream that I would hatch a wyvern and work side-by-side with Killian. He'd come around, eventually, I was sure of that. He had to. Topaz was counting on him and so was I, even if I hated to admit it.

Like today, when the corruption had pushed me into the worst memory of my life.

He'd brought me back from the darkness. I could have been lost in it forever, but he breathed life back into me.

Then there was that kiss.

"Hello, anybody home?" Lily asked, waving her hand over my eyes.

"Huh?" I asked, coming out of my thoughts.

I glanced up to see Jasmine staring at me. She smirked, pushing around her food without eating it.

When had she gotten here?

"Lance fighting, huh?" she asked, clearly amused by the idea. "Have you ever even held a lance before?"

I frowned. "No, but I'd never held a dagger before either, but I kicked your butt just fine."

Instead of being put off by my taunt, Jasmine grinned. She loved a challenge. "We'll see how you do today, hotshot."

Taking another bite of my mutton, I decided that I was up for the challenge. Maybe this was how I brought my egg back to life, by being what my wyvern ultimately needed me to be.

A true dragonrider.

CHAPTER 4

I LANCE YOU

"*I* thought you were taking a nap," I quipped when Killian waltzed across the field, lance in hand.

He grinned at me, both of us drawn together as if by an invisible thread.

"And miss this?" he said, tapping the lance on the soft ground. "I don't think so."

Whatever resentment he'd held onto seemed like a forgotten memory as we moved around each other. The professor stepped out, a tall lean man. "All right!" he barked as he spun a long lance over his head. A massive dragon groaned at his side. "Pair up!"

The rest of the students paired off, the sound of their lances tapping making my instincts go on edge.

"You're going to have to put down your egg," Killian informed me.

My hand went to the cold shell at my chest. I

glanced around, seeing if there were any other freshmen who'd come with unhatched eggs. I spotted a nest near the edge of the building where a few eggs were nestled together.

Killian offered his hand. "It's okay. Parting with it for a little while won't hurt anything. We'll be right here."

I swallowed hard, but I hadn't left the egg for more than a few seconds. "Are you sure?" I asked, a sting radiating through my chest at the thought of parting with it.

He smiled. "Yes. Do you think dragons are constantly caring for their young? They have to hunt, so leaving little ones on their own is natural." He rested his hand on my shoulder, making me flinch as energy swarmed through us. His fingers tightened momentarily before relaxing. The energy I'd gotten from the mutton helped us both. "Do you want me to walk with you?"

I glanced up at him, wondering why he was being so nice.

Flip-flop Killian. That would be my new nickname for him.

"I got it," I snapped, irritated.

Whacking him with a lance sounded pretty good about now.

I hurried to the freshmen nest and picked a spot for my egg, nestling it between a group of others to stay warm. A magical orb radiated heat from above the nest, but I wanted to be sure the cold breeze didn't get to it.

My fingers brushed the other eggs, sensing life inside stirring with strength and eagerness. They would be fine. They had warmth to spare and they seemed to welcome my egg into their nest.

Satisfied, I clutched my lance and returned to Killian.

"I'm so going to kick your butt," I said.

He smirked, his whitewashed eyes flashing with delight. "Let's see what you've got, freshman."

I lunged, surprised when Killian reacted swiftly as he shifted out of the way. His lance swung back, smacking me in the face.

"Point!" the professor shouted.

Growling, I swung again, my vision darkening at the edges. Killian sidestepped again, seeming to expend no effort in dodging me.

"You're going to have to do better than that," he taunted.

Anger boiled in me, returning a familiar hum in my ears.

I couldn't recall any fantasy novels where I'd read about lance fighting. Just jousting, maybe, so I jumped to my feet with an idea. I ran to the end of the field, ignoring shouts wondering if I was retreating.

Nope, but I was going to teach Killian a lesson.

I turned, adjusting my lance to face him as I began long strides.

One step.

Two.

Three.

I aimed at him, increasing my momentum as I ran. He could sidestep me, but I knew that he wouldn't.

He took the bait, aligning his lance to my heart and began to run.

I'd read about this once before. The trick to jousting was strength. I could already feel the weight of my lancing pulling the end down, but something in me had surged to life. That hum in my ears was my goddess blood, giving me a boost of energy that would keep my lance steady and on target.

Killian, though, I could already spot his lance dropping, which would give me the edge. He was weak, and even if I was to blame for that, I would use any weakness to my advantage. If he didn't want to lose, he should have sidestepped instead of taking my taunt.

His pride was something that kept him from accepting our mate-bond, that made him so unpredictable and worked as an invisible wedge between us.

For a Nephilim like Killian, we didn't have room for the both of us, our wyverns, as well as his pride. Something had to give and if this was what it took, then so be it.

The ground shook as Killian and I neared, shockwaves going out with each of my steps as the hum turned into a roar in my ears. My goddess blood would give out after this, but one shot was all I needed.

Killian tired at the last moment, his lance dropping just enough that I could slip the tip underneath my arm, avoiding impact as my weapon hit hard.

Snap.

It broke in half as the impact jolted up my arms. Killian roared with pain as he lurched to the side.

The roar in my ears vanished, the dark edges of my vision closing in as I hurried to his side. I'd wanted to break him, not kill him. "Killian?" I asked, worried that I'd gone too far.

He grabbed at his chest, ripping his uniform to reveal chainmail.

"That was... quite the hit," he said, commending me as he groaned and let his head hit the soft ground. He chuckled. "Stop looking at me like that. I'm okay."

I released a sigh of relief. "Good," I said, then rubbed my eyes as stars sprinkled across my vision.

"Viv?" he asked as nausea wound through my stomach.

I sank to my knees, wobbling as dizziness threatened to take me under. "Something's not right," I said as a tingling sensation swept over my body.

"What's going on?" Lily asked as footsteps sounded around us.

"Give her space!" the professor ordered. I didn't look up to see if anyone obeyed him.

"She hit me with a heck of a jousting strike, then she collapsed," Killian supplied. "Viv?" he asked again, his touch going to my shoulder.

A zap sounded as the energy between us retaliated, feeling wrong. He jerked away with a curse. I curled in on myself with a whimper as a strange sense of loneliness wrapped over me like a shroud, an inescapable sensation that threatened to take me under.

Like that night in the ocean.

"Where's her egg?" Lily asked, her voice on the edge of frantic. "She needs her egg. You shouldn't have pulled her away from it."

"I got it!" someone shouted, making me snap my gaze up as Jasmine ran to me with my egg in her hands.

For some reason seeing someone else touch my egg filled me with rage. I surged to my feet and snatched it from her, hissing like a wild animal before I crumpled to the ground, wrapping myself around the shell that seemed even colder than before.

Strong arms swept around me, pulling me against a hard chest as Killian's scent consumed me.

I'd never realized it before, but I placed his scent now. As a rider bonded to a water dragon, his scent had a musky saltiness to it.

It should have brought me back to my worst memory.

Instead, it felt right. As if he could wash away the sadness with something new.

Satisfied, I rested my cheek against his warmth, grateful to shut my eyes as he carried me back to our room.

CHAPTER 5

LIKE A MOTH
TO A FLAME

I'll never let you go again.

My new mantra brushed my lips, a promise to my unhatched wyvern that I wouldn't fail a second time.

What had I been thinking?

Leaving my egg alone in this state had been a horrible idea. I couldn't blame Killian, only myself. Maybe other dragons left their eggs in their nest for a few hours while they went hunting, but my egg needed me at all times. It had the echo of a lost soul inside of it and I was its only tether. I couldn't stop searching for it now.

Killian left me alone in my bed as I twisted and turned, lost in a fretful hibernation that took me deeper than I'd ever gone before. A horrible darkness wrapped around me, creating a permanent shadow over my mind.

His voice came to me, seeming distant as did his touch when his knuckles brushed my cheek. Sometimes he was angry, sometimes he was kind.

Flip-flop Killian at his finest.

Grief weighed me down too much to care about Killian's internal dilemma. Although grief due to what, I wasn't sure. Grief because I had failed my egg? Grief because we were both going to die?

Or maybe grief that after everything, my father would have given his life for nothing? He could have lived on with my mother, leaving me in the cold darkness where I belonged.

Distant voices woke me, their urgency forcing me to crack open my eyes. The window shades were open, leaving a view of the emerging stars that sparkled along with the light drizzle of rain. A shadow passed every now and then, making me frown until I realized the silhouettes were dragons sporting their riders for a midnight run.

My heart warmed, hoping that for myself and my wyvern, one day.

"That's your plan?" Jasmine asked, her tone sharp as her words cut through the cracked door. I craned my neck to get a better look, spotting Killian's arm as he leaned against the doorway, crossing his tattooed arms.

"You have a better one?" he asked, sounding tired.

Had he gotten any sleep at all?

How long had I been out, anyway?

"We're both going to get expelled," she said, rubbing her temples.

"So, you're in?" Killian asked.

She sighed, slapping her hand at her side. "Stealing the Dean's sword and severing a bond to save your mate, which will probably kill you in the process? No, I'm not *in*, Killian. You need to come up with a better plan."

What? Stealing the Dean's sword?

I wanted to jump to my feet and demand answers. Did Killian hate me so much that he'd rather be dead than be bonded to me for a second longer? Despite my anger, I wanted to give Killian the benefit of the doubt. Surely he had more to his plan than destroying everything we'd created and losing Topaz in the process.

He shifted, the moonlight hitting him so that I could see his grin. He didn't seem like the kind of guy who was about to lose his dragon, making me relax. "There's a Class Seven Tunnel tonight."

She stared at him. "So?"

He tapped his fingers over his forearm. "And I'm a Nephilim. I could survive a trip to the Light Realm."

She studied him for a moment before her eyes blew wide. "Wait. You can't be serious. You're going to ask daddy for help?"

"Why not?" he asked. "If things continue to progress like this, I'm dead anyway. At least if we break the bond, this will give us a chance." He unwrapped his arms, reaching up to scratch Topaz's nose. The wyvern looked smaller, somehow, and pressed in close to his cheek as he shivered. "Plus," Killian added, his voice dropping, "I can't stand seeing Topaz like this. He's not going to last much longer, and even if I have to lose him, at least he can live in the Light Realm. There's enough magic to sustain him."

Oh...

Guilt washed over me as I held my egg tighter to my chest. I'd been hoping to find some sort of magical solution, but this was what failure looked like.

Still... no. I couldn't allow Killian to sever the bond, even if he had a plan. It would break my connection to my own wyvern before it even hatched.

"What about Viv?" Jasmine asked after a moment, her tone the softest I've ever heard.

"She'll go back home," he decided, his features hard. "Once the bond is broken, the Dean won't have a reason to keep her here and they'll send her back." He cleared his throat and pushed off of the doorway. "You'll make sure she gets home safely, yeah?"

Jasmine chewed her lip. "Yeah, okay." She jerked her head, indicating the stairs. "Well, come on. Let's go get ourselves expelled. I always wanted to live in the Human Realm, anyway."

He chuckled, and moved to close the door behind him. He paused, just for a moment, to stare at me. I could feel his gaze on me, desperate, wanting. I watched him in the dark, knowing that he couldn't see me, but our bond screamed for nourishment, for connection. He restrained himself, curling his fingers into a fist before he closed the door, making a sob catch in my throat.

He was really going to go through with this.

I waited for a long time after Killian and Jasmine's footsteps had disappeared before I tested my leg. One at first, then the other, both functional, although jerky.

Needles ran up my arms as I shifted, moving into a sitting position as I clutched onto my egg. "We've been out for a while, huh?" I asked, twisting my egg so that I could warm the other side, although I wasn't sure how much warmth I could provide. I had no energy and my fingertips had gone numb.

Ignoring the dread creeping up my stomach, I forced myself to my feet, squeezing my eyes shut for a moment as a wave of dizziness passed over me, but raw determination kept me standing.

"I won't let anyone break our bond," I vowed, speaking both of my bond with Killian and my wyvern. "This isn't over yet."

I'd been paying attention to a few of the conversations about Tunnels, and I knew a Class Seven was as high as it got. While the lower level tunnels could travel to multiple realms, including the Human Realm, Level Six and Seven had only one destination in mind. I wasn't sure where they'd gone until now, with Level Seven going to the "Light Realm" as Killian had called it.

Did he mean... heaven?

If that was the case, I had to get to it first. Maybe I could find my dad... maybe he would know what to do.

With a mission in mind, I put one foot in front of the other, wincing as my bare feet scraped against the floor. Even the smooth wood felt like shards.

"We only need to get to the shore," I assured my egg, although that sounded like an impossible marathon in my current condition.

I pushed the door open, gritting my teeth as the numbness in my fingertips transformed into jolts of pain. A faint hum in my ears sounded as I pushed myself to my limits, heading through the hall and outside.

I wasn't going to last long... but maybe it would be long enough.

Seniors swept overhead in the night, riding their dragons as sentries over campus. I felt like I'd gained a sixth sense when it came to the dragons and I knew when they were about to fly in range. I hurried behind a pillar, resting my head against it as a low *woosh* sounded as a dragon swept by.

"Close one," I told my egg, adjusting it again to make sure I didn't hold it too tightly. The light cracks up its sides seemed to have grown.

Swallowing the lump in my throat, I kept up the pattern as I dodged sentries all the way to the gate. I stared up at it, woefully unprepared to jump it a second time when a loud *click* sounded, making me jolt as it swung open.

The Academy recognized me as an official student, a dragonrider who would soar in the skies and be worthy of the title.

That realization gave me a sense of pride, even if the dream might be fleeting.

If magic itself believed in me, perhaps I had a chance.

Setting my jaw, I picked up my pace, ignoring a sprinkling of rain that came in and hardened the grainy sands outside of the campus.

The wind kicked up the farther I wandered from the Academy as if the elements disapproved of my choice. It howled, throwing sand in my face and making my eyes sting. I didn't release my hold on my egg to wipe away the sand and instead I pressed on.

The water came into view and the air changed to a salty, pungent scent. I spotted the Tunnel as well, this one glowing with golden light that contrasted against the dark vortex I remembered from the previous Tunnel.

The Light Realm...

Even though I could spot my destination, hopelessness crept in. I wasn't sure how I was going to swim in my current condition. I dragged one foot in front of the other, sheer determination keeping me aloft as my vision darkened, homing in on the distant golden glow as a beacon.

Like a moth to a flame.

The phrase hit me as I dragged on, a sensation creeping over me that I was about to die if I kept this up, but I clutched onto my egg, determined that it wasn't going to end like this.

"Just... a little bit... farther," I ground out, taking one step, and then another.

My legs gave out when I reached the shore and my eyes fluttered, wanting to close.

"Please," I begged as I held up my egg to the light. The Tunnel seemed so far away, but it glowed so brightly that I felt as if I could touch it if I could just reach a little bit farther. "Please, take him. Save him." I didn't care what happened to me anymore. All that mattered was my dragon.

The golden light responded to my plea, building in brightness until my eyes burned. I watched, hopeful as warmth enveloped me.

The hum in my ears rang louder, growing in intensity with the Tunnel's brightness until it hit a climax...

And vanished.

"No..." I breathed, desperation hitting my chest and making me gasp.

I thought I'd lost everything, that the cold egg in my grip would never evolve into the wyvern it was meant to be, until my vision adjusted and I spotted a distant glowing spec.

It grew, growing in brightness until I realized it was a bird.

No... not just any bird.

"Solstice!" I cried, having never been this happy in my life to see that resilient little bird.

I jolted to my feet, swaying as I held up the egg, knowing that this was what I was meant to do.

"Go on!" I encouraged. "Fly!"

Solstice chirped, his delicate sounds echoing over the lapping waves. My heart swelled, excitement lifting me onto my toes until an explosion sounded, sending the waves crashing.

A massive dragon erupted from the waters, spraying droplets everywhere as its giant maw snapped, going for the bird.

"Solstice!" I cried, feeling helpless as I teetered at the edge of the shore. I didn't have much power left, but I reached out anyway, feeling the last of my life-force drain into the air as I urged the bird to fly.

No... not my bird.

My wyvern's spirit.

I'd been so stupid. All these years my wyvern had always been with me, always there for me and by my side with encouragement or a snarky little chirp that always made me smile.

I held up the egg, draining everything I had to give Solstice speed. His wings burst into golden flames as his dragon's form took shape, reminiscent of what he would become once he hatched.

Once he came back to where he belonged.

The wild dragon on his tail cried out as an arrow pierced its eye, having come from over my shoulder. I didn't turn to see who'd shot it. Instead I held up my egg and poured my heart into the little bird careening over the waves.

Solstice slammed into me—no, into the egg, sending light and warmth bursting through the shell. I drew in a deep gasp as if I could breathe again for the first time.

Solstice.

He's alive.

A fissure formed through the egg as if this was the moment it had been waiting for. A tiny golden snout poked through, followed by horns. I waited, wondering if I should help the creature, but my instincts said not to interfere. He needed to do this on his own or risk being weak all his life.

The pained mewl that came from Solstice's wyvern form made my heart melt, but I forced myself to be still as I held the base of the egg. His eyes remained closed as he worked, his glittering horn thrashing as he twisted, searching for a way out. He managed to hook another edge of the shell, breaking it off as he pushed all the way through.

There.

"Come here," I whispered as he climbed out, and I scooped the tiny wyvern into the crook of my arm.

Solstice mewled again, but this one was a grateful sound. He pressed against my body and rumbled a low growl that sounded like a purr. Tears stung my eyes.

The moment would have been beautiful, had it not been tarnished by another warning roar that ripped over the horizon.

"We can't stay here," I said, panic rising in my throat.

I just got Solstice back. I couldn't lose him again.

Feeling as if I could collapse, I forced myself to move. I spun, dizzy and disoriented as I stumbled into a hard chest. Killian steadied me as if he'd always been there, ready to catch me before I fell.

My eyes went to the golden sword in his other hand, a blade stained with blood. It hummed with dangerous magic that was meant to break our bond.

But not anymore.

Now, it would be the only thing that stood between us and the wild dragons that had followed Solstice to the Academy.

"Hold onto me," Killian ordered, hooking my arm around his neck. I cradled Solstice against us, careful not to drop him.

Jasmine swooped overhead, aiming her bow at the wild dragon that had surfaced again. A haze drifted over her as her dragon's wings expanded, making her look like a terrifying Valkyrie.

A cascade of mighty roars responded to the threat and burst over the sands, making my ears ring. Killian turned so that I could see the nightmare rising from the deep.

Blue flames licked at the skies as massive, wild dragons launched into the air and headed straight for us.

Killian gave me a single command, one that I was keen to obey.

"It's time to run."

DRAGONRIDER ACADEMY

EPISODE FOUR

USA TODAY BESTSELLING AUTHOR

A.J. FLOWERS

CHAPTER 1

DEATH
ON THE HORIZON

*S*olstice. You're alive.

My dragon warmed himself against my chest as I shut out the world that descended into chaos all around us. The Wild Dragons had followed Solstice's spirit to this realm. Because of me, they had found a way to use a powerful Gate to worm their way into this world.

I had to fight, or my elation at having reunited with my dragon would be extremely short-lived.

"Focus," Killian commanded as alarms blared and the roar of deadly dragons thundered through my chest. He glanced at the shore, gritting his teeth. "The bond isn't supposed to establish like this," Killian continued. "You're going to go into a coma if you can't shut him out."

I blinked up at him, my vision bleary. Even though

my mind revolted against his suggestion, my body agreed. Solstice clung to me and keened, tightening my resolve.

I would never abandon Solstice again.

Shrill alarms blared to life and my eyes darted to the horizon. Red, rolling clouds made it seem as if the sea had caught fire. Knights and Valkyries rode their wyverns, cutting through the scene as they clashed with the vicious beasts rising from the deep.

Blood painted the skies.

Death rained down as bodies thumped to the sand and crashed into violent waters.

What have I done?

"We have to get to the gate," Killian said, his voice rising over the chaos as he gripped my arm. "The Dean's erected a forcefield," he said, indicating the shimmery veil that bolstered into the clouds. "It'll hold for now, but we have to get you on campus."

My mouth opened, but another inhuman roar pierced my ears. It rolled through my body, making terror grip my heart until I couldn't move. I wasn't trained for this. I hadn't grown up with a lance in one hand and a sword in the other. The most adventurous thing I'd done during my childhood was stick gum in Julie Emmerson's hair. Come to think of it, she'd had to cut it off, so it explained her deep-seated hatred for me.

Growling, Killian snatched me up and I squeaked. "We don't have time for you to freeze, Viv."

Solstice made a sound of complaint and dug his nails into my skin as he nuzzled into my neck. Killian grunted with pain and favored one leg as he shifted my weight, betraying that he might not be much better off than me.

"Don't," I protested, but a dragon's roar washed out the sound as Killian hugged me to his body.

He marched through the sand and I didn't complain. My entire body sagged against him, weakened and full of mixed emotions. I'd spent so much time agonizing over the dead egg I had bonded to. It had drained me of my energy as I'd tried to hatch a dragon that had no spirit... something that had seemed like a fruitless activity.

Yet, Solstice had found his way to me.

I hugged the small creature as tightly as my arms would allow as Killian's speed increased. "Hold on," he shouted as he dodged left, avoiding a screeching green flame that sent the sand bursting into glass. His grip went to the sword at his hip, but he couldn't fight, not with me in his grip. He growled and shifted me closer as he resumed the trek across the sands. I knew he wanted to draw his sword and fight, but I weighed him down. I'd been weakening him ever since our cursed bond began.

The sword on his hip was his fix for everything. The sword he'd stolen from the Dean... a blade meant to separate us, to give up on Solstice and our destiny.

How could I ever forgive him for even considering giving up on Solstice... on me?

"He's doubling back," Killian shouted, his eyes on the sky, his attention fixated on the threat from above. A roar followed as a rush of heat swept over us.

The air shifted and Killian growled as Topaz hissed when the dragon circled low, then disappeared into the clouds again. Topaz curled around Killian's neck, hugging him tighter to prevent him from falling. I could sense his fatigue matched my own and the little creature wanted nothing more than to fall into his nest and dream.

We aren't going to make it.

"Killian," I whispered, his name a plea on my lips, although I didn't know what I wanted him to do. Drop me and run? Save himself? Forget I ever existed?

No, I didn't want that, as selfish as it was. I needed him and his gaze swept to mine, echoing my own roaring emotions.

"We're going to survive this," he said, his words grounding me. He kept my gaze even when the dragon swooped in for another attack, this one targeted for us.

A bright emerald blur crashed through the red clouds, a detail Killian must have seen when I'd been wallowing in my fear.

My eyes went wide when I spotted Jasmine on her wyvern's back. She hung off the side as she aimed with her bow. Her arrow released, hurling through the air before striking the Wild Dragon in the neck. A weak spot, I realized, as the creature dropped like a stone, careening across the sands before its long snout stopped just inches from Killian's feet.

Jasmine glared at us as she swung back onto her

wyvern and crouched low. "Get a move on, you morons!" she shouted before yanking on Jade's reins, redirecting the wyvern back to the sea where the worst of the fight raged on.

"Don't look back," Killian warned me, but it was too late. The sight of a wall of Wild Dragons rising from the sea like a nightmare made my heart sputter in my chest. They swarmed the beach like a hive, talons flashed and teeth tore into flesh. Knights and Valkyries on guard duty weren't equipped for a fight like this and they bled on the melted sands.

All because of me.

"I can't allow this to happen," I whispered as tears stung my eyes. "I can't—"

Warmth surged through my body as Solstice let out a sharp cry and Killian groaned. I glanced at them, realizing my mistake.

"I'm sorry," I whispered as I bit down on my instinct to draw power from the nearest source.

I'm a Conduit.

The word lingered in my mind like a curse, something that Killian would never be able to love. All I knew how to do was take.

"We have to retreat, Viv," Killian said, pulling me around the ugly maw of the wild dragon's corpse Jasmine had just felled. "Leave the fight to the students. They've trained for this. They know what to do."

It didn't feel that way, not from the death throes that echoed all around us. They weren't ready and I certainly wasn't much better. I pushed against

Killian's chest as he trudged toward the campus, although it didn't do me much good. My body refused to listen as fatigue worked its way over me like a shroud.

By the dark circles under Killian's eyes, he wasn't faring much better.

Anger surged in me. "I need to fix this," I snapped. "I should fight."

"You can't even stand up," he informed me, making me bite my cheek. "We're returning to campus and leaving the Knight and the Valkyries to do their job."

Bossy much?

Killian hoisted me up again, grunting, but I couldn't demand he put me down. My vision swarmed with black dots and Solstice keened in my grasp. We weren't going to last for much longer like this.

Killian picked his way through the sand, avoiding the worst of the attacks as Jasmine and the other students kept the horde at bay.

The waves of sands felt never-ending as we continued making our way toward the Academy's gate. Even as the chaos grew, the heat crept closer, sweat dripping down my neck as the threat closed in on us.

We weren't going fast enough.

My mind raced and panic made my senses foggy. I regretted not going to class all those weeks now. I didn't have the training for this.

Think. What have you learned?

The memory of the dwarf pouring dragon blood over the eggs in the sanctuary came to the forefront of my mind. They'd absorbed magic while separating out the corruption.

What if I could do the same?

What if I could draw power from the wild dragons themselves?

"Killian," I snapped, but he ignored me, his white-washed eyes watching for any sign of danger as he stumbled us closer to the Academy's gates. "Killian!" I tried again. "Put me down."

"We're almost there," he insisted as Solstice squeaked with warning just before a blast of heat knocked us to the sands.

Men, do they ever listen?

I stumbled to my feet, Solstice still clinging to my chest. Three dragons swarmed above us and Jasmine shouted in the distance, trapped behind a wall of enemies that had broken through the ranks.

We were on our own.

"Okay, Solstice. We got this," I whispered to him, running my fingers over his golden snout as he chirped in support.

Killian kicked up sand as he struggled to his feet and drew his sword, shouting my name.

Ignoring him, I closed my eyes and focused.

The sources of power lit up all around me. Some bright and holy, others dark and sickly.

There you are.

I focused on the dark spots, latching onto them in my mind. Instead of shrinking away, I opened myself up to it. Cold dread spread through my chest and my teeth began to chatter. Killian reached me, grabbing my hand and hissing with pain, but he wouldn't let go.

"What are you doing?" he bit out. "You're freezing."

Solstice keened and snuggled against my chest as if trying to warm me, but I knew this was our only chance. The darkness trembled and ebbed, moving away from me.

"They've stopped," Killian informed me, his grip on my fingers tightening. "Are you doing that?"

I couldn't answer him as panic choked me. A massive swarm of darkness swept over the skies, the energy unnatural and wrong. Forcing my eyes open, I blinked, my vision split between the real world and the aura of my magic.

Killian grabbed my hand, making me gasp as the flux of energy swarmed over me. He grunted as I struggled to gain control over the forces.

"Viv," he said, his voice low with warning as tiny black droplets formed over my arms.

Corruption.

I swallowed past the lump in my throat as nausea rolled through my stomach. I could use this energy, but I had to purify it first. My legs straightened and my shoulders rolled back. Breathing a sigh of relief, I embraced the rejuvenation.

"This is wrong," Killian bit out as I swiped the back of my hand over my burning eyes... My knuckles came back black.

Wiping the Corruption on my shirt, I tugged Killian

to the campus. "Trust me, okay?" I asked him, my voice hoarse.

The chaos all around us had stilled into a deathly silence.

Until a roar sounded.

"Move!" Killian shouted, his tattoos glowing blue with renewed energy. While I had drained him all this time, I could also share my bounty with him, too.

A creature dove from the clouds, spreading black horrible wings as red eyes fixated on me.

Not good!

I raced with Solstice clinging to my chest and Killian at my side. What little energy I'd sifted from the dark forces all around us I burned like a match, fueling our plight as we closed the distance to the Academy.

The Wild Dragon swooped low and the hairs on the back of my neck stood on end. It felt as if his talons could slice open my skin straight to my spine if I hesitated for even a moment. Heat unfurled all around us as it released a bellowing moan.

"Keep it up, Viv!" Killian encouraged as I realized I was protecting us from a Wild Dragon's flame.

Me. That's all that stood between us and being burned to a crisp. No pressure.

Finally at the finish line, I hurled us through the Academy's gate and into the bubble of protection with a *pop* as the magical shield closed in around us. The creature behind us roared as it slammed into the barrier, flapping his taloned wings against it before lifting off with an enraged bellow.

My lungs burned as I gasped for breath. Whatever energy I'd claimed from the Wild Dragons had been expended and my vision swarmed with bursting stars. The fight raged on in the distance and my stomach sank with a sinking sense of dread.

We'd made it… but at what cost?

CHAPTER 2

LITTLE BIRD

"*W*e need to get to the bunker," Killian said as he hauled me to my feet.

"Bunker?" I murmured as Solstice nuzzled his snout under my chin. I'd been here for weeks, maybe even months, and I hadn't heard anything about a bunker.

I wobbled as Killian led me down an eerily empty street. "Everyone not fighting or preparing to fight will be there. It's only for emergencies, and if you had attended Siege Class you would have known about it."

Right.

"Are you calling me a slacker?" I snapped as my legs gave out and Killian caught me around my waist. Glaring up at him I added, "Because this slacker just saved your life."

Take that for being bonded to a Conduit.

A *ping* sounded and Killian glanced up. A billow of red fanned out where the dragons unleashed fire onto the barrier. "If you'd prefer we *stay* alive, I suggest we move. I've never seen that many dragons in one place. The Academy's magic is weak, it has been for some time, and this barrier is not going to hold forever."

I waved one hand in front of us. "Then lead the way."

Killian jerked me along, his grip around my waist a reminder that he wasn't going to leave me behind. He could just use that sword of his and cut me free, but I couldn't make my tongue work to remind him.

We passed the cafeteria, then the armory and wyvern stables that buzzed with activity. I watched with envy as students laced up armor and jumped onto their mounts, flinging through the barrier to join the battle to protect the Academy. The shrill alarm echoed here, making the dragons impatient for their riders to finish their preparations.

Solstice keened in my ear, just a newborn wyvern with no means of self-defense yet, but that didn't stop him from wanting to fight.

Topaz's tiny wings flared, his instinct wanting to join the herd.

"Not today, Topaz," Killian said, petting the creatures small head as he tucked him closer to the crook of his neck.

"There's no time to waste!" a professor bellowed through the streets. I recognized the tall, lean professor from lancing practice. "Get in formation and pair off into teams!"

I smirked at the instruction. Jasmine had definitely not followed the "teams" directive.

Killian's hold on my waist tightened as another round of students launched into the air. "Let's keep moving," he said, his breath hot against my ear.

The smaller path between the stable and armory opened up as we rushed past the dorm building. I stumbled and Killian caught me. A sense of trepidation swept through me as I wavered and tumbled into his chest.

"Viv," he said, his voice low, "are you—"

His concern cut short as a shredding sound ripped through the air, making me cover my ears as I screamed. An influx of raw, dark energy threatened to knock me from my feet.

The barrier. They've made it through the barrier.

The alarm increased in tempo, blaring with renewed panic that matched the pace of my heart.

Killian cursed under his breath as a wave of shadow tumbled over the gates, throwing the Academy into darkness.

I threw out my hands. "No!" I shouted. "You do not get to take this from me!"

This darkness had taken so much from me already. My father had died in the darkness of the sea. My past laid buried like a nightmare that wouldn't end. My future hinged on broken promises and fear.

I couldn't live like this.

I *wouldn't* live like this.

A scream erupted from me as I pushed the darkness

out with all of my heart and soul. A roar responded in kind as the Wild Dragons forced into a retreat and the barrier healed where it had been broken.

"Viv," Killian said, his voice holding a note of awe.

What energy I had left had finally run out and my eyes rolled into the back of my head.

I wavered, but Killian wouldn't let me fall. He looped his arms under my knees and lifted me to his chest. Warmth surged as our bond flared and my heart stuttered.

My ears rang as I clutched Solstice to my chest, but I clearly heard Killian's calm voice cut through the terror. "I've got you, little bird."

My mind caught on to that endearment, even as my world dimmed.

Little bird.

The loving nickname in direct contrast to the taunt I had always endured growing up.

No longer was I the *odd bird*.

I was Killian's little bird now.

The delirious thought was the last thing in my mind before darkness took over.

CHAPTER 3

IMMORTAL

*T*ime passed as I slipped into a state between lucidity and sleep.

I couldn't move.

Black nothingness mixed with red bursts of agony in a disorienting blur.

I welcomed the absence of noise and chaos. This world was cool and peaceful; a reprieve from the fire that raged through my body.

I'd overstepped my ability as a Conduit. The cold burn came from the Corruption I'd failed to expel, but because of my actions, I was still alive. The Academy was still safe and we'd all live to see another day.

At least, that's what I hoped was the case. I couldn't open my eyes or fight my way to complete lucidity to find out if the Wild Dragons had consumed us all yet.

The pain came in waves, progressively getting worse until the darkness would take over again. I tried desperately to move or scream for help, but I was paralyzed. Forced to endure each moment. My every nerve ending burned and I was certain that somewhere in reality I must actually be on fire. I was sure that I wouldn't come out of this as anything other than a charred husk.

At first I was surrounded by unborn dragons.

The Egg Sanctuary.

That was what Killian had meant by the bunker. The most protected place on campus.

However, the tension in the air passed and eventually I must have been moved.

Brief flashes of my dorm kept me tied to reality. I caught glimpses of Killian's whitewashed eyes gazing down at me. They were filled with concern and a plea, although a plea for what, I couldn't tell. A plea to live, perhaps, a plea not to leave him, to forgive him, to forgive myself.

The weight of Solstice curled on my chest reminded me that I was still alive, that this was all for a purpose.

I had to survive, if not for anyone else, for my dragon, and for my mate.

Through one of my bouts of lucidity a distant melody cut through the murky fog of my mind. It was familiar, I decided, one that held lilting notes of a long-buried memory I couldn't quite reach.

My mind cleared as the melody grew in confidence, revealing an old image, one of my mother singing one of her favorite Celtic lullabies as she tucked me in for the night. My dad stood behind her smiling with such undiluted joy that it made me want to weep.

Yet the song kept going, pulling me out of the pit of darkness and into the light, growing louder and clearer.

I wasn't imagining it, she was here.

Mother!

My eyes flashed open and sunlight streaming in from the window made me flinch. My eyes adjusted as the song abruptly cut off and a gentle touch caressed my face.

"Vivi," she said on a gasp, diving in for a hug as she wrapped her arms around me, squeezing the tiny dragon between us. "You're awake!"

I blinked a few times as Solstice squeaked from the rough motion, making my mother laugh. When I tried to return her embrace, a strong grip held me back.

Killian.

My mother pulled away and brushed tears from my face, seemingly unfazed that Killian slept beside us, his fingers threaded through mine.

"You're here," I marveled, my voice cracking from disuse.

"Yes," she confirmed with a bright smile, as if that was to be expected. "Of course I am."

I couldn't believe it. My mother was here... but, what of the battle? My eyes went wide as I recalled my last memories fighting for my life. "The Wild Dragons!"

She shushed me, stroking my arm in reassurance. "They're not able to hurt you, Vivi. You pushed them out, remember? And the Dean was able to reestablish the barrier. It has kept them at bay, for now. They're still in this realm, but eventually they'll get hungry enough they'll have to leave."

So, this is a siege.

I swallowed past the lump in my throat. I wanted to hear everything I'd missed, how she had found her way to me, if the threat of the Wild Dragons had really passed, but most of all, I wanted to hold onto that memory that she'd awoken inside of me. "You haven't sung in years," I said, rubbing my throat as my voice came out raw and scratchy.

My mother reached over the table and retrieved a waiting glass of water, ready for me once I had awoken.

"It... reminds me too much of your father," she said, her smile tinged with sadness. "You seemed like you were drowning. I couldn't bear another second of it, Vivi, so I sang a song to bring you back to me."

Solstice squeaked again, trying to get comfortable on my lap now that I was sitting up, and nipped at Killian's hand. Topaz stirred, wrapped around Killian's neck to hiss at the golden wyvern.

"Don't do that," I chided to my dragon, directing his golden snout into the crook of my arm. He nuzzled into the warmth and vibrated his wings, which I took as a sign of contentment.

Killian still held my hand, and I squeezed it. "Is he okay?" Maybe he had fallen into a coma too.

"He's just exhausted," my mother said, making my shoulders relax. "He hasn't left your side for weeks. I kept trying to tell him to get some rest, and I guess it finally caught up to him." She smirked. "He's a devoted mate, my daughter. You have chosen well."

I kept my reservations to myself about that, but seeing Killian like this built warmth in my chest and I couldn't help a small smile.

I brushed his hair from his face, sending a sliver of my energy that seemed refueled by my mother's presence. "Killian," I whispered. "Wake up."

He groaned as his eyelids fluttered open. When he registered my face, his eyes went wide and his pupils dilated. He wrapped his arms around me, upsetting both Solstice and Topaz who screeched in protest as my mate buried his face in my neck.

"You scared me," he whispered, his voice harsh and raw, just like mine.

When he pulled away he chuckled, no doubt at the blazing state of my cheeks. I glanced at my mother, who only seemed amused by my discomfort.

My mother folded her hands while Solstice curled up in my lap again and Topaz resettled around Killian's neck. "Now that she's awake, the Riderbond magic should stabilize, yes?" she asked.

Riderbond magic?

Killian nodded and brushed his hair from his face, and I finally saw what my mother meant. He'd clearly been drained, leaving his features frail and his once feathered and beautiful hair limp and dull. It was his relief that had made him look energetic, but now he sagged against the headboard as she sat next to me.

"What does she mean?" I asked, my voice going up in pitch. "And why do you look so sickly? Are you okay?" He looked as if he'd had a brush with death and I couldn't voice the last part of my question.

Is this my fault?

"I'll be fine," he assured me, his eyes watching me from underneath hooded eyelids. "I had to share some of my magic with you during your transition, but now that you've stabilized, I'll recover what was drained."

Answer: yes, this is totally my fault.

I groaned and pulled my knees to my chest, leaving enough space for Solstice who squirmed closer to me, stealing as much of my warmth as possible through his hard scales. "What kind of transition?" I asked as the guilt rammed through me.

Killian smirked. "If you had gone to class—"

"Yes, yes, I know," I grumbled. "Just explain."

He nodded. "You were unconscious because you tried to use Dragonrider magic, something that you're only supposed to do as a full Dragonrider bonded to your wyvern. Solstice had only just hatched, and the bond is… different, in your case. There are other variables at play since you are a Conduit, but in the end, Dragonrider magic works the same. You needed power that simply wasn't there, and you needed to transition into a state of immortality with limited stores. This is typically a slow, natural process, but you've been fighting on the brink of death for four weeks."

"With Killian's help," my mother clarified, beaming with pride.

All I could do was gape at them.

Immortal?

Four weeks?

"Y-you can't just dump all of that on a girl all at once!" I cried as a wave of dizziness swarmed over me. "I'm... immortal now?"

Killian tilted his head to the side. "Not entirely, but as far as lifespan goes, yes you are immortal. You won't die from old age and you won't physically age past your thirties."

Well, that was definitely a Dragonrider perk that no one cared to inform me about.

I swallowed hard. "So, uh, I've been out for a month, turning *immortal.*"

Killian glanced down at Solstice who rested his snout on my knee. "And completing your bond with your dragon. Just take a minute to digest it, Viv. You did it. Your dragon is here." He smiled. "Does he have a name?"

I glanced down and smiled as Solstice keened at me. "Solstice," I said.

My dragon met my gaze, his golden eyes glowing with healthy magic. The thin fabric of his wings flexed under my touch and he nuzzled me, opening his mind to mine.

He'd died before I could ever get to know him, but my magic had called his spirit. He'd found me as the golden finch, fueled by the promise of our connection that could finally flourish and grow.

Then I'd found his egg... I'd found him, and he'd

done everything in his power to get back to me.

"Oh, Solstice," I said, tears streaming down my cheeks. "I'm so sorry I couldn't find you sooner."

My mother rested a hand on my shoulder. "Everything has worked out as it was meant to, Vivi. You must believe that." She smiled and rolled her shoulders back. "You must be starving. Killian, didn't we have a meal ready?"

He nodded. "Yes, I'll go get—"

The ground trembled, cutting him off as a roar pierced the air.

My mother rushed to the window and her expression turned dark. I scrambled off the bed as Solstice wound himself around my neck, the slight weight a comfort on my shoulders.

I stumbled, my legs threatening to give out from disuse and Killian caught my arm. He helped me to the window to see the battle-worn campus that cut a line of charred sand and dried blood against a shimmering barrier. Guilt surged in me and Solstice keened, his emotions linked to mine.

I was the reason the Wild Dragons had done this. They wanted me... but why?

My questions cut short as the ocean swelled in the distance, rushing up toward the Academy on a tide fueled by dark magic that felt cold and wrong. Wild Dragons circled from above, following the rush of water as it approached the Academy's barrier. It hit with a harsh *ping*, making the dragons screech as they released a torrent of green flames. My heart seized in my chest as I watched in horror.

I groaned as a new sting radiated through my chest. Each attack on the barrier felt like a knife through my body and I cried out. Killian and my mother placed their hands on me, which was a mistake. "Don't touch me!" I screamed as my magic fluctuated and searched for a source to draw from.

They reluctantly obeyed and I squeezed my eyes shut as Solstice cried out with my pain.

"Let's go," Killian said, his words cutting through my agony. "We've had it wrong all this time. It's your magic that's kept the barrier up. Let it go, Viv, before it kills you."

I didn't want him to be right, but that's why my transition had taken so long. Most of my magic went to the barrier protecting the Academy, but I couldn't keep this up and I let it go on a long exhale.

A sharp *pop* fluctuated through the air and the Academy's shrill alarms flared to life.

This wasn't a siege. This was a ticking time bomb, and now we were all going to die.

CHAPTER 4

FIGHT OR FLIGHT

"We need to move," Killian said, his tone flat. He snatched up his boots and hefted his armor over his shoulders.

"You're in no condition to fight," I said, stumbling to him. "And neither am I. Need I remind you that I just got out of a month-long coma after trying to fight them the last time?" We needed a better plan. One preferably involving military-grade weapons. "What about Earth?" I suggested. "Can't they help?"

Killian scoffed. "You mean the Knights of the Silver Order? They're too busy worrying about their own realm to care about anyone else."

"Knights of the what?" I asked.

He rolled his eyes. "After this, you're doing double-classes."

"We have to hurry," my mom said as she slipped a

jacket around her shoulders. "They're going to be coming for Vivi and Solstice."

"I know," Killian bit off.

I frowned. "Well I'm glad you guys seem to know what's going on, but I sure don't."

Killian took the golden sword and sheathed it at his hip. It seemed the Dean had let him keep it. "There'll be time for that. For now, we need to get you to Finn." He tightened his scabbard and then reached for me, only for Solstice to go rigid at my neck and hiss. He snapped, but Killian backed away in time to avoid the tiny—but sharp—baby wyvern teeth.

"Solstice!" I chided.

"It's all right," Killian said with a smirk as if he approved of the wyvern's behavior. "He wants to protect you. I can understand." He tossed me my shoes as he glanced at the window. "We've wasted enough time."

The water surged past the gates, rushing in fast as I swallowed hard. The Wild Dragons streamed in, clashing with the first wave of students in a repeat of a battle I didn't want to see again.

Death.

Destruction.

Guilt.

"Killian," I said, my tongue thick in my throat. "I don't know if I can do this again."

Killian drew me away, this time Solstice allowing his touch. My mate's appearance had changed underneath the layer of armor and weapons. His eyes held a sliver of my magic, giving him enough energy to fight. "We're not going down without a fight, Viv. The Academy has had a month to prepare for this, as have I."

The idiot, I thought. I wasn't going to let him do this. I opened my mouth to say as much.

His desire to protect me mirrored my dragon's, the strength of that emotion making me snap my jaw shut.

I knew then, without a doubt, that he would die for me. He would do anything to keep me, Solstice, and Topaz safe.

The revelation shocked me. Wasn't he going to break the bond? Where had this undying loyalty come from all of a sudden? If his feelings could change so drastically, what was to stop them from changing again?

"We need to move," my mother's voice interrupted my musings and broke the moment.

"She's right," Killian said, eyes still locked on mine. "I'll distract them from the ground while you two get to the sanctuary."

With that, he grabbed my face and pulled me in for a kiss. It was short, but passionate. He pulled away, opened the door, and walked out without another word.

I stared after him for a moment before turning to my mother, "Are you just going to let him go off alone like that?"

Mom squeezed my shoulders before moving toward the door, taking my hand to drag me behind her as she went. "Sweetie, Killian understands your importance, as well as your wyvern's. If either of you die, any hope of stopping the Wild Dragons dies with you."

I wanted to ask why. How I could be so important? I didn't get a chance as my mother grabbed my arm and dragged me out of the room. Solstice was wise to keep his teeth to himself, because my mother was a force to contend with when she set her mind on something.

Right now, that something was keeping me alive at all costs.

The sentiment rang too close to home. It reminded me of my father's death. As we fled down the steps and the roar of the Wild Dragons and battle grew closer, I couldn't help but feel that my life was on repeat of the same tragedy. Maybe my father had been the first to die in my place, but he certainly wouldn't be the last.

We stumbled down into the main street, splashing up the thin layer of intruding water as we raced toward Central hall. A dragon landed behind us, and Killian's battle cry followed next.

"Don't look back," my mother instructed, squeezing my hand. "Trust him, Viv. He'll be fine. Your presence would only distract him. You said it yourself, you're in no condition to fight."

I ground my teeth together, hating that my mother was right.

As we turned the corner around the practice fields, I spotted Lily. I couldn't help but remember the video of her standing in the middle of rubble, her school and everyone else inside it destroyed.

Reminiscent of that image, she stood, staring out at the incoming flood waters and Wild Dragons. I couldn't see any weapons on her, but she didn't seem concerned.

Just as I was about to shout her name, her skin started to glow. My eyes widened as I stared at the transitioning dragon, transfixed. Her skin faded into ruby red scales and her limbs lengthened, expanding until a full-grown dragon stood where Lily used to be.

Is anybody else seeing this?

Just then, James ran toward the huge beast. Between his strides he reached over his arm. I felt the urge to comically wipe my eyes in disbelief as I watched him pull a broadsword from his wrist. He literally just reached into his tattoo and pulled out a whole freaking sword.

He reached dragon-Lily and launched himself into the air without missing a beat. He swung his leg over her back as she took to the air. Their movements synchronized as if they had practiced this exact exercise over and over. I watched over my shoulder as they soared toward the battle.

A chirp directly into my ear broke me from my stupor. I returned to running for my life, sending a flash of gratitude through my bond with Solstice. I began running again in earnest, sloshing my way through the ankle-deep ocean water.

"Come on, Viv! We're almost there!" My mother

dragged me by the hand, speeding up as we finally came upon Central Hall.

We hurried inside, throwing the door open, perhaps with more force than necessary, then slammed it closed again. Relief rushed through me as I realized the floor was dry. Well, aside from the water we'd brought in with us. I hoped it wasn't Corrupted somehow.

A gruff sound made us both jump. "Well, come on then," Finn said. "I don't have all day."

I pulled my mom along to follow the dwarf, glancing at her only to find she wasn't fazed at all.

Things that don't surprise my mom: Dragons, touchy mates, and dwarves. Good to know.

I cleared my throat as we descended into a very empty stairway. "Where is everyone?"

"Fightin', I suppose," Finn said with a shrug. "Now that you hatched a queen, the Dean isn't pulling any punches. All hands on deck, as the sayin' goes."

I halted, only to be yanked forward by my mom again. "Excuse me… queen?"

He barked a laugh. "You didn't tell her, eh?"

My mom winced when I stared at her incredulously.

"Yeah, sorry, honey. I didn't want to tell you yet…"

I glanced down at the golden dragon peering up at me.

Apparently… Solstice was a girl.

And on top of that… a *queen*.

CHAPTER 5

HEIRLOOM

ingers curled into fists, I followed the gruff dwarf and my mother into the Egg Sanctuary. It spanned out before me in its raw grandeur, boasting shelves upon shelves of colorful wyvern eggs.

Solstice keened in approval, twisting around my neck as his—*her*, tiny claws pricked my skin.

"So, about this queen business..." I began.

"The term is typically self-explanatory," Finn said with a sneer.

My mother sighed. "Solstice is one of the last dragon queens, dear. With your heritage as an enchantress of Avalon, you were strong enough to reunite her spirit with her egg and bring her into this world. With the two of you working together, and with a Dragonrider mate like Killian on your side, you'll finally be a force powerful enough to take on the Wild

Dragon's Corruption." She rested a hand on my shoulder and gave me a sad smile. "It's why we have to keep you safe, for now, no matter the cost. You must grow in to your powers, and Solstice must come into her own as well." Her fingers trailed over my wyvern's snout, the creature nuzzling her with affection instead of lashing out.

Smart lizard.

The sounds of battle filtered into the room, muted by the walls above. I hugged myself and looked up, hoping that Killian was okay.

"I hate just sitting down here while they're all up there fighting," I admitted.

Finn scampered up a ladder and righted an egg about to fall, grumbling about inconsiderate dragons. "Best get comfortable, lass. It'll be some time before we know the outcome of this battle." He kept his gaze on the egg, stroking it gently. "If they make it down here, well, this old dwarf has one last trick up his sleeve."

A warm tattoo glowed over his arm that I hadn't noticed before, spiraling over his wrist until it formed a solid band.

My mother tugged me away, pulling me between the shelves until she found padding used for the nests. She sat me down and stroked my hair from my face. "Dwarves have an ancient power that comes from the soil and rock itself," she explained. "Nothing is going to happen to you."

I flickered my gaze up to her. "How do you know so much?"

She shrugged. "I am an enchantress myself, you know. I didn't grow up on Earth."

My eyes nearly bugged out of my head. "Seriously?"

She smiled and began the long story of her upbringing, managing to distract me from the battle that raged above our heads. Avalon had been taken over before her time, but Earth was only a place she'd discovered in her adult years. It was supposed to be part of her training, but then she met my father and had me.

"Do you regret it?" I asked, my eyes wide. "Your home realm sounds pretty… amazing."

She chuckled. "Well, the Light Fae do think very highly of themselves, but it does make one weary living in a world with no night."

"The sun doesn't set at all?" I marveled.

"There *is* no sun," she clarified, continuing to blow my mind with every breath. "Maybe you'll see it one day."

We spent the rest of the day in the sanctuary waiting for any indication of who was winning the battle that raged outside, all the while my mother taught me about the other realms she had visited. When I asked if there was such a thing as "Dark Fae," she frowned and told me they used magic called Malice, but that she didn't know much about it.

During the conversation the walls occasionally shook, making the eggs rattle in their nests. Finn moved around the room frantically when this happened, tutting that someone needed to get those

Wild Dragons under control before he slapped them upside the head.

I would have paid good money to see him try.

Sounds of the battle finally made even Finn go quiet as we tried not to glance at the ceiling. The roar of an enraged dragon. The clashing of a sword on stone-like scales. Perhaps a building falling down, or what could have been an explosion.

The sounds of the battle and the shaking of the walls kept me on edge all day. I switched between pacing back and forth and sitting, chewing on my nails.

Killian and Topaz were out there in danger while I was safe in the sanctuary. Jasmine, Jade, Lily, James and all my fellow students were all out there, too. Everyone was fighting for me while I hid. The guilt tore through me all day as I searched my mind for something I could do to help.

A thought occurred to me as I considered the rising ocean water rushing towards the Academy. "Can water get into the sanctuary?"

Finn turned to look at me briefly before turning back to coating the eggs with dragon blood. "Nay, lass. The sanctuary is the safest place on campus, both physically and magically. If wyverns didn't need fresh air, I would have insisted you did your hibernation here."

I scrunched my face in confusion. "Hibernation?"

He just shook his head at that and rolled his eyes before grumbling, "I haven't the faintest idea how you managed to hatch a fledgling queen, lass. Not even a speck."

Solstice uncoiled herself slightly to chirp at him, baring her teeth at the dwarf. I stroked under her chin. I could understand Finn's frustration with my lack of knowledge. It was a frustration I shared and intended to remedy if we got out of this alive.

I sighed as Finn went back to coating the eggs in silence.

"Come on," my mother said, "time to stretch those legs." She hooked her elbow with mine and dragged me from the table I had been sitting on. We began to walk slowly through the shelves of eggs.

"Are you going to explain any of this?" I asked, my voice was small. It was clear that my mother had hid an entire lifetime from me.

She faced me, her face the picture of guilt.

"I only intended a normal life for you," she said, as if that could defend her actions. "You were never supposed to become a Dragonrider or get involved with any of this."

"But I am involved," I said, my voice cracking. I couldn't help the accusation in my voice. What if I had been raised in a different realm? What if my father could have been saved?

The guilt in her expression said that she considered the same questions, so I bit my lip. "I should have told you," she admitted. "I should have predicted how powerful your gifts would be."

I quirked an eyebrow. "Gifts?"

She nodded. "The women in our family have gifts, yes, but they can vary. Some can see the future, some can heal, and some can even breathe underwater or conjure fire." She smiled, running her fingers through my hair.

It occurred to me that she spoke about this in the present tense. "Is your family still alive?"

"They're scattered across the realms for our protection. Until Avalon is healed, we will never be safe."

I frowned. Based on current events, that much was clear. Then another realization hit me. "What's your gift, then? Wait, let me guess. It's your grilled cheese."

She chuckled. "You got me. I'm blessed with killer grilled cheese skills." She took my hand and rubbed her thumb over my knuckles. "It's my song. My voice brings peace and pleasant dreams. It's not much, I know, but your father loved it when I sang."

I couldn't help the stupid smile that spread across my face. "So are you like… a siren, or something?"

She threw her head back and openly laughed this time. "Those with my gift have been called that, yes, but it doesn't cause men to fall in love. Well, discounting your father. He loved me *before* I sang, but after is the first time he said it."

I smirked, wishing I could have been there for that moment.

She sighed, her wistful memories fading into the grim present as the walls around us rumbled from the ongoing battle from above. "I thought your blood might be diluted enough that you could have a normal life."

"That worked out well," I said dryly.

"You're right to feel bitter," she said. She reached into her jacket. "I'm not going to hide your legacy from you any longer, which is why you should have this."

She pulled out an amulet on a golden chain. The pendent gleamed with solid gold, shaped into a Celtic knot that wound around an egg-shaped opal in the middle.

She smiled as she handed it to me. "This is an old Avalon relic that has been passed down for generations. You can use it to open a portal to wherever you want, which is how I got here once I figured out where you were. You don't have to wait for a Tunnel if you have the magic to operate it. That's what took me so long to get to the Academy. I had to salvage the magic to activate it again," she said in explanation as she gave me the beautiful necklace.

I was about to thank her for the precious heirloom when a loud boom shook the sanctuary. The shelves rattled and Finn shouted out as he caught a falling egg just inches from the ground.

Water trickled in through the door. I looked on in horror as I realized the entire sanctuary was underground, meaning it would easily fill all the way up with water. "I thought you said this place was magically protected," I shouted at Finn.

Finn cursed. "This water ain't right! Corrupted. I can feel it. It's getting past the barrier!"

I watched, paralyzed, as the cool water filtered over my ankles. The sanctuary would be underwater soon.

"Don't just stand there, ya morons!" Finn shouted. "The eggs *cannot* become Corrupted."

Even now, Finn put the eggs first.

Finn frantically rushed around the room, opening the trash hatches to release some of the water, but it did little to stem the flow. More of it flowed down the shelves, but I found myself compelled to help Finn as I picked up eggs from the lower racks and placed them higher. Solstice keened with worry, equally insistent that we save the unborn dragons.

Another loud boom shook the walls again and the trickle of water from the door grew stronger. Frustration at my helplessness built up in my chest.

I should be doing more than keeping eggs dry! I should be helping my people survive this!

Enough!

My senses sharpened as I focused solely on the door. Time seemed to slow as I wrenched it open. Water rushed past me as I forced my way up the stairs and out into the main entrance. My mother's screams that followed me out were overwhelmed by the roar of water.

The giant stone doors of Central Hall were cracked, laying in pieces as water flooded the building. I ran for the opening, ignoring my mother and Finn as they shouted for me to get back to safety.

As I crossed the threshold, the stench of charred flesh and smoke hit me in the face. The roars and clashes of swords were a deafening cascade of sound against the silence of the sanctuary. A dark landscape greeted me, brightened by the occasional spray of green fire.

A voice down the street sneered, "You think you're so special." The sarcastic laugh was punctuated by a strangled cry of pain.

I turned the corner to find a woman with blue scales towering over Lily. "Lily!" I cried, horrified by the cuts and blood crusted over her entire body. I wasn't sure how her powers worked, or why she hadn't stayed in her dragon form, but the woman attacking her clearly wasn't one of the students.

And where was James?

"Don't hurt her!" I yelled, making both females turn to face me. Solstice hissed as my anger surged.

"Vivi!" Lily cried. "Get back to the sanctuary!"

The blue-scaled woman laughed. "Well, well, well." She stepped over Lily. "Thank you for making this so easy for me." She winked, taking leisurely steps in my direction. My mother chose that moment to follow me out onto the street and I held out an arm to keep her back.

"Zelda," my mother whispered.

Did she know everyone?

The woman raised an eyebrow at my mother. "It seems my reputation precedes me. I'm not familiar with you." She flipped her hair over her shoulder. "Introductions won't be necessary. You'll be dead soon enough, anyway."

"This is a general of the Wild Dragon Queen who's

taken over Avalon," my mother hissed under her breath. "Tread carefully, Vivienne."

The woman set her gaze on Solstice and smirked. "My mission is to collect the dragon queen. You have all proved more challenge than you're worth, so if you simply hand over that creature, I might make your deaths quick."

Solstice keened and tightened around my throat. I patted her on the flank.

"You're insane," I growled. "Over my dead body."

Zelda's lips lifted to reveal sharp teeth. "As you wish," she snarled as she lunged.

I scrambled back, pushing my mother out of danger. I hadn't thought to bring a weapon with me.

Good job, Viv. Way to think things through.

Solstice growled, the noise rumbling around my neck. She coiled tighter as warmth tingled through my body. Zelda lunged for us again only to hit a shimmering gold barrier. She flew back, landing into the water with a splash.

I patted Solstice on the nose. "Good one, girl. And… sorry I thought you were a boy all this time."

Solstice trilled in what sounded like laughter.

Zelda swept to her feet, her face a mask of pure fury. She sloshed through the water when a shout overhead made us all look skyward.

An emerald dragon careened down from above, releasing a great wave of fire at the shifter.

Jasmine!

Zelda roared, a noise that shouldn't have been physically possible from a human body. She lifted her hand and sickly green water shielded her from the worst of Jade's fire. The water evaporated into a cloud of steam.

Jade swooped, revealing Jasmine and Killian on her back as she came in for a landing.

Killian shouted as he launched himself from Jade's back. I helplessly held out a hand as he fell, his sword extended and pointed straight at Zelda's chest.

Zelda whirled, twisting in an impossible maneuver that still wasn't good enough. The sword seemed to shift with her and pierced her side. Killian slammed into her next, sending them tumbling in a tangle of limbs and claws as Zelda attempted to shift.

I grappled toward them and pulled out the necklace my mother had given me. It glowed with power and I met my mom's gaze long enough so that she could see what I was doing.

I'm sorry, I thought, hoping she could understand my plan.

We couldn't keep fighting like this. We weren't going to survive.

But I'd learned something that even my mother hadn't figured out. They wanted Solstice alive... which meant this crazy plan of mine just might work.

My desperation hit my bond with Solstice, sending out a golden shockwave that rippled through the air.

"Stop, Vivi!" Jasmine shouted from her dragon. "Your bond can't handle this!"

Oh, she was wrong. Solstice coiled around my neck, her heart stronger than it had ever been.

I closed my eyes and focused all of my energy into the necklace in my grip.

Take me home...

"No!" Zelda screeched as the water at my feet swirled and rose, forming a portal.

The sounds of battle stopped and I sensed an unspoken command sweep through the Wild Dragons.

Don't let her leave.

Follow her.

Anyone I left behind would be safe. The Wild Dragons wanted Solstice, not the others.

Taking a deep breath, I stepped through the portal and didn't look back.

CHAPTER 6

HOME SWEET HOME

I flew from the portal, landing unceremoniously on the ground as I tucked and rolled, glad that Solstice tucked under my arm to stay safe.

I groaned and lifted myself onto my knees, trying to catch my breath from the forceful fall. Apparently, I needed to work on my portal-creation skills.

"We gotta move," I told Solstice. The portal behind me rumbled. I had hoped that the portal would close and the dragons would be forced to find another way to get to me. Either way, they would leave the Academy alone, that much was for sure.

Solstice screeched just as something hard hit me from behind, sending me falling to my face again on the beach. Solstice wriggled out from underneath me and hissed at my attacker.

Flailing, I worked my elbow to hit my assailant hard in the temple.

Vivi one, mysterious enemy zero!

"Ow!" a male voice said, scrambling away from me and I realized I'd just beamed Killian in the face.

"Oops, sorry," I said, wincing. "To be fair, you really shouldn't surprise me like that."

"The dragons immediately retreated, but not Zelda. She's trying to get through the portal," Killian bit out, rubbing a growing bruise on the side of his face. "Shut it down. We're sitting dragons out here."

"Sitting ducks, is the phrase," I corrected him as I glanced at the swirl of water. "Uh, I'm not even sure how I got it open in the first place," I admitted, "and—"

Killian rolled his eyes before he snatched the amulet out of my hands.

The portal immediately fell, sending water splashing all over my face.

I spit out a stream of water. "Well, that's one way to do it."

Killian pocketed the amulet, brushed himself off and then scanned the dark landscape. "So, this is your home?"

I considered the slice of land that I knew all too well. Silver Lake Resort glowed with dim lights in the distance, marking this as the place where my father died, as well as where I'd nearly drowned no thanks to Max Green and his psycho buddies.

"Something like that," I grumbled as I scooped up Solstice who trilled in response before looping around my arm. I frowned. Luckily it was nighttime, but I couldn't exactly waltz around with a dragon.

A problem to figure out in the morning.

"Let's go to my house," I said, waving Killian along. "It's this way."

I led Killian to the road, which he took his time to scrutinize. "Interesting black river," he said, frowning when I laughed.

"It's called asphalt," I said, chuckling.

He quirked a white eyebrow. "You didn't see me mocking you when you showed up at the Academy wearing underwear." He smirked, eyeing my body. "Not that I was complaining."

I rolled my eyes. "It was a bathing suit."

He smirked. "Whatever it's called, I liked it."

"You're such a guy. Come on." I led Killian off the road and through the forest toward my childhood home.

We'd just crossed to the other side where I estimated my neighborhood to be when headlights rounded the corner. We were still hidden by a crop of trees, but I wasn't going to miss Killian's reaction to cars.

I wasn't disappointed.

He immediately crouched in a fighting stance and drew his sword. "It's a demon," he said, his voice a harsh whisper as I bit back a laugh. "Or maybe even worse than that... a Light Fae."

A truck careened by us, rumbling so loudly I wondered if the muffler was broken.

"Get behind me!" Killian snapped, only to hesitate when I broke down laughing.

Killian frowned as I dissolved into a fit of manic giggles. The truck harmlessly disappeared into the night, leaving Killian's whitewashed eyes staring at me, as if illuminated by the moonlight.

"That wasn't funny," he said, sheathing his sword.

"Oh, yes it was."

He frowned while Topaz shivered, finally making me feel sympathize. I stroked the little creature and his hackles lowered when Solstice nuzzled him.

At least our dragons got along.

"So, what was that thing?" he asked.

"A truck," I informed him, able to answer him with a semi-straight face. "It's a transportation device. I really can't believe you've never seen one."

He crossed his arms. "Who needs a device when you have a dragon?"

I tapped my lip. "Fair point."

We wandered onto the dark road and for once I found myself grateful for the lack of street lights. It kept us hidden as we worked silently through my old neighborhood.

Although everything felt so different now. A lonely wind rustled the leaves and a shadow swept overhead, causing me to snap my gaze to the dark skies.

Could the Wild Dragons have followed me already?

Solstice keened and nudged my jaw, sending comfort through our bond. She didn't want me to worry, and my own adrenaline spikes were giving her a headache.

"Sorry, girl," I whispered as I scratched under her chin. She seemed to like that.

When we reached the house, it felt somehow small placed on the overgrown lawn. I fumbled underneath one of the pots and pulled out the spare key.

"Seems secure," Killian said in a mocking tone.

"Don't judge," I said, wielding the spiky end of the key at him before unlocking the door.

I stepped into my home, inhaling familiar scents. I turned on a light and walked to the dining table where mom's papers were still strewn about. I shuffled them a bit, finding a strange pit in my stomach knowing that she wasn't here.

She had finally found me again, for what? To put herself in danger?

Killian slipped his hand around my waist, startling me. "You're thinking about your mother, huh?"

I nodded, unable to speak in case I started crying. I so didn't want Killian to see me cry.

"She's the reason you could leave the Academy like that," he reminded me, patting the amulet in his pocket. "She's an enchantress of Avalon, so she is where she's supposed to be, when she's supposed to be there. The same goes for you."

I smirked, finding that level of faith amusing for a guy like Killian. "How serendipitous of you."

He smirked, but then his stomach released a violent grumble, one my stomach echoed.

I flicked my thumb at the fridge. "I say we eat something before we alert the Wild Dragons where we are by our tummies."

Killian chuckled. "Agreed."

I opened the refrigerator, finding it completely empty. Frowning, I closed it and spotted a pizza delivery number on the door. "A few weeks without me and she probably starved. Thank God for pizza."

"What's pizza?" Killian asked, making me balk.

"Are you for real right now? You're in for such a treat." I dialed the phone and ordered some food, rummaging through the drawer to find a credit card that wasn't maxed out. Yet another reason to start over my life in a new realm… no credit card debt.

After clicking off the phone, I showed Killian to mom's bathroom while I went upstairs to mine. Luckily bathrooms are pretty straightforward, so I didn't have to explain basic plumbing to him, thank goodness.

I filled the sink for Solstice and she slipped into it with an adorable trilling sound. Her leafy wings splashed into the water and I chuckled. "You like that, huh?" She squeaked at me before dunking her head, then she rolled her snout across her scales until they shined.

Smirking, I left Solstice to her bath while I cleaned up and found a new t-shirt and jeans to wear. The doorbell rang as I was putting my hair up into a ponytail. "Yeah, just a minute!" I shouted down as I scampered out of the room and down the steps.

Killian stepped out of the bathroom and I barreled into him. My hands went to his naked chest as I gazed up into his whitewashed gaze. "What was that alarm?" he asked, his voice a husky whisper. I realized that I was crushing myself against him, hesitating a moment longer than I should as I cleared my throat and untangled myself from his hold.

A shirtless Killian tended to make a girl's brain misfire. Totally not my fault.

"It's just the doorbell," I explained as I hurried past him.

I creaked the door open enough to retrieve the pizza and sign the receipt with a generous tip. What's a little extra credit card debt?

The delicious aroma hit my nose, making my knees week. I hadn't eaten a solid meal for a month and it certainly felt like it.

Mouth watering, I hurried up the steps. "We can eat in my room," I said, my stomach bursting with butterflies at the realization that this was the first time a boy would be in my bedroom.

Killian followed me silently, not seeming to understand the monumental gravity of this situation. Given that we'd technically been living together for a few months now, I guess it wasn't such a big deal, but it still felt like one.

Hurrying onto the bed, I flipped open the pizza box and offered him a slice. He simply stared at it with a raised brow.

"If you're not going to eat it, I am," I said, shoving it

into my mouth. I flinched when it burned my lip, but I was way too starving to care.

Solstice flapped out of the bathroom, glittering from snout to tail, and perched on my thigh. She reared her head back and opened her maw, so I tore off a piece and dropped it down.

Killian and Topaz both made a pained sound. "Dragons are supposed to eat raw meat."

Solstice keened and opened her mouth for more. I giggled and gave her another piece. "Well, any dragon of mine is going to love pizza." I chomped off another piece for myself, rolling my eyes back. "Sheer heaven," I said around the mouthful.

Killian pinched a piece between his fingers as cheese dripped down onto the box. "I don't see the appeal."

"Just try it," I said.

He returned the piece to the box before shifting onto the bed and resting against the headboard. He crossed his arms and stared me down. "You and Solstice have as much as you want. We'll go hunting in the morning."

I rolled my eyes. "You can't 'hunt' here."

He frowned as if I'd grown two heads.

Sighing, I ate in silence while Solstice greedily gobbled half of the box.

My gaze fell to the sword he'd rested against the door. It wasn't something I wanted to talk about, but if Killian and I were really going to do this, we needed to try to work together and understand our feelings. I sensed his deep desire to protect me. He'd more than proven that by throwing himself at Wild Dragons so I could get to safety.

Why do all of that when he'd been so ready to walk away?

"What made you change your mind?" I asked, keeping my gaze on the sword.

He shifted and didn't answer right away. He was quiet for so long that I finally looked at him. His pained expression made it clear that he was in torment over this issue.

His jaw flexed before he spoke. "You were dying, Viv. At the time... I thought it was the only way."

"You didn't even give me a chance," I shot back, hurt that he would have gone through with breaking our bond had I not reunited with Solstice that night. "Why didn't you just trust me?" The question came out quiet and I stared at my lap before meeting his gaze again.

His piercing eerie eyes held a mixture of determination and love. "I won't make that mistake again," he assured me as he reached out and laced his fingers over mine.

Our bond surged. I sensed the wave of cresting emotions when he opened himself up to me, fully and completely. I gasped as it hit me. He was more than willing to die for me, but what he truly wanted was a life with me, one where we flew in the sky with our dragons and protected the realms.

Together as one.

Heat surged over my face as I pulled away. "So... you'll trust me?" I asked.

He nodded, absolutely sincere. "Yes."

Glancing at the remaining pizza, I held up a slice and offered it. "Then take a bite!"

He chuckled and took my offering. "Very well, little bird."

My heart stuttered at that name. He ate his pizza in silence, keeping his gaze on me the entire time.

The moment would have been perfect, except for the low boom that crested across my soul.

The Wild Dragons were on their way to this realm... and I had no idea what we were going to do next.

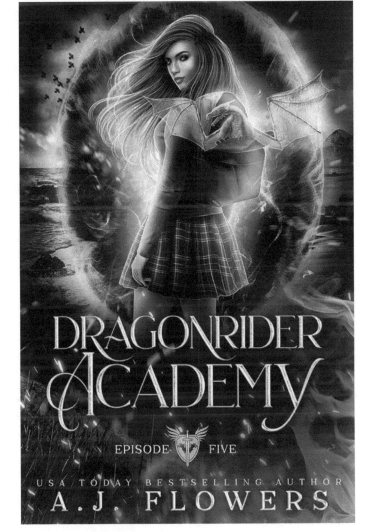

DRAGONRIDER ACADEMY

EPISODE FIVE

USA TODAY BESTSELLING AUTHOR

A.J. FLOWERS

PROLOGUE

HOME

I flew from the portal, landing unceremoniously on the ground as I tucked and rolled, glad that Solstice tucked under my arm to stay safe.

I groaned and lifted myself onto my knees, trying to catch my breath from the forceful fall. Apparently I needed to work on my portal-creation skills.

"We gotta move," I told Solstice. The portal behind me rumbled. I had hoped that the portal would close and the dragons would be forced to find another way to get to me. Either way, they would leave the Academy alone, that much was for sure.

Solstice screeched just as something hard hit me from behind, sending me falling to my face again on the beach. Solstice wriggled out from underneath me and hissed at my attacker.

Flailing, I smashed my assailant hard in the temple with my elbow.

Vivi one, mysterious enemy zero!

"Ow!" a male voice said, scrambling off of me. Then I realized I'd just beaned Killian in the face.

"Oops, sorry," I said, wincing. "To be fair, you really shouldn't surprise me like that."

"The dragons immediately retreated, but not Zelda. She's trying to get through the portal," Killian bit out, rubbing a growing bruise on the side of his face. "Shut it down. We're sitting dragons out here."

"Sitting ducks, is the phrase," I corrected him as I glanced at the swirl of water. "Uh, I'm not even sure how I got it open in the first place," I admitted, "and—"

Killian rolled his eyes before he snatched the amulet out of my hands.

The portal immediately fell, sending water splashing all over my face.

I spit out a stream of water. "Well, that's one way to do it."

Killian pocketed the amulet, brushed himself off and then scanned the dark landscape. "So, this is your home?"

I considered the slice of land that I knew all too well. Silver Lake Resort glowed with dim lights in the distance, marking this as the place where my father died, as well as where I'd nearly drowned no thanks to Max Green and his psycho buddies.

"Something like that," I grumbled as I scooped up Solstice who trilled in response before looping around my arm. I frowned. Luckily it was nighttime, but I couldn't exactly waltz around with a dragon.

A problem to figure out in the morning.

"Let's go to my house," I said, waving Killian along. "It's this way."

I led Killian to the road, which he took his time to scrutinize. "Interesting black river," he said, frowning when I laughed.

"It's called asphalt," I said, chuckling.

He quirked a white eyebrow. "You didn't see me mocking you when you showed up at the Academy wearing underwear." He smirked, eyeing my body. "Not that I was complaining."

I rolled my eyes. "It was a bathing suit."

He smirked. "Whatever it's called, I liked it."

"You're such a guy. Come on." I led Killian off the road and through the forest toward my childhood home.

We'd just crossed over to the other side where I estimated my neighborhood to be when headlights rounded the corner. We were still hidden by a crop of trees, but I wasn't going to miss Killian's reaction to cars.

I wasn't disappointed.

He immediately crouched in a fighting stance and drew his sword. "It's a demon," he said, his voice a harsh whisper as I bit back a laugh. "Or maybe even worse than that... a Light Fae."

A truck careened by us, rumbling so loudly I wondered if the muffler was broken.

"Get behind me!" Killian snapped, only to hesitate when I broke down laughing.

Killian frowned as I dissolved into a fit of manic giggles. The truck harmlessly disappeared into the night, leaving Killian's whitewashed eyes staring at me, as if illuminated by the moonlight.

"That wasn't funny," he said, sheathing his sword.

"Oh, yes it was."

He frowned while Topaz shivered, finally making me feel sympathy. I stroked the little creature and his hackles lowered as Solstice nuzzled him.

At least our dragons got along.

"So, what was that thing?" he asked.

"A truck," I informed him, able to answer him with a semi-straight face. "It's a transportation device. I really can't believe you've never seen one."

He crossed his arms. "Who needs a device when you have a dragon?"

I tapped my lip. "Fair point."

We wandered onto the dark road and for once I found myself grateful for the lack of street lights. It kept us hidden as we worked silently through my old neighborhood.

Although everything felt so different now. A lonely wind rustled the leaves and a shadow swept overhead, causing me to snap my gaze to the dark skies.

Could the Wild Dragons have followed me already?

Solstice keened and nudged my jaw, sending comfort through our bond. She didn't want me to worry, and my own adrenaline spikes were giving her a headache.

"Sorry, girl," I whispered as I scratched under her chin. She seemed to like that.

When we reached the house, it felt somehow small and rectangular placed on the overgrown lawn. I fumbled underneath one of the pots and pulled out the spare key.

"Seems secure," Killian said in a mocking tone.

"Don't judge," I said, wielding the spiky end of the key at him before unlocking the door.

I stepped into the home, inhaling familiar scents. I turned on a light and went to the dining table where mom's papers were still strewn about. I shuffled them a bit, finding a strange pit in my stomach knowing that she wasn't here.

She had finally found me again, for what? To put herself in danger?

Killian slipped his hand around my waist, startling me. "You're thinking about your mother, huh?"

I nodded, unable to speak in case I started crying. I so didn't want Killian to see me cry.

"She's the reason you could leave the Academy like that," he reminded me, patting the amulet in his pocket. "She's an enchantress of Avalon, so she is where she's supposed to be, when she's supposed to be there. The same goes for you."

I smirked, finding that level of faith amusing for a guy like Killian. "How serendipitous of you."

He smirked, but then his stomach released a violent grumble, one my stomach echoed.

I flicked my tongue at the fridge. "I say we eat something before we alert the Wild Dragons where we are by our tummies."

Killian chuckled. "Agreed."

I opened the refrigerator, finding it completely empty. Frowning, I closed it and spotted a pizza delivery number on the door. "A few weeks without me and she probably starved. Thank God for pizza."

"What's pizza?" Killian asked, making me balk.

"Are you for real right now? You're in for such a treat." I dialed the phone and ordered some food, rummaging through the drawer to find a credit card that wasn't maxed out. Yet another reason to start my life over in a new realm... no credit card debt.

After clicking off the phone, I showed Killian to mom's bathroom while I went upstairs to mine. Luckily bathrooms are pretty straightforward, so I didn't have to explain basic plumbing to him, thank goodness.

I filled the sink for Solstice and she slipped into it with an adorable trilling sound. Her leafy wings splashed into the water and I chuckled. "You like that, huh?" She squeaked at me before dunking her head, then she rolled her snout across her scales until they shined.

Smirking, I left Solstice to her bath while I cleaned up and then I found a new t-shirt and jeans to wear. The doorbell rang as I was putting my hair up into a ponytail. "Yeah, just a minute!" I shouted down as I scampered out of the room and down the steps.

Killian stepped out of the bathroom and I barreled into him. My hands went to his naked chest as I gazed up into his whitewashed gaze. "What was that alarm?" he asked, his voice a husky whisper. I realized that I was crushing myself against him and I cleared my throat as I untangled from his hold.

A shirtless Killian tended to make a girl's brain misfire. Totally not my fault.

"It's just the doorbell," I explained as I hurried past him.

I creaked the door open enough to retrieve the pizza and sign the receipt with a generous tip. What's a little extra credit card debt?

The delicious aroma hit my nose, making my knees week. I hadn't eaten a solid meal for a month, and it felt like it.

Mouth watering, I hurried up the steps. "We can eat in my room," I said, my stomach bursting with butterflies at the realization that I was going to bring my first boy to my bedroom.

Killian followed me silently, not seeming to understand the monumental gravity of this situation. Given that we'd technically been living together for a few months now, I guess it wasn't such a big deal, but it still felt like one.

Hurrying onto the bed, I flipped open the pizza box and offered him a slice. He simply stared at it with a raised brow.

"If you're not going to eat it, I am," I said, shoving it into my mouth. I flinched when I burned my lip, but I was way too hungry to care.

Solstice flapped out of the bathroom, glittering from snout to tail, and perched on my thigh. She reared her head back and opened her maw, so I tore off a piece and dropped it down.

Killian and Topaz both made a pained sound. "Dragons are supposed to eat raw meat."

Solstice keened and opened her mouth for more. I giggled and gave her another piece. "Well, any dragon of mine is going to love pizza." I chomped off another piece for myself, rolling my eyes back. "Sheer heaven," I said around the mouthful.

Killian pinched a piece between his fingers as cheese dripped down onto the box. "I don't see the appeal."

"Just try it," I said.

He returned the piece to the box before shifting onto the bed and resting against the headboard. He crossed his arms and stared me down. "You and Solstice have as much as you want. We'll go hunting in the morning."

I rolled my eyes. "You can't 'hunt' here."

He frowned as if I'd grown two heads.

Sighing, I ate in silence while Solstice greedily gobbled half of the box.

My gaze fell to Killian's sword resting against the door. It wasn't something I wanted to talk about, but if Killian and I were really going to do this, try to work together and understand our feelings. I sensed his deep desire to protect me, and he'd more than proven that by throwing himself at Wild Dragons so that I could get to safety.

Why do all of that when he'd been so ready to walk away?

"What made you change your mind?" I asked, keeping my gaze on the sword.

He shifted and didn't answer right away. He was quiet for so long that I finally looked at him. His pained expression made it clear that he was in torment over this issue.

His jaw flexed before he spoke. "You were dying, Viv. At the time... I thought it was the only way."

"You didn't even give me a chance," I shot back, hurt that he would have gone through with breaking our bond had I not reunited with Solstice that night. "Why didn't you just trust me?" The question came out quiet and I stared at my lap before meeting his gaze again.

His piercing eerie eyes held a mixture of determination and love. "I won't make that mistake again," he assured me as he reached out and laced his fingers over mine.

Our bond surged and I sensed the wave of cresting emotions when he opened himself up to me, fully and completely. I gasped as it hit me. He was more than willing to die for me, but what he truly wanted was a life with me, one where we flew in the sky with our dragons and protected the realms.

Together as one.

Heat surged over my face as I pulled away. "So... you'll trust me?" I asked.

He nodded, absolutely sincere. "Yes."

Glancing at the remaining pizza, I held up a slice and offered it. "Then take a bite!"

He chuckled and took my offering. "Very well, little bird."

My heart stuttered at that name. He ate his pizza in silence, keeping his gaze on me the entire time.

The moment would have been perfect, except for the low boom that crested across my soul.

The Wild Dragons were on their way to this realm... and I had no idea what we were going to do next.

CHAPTER 1

FLYING LESSONS

*I*t felt strange to sleep in my own bed after all this time. An eternity could have passed since I'd first gone to Dragonrider Academy. Everything had changed.

Yet, waking up from a foggy sleep as I blinked at my childhood ceiling peppered with glow-in-the-dark plastic stars made it all feel like a dream.

A pleasant one, perhaps, even if my life was now filled with danger and new threats.

Rubbing my eyes, I searched the room for my mate and for our dragons. I found the room empty aside for a discarded pizza box strewn across the floor.

A high-pitched chirp from outside drew my attention to the window. I rolled out of bed and rushed over, peering out and stopping short when I saw Solstice teetering from a large tree.

"Solstice!" I yelled, leaning over the sill. "Be careful!"

Completely ignoring me or demonstrating any sense of self-preservation, Solstice launched herself. My stomach dropped before she opened her wings with a dramatic flourish and glided toward Killian.

He held his hands out to her and she flew directly into his arms. She chirped in excitement and wriggled down immediately, making a run for the same branch she had jumped from like a toddler who'd just learned how to use the playground's slide.

I sighed as Killian glanced up at me, a glitter in his eyes I hadn't seen before.

Pride.

Topaz jumped from the same branch and glided to Killian, keeping his sapphire webbed wings open wide. Laughter escaped me as Topaz hit his rider hard, making Killian release a breath. Topaz squirmed excitedly in his arms, his flailing tail smacking Killian's face as he jumped down before making a beeline for the tree again.

Killian laughed too, ruefully shaking his head at the over-zealous wyverns. My heart swelled with happiness as I leaned on the sill and watched the wyverns attempting their first strides that would eventually turn into flight.

I longed for that day.

When Solstice chirped again with victory having completed another lap, I glanced at the privacy fence.

Maybe this wasn't such a good idea.

Just as I was about to go down and corral the creatures indoors, a portal opened.

Right there in my backyard.

Killian reacted fast, clutching Topaz protectively to his chest while he barked at Solstice to remain in her tree.

Who could it be? Was it the Wild Dragons? Had they found us already?

Tearing myself away from the swirl of red that broke the air into pieces, I dashed down the stairs, taking two at a time. I caught the rail like I used to as a kid, using my momentum to swing around to the back-door where I burst out on the yard, my chest heaving as I readied myself for a fight.

Solstice chirped several times in quick succession as she saw me. She jumped from the branch and soared through the air, changing her course to glide towards me. I held my arms out for her, anxiety making my hands shake as I darted my gaze from her to the portal vividly come to life.

It sputtered and wavered, seeming more unstable than the ones I'd used before.

A body came through and hit the ground hard, but I relaxed when I saw who it was.

"Lily!" I exclaimed, situating Solstice around my shoulders and rushing over to help my friend.

Before I could reach her, another body came crashing through the portal right on top of her. I winced in sympathy as the air whooshed from her lungs with a wheeze. I recognized James now that I knew who to expect. The portal closed behind him with an odd airy noise.

"Get off me!" Lily said as she shoved James off. She held a hand to her chest, taking in deep breaths. "I knew there was a reason Professor Finn was banned from using dwarf magic! That portal nearly catapulted me into a different realm!" She staggered to her feet and waved around a finger. "Never again!"

James laughed as he got to his feet and dusted himself off. "What happened to your sense of adventure? The Academy has made you soft."

Lily rolled her eyes skyward. "There's a difference between being adventurous and being reckless."

Killian interrupted then, asking the question I had been about to ask myself. "What are you doing here? Portal magic was banned years ago when Finn opened up a portal to the Malice Realm."

Malice Realm?

I didn't need to be a realm expert to know that probably wasn't a place to visit for vacation.

Lily nodded gravely, seriousness taking over her face as she reached into her pocket and held out a piece of paper. "We tracked Vivi's necklace to find you. It's all explained in here. I think it's best if you read it first." Her eyes darted to me, concern in her expression.

Nervousness filled my stomach while Killian took the note. His expression darkened as he read, which only served to make my anxiety worse. He frowned when he was done and then met my eyes.

"What does it say?" I asked him, trying to stay calm until I knew the situation. He solemnly handed me the note without saying anything.

I took the letter, looking at all of them warily before I focused on it. Solstice leaned from my shoulder, nipping at the corner of the page. I gently nudged her back.

"Are you already hungry again?" I asked, rubbing the long line of her snout. She chirped in response. "We'll get you more to eat soon," I promised. All that flight training had probably worked up an appetite, but right now we had a situation on our hands to deal with.

I turned my attention back to the letter, skimming the dark words as dread filled my stomach. I glanced up at Lily and James as soon as I finished. "My mother has been taken hostage?"

Lily winced, twisting her hands together, "Not exactly. There's more to it than that. She went to Vyorin as neutral ground to talk to Zelda."

I bristled. "Why would my mother willingly go talk to Zelda?" The dragon in human form had nearly killed us all.

"She's the Queen of Avalon's right hand," Lily said. "She wasn't going to leave the Academy empty-handed. We're guessing that if she had, she'd be as good as dead for her failure, so your mother agreed to go willing as leverage if they left the Academy alone."

"Leverage for what?" I asked.

Lily glanced at Solstice who'd started preening my hair.

"She's not getting Solstice," I snapped. My mother wouldn't have gone with the Wild Dragons if she hadn't had a plan.

"That's not what she wants," James interjected. He crossed his arms, his tattoos rippling over his toned forearms. "At least, not when she learned that you'd come here."

I frowned. "I thought they wanted Solstice because they needed a fledgling queen?"

"They want humanity," Killian interjected. "Lily is actually a Queen of the purebloods herself. Purebloods are dragons who can turn into humans at will. She can gift other dragons that power, or at least, she should be able to. The Queen of Avalon wants to study her and any like her. Apparently, though, they've already got a pureblood on their side because Zelda was human, and that's likely not the last we'll find. This must be about something else."

Lily nodded. "I've met other human dragons before, but they were called rogues and were permanently human. There were *Hovakim*, too, humans who traded their souls to worship the dragons in hopes that they or their future generations would be able to become dragons. Nobody seems happy with their current state, I tell you."

James nudged her side and wiggled his eyebrows. "I'm very happy."

Lily glowered at him, rolling her eyes before turning back to me. She pointed to the bottom of the note. I'd skipped that part after reading my mother had been taken hostage. "They want someone named Max Green in exchange for your mother. Do you know him?"

I furrowed my brow at her, confusion swirling through me, "What? Why would they want Max?"

Lily shrugged. "I was hoping you could tell us." She glanced at the privacy fence when a shadow passed by. "Can we go inside to discuss this?"

"Uh, yeah," I gestured to the back door that was still open. "Right through there."

Killian grabbed me by the arm. "Who is Max?" he asked, enunciating his words very carefully.

I froze. *Oh boy, this is not going to be fun to explain...*

I shuffled from foot to foot, wracking my brain for a delicate way to tell him. He narrowed his pale eyes at me and crossed his arms, "Who is he, Vivi? I will not compete with another male."

"What? No! Killian..." I hesitated for a moment. "Max is the boy who tried to drown me."

He stared at me, his whitewashed eyes shimmering with pure rage.

Well, this wasn't going to be pretty.

CHAPTER 2

COFFEE ADDICTION

*K*illian paced behind me in the kitchen, muttering furiously to himself as I poured four steaming mugs of coffee from the fresh pot I had just made.

He wasn't happy, not after I'd told him everything that had happened between Max and me. Not a fun tale, one that involved violation, near death, and an encounter with the Lady of the Lake that almost hadn't ended well.

While my fated mate brooded with murderous fury, I raised my cup to my nose and inhaled, my eyelids fluttering as the dark roast scent hit my senses.

The smell of coffee had always been a comfort to me. It brought back memories of a warm Saturday morning with my parents. Now, the memory brought a pang of grief with it. It was just me here, without them both, but my mother still had a chance. I wasn't going to let her down.

Solstice's ears perked as she sniffed. I moved the cup out of range before she took a bite out of the ceramic.

Killian stormed across the living room behind me, not looking to calm down anytime soon. I held out the cup to him as a peace offering and he glowered at me.

"You didn't tell me," he growled, an underlying tone of hurt hidden beneath a wave of anger.

He had a right to be angry. I had hidden something from him, but it had been for his own protection, as well as mine. If he caused chaos in the human realm, it would not end well for either of us.

"For one, it's none of your business," I said, shooting up a finger.

"None of my business?" he asked incredulously. "You are my mate. If someone wishes you harm, it is most certainly my business."

Narrowing my eyes at him, I shot up a second finger. "That brings me to my second point, which is as your *mate* I knew you'd react like this." It sounded like the excuse it was, but I didn't regret my decision. "This is Earth, Killian. You can't just go around killing humans."

Because after what Max did, Killian would definitely try to kill him. The Nephilim didn't know anything else. Punishment would be swift and violent in his world. There was no in-between.

"The rules are different here," I insisted when

Killian simply glared at me with murder in his eyes—precisely why I didn't want him anywhere near Max with a look like that on his face.

I glanced at Lily for support. She and James watched us, their expressions matching masks of misery, clearly wishing they were anywhere else. I handed them cups of coffee to occupy them—Lily giving me a weak smile. By the look of sheer delight on her face after she took a sip, she missed coffee as much as I did.

"Tell her I'm right," Killian snapped at James. "You lived in this world. How do humans deal with their worst? Kidnappers and ra—"

James shot up a hand. "I'm upset too, Killian, but we can't lose focus. We need to know what the Wild Dragons want with this human, regardless of what he's done." He leaned in, threading his fingers together as he rested his elbows on his thighs. "Think about it. We find out what the Wild Dragons want with him. Then, one possibility is that it's nothing to worry about and we hand him over. In that case, he'll meet his fate and we get Vivi's mother back."

Killian sniffed at that idea, the flare in his eyes saying he'd find that a fitting punishment. "That's the preferred outcome."

Lily set her coffee on the side table. "Or, there's a reason we have to keep him," she said, voicing the alternative. "In which case he will be dealt with by the Dean."

And my mother would be on her own while the

Dean dealt with Max.

We all shivered at the thought of being at the Dean's mercy, an ancient Viking who had a penchant for swords.

Killian's shoulders lowered. "Well, I suppose we can focus on the task at hand. For now." He glanced down when I offered him the coffee again, in desperate need of a distraction no matter which route we wound up taking. He glared at the offering. "What is that and why is it black? Are you trying to poison me?"

"It's coffee," I said as Topaz sniffed at it and Solstice growled. I swatted at her. "Our wyverns seem to like it. Why don't you give it a try?"

He gave me a raised brow. "It looks disgusting."

"Trust me," I said on a laugh, forcing the cup on him.

He lifted to his nose and his nostrils flared. "Smells interesting," he agreed.

I nodded, waving him on with encouragement.

He took a small sip, all the while his gaze remained locked onto mine. His face transformed into a grimace as he spat it out and wiped his mouth. "You *are* trying to kill me!"

Topaz trilled with interest as Killian held out the cup, skittering down his arm to dunk his snout into the mug.

"Topaz seems to like it," Lily pointed out with a laugh.

The wyvern slurped away at it happily, making contented gurgles.

Solstice chirped at me with complaint, so I sighed and offered her my mug. She drained it in seconds. "Pace yourself, girl," I said, chuckling.

James cleared his throat. "So, tell us more about Max. We need to figure out why the Wild Dragons want him before we can decide what to do with him. He *is* human, right?"

Human? I thought. Theoretically, sure, but after what Max had done, groping me and nearly drowning me, he seemed anything but human to me.

"He's a monster," I murmured.

Killian's gaze darkened as Solstice keened.

As though she could feel my mood sour, Solstice nuzzled my neck right over a ticklish spot. I laughed, rubbing the sweet wyvern in gratitude.

I set my coffee mug down and Solstice flapped down to the table, sniffed at it, then voiced her complaint when she found it empty.

Topaz chirped at her, scampering onto the table and inching over towards my cup now that Killian's had been drained.

"He's a monster, yes, but also human," Killian decided.

James gave him a raised brow. "What makes you say that?"

Killian kept my gaze locked on his as he recounted his interpretation of my story. "He wanted something from Vivi, but if he'd actually wanted her dead, he wouldn't have brought her to the water where the Lady of the Lake knew to watch for her. She's always been on the Academy's recruitment list, but thanks to her mother she had no idea she was supposed to meet with the Lady of the Lake anyway."

The accusation in Killian's tone made me bristle. "My parents are the only reason I'm still alive," I growled. My father had given his life to protect me from all this supernatural crap. Maybe it was to keep me away from the Academy, or maybe it was to keep me off of the Wild Dragons' radar for as long as possible. I had a sneaking suspicion of who had killed him now, and I meant to get even.

The memory of the night when my goddess blood had activated burned itself into my mind, having come to me during the feverish fit when I had bonded Solstice's empty egg. Retrieving my wyvern's lost soul had nearly killed me, but surviving it had taught me a lot—such as my destiny was so terrible, my parents were willing to die to protect me from it.

I'd already lost one parent. I had no intention of losing another.

"My mother is a hostage and we're going to get her back," I said, giving Killian a level stare. He had to know I was serious about this, regardless of what Max deserved. This wasn't about a dumb jock from Oakland High. This was about my family.

"We are," Killian agreed, "starting with figuring out why the Wild Dragons want this human in the first place." He tilted his head as if something occurred to him. "You say he forced you under the water." His irises burned with inner heat at that statement and all that it implied, but he had a point to make. "That's the only reason you came to the Academy in the first place, isn't it?"

I swallowed past the lump in my throat. I hadn't considered that Max was the only reason I'd gotten into all this mess. It wasn't some sort of twisted destiny or fate, but Max's arms shoving me into the water and driving me to the Lady of the Lake, and into this new life where I'd been on the run with few breaks in-between.

"Although his actions are monstrous," Killian continued, "he's human. At least, from what I can tell." He turned to James. "Why don't we just hand him over to the Wild Dragons, then?" Murder glazed over his eyes. "That would be a better fate than what I would do to him," he balled his hands until his knuckles turned white.

Lily clutched the arms of her chair; her nails having extended to claws. Her eyes flashed gold as she considered Killian's proposal. "Unfortunately, we can't just hand him over without knowing *why* they want him, even if he is mortal." She squirmed in her seat, as if struggling with the logic of her statement. "Though, I would like nothing more than to rip him to shreds, if I'm being honest."

James listened to the conversation all while he rested his elbows on his knees. He clasped his hands, his expression turning grave. "Lily's right. That's why we're here. We could have delivered a message to you using far less magic than portaling in, but the Dean knew this was important enough to send reinforce-ments." He glanced at me, his blue gaze intense. "Your mom can't stay with the dragons, especially when they have likely figured out what she is by now. They won't give her up in an honest trade even if we did hand over this human. I can't imagine what would be more valu-able than a full-blooded descendant of the goddess."

I scratched the burning swirl on my left shoulder, the birthmark having come alive since our return to Earth. Dragonrider Academy uniforms typically kept it covered, and at times I forgot about it, but now in a loose t-shirt I was painfully aware of what my lineage entailed.

"It doesn't make sense," I agreed.

"They might not be able to use her like they could use you," Lily said, her skin shimmering with ruby tones as scales threatened to erupt over her body. She drew in a deep breath as if to calm herself from transi-tioning. "A full-blood is a powerful resource, and in full control of their gifts. But a Halfling?" She glanced at me, her pupils dilating into slits. "Your power is less protected, in that way. Dragons are a parasitic species, at their core, and they will eventually find a way to use it to their advantage. Maybe this is just an elaborate trap to get you back into their clutches." Her gaze shimmered with heat as if she spoke from experience. Being a dragon herself, I knew she meant every word.

"Then why don't they just come for me? Why this ruse to trade my mother for a human?"

"Oh, they want him," Killian concluded. "There are

multiple angles at play here. We need more information."

"But my mother—" I began.

"Your mother knows how to fight back," Lily cut in. "She'd rather die than give up her magic, if she's truly a descendant of the goddess. They won't get anything from her and until they have you, they'll keep her alive."

Solstice keened as panic threatened to swarm through my body, reducing me into a useless pile of flesh.

Killian took my hand and warmth chased away the cold, the power of our shared rider bond mixing with the golden magic of my lineage.

Urgency filled me, bursting through in a desperate statement. "Then we have to do something!"

Lily nodded. "Agreed, which is why we're going to go undercover at this high school of yours and get to the bottom of it."

Frowning, I tugged Killian closer to my side, not wanting to let go of his encouragement just yet. "How? We can't just waltz into the school. I disappeared, remember?"

Lily grinned, small fangs poking from her lips. "I'm a Dragon Queen, remember? I've come a long way from my human days." She glanced at James, who gave her a knowing smile. "Dragonrider Academy is a unique place, one that has taught me how to use my gifts. I'm able to use basic compulsion enchantments."

James hummed in agreement. "She'll be able to

convince the staff that we're students, as well as place a fog over the school to encourage a general disinterest of our presence. Knights of the Silver Order have dragon allies and have solicited such services."

Lily snorted. "You sure did stand out to me at Nimrock High. You must not have used a very powerful dragon."

He tilted his head. "That's because you're my Queen. There's no fooling you, even if my mother had hired out a rogue in exchange for amnesty." He rubbed his chin, his tattoos peeking out from under his sleeve. "Evelyn's a powerful dragon with the amount of loyal *Hovakim* in her nest, but apparently not powerful enough."

Killian and I glanced at each other, an unspoken conversation seeming to go on between us.

Even if Lily could convince the school that we belonged there, Killian would no doubt blow our cover in two seconds flat.

My anxiety trilled in the back of my mind as Killian's thumb stroked my knuckles. Our gazes went to our wyverns who were now tumbling over the floor fighting over the last drop of coffee. After the copious amount of caffeine they'd already had, I doubted they'd nap today like they usually did.

I doubted Lily's compulsion could hide Solstice and Topaz, and we couldn't very well leave them here. No telling what kind of trouble they'd get into.

I rubbed my temple, which was starting the throb. "And what do you propose we do about *them?*"

CHAPTER 3

BLENDING IN

*L*ily's solution to our wyvern problem made me feel uneasy, mostly because I didn't like Solstice being in such a vulnerable form.

She flitted around my head before landing on my shoulder, her golden finch glamour a purely visual magic that hid what Solstice really was to the naked eye, yet she felt just as heavy as she always did as she nuzzled up to my neck. Lily couldn't make her entirely invisible, not when Solstice was a fledgling queen in her own right.

Topaz, however, seemed to be having too much fun being invisible as Killian cursed, the lobe of his ear shortly after turning bright red. Irritation made Killian's tattoos flush with blue magic in response, although Lily had assured me that she could convince mortals it was only a trick of the light.

"I think he wants more coffee," I offered with a chuckle.

Killian only glared at me. "No more *coffee*. Ever. Again." The wyverns were indeed unruly after the addicting drink, chirping at us nonstop for more. I had to agree, maybe coffee was not the best thing to give a mythological lizard.

Lily clapped her hands as she marched down the street. "Enough dilly-dallying! We're going to be late for homeroom if you two keep flirting."

"I'm not flirting," Killian ground out.

James slapped him on the back, making Killian buckle. A tear formed on my mate's sleeve, an invisible Topaz likely stubbornly maintaining his perch. "You'll get used to the human uniforms," he promised, his gaze falling onto Lily with interest. Her skirt ran high as her gauzy blouse lifted to expose her midriff when she walked, perfect for fitting in with the cheerleader crowd.

Killian likewise had a hungry gaze that ran over me. "I remember the last uniform," he said, grinning as he confidently snaked a hand around my waist. "You showed up on the Academy's beach naked, practically begging to be my mate."

I huffed out a breath. "I wasn't naked. I was wearing a bathing suit." I shot up a finger. "And there was definitely no begging."

Killian shrugged. "If you say so." His hand slipped to the small of my back, making my brain turn into scrambled eggs. It was hard to stay mad at him when he knew exactly how to break down my defenses.

Plus, Lily's idea of making Killian fit in practically had me drooling. Lily had conjured them all new outfits. Killian in particular sported a Radiohead t-shirt —courtesy of one of my favorite bands—the sleeves short to show off his tattoos. She'd tucked his white hair behind his ears and after some fussing, decided he had to go punk. No amount of glamour would hide his Nephilim eyes, or his rider bond tattoo, and suppressing its typical glow when he got emotional was all she was able to do.

His jeans ran tight around his hips and he pulled me in close, grinning as if he knew the effect he was having on me.

A car sped by, making Killian flinch, but I gave him some credit for acclimating faster than expected to the modern technology. His ear turned red again and Killian flicked at the air with a hiss. "You are taking advantage of this invisibility to mess with me, you mischievous little lizard."

I chuckled as Solstice chirped at Topaz, which I imagined was her version of a chide to keep the wyvern in line. I reached up and rubbed her head in response.

The school came into view as the tree line broke on the horizon. "Are you absolutely sure this is going to work?" I asked. We'd be in full view of the student body in the next ten minutes, and there would be no going back. We only had one shot to get at Max, and if word got out what was going on, I had no doubt his father would keep him out of harm's way. He could afford private school if necessary, and from my knowledge the only reason Max went to Oakland High was because he liked the sports team.

Killian stiffened when we stepped onto the asphalt parking lot and the students paused, their conversations dying as they turned to us.

"I knew this wasn't going to work," I hissed as all eyes turned our way.

"Uh, pretty sure it's not us they're staring at," James said, glancing behind us in much the same way as the rest of the student body.

I turned to find a striking female flanked by two males on either side—all of them just as ethereally beautiful as she was.

She didn't even attempt to hide her dragonesque features, jewel-toned scales glittering in patches over her skin as she walked. Her slitted pupils dilated, slicing through emerald eyes that snapped on me in an instant. She grinned, her smile framed by petite fangs as she came to a stop just out of reach. She ran one finger through her hair, snagging her horns as if to taunt me.

"Well, hello there," she said, an Irish accent capping off her otherworldly aura. She leaned to get a look around me, her smile widening. "Lily, is that you?"

"Evie?" Lily asked, aghast as she shoved around me. Solstice squeaked in protest, clinging painfully to my shoulder as I regained my balance. "What the heck are you doing here?"

By her friendly tone, I shouldn't have been surprised when Lily threw her arms around the dragon shifter, making my eyebrows shoot up my forehead.

The four guys behind her watched the friendly exchange, before taking us all in. They seemed particularly wary of James, the Knight of the Silver Order who knowingly rubbed his wrist—the place where his magical sword would come out if provoked.

I glanced behind us, finding all of the students whispering and I knew the gossip was flying.

Whelp. So much for blending in.

CHAPTER 4

HOVAKIM AND
HASHBROWNS

*B*ased on the fact that nobody ran screaming for their lives, it was apparent that Evie maintained some sort of glamour that hid her dragon traits.

She seemed to enjoy the fact it didn't work on me or any of my friends as she grinned at me across from the cafeteria table. Solstice flapped at the outside window, eager to get back to me, but I couldn't rightly explain why I had a pet finch on my shoulder, so I'd agreed when Lily suggested that he wait outside.

By the sound of his very loud chirping, he wasn't too pleased about the predicament.

"You're here early enough for breakfast," Evie praised as she took a muffin from her tray, but she didn't bite into it. Instead she turned it around in her palm, seeming to admire it. "I do miss a good human breakfast."

"Oakland High breakfast, you mean," the redheaded male named Yosef corrected her as he glanced around the open space. While everyone was interested in the newcomers, no one was brave enough to come within earshot.

His twin, Jakob, waggled his eyebrows as he snatched up the muffin and took a bite. "You worry too much, Yosef. Evie's glamour works on auditory senses now, too. Nobody is going to hear us. Even if they did, though, we have *amnesty*. Evelyn could light up this place and we'd walk out without even one knight on our tail."

James rubbed his wrist and gave Jakob the full force of his disapproving glare.

Jakob swallowed his bite. "Okay, well, maybe *one* knight."

"No fires," a muscular male declared as he crossed his arms. I wasn't sure if that one was Liam or Marcus, the two brothers weren't twins but they both looked like they could benchpress five times my weight. "We're here to finish our assignment, then go back to Avalon."

I slammed down my orange juice. "You work for Avalon?" I shot back. The only reason I hadn't taken care of these guys was because Lily seemed to trust the dragon, but maybe I shouldn't trust any dragons. "Tell me one reason why I shouldn't kill you right now."

As if hearing my train of thought, Lily gave me a frown, her eyes filled with hurt. "Because Evie is my friend, Viv, and her *Hovakim* are her family. They can be trusted, too." She reached out and placed a hand over mine, her touch pleasantly warm. "She's a double agent. We can learn things about the Wild Dragons and gain an edge."

"Or the Wild Dragons can learn things about *us*," I shot back, glancing at Evie. "Such as my relationship with Max Green." I tilted my head. "If you're really here to help, then tell us, why does your Queen want him?"

Evie kept a level stare on me, unflinching in an eerily reptilian way. "I promise you I'll tell you what I know, but if you continue to utilize your goddess magic you're going to blow our cover."

I glanced down, noting the sharp glow on my left shoulder bleeding through my shirt. I clamped a hand over it and frowned.

The tension at the table was palpable. James glared at Evie, folding his tattooed arms over his chest. Killian didn't look any happier as he studied the group across from us.

Killian gave Lily a raised brow. "Are you going to explain how you two became friends?" He gestured across the table. "I know you're a dragon, but the Academy accepted you because you had a Knight for a mate. This chick has four human *Hovakim*. Not exactly approved behavior according to the Dean."

"Why aren't they approved?" I asked, honestly curious.

Killian didn't take his glare off of Evelyn. "They're slaves who sold their souls to the dragons for longevity, health, and madness."

One of the dark-haired muscular males paused from his food to retort, "I'm quite sane, thank you."

The red-headed twins nodded their agreement and the other muscular one just glowered at all of us like he wanted to be anywhere else.

Evelyn seemed at ease between her four mates, quite content despite the growing tension. She reached for an apple, jerking back when an invisible Topaz devoured it.

She raised a brow and turned to Lily. "Your powers have evolved."

Lily smirked at Evie's horns. "As have yours."

Killian scooped up Topaz, the wyvern's location given away by a leftover stem. He crooned at the wyvern and scratched his favorite spots. "Good boy."

Lily sighed. "Killian, Evie and her mates have been helping out with intel on Earth with the rogue dragon influence. As have Yosef and Jakob." She pointed to the identical redheads, then gestured to the muscular males. "Marcus and Liam likewise offer their protection. They're on the inside with Avalon's queen providing invaluable intel." She straightened her back and stared defiantly at my mate. "How did you think I knew to come here? The only reason we received a ransom note was because Evie convinced the Queen it was the best course of action. Otherwise she would have just killed Vivi's mother and gone after Max herself." She glanced at me as I swallowed. "Ever since the incident at Nimrock High, I knew it was just a matter of time before the dragons came for me. They wanted me, and I left, and the moment I returned to Earth they sensed it, but I'm not going to let Vivi face this alone for a second."

James glared at her. "You didn't tell me you were keeping up with a dragon. Or the danger you'd be in if we came back."

Lily sighed again, turning to face her mate with the same defiance. "I'm a Dragon Queen, James. Deal with it. Not all dragons are bad, or you wouldn't have let me live. And Evie made sure she was the one put on assignment for this job to ensure my safety, as well as Vivi's, right Evie?"

Evelyn nodded, looking between the four of us. "More or less. I had to ditch my partner, but for now I'm the only dragon you have to worry about." She shrugged. "For a few days, anyway."

James narrowed his eyes. "Partner?"

Evelyn released on long breath. "That's right. I might have the Queen's ear, but I'm not in charge. The Queen had me pair up with Zelda." She rolled her eyes toward the ceiling. "She's crazy. It's little wonder she hasn't found any mates. The only reason I was able to come alone was because I got her into trouble. She wasn't supposed to try and kill Vivi. The Queen wants her alive, so she was pretty ticked off about all the massacre and fire and whatnot. She thinks only Vivi is strong enough to kidnap Max, which very well may be true, if my suspicions are correct."

"And do you care to enlighten us about your suspicions?" I asked.

Evie rested her elbows on the table and leaned forward. "We'll get to that, but first, you have to know what's at stake here and that *I'm* not your enemy. Avalon's Queen has more ambitions than just taking over Avalon. The Wild Dragons are planning an invasion of all the realms and attacking Dragonrider Academy was only the first phase. They are after all Dragon Queens."

Lily flinched. "That's why Zelda went after me."

Evie nodded in grave confirmation. "Correct. I only found out recently her plan to overcome the balance by hoarding power."

James grunted. "Dragons do love their hoarding."

Ignoring him, Evie continued. "Avalon's queen wants all realms to bow to her. She believes that if she gathers all the Dragon Queens and makes them bow, she can achieve her goals by absorbing their collective power." She glanced between Solstice at the window, the golden finch a creature she clearly hadn't missed, then her gaze fell on Lily. "Two queens in one place is going to make her salivate, but there's only one thing she wants more right now. And that's keeping you safe." She turned her gaze to Max who was across the cafeteria joking with his buddies. I followed her gaze and stiffened as flashes of that night rushed through my head.

Killian turned in his seat, his gaze turning dark. "That's him, right?"

Before I could reply, he shot up from his seat, clearly having menacing intentions towards the group of humans. James followed him and put a hand on his shoulder, pushing him back down. "Stay."

Killian growled. "I'm not one of your dragons you can boss around, Knight."

James didn't flinch. "Now's not the time, Killian. We'll deal with Max and his buddies later, I promise you. They will get what they deserve in due time."

Killian and James glared at one another, seeming to have an unspoken conversation before Killian finally backed down, settling in his seat as his fists clenched.

"We could just take him now," Killian complained.

"You couldn't," Evie retorted.

"Why?" I asked. "What could Max do to possibly fend off a pissed off Nephilim Dragonrider?"

Yosef met my eyes. "Max isn't what he seems."

"And what *is* he?" I demanded.

Jakob rubbed his chin. "We suspect it's an inactive dragon gene that triggered the Queen's search for powerful dragons, which would make him unpredictable and dangerous." He glanced at James. "I'm surprised the Knights of the Silver Order aren't involved in this."

James crossed his arms. "They probably are, if what you say is true."

Evie grinned, showing off teeth. "Ah, so there's a little family drama now that you've mated the enemy? Keeping you out of the loop, are they?"

James glowered in response. "They try, but they don't hide their activity very well. If Max has the gene, then the Order is going to be all over this. My brother has the Silver Order keeping a pretty strict lockdown on Earth's realm. Any dragon who harms a human or is suspected to be dangerous is hunted down and taken out."

Lily bopped his nose with her finger. "Or so they might try."

He smiled down at her, wrapping his arm around her waist. "Some dragons do prove to be rather resilient, I agree."

I raised an eyebrow. I'd heard about their history, but I hadn't realized the dire terms of how James and Lily had met. "So… Lily was your target?" The unspoken question lingered underneath my words. If James had been sent after her… that meant that he should have tried to kill her.

Lily ran a finger over his wrist, a faint blue glow smoldering like fire underneath her touch. "I was, and he succeeded at first."

James ran his thumb over her lower lip. "Good thing death doesn't take with you."

Killian and I shared a look while Lily chuckled as if amused, leaning in to kiss him. James took full advantage of the moment, deepening the innocent display of affection into something more.

And I thought my relationship was messed up.

While Evie seemed enthralled by the display of affection between dragon and Knight, my gaze fell to Max again, as if drawn by his mystery and darkness. Thanks to Lily's magic, he hadn't yet noticed me. He joked with his buddies just like I always remembered, drawing the attention of the room by his noise and popularity. Everyone loved him.

But nobody really knew him, not like I did.

And my guess was, even he didn't know how special he was. Figuring out what exactly the Avalon Queen wanted with him might prove to be a challenge, but if it meant getting my mother back, I'd find a way to delve into his black soul and unravel all of his secrets.

The morning bell rang, breaking me from my thoughts. We all stood and made our way to our first class.

Solstice chirped at the window, reminding me that unlike the last time I'd been a student here, this time I wasn't alone.

CHAPTER 5

A NEW STUDENT

"*H*uh?" Sally asked when I tried to get her attention for the third time. Everyone I had talked to today seemed to struggle to pay attention to me, which at first I thought had been because of Lily's glamour, but now I was starting to suspect something more was at play.

"Max Green?" she repeated, seeming to be able to focus better when the conversation wasn't about me. Nobody seemed to know anything about my disappearance, or even be able to talk about me, or *to* me for that matter. Sally wouldn't even look at me, being one of the cheerleaders, that wasn't odd, but it seemed to prove useful in getting someone to communicate with me. "I haven't noticed anything out of the ordinary." She leaned into her locker to pluck out an English book. A Vogue magazine stuck out from the pages. She peeked into the mirror and adjusted her ponytail, not making eye contact with me. "He's got another party coming up, but it's invite only." The tone in her voice suggested she knew I wouldn't be invited, someone so inconsequential that she couldn't even look at me—even if she didn't realize that was because some sort of compulsion magic was at play.

Not that I exactly wanted an invitation. The last time I'd gotten one I'd nearly been violated and murdered. Not exactly what I'd call a great time.

"Thanks," I muttered, backing away when Sally waved excitedly at one of the jocks. They all looked the same to me, except for Max and his buddies that I'd made a point to avoid while I did recon.

I dragged my feet as I headed to my last class of the day, feeling defeated that I hadn't learned anything new. Solstice followed my path from the windows, her muted chirps coming in to remind me that I still wasn't alone.

Sighing, I glanced up and waved at her. "Yeah, thanks girl."

She was ready for me to be done for the day, and so was I, but I had hoped to find at least *something* useful. We were on the clock as it was.

Biting my lip, I realized maybe I *had* learned something interesting. None of the students seemed to respond to information about my disappearance, which I suspected went beyond Lily's glamour.

Their memories had been altered.

If that was the case... who could have had the

power to alter memories? A dragon, surely. Maybe Evie? I made a mental note to ask her about it later.

The day dragged on, resuming an academic monotony I'd forgotten how much I'd hated.

Mostly because I didn't need classes. I never had, which was why I had retreated to Oakland High's library every chance I got—begging Miss Jenny to order new dragon fantasy fiction novels as often as possible.

Solstice pecked at the window, reminding me that I didn't need any of those novels anymore. All those adventures I loved reading about? Yeah, I was living it.

Except now my mother's life was in danger.

And my mate wasn't in the majority of my classes, making me desperately worry how he was fitting in.

Lily had managed to get me two classes with Killian, first our homeroom and then he was on his own until the last hour in algebra. The latter of which I decidedly did not miss. She'd probably done it on purpose to help us "split up," but I still felt she underestimated Killian's ability to act… normal.

He demonstrated his inhuman nature by solving an entire worksheet in ten seconds flat, earning gaping looks from the students and the teacher as he eased back in his seat.

Lily sighed from across the room and her scales briefly glowed. A warm shockwave swept through the air, then the attention melted away from us, allowing me to glare at my mate.

While academics didn't challenge me, my worksheet remained half-finished. I couldn't complete such complex problems *that* fast.

"How did you do that?" I asked, curious where a Nephilim Dragonrider would have learned Algebra.

He rolled his eyes to regard me, as if the answer to my question should be obvious. "I already learned this sort of "basic" math when I was a child."

I crossed my arms. "This is advanced math. We're in an advanced placement course for college prep."

He swatted at the air, likely at Topaz nipping at his ear again, bored with staying in one place for too long. "Maybe for a human," Killian said as he lowered his voice. "But if you'd grown in Paradiso like I had, you would have been actually challenged instead of bored out of your skull." He glanced down at my worksheet. "You've managed to learn the basics even with such rudimentary training, but had you been able to grow up in Avalon, you would have been with others of your kind. Understood. Respected."

That sounded…. well, amazing. I tried to keep my expression flat. I didn't want Killian to know how much it pained me that I would never have the picture he'd just painted. My upbringing had been isolating and lonely, painful and dull with only a few bright moments of excitement.

Even now, my adventures came with the weight of lives in the palm of my hands. If I messed this up, my mother could die, just like my father.

"Tell me about Paradiso," I said, instead wishing to

keep the conversation on my mate. He fascinated me and I still felt like I knew so little about him.

He smirked and waited, making me wonder if he wasn't going to tell me. His white-washed gaze met mine, as if searching for something. "You could see it for yourself, you know."

"Perhaps," I agreed, "but that won't be for a while. I'd like to hear about it from you, first."

He nodded, acquiescing to my request. "It's another realm, one made for Nephilim like me. Angels aren't supposed to procreate, but for those who have free will, sometimes they bend to temptation. I never knew my parents. They were forced to send me to Paradiso for my protection. I was raised by the community of Nephilim like myself, those who understood exactly what I was and what I needed to thrive—and they provided the necessary training to protect myself."

"From what?" I asked, my eyes going wide.

He waved a hand in dismissal. "There are many threats throughout the realms. Nephilim have natural enemies, but the Wild Dragons have become a growing concern that needed to be dealt with. When I came of age, I had a choice. Join the Holy Army, or join Dragonrider Academy." He leaned back in his chair, crossing his arms. "It seemed like an easy choice at the time."

"And now?" I asked, literally on the edge of my seat. "Do you regret not joining the Holy Army?"

He shook his head. "No. They are busy dealing with other threats—one potentially worse than the Wild Dragons, if you can believe it, but that isn't your concern for now. My kind underestimates what the Wild Dragons are capable of. If the Avalon Queen succeeds in getting what she wants, she'll be more powerful than anyone could have imagined possible." His jaw flexed, his gaze going distant. "I made the right choice. The Wild Queen has to be stopped, or else all of the realms will be in danger of falling."

The Wild Queen.

That made our mysterious enemy sound terrifying, and I imagined she was. I wouldn't underestimate the threat, not like Killian's family. I would do everything in my power to make sure no one else suffered like I had.

He studied my worksheet. "Do you want help solving your algebra problems?"

I sighed, "I don't see the point. It's not like I need this to kick Wild Dragon butt."

Killian grinned. "You'd be surprised. It's good for the mind."

I snorted. "It's good for a headache."

A scratching sounded from Killian's desk and a portion of his worksheet disappeared as an invisible Topaz chomped at it. Killian cursed and pulled him away.

I couldn't help but laugh. "I stand corrected. Apparently, it's also good for a wyvern's snack."

Solstice chirped from outside the window, the noise a clear complaint that he couldn't be inside with us, especially now that Topaz found something to eat.

Despite Lily's glamour working its heat through the

room to keep us undercover, I felt eyes on me and looked up, catching Julie Emmerson glaring at me, a suspicious look in her eyes.

I leaned over to Killian, whispering. "I think we have a problem."

Killian just smiled at me, "She's probably just pushing against the glamour. When emotions run high, it makes it more difficult for dragon magic to hold. It doesn't matter if she remembers you actually left though. Who would believe her? One person doesn't matter so much. It's when the breeches happen in mass quantities that the Silver Order steps in."

"The Silver Order is where James is from, right? Is he important to them?"

Killian barked a laugh. "You don't know who he is? That explains a few things."

I rolled a pencil back and forth on my desk. "You know I'm not from your world, Killian. Stop teasing and enlighten me."

He bent his head in apology. "James is royalty. He abdicated the throne when he mated a dragon. Now, his brother Ivar is the king of the Knights of the Silver Order. Their mission is to keep humanity safe from dragons—and there are conflicting views on how to accomplish that."

I hummed in thought. "So, James was sent to kill Lily, but he didn't?"

"Oh, he did," Killian retorted, blowing my mind. "She's a powerful Dragon Queen. It'll take more than a Knight like James to truly end her life. She'll most definitely be one of the queens that the Wild Dragons will be after, so we have to remain vigilant."

"That's nuts," I said.

Killian grinned. "If you think James is bad, his brother is much worse."

"How could he be worse?" I asked, bringing the eraser to my mouth.

"He's a Traditionalist," he said, snatching up my pencil before I could chew on it. "Ivar believes that all dragons and their allies much be eliminated. James, however, is a Loyalist, a Knight who bases his decision on the code of Excalibur and the Lady of the Lake. James doesn't talk about the code, but from what I've gathered it is a vague set of values, ones that can be interpreted differently. He views dragons like Lily as reformed and evolved creatures, ones worth protecting. Lily doesn't want to kill the Wild Dragons—she wants to save them."

I grunted at that. "They can't be saved."

"I agree."

We went silent, the conversation giving me a lot of food for thought. I couldn't say I agreed with Ivar. Lily was my friend. I would never harm her, but the Wild Dragons were soulless, evil things. They had taken my father away from me and they would pay the price for that.

If my mother died too... I would show them no mercy.

The teacher clapped her hands, calling for the worksheets and we passed them up the rows. The class quieted, making it impossible to hold a conversation about the supernatural without being overheard even with Lily's glamour.

Killian flinched when the teacher flipped on the TV, the next task an educational video explaining the problems we had just attempted.

Killian's eyes remained glued to the moving images, his frown deepening when a cartoon letter "X" sauntered across the scene. "What in all the realms is that creature?" he asked, making me laugh.

Halfway through the video, the door opened and all eyes went to the newcomer. We all stared at the tall, gorgeous boy with ice-blue eyes and blonde hair as he walked in. He was unmistakable, with glowing silver tattoos along his arms as a Knight of the Silver Order.

Killian sighed, shoulders slumping in annoyance. "Great. Ivar is here."

CHAPTER 6

DUEL BY
BEER PONG

*I*var sure knew how to make an appearance. He hadn't solicited any sort of glamour protection and now Lily swiped her face in frustration as James dragged us all to the courtyard, our classes finally done for the day.

"What do you think you're doing?" he snapped at his brother.

Ivar jerked his arm away, defiance radiating in his gaze. "You don't get to boss me around any longer, James, not after the stunt you pulled." He glared at Lily for good measure, who maturely stuck her tongue out at him.

The students gave us a wide berth as we gathered under the shade of one of my favorite oak trees, a place where I would have read for hours losing myself on a fantastical adventure between the pages of a good book.

Now, I growled with frustration as obstacles continued to prevent me from getting anywhere with our mission. We hadn't been able to learn anything useful and supernaturals kept getting in the way.

Dragons. Knights. Kings. What else could go wrong?

I noted that Evie and her *Hovakim* stood some distance away as they watched the exchange. Meanwhile Max and his buddies sat at a table across the courtyard, their attention drawn to us despite Lily's efforts.

"You guys need to figure this out," she hissed. "You're drawing way too much attention."

Solstice keened with agreement in my ear, her finch form struggling with how much Lily was having to cover for us right now. My wyvern shifted on my shoulder and I switched her to the other one. She was getting too heavy to sit on my shoulders for much longer at the rate she was growing. No wonder she and Topaz were always starving.

Ivar handed Killian a letter, pointedly ignoring his brother. "The solution is simple. You all need to leave."

"Why?" James growled.

Ivar pretended his brother didn't exist, instead directing his response to the rest of us. "You're all in violation of Article Eight, Section Five of the Realms Agreement between Dragonrider Academy and the Knights of the Silver Order. Every one of you must return to your own realm immediately." He narrowed his eyes at me. "Including you. This isn't your world anymore, Dragonrider."

Killian glared back, balled the paper up, and lifted it to his shoulder where Topaz's form shimmered. The notice disappeared a second later, likely eaten by the starving wyvern. Ivar's expression darkened.

James crossed his arms. "We have business to attend to and we will leave when we are ready to leave. I speak for the Order just as much as you do, and Article Eight does not apply in this instance. We are not in your jurisdiction, therefore you can't tell us to back off."

"This entire realm is our jurisdiction," Ivar growled, finally facing his brother. "You're not even allowed to be here. You and I will settle this with a duel and your betrayal to our kind will be dealt with once and for all."

I threw my hands up in exasperation, stalking over and plopping into the swing hanging from the tall oak tree. "Great, more duels. Don't you people settle disputes with anything more modern? What about a game of darts or something?"

Killian gave me a perplexed look. "What are darts?"

I sighed and shook my head. Ivar glanced at us and then turned his attention to Evie who wiggled her fingers at him.

"I've ordered the death of your rogue dragon friend and her allies in this realm—I didn't expect those allies to be you."

That was interesting information, and likely the reason we'd gotten a personal visit from the new leader of the Knights of the Silver Order. Maybe he cared more about his brother than he would openly admit.

"She has amnesty," I clarified, remembering one of her *Hovakim* bragging about that fact.

Ivar shook his head. "Not anymore. Not after she allied herself with the Avalon violators who've been rampaging the realms. While that might *fly* in other kingdoms, Earth is off-limits and swift action will be taken against offenders."

Lily snorted. When Killian raised his eyebrow at her, she added, "He said *fly*. Get it?" He stared at her. "Dragons... fly? Never mind."

James scoffed. "The rogue dragon is working for us, you dimwit."

Ivar clenched his fists. "Say that to me again when we're in a proper duel and I can knock you off your feet. I'm not a child anymore."

James pushed into his brother's face until their noses brushed. "Try me in a duel, little brother. See what happens."

I rolled my eyes. "It sounds like we all should just work together. The Wild Dragon Queen is holding my mother hostage and wants a student from Oakland High in return. We need to understand what she wants to do with him before we go through with it." Ivar seemed to mull over my words, his blue eyes calculating.

Killian added his explanation, detailing the invasion at the Academy and my mother's abduction and ending with Max. He emphasized that we couldn't leave until we at least had more information.

Ivar nodded in understanding as Killian finished, then he turned to me. "Your mother," he repeated, his eyes growing dark. "And they want this human in exchange? That's odd."

"Yeah, we can't figure out why they would want him," I said, glancing over at the human in question.

Ivar's face scrunched in confusion and I was disappointed that he seemed just as clueless as we were. I had been hoping that the Order would prove useful.

"I don't know the significance of this human or why they would want him," he said, "but something does seem off about him..." He squinted at the table full of teenage males.

Frustration filled me as another person agreed on Max being off. Why couldn't I see it too?

As if he could sense us talking about him, Max looked over, catching my gaze for the first time. Recognition seemed to roll over him and Lily cursed from my side.

He got up from the table and jogged over to us. Panic made my stomach flip as I reached out to Killian for support.

Max slowed to a stop in front of me, giving me a sleazy smile and ignoring Killian and Ivar. "Hey, babe. I haven't seen you around in a while. How was your vacation?"

His voice and proximity were enough to make me start shaking. I hadn't been this close to him since he violated and then tried to kill me. I glanced at Lily, wondering why her glamour wasn't working anymore. She gave me a helpless shrug and mouthed an apology.

Killian slipped his arm around my waist and glared at the human with murder in his gaze. "She's not your *babe*."

Topaz hissed, but Max didn't seem to be able to hear him.

Max smiled and lifted his hands up in surrender. "Oh, sorry! I didn't realize she found a new boyfriend." He playfully punched me in the shoulder. "Good for you, Viv." He scratched his head. "Although, now that I think of it, I don't remember where you went on vacation. Was it a beach…" He snapped his fingers. "That reminds me, you didn't get to come to my last resort party. That's really too bad, it was fun, although I don't remember most of it. I must have blacked out from drinking."

Right, more like Dragonrider magic.

"Too bad," I mumbled. "I'm sure it was a good time."

He hummed in agreement. Killian looked ready to punch him in the throat, but the idiot was talking. Maybe the only way we'd learn anything about him was directly from the source, so I squeezed Killian's fingers around my waist and listened.

"Like I said," Max continued, "we all had a really good time. I'm having another party at my place this weekend, you're welcome to come. You know where it is, right?" He glanced at Killian, then Ivar and James who all looked sorely out of place amongst the students. "Uh, your friends are welcome, too."

My heart thundered in my chest as I forced myself to meet his gaze. He pointedly waited until I replied, "Oh, um. Yeah, sure. I know the place." The Green mansion was hard to miss, a jewel that sat atop the horizon at the end of Silver Lake.

He grinned, giving me one of his charming smiles that I once would have melted for. "Awesome! I'll see you there."

Killian stared after him as he walked away, probably imagining all the ways he could torture him, before he looked back at me. "We aren't seriously going, are we?"

Ivar nodded at him. "Oh, you're going, as am I. I fully intend to make sure this business is taken out of my realm." He glared at his brother for good measure. "And we still have a duel to schedule."

"Duel by beer pong?" I offered with a chuckle while Killian gave me a questioning look.

The prospect sounded hilarious, even if it was going to be at another one of Max's parties.

Hopefully no one would try to kill me this time.

CHAPTER 7

A PARTY
TO REMEMBER

*T*he rest of the week dragged on and I found myself counting down the days until Max's event. While I wasn't looking forward to reliving the worst night of my life, I knew this time would be different. I had Killian. Solstice. Lily and all of my friends who would rather take a beating than let anything bad happen to me.

Plus, I had faced literal dragons and survived. Dealing with Max was good for me—an exercise to face my old fears.

We fell into a strange sort of routine, one spent joking in the evenings, eating lots of pizza, followed by classes as if nothing had ever changed.

Except everything had changed, and maybe it was for the best. I liked this new life, one with laughter and friends.

Before I knew it, Friday caught up to us and Max's party stared me straight in the face.

My heart thundered in my chest as we walked up the polished hill, the mansion a place I'd seen like it was a distant postcard, but I'd never been there myself.

Until today.

"Okay, maybe I'm not ready for this," I admitted.

Killian kissed the crown of my head. "I've got your back."

I squeezed his hand in return.

"Zelda is here, just so you all know," Lily said from beside me. "Evie told me she will be attending the party."

"Great. Just what we need. More dragons." Killian rolled his eyes and shook his head, gripping me tighter.

"She will probably be pretty focused on Max," Lily reassured us. "We're all working together at this point, so she shouldn't cause too many problems."

I huffed a laugh. "So you're just going to ignore the fact she tried to kill you?"

Her eyes slit before returning to normal. "Most definitely not, but I'll deal with her later."

Noted. Don't get on Lily's bad side.

Techno music rolled down the hill as we immersed ourselves into the thrum of dancing life. It felt like the entire school had been invited, but I didn't recognize all of the faces. The Resorties tended to attract families who vacationed on the lake for the summer, so there was no telling who was in attendance tonight.

Then I noticed the shadows around the perimeter. Guards suited up for Resort Security kept a watchful eye on the event, surprisingly seeming to be here to help, not to report the underage drinking.

"I'm not sure how we missed them," Killian remarked, noticing the heavy security the same time I had.

"It is strange," I agreed. A group of Dragonriders and our wyverns had missed the guards, which rang my supernatural alarm bells and enforced the theory that Max and his family might not be entirely human.

Music blared as someone shoved a drink in my face, interrupting my musings. Killian swatted it away and threatened the partier's life.

"It's not worth it," I told him. "We have a mission. Stay focused."

Killian growled, but nodded before we worked our way up the steps and into the house.

Max's parents clearly weren't here. They were most likely off on business, as usual, buying up more resorts or doing something otherwise nefarious. Silver Lake Resort was only one of the many resorts they owned and managed. Human nor not, they had to keep up their wealth somehow.

We walked through the foyer; the loud music almost deafening. I scanned the room, clutching Killian's hand so I didn't lose him in the crowd of drunken people. I spotted Evie in all her gorgeously glamoured glory, surrounded by her *Hovakim* and several of the jocks as well. She smirked at them all, a glint of mischief in her eyes.

I leaned up to Killian's ear, cupping my hand around my mouth so he could hear me. "Let's save those poor humans from falling completely in love with Evie."

He followed my gaze and then grinned. "They don't know what they're getting themselves into, but we have work to do. They'll figure it out."

As we made our way into the extravagant living room littered with expensive sculptures, a female stepped into our path. I recognized Zelda immediately.

My heart stuttered, and then picked up pace as I thought of the last time I had seen this particular pure-blood. She smiled at me, though, her grin more feral than friendly.

I noticed, then, that she was flanked by Julie Emmerson and the rest of the cheerleaders.

Of course they would be friends.

"What's taking so long? Don't you want to save Mommy?" Zelda leaned in close, her face twisted into a sadistic smirk.

Fury filled me and I couldn't help balling my hands into fists, mistakenly squeezing the life out of Killian's fingers.

"We're working on it," I bit out, gritting my teeth at the effort it took not to lose it.

Her smirk widened. "Well, don't take too much longer, or your mother...." She trailed off at the end and drew her clawed finger over her neck, making sure

I understood the stakes. "Two days, *Vivi.*" She drew out my name with cruel intention.

Zelda threw her head back in laughter. The cheerleaders likely hadn't been able to hear her, either through the music or through the dragon glamour, but they still all followed suit even though there was no way for them to know what they were laughing at. It was a blatant display of power, a show of how charming dragons could be. She could turn the entire school against me if she wanted.

Point made, Zelda winked at me, and then turned on her heel and walked away with Julie and the cheerleaders trailing behind her.

I stared after them for a moment before Killian gently tugged my hand, making me realize I was still squeezing the life out of him. I eased my grip and he bumped my shoulder with his.

"We *are* going to free her, Vivi. Don't worry," he said, leaning down so I could hear him. I met his eyes, and the confidence in his words and expression calmed me enough to get my mind back on our objective for the night.

I gave him a jerky nod, took a deep breath, then refocused. Solstice clung like a heavy weight on my shoulder, offering her own support as she nibbled on my ear. I didn't care if it looked odd if i had a finch on my shoulder, I needed her strength right now.

I nodded once jerkily, took a deep breath and then got down to business.

"We need to find Max," I decided as I took the lead.

We walked through several rooms before I finally spotted him in front of a beer pong table filled with red cups. I studied the scene for a moment and then turned to Killian.

"Do you think you can distract him for long enough for me to snoop around for some kind of information on why the dragons want him?" I asked.

"Distract him how?" he asked.

I glanced at the jock, knowing that only two things would occupy him. Boobs, or a fight.

I couldn't stick around, and I wasn't about to subject Lily to such torment, so a fight it was.

"Rile him up or something," I said, then pointed a finger. "But don't go too crazy, okay? This is just a diversion."

Killian's lips twisted into a wicked grin. "You got it, *babe.*"

I rolled my eyes, about to tell him not to call me that before he released my hand and stormed his way to Max, definitely thrilled to have been given permission to indulge in his need for violence against the male.

He reached him and grabbed his shoulder, jerking Max around to face him. Killian started gesturing wildly, and then jabbed Max in his chest with his finger. Max's expression was the picture of confusion at first, and then he got angry. The change was so quick, it was almost as if a switch had been flipped. Max took a swing at Killian, and Killian ducked underneath it before slamming his fist into Max's face. I slapped my hand to my forehead and shook my head at my mate's 'distraction.'

I guess I should have seen that one coming...

Like most drunken fights at a party, the violence spread. Soon there was a full-on brawl, with people forming a circle around the fighting and chanting. I backed out of the room and made my way up the stairs, looking around to be sure that no one was paying attention to me. Though, by that time, most people were too preoccupied either participating in, or watching, the brawl.

I walked through the hallway, peeking into each door I passed. After walking for a while, I finally found what seemed to be a master bedroom.

Hmm, maybe this belongs to his parents?

I walked in slowly, closing the door behind me and locking it to make sure no one walked in on my snooping.

I made my way to their closet first, shuffling through clothes and boxes, looking for anything suspicious. I worked through the rest of the room as fast as I could, conscious that I probably didn't have much time. Fights were good distractions, but they didn't generally last very long. At least, I imagined that would be the case with Killian at the helm.

Frustration filled me as I closed the bedside drawer and ran my fingers through my hair. Nothing.

A chirp from behind me got my attention and I

turned to where Solstice was fluttering in her golden finch form. She hovered near the base of the bookshelf, chirping incessantly.

"Did you find something?" I asked, rushing over to her and kneeling beside the bookshelf. She bounced over the floor and I followed the trail with my fingers, finding a groove in the wood.

The bookshelf opens!

"Solstice, you wonderful little wyvern genius!" I exclaimed, beginning to pull books from the shelves. She chirped at me happily, swirling around my head. I felt a *click* as I pulled a red book back and it stuck in an angled position.

The bookshelf groaned and then began to swing toward me, the bottom scraping against the floor in the same place as the groove. When I glimpsed the secret room, my jaw went slack.

An obscene number of weapons glittered on the wall. Guns, knives, swords, bows—and... was that a grenade launcher?

"What the heck?" I murmured as I stepped into the weapons closet.

After my shock at the weapons faded, I noticed the safe built low into the center wall. Excitement rushed through me as I realized we might have found what we were looking for.

I knelt in front of it and stared at the lock for a moment. My shoulders slumped in disappointment as I remembered I was not, in fact, a master safe cracker.

With as much money as the Greens had, this safe was guaranteed to be high quality.

Solstice chirped from my shoulder and flew over to the lock. A gold light burst into life at her beak, and then the molten energy slipped into the safe. A moment passed in silence, and then the safe swung open.

"Go Solstice!" I said, patting her before checking out the contents.

While I expected more weapons, or maybe jewels, I raised my brow at a simple filing cabinet. I thumbed the tabs until I came across one that took my breath away.

Reid, my last name.

I grabbed the folder and slowly opened it, not quite sure what I would find. The first document in the folder was dated over a decade ago. Anger rose like a tidal wave as I read the page. My dad's death had been no accident, and Silver Lake Resort had covered it up. Specifically, *Max's parents* had covered it up.

"Bastards," I growled.

I stared at the page stunned, re-reading the words. Then I saw the letterhead.

Knights of the Silver Order.

Max's dad was a Knight of the Silver Order, and he had covered up my dad's death.

The next document told me why.

Me.

As an undercover Knight, Mr. Green had felt my connection to dragonian magic and proceeded to make a deal with the water dragons to drown me before I could grow into it. My dad had died saving me from his treachery, so of course he had to cover it up.

The document detailed his original deal with the water dragons and also his complicity in the actual ordeal. As it appeared, he was the one who had restrained the Lady of the Lake so that she couldn't help—at least, not that night.

Document after document cemented the fact that Max's parents were unhinged. They were Traditional-ists who, after the ordeal with James and Lily and the destruction of her high school by dragonfire, thought Ivar had become too soft. They were planning a coup, ironically with the help of the dragon magic they so despised, something Ivar himself was unwilling to do.

When the initial attempt had failed, they began work to frame my mother for tax fraud, hoping to work the system against her to put me into the foster system. Then, if something happened to me, it would have been covered up as a run-away, another missing child cold case for the books.

A devious plan, all because of what I was. A girl with a dragon for a soul.

Ironically for them, killing my father was what had awakened me. I had created Solstice's finch form, called her soul to me to seek justice.

Justice I still intended to get.

As I was putting the folders back, I saw a black file I had missed. When I opened it, the hairs on the back of my neck raised.

It contained photographs of me and my mother. In our home, at school, at work. Anywhere we had been in the last decade, there was a photo for it. They especially liked to photograph me with Solstice in her finch form. On one of the pictures with her golden form, there was a giant question mark.

They'd known.

And they'd tried to end it.

Cold fury ran through my veins, and I worked at calming myself before realizing that Killian's distraction wouldn't last forever. I put everything back how I had found it and shut the shelf behind me. I put all the books back in their places, to the best of my memory at least.

As I made my way back down the stairs, I passed framed photos that I hadn't noticed before. They stuck out to me this time though, and my fury grew every time I saw a photo of the Greens looking like a happy family when they had torn mine apart.

I walked into the room where the fight had been to see that it had been calmed, with Max on one side of the room held back by his jock buddies and Killian on the other held back by Evie's *Hovakim*.

Police sirens sounded from down the road making the whole room full of underaged drinkers scramble. I pushed myself through the chaos towards Killian and grabbed his arm. I ran for the kitchen, dragging him out the back door and around the property to the main road, for once glad that I grew up here and knew my way around.

"I'm not done with him," Killian growled.

"You're done," I said, my words an order.

We couldn't afford to get locked up in jail or we wouldn't get anywhere before it was too late and my mother got hurt. Or worse.

CHAPTER 8

TRADITIONALISTS
&
LOYALISTS

*K*illian stopped in place as we turned left onto the main road. "Where are we going? Your house is that way, isn't it?"

We'd lost everyone else in the chaos, but my mind was spinning too hard to care.

"We aren't going to my house," I sputtered, my brain screaming at me to hurry before Max's parents found out I was back in town. They weren't human, and I didn't know if Max was in on their plans or just a pawn. Either way, I had to get to the bottom of this —fast.

"We're going to Silver Lake Resort. Max's dad is behind this. All of it," I bit out between clenched teeth. "If we are going to find any more information about what's really going on here, that's where it will be."

Killian questioned me about what I'd found, and I told him everything I'd seen.

"We should go to James with this," he said, his words a low, murderous whisper. If he'd been angry before, now he was pissed.

"No." I wasn't going to let anyone else deal with my problems. Max's parents had taken my father away from me. They were the reason I'd suffered and now I would deal with them myself. I couldn't risk Knight politics getting in the way of justice—as ironic as that sounded.

Plus, the Wild Dragons wanted Max. I still didn't know why, but somehow, this was all connected.

It had to be.

Killian stopped in his tracks, his eyes growing wide as a new revelation seemed to hit him. "That's what she meant."

I paused. "Who?"

He glanced at me, his eyes nearly glowing in the diminishing light. "The Lady of the Lake. She told me that her hands were tied, that the war between Knights had gone too far. I thought she meant the war between the Knights and the dragons, but she was referring to an internal battle—one between the Loyalists and the Traditionalists."

"The Greens are Traditionalists," I said, frowning. "According to their beliefs, anything remotely related to dragonian magic needs to die, by any means necessary, and I was harboring a Dragon Queen's spirit right in their backyard."

They wanted me dead because of who I was, because my soul had bonded with Solstice.

She keened in my ear. I reached up and scratched her head. "It's okay, girl. It wasn't your fault."

Killian scoffed. "And they were willing to work with the Wild Queen to take you out, a harmless child?"

I ground my fingers into fists. "Not so harmless anymore." They had pictures of my mother, too. I suspected they knew what she was, which meant they knew what I could become.

To them, mixing dragonian magic with goddess blood—the same blood that created Excalibur—would be blasphemy.

"Come on," I said, my decision made. "Let's find what other secrets they're hiding."

Because Max was still a question mark, one I intended to figure out.

We walked the rest of the way to the resort in silence. When we reached the grounds, I cut left and led us through the forest, this time keeping an eye out for security, although it felt like we were very much alone.

"Do you know where you're going?" Killian asked.

I knew this forest like the back of my hand. "I grew up here," I explained. "Solstice and I would play through these woods, finding secret paths." Including a backdoor into the resort to visit my mom before she'd started working from home.

That's where I led Killian, bypassing all the security at the front gate. Solstice had been the one to find the loophole, now that I recalled my childhood adventures. I'd never realized just what she'd been up against, that even back then, she was trying to help me survive.

I found the same old window with the broken latch in the back, jiggled it free, but frowned when I slid open the glass. It wasn't as much space as I remembered it being.

"I'm too big to fit into this opening anymore," I realized, glancing at Killian. "And there's no way you're getting in."

Killian chuckled. "No, I imagine not."

Solstice chirped and pecked at the lock on the door, blasting it with golden energy. I raised an eyebrow at her, then tested the knob. The door gave way without protest. "Good girl," I whispered.

We made our way up the stairwell until we reached the executive floor. Security was nowhere to be seen, likely still prowling the mansion grounds instead. If they knew our target was Max, then they'd stick with him, luckily for us.

Taking advantage of the opportunity, I headed straight for Mr. Green's office. I remembered it from my visits as a child, and found the same gaudy nameplate glittering above a set of double doors. Solstice worked her magic again on the lock and we hurried inside.

We spread out, the four of us including Topaz whose glamour had worn off, to search for what the Greens might be hiding. I walked the perimeter of the room looking for grooves in the floor. This time, I found them in front of the fireplace.

"Got you," I announced.

I pushed bricks and moved the things on the mantle trying to find the trigger. Topaz jumped from Killian's shoulder and rammed the poker standing beside the fireplace. The stick went back at a forty-five-degree angle and the fireplace grated as it swung across the floor.

"Oh, you genius little dragon!" I cooed at him, scooping him into my arms to give him scratches. He basked in my affection, especially when Solstice swirled around my head chirping her jealousy.

The room spanned out, reminiscent of the one I'd found in the mansion's bedroom, only larger and boasting a small desk at the back.

Killian whistled at the arsenal hanging on the walls.

"They have just as many in their home," I said dryly.

Killian and I got to work, starting with opening filing cabinets. We found more photos of my mother and I, some of Solstice as well in her tree near my window, and her favorite perch by the lake.

"Did they ever go after you, girl?" I asked Solstice, concerned what might have happened when I wasn't watching. The golden finch had only appeared to me randomly, otherwise disappearing for hours at a time before I'd known what I was.

She keened, her sounds suggesting that she'd done her best to stay out of harm's way, but there had most definitely been a present danger.

Killian growled low in his throat at whatever was in the file he was reading, fury rolling across his face like storm clouds. I read over his shoulder and gasped.

It was the file for my murder that involved Max—the one that had almost succeeded.

Except... Max hadn't known about any of it. He'd been used, manipulated by a shard of Excalibur, the sketch of it a dark splotch on the paper.

"The Order most definitely would not have approved of this," Killian bit out, holding up the offending document. "Can we get James involved now? This is sick." Killian pointed at the inscription. "This spell is permanent and it's a powerful weapon against dragons, which would make complete sense as to the reason why the Wild Dragons want Max."

"So, he can kill them....?" I asked, confusion filling me. I couldn't imagine why the dragons would want a weapon designed to be used against them.

"Dragons are a parasitic species. They consume and absorb. The Wild Queen has proven what she's capable of and she wouldn't care about the side effects of absorbing the power that's inside of Max green. If she gets her hands on him, she'll extract his magic and use it against the Knights of the Silver order, and against the Dragonriders."

"What does the power do, exactly?" I asked, my eyes wide.

He frowned, pointing down at the page. "This is corruption merged with a shard of Excalibur. It's a twisted form of magic, one that uses the power of madness and turns it into a weapon. The Wild Queen would be compatible with it, if she's willing to go even madder than she already is—which I imagine isn't a problem."

"Great," I huffed. "So, what do we do? We can't just hand Max over to her."

"No," he agreed. "Not without a means to restrain the madness inside of him."

"And how do we do that?" I asked.

Before Killian could respond, a loud bang sounded from the main office. My heart raced and my stomach dropped as Max came into view, looking positively menacing with a black eye shadowed into his face and blood splattered on the front of his blue t-shirt. Killian shot up, putting himself between Max and I.

Max approached us, his gaze tearing away to stare at the weapons on the wall.

"What the heck?" he whispered, his face slack. Then he took in Topaz and Solstice who hissed at our feet. Topaz had turned entirely visible while Solstice shimmered between finch and wyvern. Max backed up a step, his eyes growing wide.

"You didn't know about this place?" Killian asked, skeptical.

"You're..." He shot out a finger, snapping his gaze back up to us in shock. "You're Dragonriders. Real Dragonriders, aren't you? My father told me about you... He said you were dangerous."

"He's the dangerous one," I shot back. I pushed around Killian and shoved the file at Max. "He's been using you. Read for yourself."

He took the file hesitantly, looking back at us before he opened it and began reading.

His face slackened, and then fury grew in his expression. He was shaking by the time he finished flipping through the pages, ending on the sketch of the shard.

"I've seen this," he murmured, his gaze dark. "I thought it was just a bad dream."

"It's real," Killian said, the murder in his gaze promising me that Max wasn't quite off the hook just yet. "You have darkness in you, Max. Darkness that has hurt someone I care about." He drew one of the blades off the wall, wielding it at him. "I can't let you walk out of here."

Max might be a bully, and a cocky jock, but one thing he was not was a trained warrior. He stared at Killian, eyes wide, stunned and speechless.

I rested a hand on Killian's wrist, lowering his weapon. "There must be another way," I said. "Let's take him back to the others. Maybe James will know what to do." Plus Max was my only chance at getting my mother back. I couldn't let Killian kill him, even if I wanted him to.

Killian sniffed, considering it before relaxing. "Fine." His eyes narrowed at the shadows that snaked around Max's wrists. Corruption seeped from him in visible form, swirling around him in lazy waves. "You have control over it, don't you?"

Max glanced down and flexed his fingers. "I thought I was going crazy," he admitted. "I kept seeing glimpses of the ocean... of doing something I..." He glanced back up to me. "That wasn't me, Vivi. I swear it. I—"

I shot up a hand. I didn't want his apologies, and I certainly didn't want to relive those particular memories. "You want to make this right? You come with us. You cooperate."

He met my gaze, his face twisting with rage before he turned and punched the back of the brick fireplace, leaving a dent in the brick with several pieces flying in all directions.

So, definitely not human.

Killian pushed me behind him again, spreading his arms in an effort to make sure I was safe. "The corruption is fighting his free will to work with us," Killian said as the temperature in the room plummeted. He drew his weapon again, resuming a warrior's stance.

Max roared and Solstice burst into wyvern form, shedding the last of Lily's glamour.

Solstice jumped from the floor and flapped onto Max's head. The sudden weight of my dragon made him freeze, and then her golden magic shone down on him like a sunrise.

His skin sparkled and shone with her light, and he made a strangled sound as his arms began to glow. A black shard smoldered inside his chest, sizzling against the light.

Solstice screeched and stomped her foot on his head, clearly telling him to stay still. Surprisingly, he got the message and obeyed.

Solstice closed her eyes and spread her wings. The light increased in brilliance. Several moments passed and then the gold began to travel along his body, all of it appearing to gather over his heart before it burst out in a blinding flash.

Max stumbled back from the force of whatever my wyvern had just done and Solstice fluttered off of his head. He turned to face us, and all the crazed anger gone from his expression. All that remained was sadness, grief, and regret.

"Oh my God, Vivi. Oh my God. What have I done?" He stared into my eyes, his face breaking. "I remember it all so clearly now. The party, swimming, and... everything else."

I winced as the memories rushed through me. Even knowing that he hadn't actually been in control of himself at the time didn't help with the trauma I still needed to deal with.

"She cleansed his corruption, at least temporarily," Killian explained, giving Solstice a nod. "It'll help him cooperate for now."

Max shook his head as if trying to clear it. "I'm so sorry. I can't understand why my father would do this to me. Why does he want you dead so badly? It doesn't make any sense. The Knights of the Silver Order are a force for good. We protect the innocent." His jaw flexed. "Instead... he tried to make me snuff it out."

Killian and I locked eyes for a moment, mutually gauging how much we should tell him. Killian nodded at me, and then the male. I sighed and turned back to

Max, beginning my story after I emerged from the water in another realm and ending with the information that we had just learned ourselves.

He had a determined look in his eyes when I finished. He nodded at me without hesitation. "I will go."

"Go... where?" I asked, not sure if I'd heard him correctly.

"To Avalon." The surprise must have shown on my face because he doubled down. "I *will* go. I have to. Helping you get your mother back is the least I can do after everything my family and I have put you through."

"Thank you," I said, not knowing what else to say.

"Right now, though, we need to go," he said, ushering us out of the room. "You triggered a silent alarm when you broke into my dad's office. That's how I knew you were here. Local security, my parents, and I all have apps that notify our phones if any alarm is triggered. So, security won't be far behind. They were at the mansion on my father's orders to stick with me, but I lost them when I was in the woods looking for you. They'll realize where I've gone and this place will be swarming with them soon." He backed out of the room. Killian took my hand, drawing me out, but I pulled back.

"One thing," I said, grabbing a file.

Killian gave me a raised brow, but I didn't have time to explain. First, we had to get out of here without getting caught.

We rushed through the hallways and down the stairwell. We ran straight into security, but Solstice released another blinding wave of light, stunning them and giving us a chance to escape.

Even as we ran through the forest with the threat on our tail, relief ran through me.

Max had agreed to go.

My mom would be safe.

But first... we had to make sure that Max wasn't a weapon that the Wild Queen could use. I had a feeling that Evie might just be able to help with that.

CHAPTER 9

THREE LITTLE
WORDS

*W*e made it back to my house after finally losing security. As we walked through the door, I smiled at our weary greeting party. James and Lily sat together on the love seat, and Evie and her four guys were all sprawled on the couch. Their conversation stopped as we walked into the house, Max in tow.

"Well, look what the riders dragged in," Lily said dryly, eyeing Max with a raised brow. "I thought he was the enemy."

"Maybe not," I explained. "Max wasn't in his right mind when everything went down at the beach. He was... corrupted."

The three of us sat down and I explained what we had found out. By the end of it, James was on his feet pacing and Evie was beside Max, peering into his eyes as if fascinated.

Max stared back at her, equally enamored, but Evie seemed to always have that effect on males.

"Green! I never liked that man," James ranted as he paced. "Of course he would be the one behind all of this. Why didn't anybody tell me Max's last name? I could have told you who he was."

Killian gave James a flat stare. "We did, actually. You were right there when we read the ransom note. Maybe you should pay better attention."

James growled. "I was a little preoccupied unscrambling my brain from Finn's idea of portal travel. Excuse me for not catching that right away."

"So, you've agreed to be traded for Vivi's mother?" Evie asked Max, her fingers slipping up his wrist as she completely ignored the testosterone competition between James and Killian. Max relaxed under her touch.

Max relaxed under her touch. "It's the least I can do to atone for everything she's been through because of me and my family."

She looked at him for a long moment, seeming to be thinking hard on something, "Well, dragons are not typically gentle creatures, especially where you're going. If you go in alone with no one to protect you, you probably won't survive long." She straightened, giving him a toothy grin with fang. "I can provide you protection, if that's something you might be interested in."

Max met her gaze and then nodded again.

"You'll become a part of my *Hovakim*," she decided, earning a raised brow from me. How many worshipers did the dragon need? "You will be protected as one of my own, and you will never be alone again." She smiled warmly at him and gestured to the rest of her partners.

Lily rolled her eyes while James snickered. "Heavy deal, man, but one I would take if I were you."

Killian hummed in agreement. "It would bind Max to her and keep the Wild Queen from absorbing the shard's power." He tilted his head. "Well, she could kill him and extract it that way, perhaps."

"It would destroy the shard," James remarked. He snapped his fingers and gestured for Max to stand up. Max obeyed and James flicked his shirt collar aside, pointing at a dark vein that streaked down his torso. "This is a spell that binds the shard to the heart. If the heart stops beating, the shard will shatter and the power within it will cease to exist." He drew his hand away. "How did you come to possess a corrupted Shard? Ivar would not have authorized this sort of magic within the Order."

Max rubbed the back of his head. "I didn't even know about this. My father did it to me... maybe when I was asleep?"

Evie hummed as she stepped around him, analyzing him as she twisted with liquid, reptilian movements. "There's dragonian magic on you. Your memories have been altered. Your father did this with a dragon's help."

Not good.

"Would it have been the Wild Dragons?" I asked.

Lily bit her lip before nodding. "Yes, it must be. The Greens have been working with her."

James shook his head. "That's the thing with Traditionalists. They believe the ends justify the means. They would be willing to work with the Wild Dragons if it benefited them." He clicked his tongue. "That's how the Traditionalists have been trying to overthrow my brother. Idiots."

The conversation dwindled into the inevitable course of action. Evie would convert Max as one of her *Hovakim*, a process I was told would take the entire night, leaving the rest of us to get some rest before we would splinter off. Evie was still under the guise as one of the Avalon's dragons, and she would return to them with the story that she'd saved Max from certain death by bonding with him. It wasn't a hard story to sell, given how much Killian hated him, regardless of his intentions.

Evie and her *Hovakim*, including Max, retired to the master bedroom they had been using all week. Lily also convinced James, who was still fuming, that they should sleep as well on the couch.

Just like that, it was just Killian and I, which wasn't new but it felt different this time. We had found what we needed. Max was here and ready to go to the dragons voluntarily. The stress we had been facing for months was finally coming to an end, which left room for other neglected emotions.

Such as our feelings for each other.

Killian stood from the couch and held his hand out for me. "We should head to bed too. We all have a busy day tomorrow."

I let him pull me up and we made our way to my room. We got ready to sleep in silence, taking turns in my bathroom, before we settled into the bed with our wyverns curled up between us.

I stared at Killian, studying his face. He was so beautiful to me. Of course, he was literally half angel, so it made sense. The cut on his lip drew my attention and I raise my hand to brush it lightly with my fingertips.

"Why did you think starting a fight was the best idea?" I asked him, exasperated that he got himself injured.

"He hurt you," he replied simply. He brought his hand up to cup my cheek. "Vivienne Reid, you are the most important person to me. I can't bear the thought of you being hurt, and I would do unspeakable things to anyone who was the cause of it."

My heart fluttered at his declaration. "Let's just hope it doesn't come to that."

His gaze met mine and I couldn't look away. My world closed in around me, leaving nothing else except his soul and mine, two sides of a coin meant to be together forever.

I'd bonded with him, with Solstice and Topaz who curled up between us. We were a family, and he was my mate.

When he pulled me close and pressed his lips to

mine, it felt right. I closed my eyes and fell into the sensation that overwhelmed me every time our skin touched—a blazing heat that snapped through me like fire and ice. Electricity blazed along my fingertips and Solstice stirred in her sleep, keening with approval of the unification of my bond with Killian. Our connection fueled our bonds and our dragons, strengthening us all with life.

My goddess blood should have been a hindrance, a drain, but something inside of me was changing.

Maybe our fated match wasn't doomed after all.

Fireworks went off behind my eyelids as he deepened the kiss. Tingles ran along every inch of my body as his emotions invaded mine, our bond allowing me to feel everything he felt. What struck me to my soul was how strongly he meant every word he'd just said. I opened myself up to him in turn, letting him feel just how grateful I was that he was here with me. That he'd reached a point where he could forgive me for trapping him in this relationship—and for trusting me long enough to bring Solstice back to life.

He made me feel like I could do anything with him and our wyverns at my side.

He pulled away before we both drowned in sensation, leaving me breathless as he pulled me closer. He tucked his arm under my head and cradled Solstice and Topaz around our middle.

I smiled as I watched him, never wanting this night to end.

He didn't have to speak the words. I felt them.

I love you, Viv, now and forever.

You are mine.

CHAPTER 10

JUSTICE

*T*he file I had taken from Mr. Green's office was one of the original police reports from my dad's death that had marked it as a potential homicide. I couldn't prove that Max Green had covered it up, but I had a report that likely had his father's fingerprints all over it.

It was extremely satisfying to go into the police station and give them all the evidence they needed to put Mr. Green away for a long time. Though, I felt bad for Max when he watched his dad brought in and shackled in handcuffs.

I'd never met him, I realized as I watched the blonde-haired male stiffen as the police rattled off his rights. The billionaire towered over the civil servant, and his arrogance reeked off of him, assuring anyone watching that he would hire the best lawyer money could buy.

His blue gaze found mine, his eyes narrowing in recognition.

You, as if he seemed to say. *This is not over.*

I had a bad feeling that the police wouldn't hold a Knight of the Silver Order for long—especially a rich one—but James had gone to talk to his brother, so it would get sorted out one way or another. A coup would not be tolerated, especially with the evidence of a corrupted Shard of Excalibur being used in such a manner.

We gathered in my backyard after all the legal stuff had been sorted, both human and supernatural. As much as I wanted to make sure Mr. Green got what he deserved, I had a mother to save.

I took my necklace out from under my shirt with mixed feelings.

Solstice keened. "Yes, yes," I said, rolling my eyes. "I'll make a better portal this time."

Evie tucked her arm around the crook of Max's elbow and he smirked at her, a new familiarity between them growing. The other males crowded around them, patting Max on the back and welcoming him into their strange but tightly knit group.

"Are you sure that the Wild Queen won't be able to use the corrupted shard that's inside of Max?" I asked under my breath.

James gave me a grave nod. "He's one of Evie's, now. We'll hold up our end of the bargain without giving the Wild Queen anything useful in return." He glanced at the gorgeous dragon. "Evie might pay a price for putting up that obstacle, but I prefer to let the dragons play their own political games. It'll buy us time, at least."

"Time for what?" I asked, not having thought further than getting my mother back.

He grinned. "To get you fledged as a true Dragonrider. You're going to save us all, Vivi, and I'm going to do my part to give you a fighting chance."

Lily smiled, snuggling into his side. "Agreed."

That thought warmed me and I closed my eyes, letting out a long breath I'd been holding.

Energy funneled through my fingertips into the metal brushing against my skin. The portal opened on my command, swirling like a whirlpool, and one by one we all jumped through.

Without the stress of Zelda trying to murder me and an army on my tail, the tunnel walled in around me, stable and serene. We walked through, a proud thrill rolling through me that I'd done this. Solstice wrapped around my neck, her tail curling along my collarbone like an ornament as she fed me golden power.

And I had a feeling this was only just the beginning.

I took in the Academy for the first time in over a week and smiled to myself. It felt like home now. A place where I finally belonged.

Glancing around, I found the welcoming party at the beach sorely lacking. A hot breeze curled underneath my hairline and the roar of dragons rumbled in the distance, an oddly comforting sound to me these days. "Where are they?" I asked Evie, figuring she would be the most likely to know how the hostage exchange would be handled.

Evie held up a necklace with a black stone, one similar to mine. "We call them."

I raised my brow at the trinket. "You have enough magic to summon a portal?"

She shook her head. "Not a portal—a Tunnel."

Lily winced. "Those are unstable. Tunnels are meant to be natural breaches in time and space. Forcing one without the wall barriers like Vivi's goddess magic can do is dangerous."

Evie smirked. "I like dangerous."

She clutched the stone with her fist, her skin crawling with dark magic as her features changed. Scales erupted across her skin and a phantom shadow of wings spread from her back.

It was oddly beautiful... and terrifying.

The Tunnel burst to life, swirling with black mist as the air itself groaned. A few short moments later Zelda stepped through, her pace matched by two larger dragons dripping with corruption.

We all moved into fighting positions, not trusting the Wild Dragons to hold their end of the stalemate.

Zelda ignored our aggression and instead her gaze landed on Max. He shrank back as a malicious grin spread across her face.

I narrowed my eyes at her. "Where's my mother?"

She tore her gaze away from her prize to regard me, seeming irritated by my presence. "Safe, for now."

Zelda drawled. "Once the human returns with me, we'll make the exchange."

"You'll bring her now," Killian demanded.

I clenched my fists in grim agreement.

Evie stepped forward, her *Hovakim* moving with her as one. Max walked with her, chewing his lip as he took in Zelda's dragonian appearance and long fangs.

"I can guarantee his security," Evie said, straightening with her regal form. She wasn't a queen, but she sure did act like one. "Max is now one of mine."

Zelda raised her eyebrows. "I don't think the Queen will be very pleased with you taking the target as one of your *Hovakim*."

Evie turned a glare on us as if everything we did disgusted her. "They would have killed him had I not gotten to him first, but I managed to make them honor our original deal. Max is coming with us and they won't come after him again if we hand over the siren." She raised her chin at me. "Right, Dragonrider?"

I gave her a jerky nod. "That's right. If you turn over my mother, I won't come after Max again."

Zelda watched our exchange. I wasn't sure if she bought the act, but all she seemed to care about was getting Max to Avalon. "Very well." She turned to bark an order at one of the dragons. "Bring the girl's mother."

The dragon slunk back through the portal and when he emerged again, he was dragging my mother with his teeth. I looked her over, trying to discern whether she had been injured or not in the week she'd been held captive. Aside from a few scrapes and bruises, she seemed relatively unharmed.

The dragon dumped her on the ground and I flinched, but she smiled at me, reassurance in her gaze.

"Don't get too comfortable," Zelda said, grinning in what was more of a snarl than a smile. "Our Queen won't stand for Dragonrider Academy's blasphemy for much longer. You *will* bow, one way or another."

I glared back, defiance in my gaze.

I would bow to no one.

The dragons left, the Tunnel hissing until it disappeared into nothing.

Running to my mother, I crashed to my knees and wrapped my arms around her neck. "Are you okay?" I asked, my voice suddenly hoarse and scratchy.

She stroked my hair as Solstice keened between us. "I'm fine, dear." She pulled me away, tears in her eyes and she cupped my face. "You did well. I was afraid you would turn over the boy without understanding what he was." She glanced at Killian, James and Lily. "I should have known that your friends wouldn't let us down. Thank you, all of you, for everything."

Dragon roars pierced the skies, a welcoming party on the way from the Academy. I spotted Jasmine riding her emerald dragon Jade, and Vern behind her with his dragon that glittered like midnight. Wings spanned the horizon, a collective roar trumpeting our return and I smiled.

Killian rested a hand on my shoulder, the energy

between us burning hot as our wyverns joined in the call of their brethren.

Finally, my loved ones were safe and I could figure out how I was going to live in this new life of mine.

Until the Wild Dragons decided to strike again... at least.

EPILOGUE

Two years later...

The sun warmed my face as I closed my eyes and breathed in the mountain air. Peace filled me as I laid on the mountaintop next to my mate. We had decided to play hooky today and had escaped to Vyorin, the beautiful realm that Lily was from. I'd never been brave enough—or powerful enough—to make the trip.

I'd grown in my powers, that much was clear. The strain on Solstice's growth had gotten easier and even though I was a Conduit, Killian and Topaz seemed to thrive the closer I got to them.

I wasn't sure what had changed, or how I no longer drained them of their energy—rather I seemed to sustain them. Perhaps it was kismet, or maybe something else had happened within me that I didn't yet understand.

Whatever the cause, I had a feeling there was yet another secret about myself that I would soon figure out.

I opened my eyes in time to see a massive dragon swoop through the red sky over us. I stiffened as fresh fear swept through me.

Killian nudged my shoulder and nodded toward the dragon I hadn't seen before. "That's Damian. He was Lily's high school friend, and probably one of the best people I've ever met." He tucked me against his chest. "He's one of the reasons that James decided to stay at the Academy. He met him when his dragon side had been suppressed, got to know him, and realized that Lily wasn't the exception. Other dragons can be like her if properly guided. She's a pureblood with a kind heart."

Our peaceful conversation was interrupted as a roar came from the skies. Topaz and Solstice soared overhead, play fighting with each other in mid-air as the Vyorin dragon ventured off into the horizon. Ignoring his departure, they swooped and dived, nipping at each other's tails as they raced around the sky.

I loved seeing them like this. Happy and free.

They were both oversized now, though they seemed to forget that at times. They dived toward us, flashing their wings out to catch themselves at the last moment causing a blast of wind to hit us.

We laughed and threw sand after them as they looped back up, still play-fighting.

"What are we going do with them?" I laughed as I sat up.

He smiled back at me, his eyes shining with happiness. "We are going to ride them instead of being the targets of their air bombs. Then, they'll have to listen to us."

"Right," I said, skeptical that Solstice or Topaz could be tamed.

Killian squeezed my hand, that familiar energy zinging through my heart that never ceased to take my breath away.

Or perhaps I was just excited about the ceremony next week. The wyverns were finally big enough for us to saddle, and we would get the chance to ride them for the first time at the Academy's celebration for Juniors.

I couldn't wait to fly through the sky with my wyvern under me and my mate at my side.

It was time to become a fully-fledged Dragonrider.

It was time to fly.

DRAGONRIDER ACADEMY

EPISODE SIX

USA TODAY BESTSELLING AUTHOR

A.J. FLOWERS

CHAPTER 1

HARD LESSONS

"*T*wo years of training and you still aren't paying attention," Jasmine chided.

My breath whooshed out of me as I hit the ground with a painful thud. Jasmine blocked the sun as she leaned over me, sighing because I should have blocked that blow.

We both knew it.

"The sun blinded me," I ground out, taking her hand as I struggled to my feet. I brushed Dragonrider Academy's sandy dirt off of my training pants. She glowered because I was just making up excuses. Sighing, I added, "I'm just… distracted."

She relaxed. "Understandably," Jasmine said, being uncharacteristically nice to me. She motioned down the field. "Those dark circles under your eyes could rival charcoal. Why don't you get some rest and we'll try again tomorrow? I'm still on campus for another few days."

"Sure," I murmured.

My heart twisted every time Jasmine or anyone else gave me that sympathetic expression. It was the same one I'd gotten when my father had died and it was all I saw now that my mother was sick.

I hated it.

"Put ice on that leg, okay?" Jasmine asked as she turned toward the sunbathing wyverns at the end of the training field. A splash of green and golden scales shimmered in the sunlight as Jade and Solstice yawned.

At least those two got along.

Murmuring my assurance that I'd get some ice, I followed her toward my dragon, grimacing as a sore ache blossomed across my thigh where Jasmine had punished my distraction.

She might be sympathetic, but she trained me hard. Perhaps even harder than she ever had before, and that meant that she was scared.

If Jasmine was scared, then I knew we were in for it.

She didn't even have to be here. She'd graduated from the Academy a year and a half ago and went on regular missions. She loved patrol duty, but she made special visits to help with my training. We'd come a long way from our initial sparring session. When it came to combat, Jasmine knew how to help me learn how to use my small body against larger opponents.

I couldn't keep relying on my Goddess blood, especially now that it felt like it was diminishing along with my mother.

Solstice leaned her long neck down as I approached her, peering at my uneven gait with concern.

I tried to give her a reassuring smile. "I just wasn't paying enough attention and earned myself a few bruises. I'll be fine after a long hot shower and some food."

She snorted at me, steam rising from her nostrils. She didn't believe me, but she wasn't going to argue.

With that, I turned and began down the path to the dorms. Solstice walked with me as far as she could, Topaz not far behind, the ground rumbling under their heavy steps, but Solstice couldn't go with me. She and Topaz had moved to the wyvern quarters last year when they'd gotten too big to comfortably fit in the dorm room.

I gave Solstice a kiss on her flank as we parted ways, she snuffed steam into my hair for reassurance, and then I continued into the dorms while she ventured to the wyvern stalls for the night.

I glanced back at her as she walked, that confident gait with Topaz, her bonded wyvern. Because of my relationship with Killian, we were a family.

My mother was a part of that family, too, and my heart ached thinking I might lose her.

The pale image of her frail body haunted me whenever I closed my eyes. When confronted, she would wave away my concern with a smile, insisting that I had more important matters to concern myself with.

Perhaps she would finally see her own lunacy and

would agree to go to a hospital back on earth. If modern medicine couldn't fix it, then surely there had to be some magical cure here. If only she would acknowledge she needed help.

I made the sharp turn to the dorms and scampered up the steps. Once in my room, the comforting musk of Killian's aftershave made me relax, but he wasn't home. Unlike me, he probably was finishing up his lessons for the day without having a total meltdown.

My body ached, but so did my heart. I couldn't mend my emotional bruises, but I could at least take care of the physical ones, so I undressed and jumped into the shower.

The warm water beat against my aching muscles and I closed my eyes, leaning my head back as I let the water run over me. The white noise served a dual purpose.

On the one hand, I felt more grounded and in control.

On the other, the sensation of water on my skin and the crash of it all around me brought me back to when I'd been underwater, both when my father had drowned trying to save me, and when I had made the journey to Dragonrider Academy for the first time.

While unpleasant, I sought out those memories. I wanted to know who was responsible for all of this.

Revenge wouldn't give me peace, but it was a good start.

I relaxed, swimming in old memories until the water ran cold, the magic used to heat it through the dorms straining against its limits. Even though we'd been free of major Wild Dragon attacks, the Academy still hadn't recovered from the magic shortage and even things like warm water were on limited quotas.

Pouting, I turned the knob and finished my normal afternoon routine, drying my hair with a towel and pinning it up so that it was out of the way. It would come down curly, but Killian liked it that way and I secretly did too.

Sitting on the bed, I watched the dragons practicing their rounds outside. My somber mood had returned and I needed another distraction.

Glancing at the desk, my mountain of homework didn't promise the kind of reprieve I was looking for, but I needed to study. Finals were in the next few weeks and if I wanted to take on Avalon with the dean's support, I needed to pass every test she threw my way.

I spotted Jasmine on the streets below and I scampered to the window. Leaning out, I took note that she turned and entered the building that housed the Dean's office. I frowned, hoping she wasn't about to rat me out about my struggles in the sparring subject.

Although I was struggling in all of my studies, so unless I completely aced my exams, I doubted the dean was going to allow me to go anywhere this year.

Thinking of suffering through another year without any resolution, especially if my mother wasn't going to be around to see it, made me feel sick.

The door slammed open, making me jump with a

screech. Killian rushed in, immediately going to me as his hands hovered over my body. He pulled aside bits of fabric, examining me. I batted him away. "Do you mind?" I spat.

He frowned. "Solstice told me that Jasmine was too hard on you during today's training. She said you were limping." He cursed when I staggered. "I told Jasmine you were distracted right now. She needs to give you a break."

A new sort of anger blossomed in my chest. It was nice that our riderbond had evolved so that Killian and Solstice could converse, maybe not exactly in words, but with images and feelings. No telling what Solstice had shown him, and in situations like this, Solstice's perspective could be a bit overprotective.

"Who wouldn't be distracted, Killian? And seriously, I'm fine, okay? Solstice is just being overdramatic. It's just a couple of bruises."

"We just want you to be safe, Viv," he said, tilting his head, his gaze still roaming over me looking for injuries.

This over-the-top concern from Solstice and Killian had only gotten worse the past few months. The way they watched me and worried made it seem like they thought I was going to have a complete breakdown.

And maybe I was, but that was my prerogative.

"Then it's a good thing I have you guys to obsess over me," I said with a smirk. "You could put me in bubble wrap. Would that help?"

Killian backed up to the bed and slumped down with a sheepish smile. "What's bubble wrap?"

Rolling my eyes, I sat down next to him and took his hand. "Next time we head to Earth, I'll get you some. It's very therapeutic and addictive when you pop it."

Killian hummed with interest. "If we ever get back to Earth."

I leaned my head on his shoulder. "We will."

While the Academy had a stable truce with the Wild Dragons, travel between realms had gotten exponentially worse. We couldn't go anywhere without running into a fight and I was starting to feel isolated.

If my mother actually did agree to go to a modern hospital, I would fight all the Wild Dragons in the realms if I had to.

"You've been pushing yourself so hard," Killian said, rubbing my arm. "With everything going on with Marigold, I worry about you."

"We'll get through this," I said, more to convince myself than him.

He hugged me and ran his touch over my birthmark out of habit. The magic that regularly coursed between us was a comfort now, one that warmed my body and fueled my power. Without Killian, I would have withered into nothing.

"What about a break?" he suggested. "It's been months since you've had a day off. You don't want to be burnt out for your first flight." He smirked. Of course I couldn't forget that I would get to ride Solstice for the first time in just a few short days.

"What about the trip to meet up with Max?" I asked, perching my chin on his shoulder. "We're supposed to get an update on what's going on from Avalon." We didn't get updates often, so I was particularly looking forward to hearing from Max again.

Definitely not something I would have thought possible a few years ago. Max had become an ally, one that worked on the inside feeding us valuable information on the Wild Dragons. It helped that he was with Evie who occasionally deigned to feed him some of her higher-level intel for us. So far from what we could tell, the Wild Dragons were getting stronger and they needed to be stopped.

We had a plan, but we couldn't just barge in and face the Wild Dragons head-on. That hadn't worked the last time and had nearly wiped out the Dragonriders altogether. We had to be careful about how we approached this war.

"I can take Lily, or James, or even Jasmine," he offered. The calm determination on his face making it clear that he had already thought of solutions for all of my foreseeable protests.

I sighed, deciding to give in to his request mainly because I was too exhausted to fight him. The mission was a simple day trip away from the Academy anyway. I wouldn't miss anything that they wouldn't tell me as soon as they returned.

While Killian was doing that, I could talk to my

mother again and see about convincing her to get some real help.

"Okay. I will rest this weekend," I said, a half-truth, "but you have to promise to stop being so over-concerned after my weekend of relaxation," I told him, raising my eyebrow as he opened his mouth to protest.

He snapped his mouth shut as he took in my expression and finally nodded at me.

"You have my word," he grinned, clearly happy with his small victory.

He could win this battle. I would win the war.

I leaned into his familiar warmth and he wrapped his arm around my shoulders, holding me tightly to his side. The position put pressure on some of the more sensitive spots on my body, but I made sure I didn't show any sign of pain. I had just gotten him to agree to stop worrying, I wasn't about to give him a reason to start up again.

He leaned his head on mine and pressed a kiss to my still-damp hair. Relaxing into his embrace, I couldn't help but release a sigh of contentment. No matter what was happening, Killian could always make me feel like everything would work out.

"I just want to make sure you understand that you aren't alone," he said, his low voice in my ear. "You seem like you are carrying the weight of the world, but you don't have to carry all of it. The wyverns and I are pretty strong, too. Not to mention all of our friends who adore you." He put his other arm over my front, securing me in a circle of his arms.

I didn't have a response for him, so I just laid my head on his chest and enjoyed the closeness.

And secretly in the background, I drew on the power his touch provided. If I was going to jump realms, I was going to need every drop.

CHAPTER 2

NIGHTMARES

Later that night...

$\mathcal{T}$he chase was on.

Flying high through the sky by myself, with no wyvern underneath me, I could feel myself being tugged through the air. My surroundings had a hazy appearance that made every detail difficult to concentrate on.

A dark kingdom spanned out beneath me, a realm that I knew was full of danger and shadows. It pulled against me, making the air thick and I struggled to breathe. Dark onyx spires pierced the cloudy skies, daring me to breach its walls.

But I was close.

To what, I wasn't sure. But I had to keep going.

To save... her?

The stale sickness in the atmosphere threatened to suffocate me. Panic began to flood my veins when I couldn't draw in a full breath, but it didn't feel like my panic. It was an outside sense of urgency, and a misplaced sense of innocence.

The purity of a soul at a complete dichotomy to the corruption of the land around me.

Then it was gone. The draw, the innocent presence, and also whatever magic had been keeping me afloat.

I fell.

A strangled scream rushing from between my teeth. The ground rushed up to meet me and I braced myself for impact.

Shooting up in bed I clamped my hand over my mouth to stifle my screams. Drawing in deep, gulping breaths, I lowered my hand and glanced around the darkness, desperately hoping that I hadn't woken Killian.

All I needed was for him to find out I was having nightmares.

He slept soundly on the bed adjacent to mine. It was how we preferred it, to be close, but not to be too intimate, at least right now. Sometimes I slept in his bed or he slept in mine, but there was a special ceremony that resembled marriage we hadn't undergone yet. While we hadn't exactly waited to do most intimate things, I liked the idea of taking it slow and making our eventual completed bond that much more special.

Dragonrider Academy left it up to the students how individual riderbonds were emotionally and physically developed. Students like Jasmine jumped straight into bed with Vern, her latest bondmate who had still stuck around. There was nothing wrong with that, but Jasmine and I were different in a lot of ways.

Killian and I cared deeply for one another, and expressing that physically was important and natural, however it could be overpowering at times. Our situation was special. I had goddess blood in my veins and Killian amped up that magic within me through physical touch. I wasn't sure what true intimacy would really unleash, or if I was ready for it.

I must not have screamed very loud, because Killian rolled over, not having even opened his eyes. I smothered a chuckle. Some guardian he made.

Yet, the dream lingered with me, the complicated emotions still raw. The terror of the fall felt like a symbol of something to come.

And the sensation that someone had been calling me didn't feel like a dream.

It felt real.

Sitting up, I dangled my feet over the side of the bed as I frowned.

I knew that realm, somehow.

I wracked my drowsy brain for the descriptions of the different realms. Realization finally hit me when I thought back to those onyx spires.

The Malice realm.

As soon as I realized where my dream had taken place, I began to feel it. That same tugging sensation from the dream. The same draw to that innocent presence surrounded by darkness. That same sense of urgency.

Someone needed my help, and they were in the Malice realm calling for me.

I glanced at Killian again. I couldn't tell him about this. He wouldn't even entertain the idea of helping a stranger right now, not when I was in such a fragile position. I considered the Dean, but she would probably be even worse. Her focus remained on Dragonrider Academy and the bigger picture. Sacrifices had to be made and war had casualties—her words.

This was something I would have to do on my own.

I tilted my head, spotting a dragon soaring in the night sky.

Well, Solstice might understand.

Decision made, I jumped to my feet and quietly went to the closet, pulling out my rider clothes that had been set aside for the big day. A plan formed in my head, one that involved a rescue in the Malice Realm and returning before Killian had his rendezvous with Max.

No one had to know.

I quickly braided my hair in a long rope down my back to keep it out of the way, and then pulled on my boots. Grabbing a dagger and a small set of throwing knives for good measure, I strapped the weapons to the leather holsters around my legs before turning to the door to begin my mission.

The campus was quiet when I stepped outside, only a few students were out and about doing midnight chores. The Academy never slept and there was always something to do, a gate to guard, a pathway to maintain, a dragon to ride.

It was what I loved about this place, but right now that worked against me. I rolled my shoulders back and walked confidently toward the stalls, glancing over my shoulder now and again to make sure I wasn't being followed.

The tugging sensation of the calling grew stronger with every step. An itch formed inside my chest and I scratched at it, my pace quickening to a brisk walk as I turned sharply toward the stalls—and collided with a tall female.

"Whoa!" Dean Brynhilde exclaimed as my stomach dropped. She boomed with laughter as she steadied me.

Leave it to me to cap off a stealth mission by literally running into the leader of Dragonrider Academy.

"Sorry," I murmured as I rubbed my aching nose.

The Dean backed away and appraised me. "No apologies needed. You seem like you're in quite the hurry. Where are you off to? Is everything okay?"

I rubbed the back of my neck. "I, uh, was just having trouble sleeping so I wanted to take a walk on the beach with Solstice. You know, dip my toes in the water and all that." I gave her my best smile, hoping that sounded believable.

She raised an eyebrow. "But you hate the water."

Oh, right.

Then she smiled. "The salty breeze always does me good, though. It's worth a try. With everything going on, you have a lot on your mind." She winked. "Solstice is a wonderful dragon. She'll love the personal time."

Giving her an awkward wave as we parted ways, my heart pounded in my chest.

I'd just lied to the dean.

There was no way she was going to graduate me now.

But that didn't matter. I scratched my chest again as the sensation grew. I knew what I had to do.

When I reached the stalls, the scent of fresh straw and raw meat made my nostrils flare. I wasn't a fan of the scents, but Solstice loved it, and that's all that mattered.

I found her awake as she paced the massive stall, a concrete sphere in the ground that behaved like a massive nest. Topaz slept just as hard as Killian one stall away, making me chuckle.

I opened the gate and Solstice climbed out, butting my shoulder with her snout.

Images of flight and an onyx tower entered my mind. I rubbed her warm scales and nodded. "Yes, girl. You saw it too, huh?"

She butted me with her head again and then marched out of the stalls. The other wyverns preened and chirped their goodbyes, all of them seeming fond of her.

Solstice was my hero. It didn't surprise me that she was popular among her kind, even viewed as a leader. She was a queen, after all.

She glanced back when we'd left the stalls, an image of Topaz entering my mind.

I rubbed her flank. "I know. We can't bring him, though. He would alert Killian and you know that he wouldn't agree to this. He'd say that it was too dangerous, but you feel it too, right? Someone is calling for our help."

Solstice shifted her weight, then snorted her agreement and proceeded down the Academy streets.

The Dean waved at us from her perch outside the office building. She liked to oversee the students and I wondered if she ever slept. Maybe as an immortal, she didn't require sleep, or at least, that's what she wanted us to believe.

We were going to the beach anyway, so I waved back at her and then hid behind Solstice so I didn't give anything away.

The sea breeze battered me as I stepped through the sand, going out further than was usual for just a walk on the beach. I didn't want anyone spotting my portal.

"Ready?" I asked her when we found a good spot behind some dunes.

She sent me a wave of uncertainty mixed with loyalty. She wasn't sure this was a good idea to go into a dangerous realm without any backup, but she trusted me.

The responsibility suffocated me for a moment before the tugging in my chest ramped up again, this time tinged with the same foreign panic I had felt in my dream.

We had to go... *now*.

Centering myself, I concentrated on the Malice realm. I tried to pull every small detail I could remember from my dream into focus. The closer I could get us to the soul, the less time it would take us to get back. Once I had the place firmly solidified in my mind, I willed the portal to open drawing power from my amulet. The effort drained my energy, but I'd taken more than what I needed from Killian for the roundtrip. A *woosh* swept over the sands as a portal blazed to life in a spiral of power.

The swirling air expelled from the portal radiated the same sickly darkness I'd seen in my dream. Falling back a step, I took in the full scope of what I was about to do.

This was the *Malice realm.*

A place of literal nightmares that I didn't know much about. Going in with just Solstice and I, completely unprepared, sounded like a bad idea, but what choice did I have?

A small cry sounded through the portal, solidifying my decision.

Solstice keened in response, having heard an innocent soul calling out for help.

"We got this," I told her. Though, even to me, it sounded like I was trying to convince myself of that more than her.

Before I could change my mind, I launched myself through the swirling dark air.

I'd never get used to the feeling of falling that came with realm transit. The entire world dissipated, leaving me in a tangle of time and space that didn't feel right. It was a place of nothing, a place of in-between.

The sensation didn't last long. I'd gotten better at making portals thanks to our trips to Vyorin to meet with Max. I landed hard on the ground, rolling to absorb the majority of the impact, a tactic that I'd learned how to do.

Immediately scrambling out of the way, Solstice came through next, barreling into the dark space after me as she launched into the sky, the maneuver meant to avoid me had I still been in the way.

Then the portal vanished, leaving us in heavy silence.

I turned in a small circle and evaluated our surroundings. It looked exactly like my dream, darkness everywhere with a suffocating density that hit me even harder in reality. I couldn't see any onyx spires, but that itch inside my chest grew in intensity, guiding me through the darkness.

Solstice landed next to me, butting my shoulder to let me know she was ready.

I concentrated on the pull, trying to decipher an exact direction. The feeling was much stronger here, so I had no trouble honing in on that feeling as I set off at a brisk jog.

We moved in the same direction, following the mysterious pull on my soul for what seemed like forever before we saw any sign of life. The tug had become more of a buzz in my veins the closer we got to our destination.

Just when it was becoming unbearable, we crested a hill, and there it was. A giant castle with tall onyx towers loomed over us. I'd never seen anything so dark or haunting, something of nightmares that would stick with me for the rest of my life.

The smooth stone shapes formed five main towers with four smaller pikes breaching the sky on the perimeter.

Solstice slowed as she took in the foreboding structure. Her unease bled through the riderbond, giving me a share of her anxiety. I reached over and gave her a comforting pat on her flank.

"Whoever we are here to help is in that castle," I told her in an urgent whisper. Her worry spiked and I grimaced. She couldn't come inside the castle with me and we both knew it. I would be on my own.

Just as that thought occurred to me, the ringing of a bell sounded all around the castle. Shouts filtered through the air and my heart skipped a beat.

I crouched, trying to figure out what was happening, before realizing that I would never be inconspicuous with a giant golden wyvern standing right next to me.

Terror filled me as dark figures swarmed out of the castle gates, rushing towards Solstice and I like a great tidal wave.

Dark elves.

There was a whole garrison of Dark elves about to surround us.

My mind raced as I tried to come up with a solution. They moved too fast for me to outrun them and I definitely couldn't take on that many at once with just my dagger and throwing knives. Though Solstice could do some damage. The thought of my wyvern sparked a tenuous plan that might be our only shot at survival.

Solstice was matured enough now. We could fly!

I turned to my wyvern and was relieved to see she had caught my thought and already knelt down, offering one wing for me to use as a ladder. I risked a glance at the advancing elves and blanched as I realized they would reach us within seconds. They wielded long, spears that looked to be made of sleek black stone.

Malice solidified.

I scrambled up Solstice's flank, using her wing as a step. I flung myself onto her back and gripped her ridges as tightly as I could. I tried to secure my knees as well, but that proved more difficult.

We were supposed to learn how to ride our dragons in a few days.

This would have to be my crash course.

Solstice seemed to be waiting for me to find a secure spot before she took off, but we didn't have any gear and I was about as secure as I could be without it.

"Go, Solstice! Fly!" I shouted as the elves closed in all around us.

She stood up, nearly jostling me off her back with the sudden motion. Anxiety shot through me at the thought of flinging through the air without even a saddle to hold onto, but the shouting garrison didn't give us a choice.

Solstice turned and took a running start, unsteady on her feet as she figured out her new center of gravity now that she had a passenger. I clung to the ridges down her spine, my whole body tensing as she beat her wings once, twice, and then we were airborne.

My stomach dropped as she dipped down erratically. She'd practiced flying plenty of times, but she'd never had a rider. She adjusted for my extra weight and rebalanced herself with impressive speed. She gained elevation slowly, catching a rhythm that seemed to work before trying to circle back towards the towering castle.

She turned a little too sharply and I squealed as I slid to one side, my hands sliding on her shiny scales as I scrambled for a handhold. I managed to catch myself and get back into a centered position, though I couldn't help shaking like a leaf and death-gripping her with all of my limbs as I squeezed my legs as hard as I could.

She adjusted her error and turned in one sweeping arc back toward the castle and the object of our mission. This time without nearly throwing me off of her back. Shouts rang up from the ground and dark weapons careened through the air, forcing Solstice to fly higher. I screeched and crouched low.

She sent me disgruntled emotions through the bond as she sensed my complaint that she wasn't warning me.

Then she tried something new. She sent me an image of moving to the left, then she did so in reality. Prepared, I kept my balance better this time.

She did the same for the right.

A grin spread across my face. It was working.

Steadier now that she had figured out how to adjust for me, I relaxed just slightly. Enough to look over her side and see the crowd of elves on the ground below us now. They all shouted and waved their weapons at us, but we were too high up for them to waste their spears.

The tugging in my chest caught my attention again and I turned back towards the castle, studying the best way to get in from the air.

A flash of light caught my eye. It harshly contrasted against the dark, dreariness of the castle and surrounding atmosphere as it beamed from the tallest tower, shining with clarity as if it had just burst to life.

That was the soul shining out to be saved, giving a last burst of life before the darkness closed in around it forever.

"Look!" I shouted, pointing as the harsh, icy wind lashed at my face, sending loose strands of hair escaping from my braid.

Solstice angled closer as she circled the tower, higher and higher until we reached the top and I could finally see the object that had called us across realms.

A dragon egg.

It balanced at the very top of the spire, shining like a crown jewel against the dark stone. The tugging in my chest reached a fever pitch as Solstice hovered close enough for me to reach out and grab it.

"Got you!" I shouted as I wrapped on arm around the egg, pulling the jewel into my chest to keep it safe.

Now I only had one hand to hold onto Solstice, but we'd found a balance and she fed me warning pictures of her movements as she retreated away from the castle.

The nagging ache in my chest disappeared instantly, in its place swelled warmth and gratitude.

We'd done it.

My celebration was cut short when Solstice let out a panicked roar. I glanced back the way we had come, spotting an inky black cloud billowing from the empty spikes where the egg had been encased.

I realized with sick dread that the Dark Elves had been drawing power from this egg, using it for their own motives.

And they weren't going to let us take it without a fight.

After triggering the castle's defense mechanisms, I leaned low on Solstice's back and urged her to hurry. "Fly, girl," I whispered, and she obeyed.

The inky cloud released a series of thunder and lightning that flashed in its midst, a dark hand reaching out toward us.

Solstice picked up her pace, making me lean down to avoid the wind pushing me off her back as I coddled the egg protectively to my chest. The dark hand reached out to us, snapping just inches from Solstice's tail.

I wasn't sure how I had pictured my first flight with Solstice, but this was not it.

We raced toward the direction I'd created the original portal. I couldn't make one here, not without risking my life. The initial portal had ripped a veil through time and space and it would be safest to return through it.

Assuming we could make it.

The shimmer in the distance gave us hope as a nightmare followed us from behind. I frantically pushed energy from my amulet, reopening the portal right in front of Solstice and I so we didn't even have to land.

The falling sensation was even worse as we simultaneously entered the swirling vortex. The dark cloud slammed against the portal behind us, unable to enter, but it clawed at it, piercing the veil.

I lifted a hand and released a blast of instinctual magic. My birthmark burned with power as goddess blood activated in my veins, stitching the portal closed behind us.

It was probably a dangerous move, but Solstice flapped her wings and powered on, keeping ahead of the unraveling tunnel until we sailed through the air, bursting into a comforting wave of salty welcome.

Home.

But we had too much momentum. We slammed into the sand and I rolled off her back, curling myself around the egg to keep it safe.

When I tumbled to a halt, I rested my head against the sands and blinked at the night sky, drawing in deep breaths.

We'd done it.

Somehow.

Solstice flapped through the sands, then sneezed, sending small grains spattering all over me.

The whole thing was so comical that I fell into a fit of laughter, my terror and disbelief coming out all at once.

Solstice's ears flicked as she stared at me, concern running through our bond.

"I'm not crazy, you big lizard," I said, choking out the words as I struggled to my feet. "I just... I can't believe that really just happened."

Solstice shook herself, flinging off the rest of the sand, and then glanced at the egg on my chest. It glowed softly with life, warmth radiating through my touch.

It was alive.

But how had the Dark Elves gotten their claws on it in the first place?

And what did they use it for? Something nefarious, to be sure, but a mystery to figure out later. For now, the important thing was to keep the egg safe.

"Vivi!" Jasmine yelled atop Jade, landing hard on the sands.

Jasmine swept her leg over the wyvern in a practiced move, bounding to the ground and running to my side. I hid the egg in my arms so she couldn't see it.

"It's not what it looks like," I began. Surely she had heard the portal or sensed my distress somehow. Maybe the Malice had somehow escaped and was now plaguing the Academy.

She waved away my words. "I don't care what

you're up to out here. I tracked you down because you need to come back on campus right now."

"What's going on?"

She drew in a deep breath, her jaw tensing before she faced me. "It's your mother."

CHAPTER 3

DESTINY

*M*y heart pounded in my chest as I ran, full tilt, toward Central Hall, still clutching the egg tightly to my chest. My thoughts came in frantic fragments.

My mother.

Trouble.

I wasn't here when she had needed me.

I burst through the doors, skidded around a corner and up the stairs to the guest suite where my mother stayed. I rushed in without knocking and stopped short when I took in the changes in the room.

The room gleamed with brilliant white shades. White furniture, white walls, a white comforter. My mother preferred earthy tones, but now it was as if she had sensed the darkness I would face today and repelled it in the only way she knew how.

She sat in a recliner facing the large window, overlooking the campus and a beautiful view of the glittering ocean beyond that.

Then I realized she would have seen me, the disheveled sands marking where I had portaled in.

Wincing, I drew closer to her and sat on the windowsill. "Mother?" I asked, attempting to draw her attention.

She rested in the chair, holding onto the sides as she struggled to breathe. Her frame had gotten impossibly thinner since I'd seen her before my training session with Jasmine.

I took her hand in mine, stroking her leathery, ashen skin. She finally looked at me, the dark circles under her eyes betraying that she hadn't been able to sleep at all.

"My baby girl," she said with a heartbreaking smile. Then she glanced down at the egg in the crook of my arm. "You found her."

Of course my mother would have known about the dragon egg. She seemed to know things she shouldn't because of what she was. "Why didn't you tell me?" I asked as Jasmine took note of the egg, then left the room, slowly closing the door behind her.

She was probably going to run straight to the dean, but I didn't care. A dragon egg would be protected here and my disobedience would be justified... hopefully.

"You wouldn't have understood," my mother said with a weak smile. "This was the way it was supposed to happen." She closed her eyes and drew in a struggling breath.

My heart twisted. "Are you talking about the

dragon egg, or are you talking about something else?" My mind couldn't even process the other possibility.

She took a deep breath. "I'm dying, Vivi."

My mind rejected the thought immediately. She couldn't be dying. I needed her here with me.

"No you're not," I exclaimed, feeling myself teetering on the edge of that break everyone was afraid I would have.

"Let me finish, Vivienne," she scolded. She sounded so much like her old self for just that second that a sharp pain went through my chest.

I leaned back and coddled the egg close to my chest, waiting for her to continue.

"Decedents of the goddess are given a gift. When we need it most, a vision will come to us. A vision of the one moment in our life that will have the biggest impact than any other. I had my vision. I saw the moment that would define my life." She paused, seeming to struggle to find the words. Or maybe she was struggling for the energy to continue talking. "I saw you die," she said, pain cracking in her voice. "I saw you die and it shattered me. I knew I couldn't let my vision become my reality. But that is why we receive these visions. We can either prepare ourselves for the outcome... or we can make our best efforts to change it."

She paused then to catch her breath, clearly exhausted just from the simple act of speaking.

"When did you get this vision?" I asked after a moment.

She chuckled. "You're always so perceptive. I saw it the moment you went to the Academy. The choice was simple. My life or yours, which was really no choice for me. I took the amulet and I poured every bit of my goddess magic into it, then it brought me to you."

I stared at her, stunned and betrayed. "You intentionally did this to yourself?" Tears pricked at my eyes. "You were willing to leave me? You have turned down any efforts to help because you *want* to die?"

She shook her head. "Of course I don't want to die, sweetheart. But I have lived a long, happy life, my dear. You have a destiny to fulfill, and mine was to see yours come to fruition." She held out her hands, beckoning me to come closer. Fighting tears, I knelt as she cupped my face in her hands. "This is the way it was meant to be, my daughter. I didn't accept help because there is no help for me. I just want you to know Vivienne, I don't regret it. I would go back and do it again in an instant if it meant you get to live."

My thoughts raced as I came to terms with what she was saying. My brain couldn't quite process the fact that my mother had sacrificed herself for me. She had literally given her life for mine, just like my father had so many years ago in that lake.

I choked back a sob. "No! No, Mama. You can't die. I need you here!"

My words dissolved into barely intelligible sentences between gasps for air.

"Shh, shh, baby. It's going to be okay. You're so strong. You can do anything." Her words were a whisper as she cupped my face, wiping my tears with her thin, shaking hands. "I love you, Vivienne, and I'm so proud of you. Never forget that."

As if those final words had stolen the last of her energy, her hands dropped limply from my face. Her eyelids fluttered closed. A sense of finality hit me and I backed away from the chair, shaking my head and releasing a broken sob.

I knew she wouldn't wake up again.

She was so still, her chest barely moving to indicate she still breathed. So still, and small, and close to death.

I paced her room, anger suddenly taking the place of my overwhelming grief.

How could she do this to me?

How was dying going to make anything better?

Fury flooded through my veins and I welcomed it, desperate for anything other than the soul-crushing sadness.

I had to get away from here.

Turning on my heel, I headed for the door, then remembered the egg. Swiveling back, I scooped it up, my heart breaking for the fragile, innocent soul that needed me right now. But who was going to keep me from falling apart?

A sensation entered my chest, and at first I thought the small voice came from Solstice. I couldn't make out words, but I could sense a desire to stay.

I glanced down at the egg. It was trying to talk to me.

The Dark Elves had been using it for energy. An

idea hit me... perhaps my mother needed this egg more than I did.

And perhaps this egg needed her.

With a little hope in my heart, I pulled back my mother's blankets and placed the egg onto her lap. I tucked her back in and left the room before I fell apart.

I walked with deliberate steps all the way to the training grounds. I picked up a wooden sparring sword and approached a random practice dummy.

Swinging as hard as I could, I let loose a high-pitched yell of fury. The dummy flung to the side from the blow, absorbing my fury and rage.

I hit again.

And again.

My arms were shaking as I lost myself, swinging and yelling and cursing all the realms for my screwed-up destiny.

It felt like eternity and a second all at once. The anger seemed to be a never-ending well, and I wasn't sure I wanted to reach the bottom anyway. That's where the grief had to be.

Suddenly, there were arms around me. Someone pried the wooden sword from my hands and trapped me in a circle of warmth and muscles. I immediately knew it was Killian and sank into his embrace. My knees gave out and I slid to the ground as a fresh sob took over. Killian followed me down, still holding me close to him. I realized then that I was shaking uncon-trollably and gasping for air. Sweat soaked my clothes and hair, and tears streaked my face.

Killian stroked my hair and rocked me back and forth, shushing me. "I'm here, love. I'm here. It's going to be okay."

His whispers continued in my ear and the safety I felt in his arms released me. I sobbed, great heaving, gasping sobs that overwhelmed me like a tidal wave.

Killian held me tightly as I let all of my grief out at once. I grieved for my mother, I grieved for my dad, I grieved for my old life that was so much simpler than this tangled mess. I'd hated it, once, but now I craved for those simple days where my family laughed at the dining table, playing a board game.

Those days were gone.

Slowly, I came back to myself. I felt wrung out, like I had cried every last tear I had. My shaking had calmed and I slowly brought my breathing back down to normal.

"I'm sorry," I croaked out at Killian, without lifting my head from his chest.

"Never apologize for allowing yourself to feel. I'm here when you need me. We all are," Killian tightened his hold around me. I lifted my head then and saw that Topaz and Solstice had coiled themselves around us, creating a warm little cocoon of comfort and warmth.

I leaned back into Killian, content to sit here for a while.

"Uh, Viv, can I ask you a question?" he hesitantly asked after a moment.

"Hmm?" I responded, my eyes still closed.

"Why do you smell like realm magic and burnt metal?"

My eyes flung open. "Right…"

I guess it was time to tell him about the Malice Realm.

CHAPTER 4

IT'S TIME

*B*efore I had the chance to confess my successful, though reckless, adventure, a voice shouted over Solstice's back.

"Are you two going to the assembly?" Lily called from a distance as the sun crested over the clouds. "The Dean pulled ahead the First Flight ceremony preparations, isn't that exciting!"

I turned to Killian, wide-eyed at the news.

"Jasmine," he said with a sigh.

Of course, after hearing about my exploits, the Dean would have had no choice but to pull up the ceremony. The Malice Realm would be coming for the egg I saved, and we all needed to be ready.

Amusement flowed through the bond from Solstice at the thought of our "first flight" ceremony. If we had survived the Malice Realm, we could handle anything the Dean threw our way.

"We'll be there in a minute," Killian called over loudly to Lily as a perplexed look lingered in his pale eyes. "Are you going to explain where you were? I woke up and you were gone, then Jasmine found me and told me she had spotted you escaping an unstable portal. You're lucky to be alive."

Nervous energy ran through me. How mad was he going to be when I told him what I had done? He wasn't a fan of me being in danger, and that's when we were prepared. I had been too reckless today. My only saving grace was that I had completed the mission and saved the dragon egg from the corruption of the Malice realm. I would make sure to emphasize the success of the unsanctioned excursion and minimize the danger. Killian didn't need to know how close we had come to being hurt.

"You realize that the assembly starts like... now. Right?" Lily called again from the other side of Solstice. "I know it's just prep for flying, but you guys are getting your saddles!" As a dragon herself, she didn't need a saddle, but she seemed excited about it regardless.

I seized the opportunity to postpone my confession. I jumped up and dusted the dirt and grass from my pants before holding my hand out to help Killian.

"Come on. We don't want to be late," I told him and made my way swiftly through the opening Solstice and Topaz made as they both stood.

"Fine. This conversation isn't over though," Killian grumbled and followed me toward Central Hall.

We stepped through the double doors of the Grand Assembly Hall, a portion of Central Hall that had no ceiling, and hurried down an aisle to our left. I sat in the first available chair I found, and Killian grabbed the seat next to mine. The voices of our classmates buzzed throughout the auditorium style room as a bright light focused on the stage.

I leaned my head back in my chair and closed my eyes. The darkness of the room, white noise of conversation, and cushioned chair seemed to remind my abused muscles that they were tired.

And that I'd hardly slept.

Killian nudged my shoulder. "It's the Dean."

I jerked up, blinking awake. I needed to pay attention. This would be the foundation of my flying skills, which had already proven useful for getting out of the messes I seemed to attract.

The buzz of voices slowly faded as everyone realized Dean Brynhilde was standing on the stage waiting for our attention.

"Good morning, students! What an exciting week it's going to be for you all," she grinned as cheer and applause rang out from the crowd of eager fledgling Dragonriders. "Before the exciting part can happen, though, we have to get through all the ceremony and tradition."

With that, she broke down how the ceremony would work, how to clean and care for our dragons and their tack, safety protocols when actually in the air, and everything in between.

She didn't mention the images, though, that had made flying with Solstice so effective.

From the preparation, to the execution, she covered everything else I would need to know. I desperately tried to focus on what she was saying, but the exhaustion in my bones made it difficult to concentrate.

Professors handed out stacks of worksheets, then one-by-one we all came up to the stage with our dragons and went through the protocols, then fitted our new saddles to our wyverns.

Solstice glanced at me with a glint in her eyes. A saddle would make clinging to her back so much easier.

Several hours later, we were done with our first lesson and dismissed for lunch. I returned to my mother and checked on her, finding her sleeping with Finn keeping an eye on her. The dwarf had taken a liking to my mother and didn't leave her side for long, except to care for the eggs in the Egg Sanctuary.

He remarked on the egg I had found, but said my mother was doing a good job of keeping it warm. He wanted me to talk to the dean about it, and explain where I had found it, then he grumbled on about how understaffed the sanctuary was and left to get my mother some food.

After he returned, I left, feeling heavy-hearted, but hopeful that the egg could do something for my mother she hadn't foreseen. Dragons had a funny way of altering destiny.

Killian accompanied me back to our room and I couldn't stay awake a moment longer. I passed out, for once enjoying a dreamless sleep.

CHAPTER 5

ALARM CLOCK

*C*urled up in Killian's embrace, I frowned when a banging on the door intruded on the best sleep I'd had in a while.

"Go away," I grumbled, then snuggled closer to Killian.

The door burst open, ignoring my request, as Jasmine stormed in, rushing to the windows. She jerked open the curtains and spilled sunlight onto my face.

"Jas," Killian complained as he buried his face into my hair. "Five more minutes."

She scoffed. "Both of you are useless. If you ever want to graduate, you'd better be grateful you have friends like me willing to get your butts up!" She yanked the bedsheet, making Killian and I groan. "It's the middle of the day! Why are you guys sleeping?"

I struggled into a sitting position and rubbed my eyes. "Nightmares," I said, only capable of single-word sentences at this point, and glowered at her.

"Don't look at me like that," she chided. "You were supposed to be washing and saddling up Solstice over half an hour ago."

My eyes went wide. "Wait, that isn't tomorrow?"

Jasmine rolled her eyes and propped her hands on her hips. "No! Everything got pulled up because of the stunt you pulled. You went to the Malice Realm, right? That's a nasty place. If you took a dragon egg from them, they're going to try and get it back."

Killian shot up. "Malice Realm?"

Jasmine rolled her eyes. "You guys really need to work on your communication."

Cursing, I dashed to the bathroom for my toothbrush. I was already dressed in my rider gear, having been too tired to take it off. Black streaks licked across the leathers, betraying that I'd been in a battle already.

Not exactly ceremony-worthy, but it would have to do.

"I was just supposed to show you how to put on Solstice's turning gear," Jasmine said, "but I guess I'll explain alarm clocks too." She leaned against the doorway with a smirk.

I rolled my eyes as I turned to her. "I don't need turning gear." I knew the equipment she referred to. Two hooks clamped onto the wyvern's horns at their snout, hooking to the rider's saddle to be tugged to indicate left and right.

I understood why the Dean hadn't covered the workaround that Solstice and I had come up with. Most riderbonds probably weren't strong enough to convey that kind of communication between dragon and rider in real time.

She raised an eyebrow. "Now this I gotta see."

Killian chuckled, engaging in a verbal sparring match with Jasmine about finally getting to pit Topaz and Jade in a sky-race. I had no doubt that Jasmine would win, but it was fun to hear them banter.

"The wyvern stalls, right?" I asked Jasmine as we walked out of the dorms.

"Right," she said from beside me.

The light run seemed to wake up my muscles so I sped up a little, stretched out my legs and enjoyed the burst of energy a power nap seemed to have given me.

The sight as I rounded the corner into the wyvern's quarters stopped me short. Soaked students and dragons ran through the field in front of the stalls. Wet, soapy sponges were being thrown through the air, buckets full of water thrown over our heads, and piles of bubbles everywhere. Laughter rang through the air as my classmates all ran around creating as much havoc as they could with only soap and water at their disposal. I couldn't help but smile at the simplistic joy.

Malice hadn't found us yet.

Now, it was time for play.

"You didn't have to be here yet," Jasmine admitted with a wry smile, "I just thought you could use some fun."

I bumped her shoulder with mine and gave her a mischievous grin. "Sounds fun to me."

Spotting a sopping wet sponge at my feet, I

scooped it up and hurled it at her. She squealed a high-pitched tone I'd never heard before, dodging just in time.

Laughing at her disgruntled expression, she searched the ground. When she spotted another sponge, I knew it was time to run.

Killian openly laughed as Jasmine went on the chase, tossing soap bombs at me as I fled through the stalls.

Killian followed at my flank, catching up to me as he rushed through a shortcut, bounding over a sleeping wyvern who keened with irritation. He launched at me, barreling into me as we crashed to the soft piles of hay in a fit of laughter.

"Now you've done it," I said, plucking strands of hay out of my hair.

He grinned. "I guess you need a shower." His rich laughter made my stomach flutter. Those butterflies went on overdrive when he gave me a long kiss.

Jasmine dunked us with a soapy bucket of water, making us both sputter. "You wanted a shower," she said with a grin.

"Get her!" Killian shouted, and Jasmine booked it down the stalls, all of us screeching as we engaged in a new game of chase.

I loved it.

This was exactly the distraction I needed.

Jasmine ran straight into Vern who scooped her into his arms. "Captured!" he shouted with a massive grin.

Killian laughed and crouched. "Oh, is that the game? I spot a dragonrider that needs to be captured."

Squealing, I ran from him and searched the ground for soapy defenses. Lily tossed me a sponge and I caught it with a triumphant whoop, launching it back at Killian. His eyes widened and he tried to duck unsuccessfully as the soapy sponge slammed into his face.

I burst into laughter, holding my stomach and watching him wipe his face and slowly bend to pick up the sponge. My laughter petered out as he looked up at me and grinned.

"Uh oh," was all I said before I turned and ran, pealing laughter following me.

I caught a glimpse of gold out of the corner of my eye and turned toward what I knew was my wyvern. I could feel her amusement through the bond. I dodged around her, eager to see what was so funny and take cover from Killian at the same time.

Solstice laughed at Topaz as he ducked his head into the water pond, gathered water in his great mouth, and then shot it out like a fire hose at anyone in his vicinity.

Killian rounded the corner and saw his wyvern's trick. He smirked at me. "Topaz! Get Vivi!"

Before I could dive for cover behind Solstice, my mate's wyvern turned his water canon on me and absolutely soaked me to the skin. I let myself fall back into a sprawl on the ground and laughed. It felt good to release energy in a positive way. It felt like it had been years since I had actually laughed like that.

"That's a beautiful sound," Killian said, smiling down at me softly, water and soap dripping from his silver hair.

I blushed, and my laughter calmed enough for me to catch my breath. I pushed my soaked hair out of my face, and sat up. The water fight was calming down, everyone returning to their actual tasks, but the light-hearted atmosphere stayed.

I smiled up at Killian and leaned back on my elbows. "Why didn't you wake me?"

"You were out cold. I figured you needed some time," he told me, his eyes gentle.

"I do feel better. No crushing exhaustion," I said with a lopsided grin.

"Good. I'm glad I let you sleep," he held his hand out to help me up as he spoke. He handed me a sponge, a small bristled brush, and a bucket full of soapy water. He wagged his finger at me when I wiggled my eyebrows and feigned dumping it on him like he had done to me. He chuckled, "That's for washing Solstice, not washing me."

I grinned at him and then turned to my bonded dragon. She bent her head and nuzzled me, leaning into my hand when I stroked her face.

"Ready to do this?" I asked her, then lowered my voice so only she could hear me, "For real this time?"

She sent encouraging feelings through the bond and I smiled at her. Then, I started cleaning her. I washed her down with soap, then thoroughly brushed out her scales, getting lingering dark stones from her flank, before rubbing in the scale oil that gave her a little extra shine. She looked like molten gold in the sunlight by the time I was done.

I glanced over at Killian, only to find him done with his task. Topaz gleamed like a gem beside him, both of them just watching Solstice and me at work. Killian's gaze was contemplative and I made my way over to him, nestling into his lap as I leaned my head against his chest.

Topaz and Solstice basked in the sunlight, warming their scales as their wings fanned out, releasing the last of the moisture.

"So, the Malice Realm," Killian began.

I winced, but his tone was soft, not lecturing.

"Yes," I confirmed.

"Why?" he asked.

Sighing, I leaned into him. "This'll sound crazy, but there was a dragon egg calling to me. I didn't know what it was at first, just an innocent soul that needed help. So I left." It was as simple as that, but I didn't expect Killian to understand.

He snuggled me closer. "That doesn't sound crazy at all. It sounds like... a miracle." He tilted his head, leaning his cheek against my hair. "Where is it now?"

"With my mother," I explained that it seemed to be stabilizing her, at least, she hadn't gotten any worse. She'd slipped into a deep sleep, but something told me that this was a chance to keep her alive.

He hummed in acknowledgement. "I hope it helps."

I leaned up to look at him. "So, you're not mad?"

He kissed me on the forehead. "I'm furious, but I understand." Then he chuckled.

"What's so funny?"

He tucked a strand of hair behind my ear. "I'm supposed to be the part-angel doing the miracles, but you always seem to be a step ahead of me." He relaxed against me. "That's what I love about you, though. You amaze me every day." He nodded reluctantly and kissed my forehead, "Can you just promise you'll wait for me next time? Don't go alone?"

I leaned into his kiss and sighed, "Okay. I promise."

I tilted my head up then to kiss him in return, only to be interrupted by a throat clearing nearby.

We both looked over and saw Jasmine standing there, two large saddles at her feet.

"Come on, lovebirds, time to put on your tack," she told us and then clapped her hands as if to hurry us along.

Jasmine spent the next hour supervising our work to see what we remembered from the dean's assembly. Killian saddled Topaz without a problem, although I couldn't remember the exact order the straps were supposed to go.

She had made sure to stress the importance of following the steps exactly. She made it a point that we never attempt to ride bareback unless we wanted to fall to our deaths. Dragons didn't have much to hold onto.

I had to stifle my laughter as I thought of myself clinging to Solstice's ridges without a saddle just last night. Solstice nudged me with amusement in her mind as she caught the directions of my thoughts.

By the time we were done it was mid-afternoon. Solstice and Topaz looked like true warrior dragons. They were fearsome and ready for battle in their leather armors and riding saddle.

"Now, you just need to make yourselves presentable for the annual feast," Jasmine said, scrutinizing our soaked uniforms and disheveled hair once she was satisfied with our dragons.

Killian threw his arm around me and we made our way to the Dining Hall, my stomach rumbling at the idea of a feast.

CHAPTER 6

FIRST FLIGHT... AGAIN

"*I*'m starving!" Lily exclaimed, ushering us to our table.

James sat next to her and Jasmine directly across from us, fork and knife at the ready.

We had been some of the last people to show up, so thankfully we didn't have to wait long to dig into the food that was taunting me from the center of the table.

"Attention, everyone!" Dean Brynhilde stood from her seat at the head table. She lifted her glass and smiled at all of us. "I would like to make a toast. Every year, there's a new batch of second years who are ready to fly for the first time. Every year, I officiate the ceremony and get to watch all of you get your wings. Every year, I am just as proud as I was the year before. This ceremony may happen annually, but I treasure every First Flight as if it were my own. You have earned your right to be here. You have proven your worthiness to be a dragonrider. Tonight, you take to the skies with your bond mates. Tonight, you take your rightful place among us. Congratulations to all of you. You've earned it." She beamed at us as she finished and lifted her glass. Applause and sporadic cheering broke out over the room. "Let's eat!"

Everyone dug in and the next few hours were filled with wonderful food, raucous laughter, and great conversation. Even the Wyverns were permitted to join today, their meals in massive piles of meats at the perimeter. Solstice and Topaz shared a long slab, making Killian and I laugh.

Bellies full and hearts content, it was time to fly.

The students walked as a group with seniors taking to the skies.

I flanked Solstice at the beach, having ample room around us for our first attempt over the water. Large wooden towers gave us some height over the waves, the structures allowing the dragons to glide over the invisible ocean drafts for a first flight.

Definitely a better situation than launching from the ground in the Malice-infested atmosphere.

Killian waved at me, standing next to Topaz on his tower as the other students prepared.

The most interesting pair was Lily and James. While I was pretty sure I'd seen them fly before, they took part in the ceremony, Lily transforming into a gorgeous dragon as she took the stand.

My nerves hummed with energy, even though I knew Solstice and I would do just fine. That had been in a life or death scenario, though, and I had a penchant for falling on my face in front of large crowds.

A whisper of encouragement came from my dragon as I leaned against her for support.

Dean Brynhilde mounted her dragon, a beast I hadn't had the pleasure of seeing before. A gorgeous, ancient wyvern with strong tusks lowered his head as the dean surveyed the students.

"Mount!" she shouted, raising a fist into the air.

My stomach twisted, but I turned to Solstice and wrapped the strap around my forearm that hung from her saddle. Pulling myself over her side in one fluid motion, I perched onto the saddle and checked all the buckles like Jasmine had taught me. I found one on the wrong loop and I secured it in the correct place.

That done, I glanced at Killian, then resisted a grin as he awkwardly heaved himself onto Topaz. He caught my amusement when he seated himself upright. He winked at me and I blushed, looking away.

"Wyverns!" the Dean shouted. "Prepare for launch!" She spread her arms wide and her dragon fanned out his wings. All the wyverns followed suit, preparing for the First Flight.

Energy and excitement hummed in the air.

This was it.

Solstice stood slowly, doing her best not to jostle me. This time though, I was secure in the straps of the saddle.

Solstice mirrored my excitement back at me and knowing that she felt the same only amplified my emotions.

The dean clapped her hands. "Remember! We open

the portal to the Sky Realm only once a year. If you can make it into the portal, you have passed your initiation." She held up her hand, keeping it flat, then shot it down. "Go!"

Solstice launched from our tower, her wings snapping against the warm draft of ocean air as we surged upwards.

I forgot all of my training and clung to the straps for dear life, then Solstice's images filtered into my mind, assuring me of which direction she was going to take next.

We bobbed as she adjusted for my weight, and I glanced over to find Topaz had taken flight as well. Killian grinned as he crouched, an expression of sheer joy on his face.

My heart swelled three times its normal size to witness that.

The wind whipped against my face and the waves stretched out below me. Suddenly the world looked a whole lot bigger. I lifted my arms over my head, releasing a cry of joy. Solstice sped up as she fed off of my excitement.

The four of us flew through the sky, that moment one of utter perfection.

Electricity charged and snapped through the air as a portal opened, releasing strong winds from the Sky Realm. I had dreamed of visiting that place ever since I'd heard about it.

Dragons of all colors began flocking towards it,

taking their riders with them as they disappeared into the swirling vortex.

"Are you ready?" Killian shouted at me over the wind.

I didn't answer, I just sent him a wink and then nudged Solstice through our bond. My playful urgency tipped her off and she shot off like a rocket.

"Race you!" My voice trailed behind me in a half yell, half scream as Solstice reached new speeds.

We approached the cyclone and Solstice followed the curve of the wind for a moment, almost seeming to pause in mid-air. Then, she dove straight into the portal. The familiar weightless feeling of tunnel transit enveloped me and then there was only air.

I breathed in deeply, in awe at the freshness of it filling me. It was the purest air I had ever breathed and I couldn't get enough. It was thicker than I was used to, with an electric energy that made it feel slightly like my skin was tingling where the air touched it. I looked around me in wonder at a realm that literally only had an endless sky. There were clouds below us for as far as I could see, stretching out like a dream.

Beautiful.

Solstice moved from side to side, catching air currents moving at varying speeds. The currents let the wyvern glide without having to flap her wings. She could theoretically ride a current forever.

"Cheater!" Killian called as he and Topaz passed us on a particularly fast air current.

I nudged Solstice through our bond again and playfulness answered me. She angled herself towards the faster current and then we were rushing through the air again. She flapped her wings now too, riding the current but adding in her own power. We gained on Killian and Topaz quickly and I grinned in anticipation.

Solstice sent me a mischievous nudge through the bond, mixed with caution. She was going to do something and wanted me to hold on. An image of us plummeting wavered in my mind, and I immediately tightened my grip on the saddle's handles and gripped my knees tighter.

Satisfied that I was safe, she picked up her pace. Then she dove straight down, passing in and out of various currents. I held on for dear life, yelling my exuberance to the endless sea of clouds coming up to meet us. As suddenly as she dove, she was climbing again. I grinned as I caught on to her trajectory.

We gained altitude fast. I looked straight above me and smirked as I saw Topaz's belly. Solstice surged upward, flying vertically right in front of Topaz who released a startled cry.

My laughter rang out, mixing with Killian's shout of surprise. Solstice flipped upside down over Topaz and completed a full loop around him, ending back underneath him.

My stomach dropped at the split second I had been upside down, the exhilaration making me breathless.

Topaz suddenly jerked up, much like Solstice had

done, making a loop of his own and pulling up along-side the golden dragon.

It was a competition then. The wyverns challenged each other over new and difficult maneuvers. Killian and I were just along for the ride, and what a ride it was.

When the wyverns grew tired, we relaxed on the wind currents, getting low enough to run my hand through the clouds.

The air changed without warning, breaking the serene moment.

Stale metal tinged my tongue.

"Vivienne," Killian warned, and Solstice drifted to Topaz's side.

I shuddered as the familiar whoosh of a forming portal broke the air directly in front of us. Solstice tried to drop, but it was too late.

The currents pushed us into the tunnel, and we fell right into the trap.

CHAPTER 7

MALICE THIEVES

*M*y scream caught in my throat as we flew into the Malice Realm. Both Solstice and Topaz backpedaled, beating their wings rapidly in an effort to change direction. The air was a stark contrast to the purity of the Sky Realm and I sucked in a few breaths, adjusting to the change.

A pit formed in my stomach as I took in our surroundings. On the ground below us, a massive force of Dark Elves stared up at us.

They didn't try to throw their spears, because they didn't need to. All around us in the air hovered Wild Dragons of all shapes sizes and colors. I could feel the corruption in their magic, making me shudder.

The realization that we were trapped made my heart race. I reached for my daggers, only to remember that I hadn't brought them with me. This was supposed to be a fun trip to the Sky Realm. Not another ill-advised trip to a world of nightmares.

"Land now, or we will make you," a booming voice

from the ground called. A figure strode through the rows of Dark Elves, the soldiers parting like water for who appeared to be their leader.

I looked at Killian, not finding much comfort in his equally panicked gaze. One of the Wild Dragons let out a bone chilling roar when we made no move to follow the order. I flinched, and then nudged Solstice through our bond. I could feel her terror, but we had to stay calm.

As we descended, I strained to see the man in charge.

A tall male with dark skin and a crown of onyx awaited us. His black eyes followed my movements, his handsome face one of sharp angles and regal lines.

I'd never seen anyone so beautiful and terrifying in my life.

We landed in the circle formed by the legion of Dark Elves. I stayed on Solstice's back, so if we had a chance to escape, we could take it. Killian obviously had the same thought, as he didn't move to get down either. We both turned to face the being who had brought us here, and now held us hostage.

"You have taken something that belongs to me, younglings," he said with a dangerous smile. "I want it back." I suppressed a shudder at the death his voice promised if we didn't comply.

"If you're referring to the dragon egg, it was never yours," I stated, proud at how calm my voice had come out.

That was the only thing that seemed to be helping

my mother. She had been willing to give her life for me, and if I had to undo her destiny by sacrificing myself here and now, I'd do it in a heartbeat.

My heart twisted when I glanced at Killian who reached for his blade. Unlike me, he kept his sword on hand at all times.

The male grinned as he held up a hand, keeping the Dark Elves from advancing on Killian. "It seems you don't know who I am, or what I'm capable of. Perhaps a demonstration is in order."

The measured calm of his anger was somehow more terrifying than if he had lost his temper.

Shadows swirled all around them, forming fabricated dragons that roared and bled red eyes. I stared at the display with shock and fear.

"I am the Malice King," he said matter-of-factly. "Everything in this realm belongs to me. You found a dragon egg here that did not belong to you. In fact, it was placed at the crown of my castle." He rubbed his chin. "So, you're a thief. While I have a liking to thieves, it is not wise to steal from *me*."

"You don't understand," I said, my voice going shrill. "My mother's dying and that egg is the only thing helping her."

He gave me a flat stare. "This may surprise you, but I do not care, youngling. Return it, *now*," the last word was said on a growl.

"And if we don't?" Killian spoke, his voice as hard as steel as he challenged the ruler of Malice.

"I believe that's where I come in," the familiar sultry

voice came from behind us and I just barely held back my curses as I turned to confirm.

Zelda was here, walking towards us with the same confident sway as she had two years ago. My mind reeled as I tried to figure a way out of this mess. We were well and truly trapped and at the mercy of the Malice King and Zelda.

Zelda kept speaking, "You see, my queen is quite invested in that egg and others like it. We were working out a deal with the Malice King for a trade. I may have to resort to drastic measures if you don't give it back voluntarily."

Her voice made it no secret that she would prefer those 'drastic measures' over having to make a bargain with the Malice King.

"No," I snarled, my decision final. I would rather die than return an innocent soul to these creatures.

Zelda smiled, vicious in her beauty, and the Malice King raised a hand.

A signal.

One to attack.

The world around us blurred as Wild Dragons and Dark Elves alike moved in for the kill. We'd been trapped here not to bargain with, but to pick off. A force like this would be able to invade the Academy and a few less Dragonriders in the world would only make it easier for them.

There were other dragon eggs in protection at the sanctuary, and my heart twisted at the thought of these beasts getting their claws on them.

It was enough to awaken the goddess blood in my veins.

My birthmark burned as Solstice bumped closer to Killian, allowing me to touch him as a blast of power flowed out of us in a powerful shockwave. It slowed time, or at least everyone around us, and allowed me to shift into a battle-trance that bound me closer to Solstice.

Everything ran clear in this state. I saw the world through her eyes as we launched into the air. Topaz beating his wings, preparing to follow.

We couldn't stay and fight, but we could survive.

A sharp cry rang out from beside me, and pain flooded the bond between me and Killian before he shut me out. My eyes flew open and I struggled to keep hold of the magic swirling inside of me as I saw the sword impaling Killian's side. The Malice King pulled his sword out of my mate at reduced speed, and I was sure that if he hadn't been strapped in, Killian would have fallen off his wyvern.

Topaz shrieked and snapped at the Malice King, managing to launch before the Dark Elf got another strike in.

The others were bound by my magic, but in his home realm, he was too powerful. His body blurred, speeding up, then slowing down, fighting against the effects of my power.

Killian cried out and grabbed his wound, hissing from the pain as he clung to Topaz. "Go!" he shouted.

The sight of him hurt was all it took for me to

explode. Solstice added her power to mine and boosted the rush of magic that flooded through every being in sight. Golden and silver light burst out of us in a giant dome. The intertwined energies collided with the enemy and knocked them toward the horizon. Wild Dragons fell from the sky or were thrown through the air as Dark Elves incinerated on the spot.

This was the power of a dragon queen and a descendant of the goddess.

Unfortunately, it had taken Killian's sacrifice to unleash.

Determined to get Killian to safety, I kept a small part of my power within me, and when the enemy had been pushed back by the magic, I forced open a portal home right in front of us, ignoring any efforts to find the old veil I'd used previously to get back home.

Dizziness washed over me as the overextension of my power made me weak.

"Go Topaz!" I yelled. I had to make sure Killian got out of here before I could leave. My injured mate and his wyvern disappeared through the portal. Solstice wasted no time following them.

Relief rushed through me as we jumped out of the portal and landed in the sand in front of the Academy. I yanked the portal closed before anyone could follow us through.

My relief was short lived as the sounds of battle reached my ears. All around us, Dragonriders fought off the Wild Dragons.

They were here.

The Malice King had only been a distraction.

Fire rained down on the sand and bodies fell from the sky.

The egg.

They must be here for the egg.

Killian groaned from Topaz's back next to me. A diversion that got my mate gravely injured. Panic filled me as the image of Killian impaled on that Dark Elf's blade rushed through my mind. I just knew that was a picture I wasn't going to get out of mind anytime soon.

I was torn between going after the egg to ensure its safety, and that of my mother, and taking care of my mate. He needed to get to the healers in the infirmary.

"I love you, Vivi," he rasped out, breathing labored. I could tell what he was doing. He was saying goodbye.

"No. You aren't going anywhere. We are going to get you a healer," I told him. "Solstice, Topaz, to the infirmary. Fast!"

They didn't have to be told again, both of them feeling the same urgency that I did to save Killian. We weaved in and out of battle, doing our best not to engage. I was singularly focused on getting Killian the help he needed.

When we reached the campus Wild Dragons blocked out the sun, making me feel sick.

This was all my fault.

We were close to the infirmary but a massive dragon blocked our way. Pure, undiluted fear poisoned my mind. I froze, unable to move as black spots sprinkled across my vision.

Just as it advanced, I threw out my hand reflexively. The goddess blood in my veins still burned with activated power. I could feel the life force of every creature around me, even this beast. I grabbed at it, frantically tearing at the strands until the beast roared in pain, then collapsed and fell to the ground.

Nausea wound through my stomach and I coughed up dark sludge.

Corruption.

I couldn't force that trick again, not unless I wanted to become corrupted myself.

Topaz and Solstice didn't pause in their mad dash for the infirmary and I almost sobbed in relief as we landed in front of the building. Healers rushed onto the street, pulling Killian out of his saddle, being careful not to jostle his injury.

The healers grabbed at me, fussing at the dark sludge at my mouth. I batted them away, screaming for Killian.

"We'll take good care of him," a female assured me. "Now, we need to see to your affliction. Can you come with us?"

I blinked as I watched Killian being dragged inside.

He was going to be okay.

But my mother was still left unprotected.

My gaze shot toward the buildings as I searched out the right one. I couldn't stop now. Even though my vision wavered, I had to make sure the Wild Dragons didn't get to her.

If they were going for the egg, then they were going for my mother.

Solstice felt my thoughts and panic and took to the skies immediately, abandoning the healers below. She flew as fast as she could, dodging the claws and teeth and fire of the Wild Dragons that we passed on our way to the Central Hall.

My mind was a jumble of anxiety as Solstice landed in front of the tall building. I tugged and fumbled with the straps of my saddle now, uncoordinated in my haste to reach my mother and the egg.

I finally got free and slid down Solstice's side, hitting the ground at a run. I rushed through the double doors. Déjà vu hit me and I realized I was running down this same stretch of hallway for the second time.

For the same reason.

My mother was in danger.

Only, when I finally burst through the doorway to her room, I stopped in my tracks at the sight that awaited me. Disbelief filled me, and tears pricked my eyes.

The walls remained pristine white, untouched from the chaos outside and my mother stood in a silk dress. A magical wind wrapped around us, sending the fabric dancing around her legs and her wild red hair whipping around her face.

A sheen of power encased the room, familiar magic that matched my own.

Goddess magic.

"Mom?" my voice cracked with emotion as I took a step toward her.

"Vivienne," she replied with relief and sorrow.

She was alive.

I stared at her, unable to understand the transformation. It was as if someone had taken that sickly, dying creature and transformed her into the mother I remembered from my childhood.

Strong. Tall. Beautiful.

Except crystal tears streamed down her porcelain face as sorrow tinged the air.

"They took my egg," she lamented. "It... hurts."

I didn't understand at first, then I spotted the black streaks that clawed around the window.

"They took my dragon," she said, turning to gaze outside.

I ran to her and clung to her side. She was a Dragonrider now, reborn and rejuvenated.

I'd done it. I'd saved her, but now we had to save her dragon.

"We'll get her back," I vowed. "I promise."

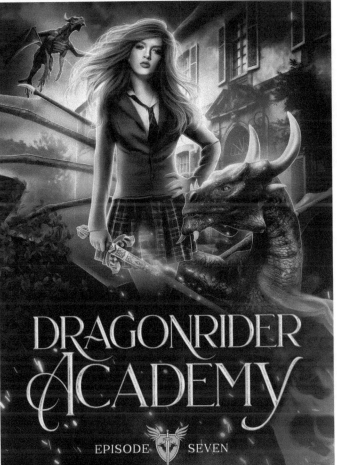

DRAGONRIDER ACADEMY

EPISODE SEVEN

USA TODAY BESTSELLING AUTHOR

A.J. FLOWERS

CHAPTER 1

STOLEN QUEEN

*M*y mother trembled as if in pain, but I couldn't find a mark on her.

Everything about her was transformed. She glowed with an inner light, radiant with youth and beauty I hadn't seen in her since I was a child. After my father had died, grief had aged her.

Now, her rejuvenation clashed with the panic in her bright eyes.

"My dragon," she said, her words pained as she slumped to the floor. Her renewed radiance clashed against her crestfallen expression. "They… took her."

My eyes grew wide. She was right. Her egg was nowhere to be seen, and somehow, my mother had bonded with it, meaning she was a Dragonrider now, just like me.

The thought of being ripped from Solstice made my heart twist. If my mother had truly bonded to the wyvern's soul inside that egg, then I would retrieve it for her, no matter what. I wouldn't wish that agony on anyone, especially my mother.

"Tell me exactly what happened," I said, keeping my words steady as I lowered to her level. "Every single detail that you can remember."

She studied me for a moment, then nodded. "It was… amazing." She smiled, her eyes lighting up. "Such warmth, love, and acceptance. I felt like I was being… reborn."

I knew that feeling all too well.

"Then they took her," her features falling. "They were masked. I couldn't see their faces. But they took the egg just after I bonded to her and this happened." She held out her hands, indicating her rejuvenated health.

I chewed my lower lip. "She must have been a queen, then."

My mother lowered her hands and nodded. "A Lost Queen, yes." She threaded her fingers through mine, her touch blessedly warm. "She's in danger, Vivi. I feel her fear." Tears crested over her cheeks. "I have to get her back."

I rubbed her arms, hating to see her in pain like this. "We'll get her back. I promise."

She shook her head. "Not *we*, sweet dear. *Me*. She's my responsibility, Vivi. I have to go. I won't put you in danger." She forced herself to stand, her legs shaking with the effort. While the dragon queen had rejuvenated her, the sudden separation could easily undo the good the dragon had bestowed.

"No," I said, forcing her to the bed. "I'm not a little child anymore. I can handle this, okay? Please, don't insult me by suggesting I can't."

She looked at me, really looked at me, as if she was seeing me for the first time. "My daughter's all grown up," she said, a weary smile on her face. "A savior to be heralded through the ages."

Her words held a tone of prophecy to them that sent a chill up my spine.

Settling her on the bed, I rushed to the window and peered out into the streets. The battle had retreated, leaving behind blood and the dark sludge of corruption.

If they'd gotten what they'd come for, then the egg was long gone, already sent back through the portal to the Malice Realm and their cruel king.

"No sign of them," I said, my fingers clenching. "It doesn't mean this is over."

I ordered my mother to rest, not that I expected her to listen to me, and then I rushed out of the room.

CHAPTER 2

MATURE DECISIONS

*A*fter a raging battle, the eerie silence on campus made me uneasy as Solstice shadowed me from overhead. I ran through the courtyard outside Central Hall, sifting through warriors and Valkyries cleaning up the carnage.

Injured were rushed to the infirmary while the rest tended to their dragons and a few of the younger students mopped up the black sludge before it soaked into the ground. It would leech what was left of the Academy's magic if left unattended.

I searched the crowd for a familiar face, needing someone to help me formulate a plan. Even Dean would have to understand the gravity of this situation. Where was she? I needed her.

Because I'd already charged into the Malice Realm once, and I'd been dragged in unwillingly a second time. Whatever waited for me on the other side wouldn't be good. I didn't have the element of surprise on my side and if I was going to retrieve my mother's dragon, then I needed help.

A lot of it.

That's when I spotted Killian in the crowd.

I ran to him and growled. "What are you doing up? You were *stabbed,* or did you forget?"

He shrugged, then winced. "I'm fine. Healers have magic, you know? I'm good."

While I didn't believe him, I knew there was a difference between being healed and being one hundred percent. "You're not okay," I observed when he held his arm to his chest. "But luckily for you I need your help right now."

I explained everything I knew, that this had all been a massive diversion to retrieve my mother's egg, one that had miraculously healed her and bonded to her.

A Lost Queen.

Killian's eyes went wide. "Let me get this straight. The egg we found is a queen and it bonded to your mother. It's now presumably in the hands of the Avalon Queen, then?"

I shook my head. "Wouldn't it be returned to the Malice Kingdom?"

He shook his head. "No. The Wild Dragon Queen wouldn't let a rare egg like that go without a fight. It's going to be with her. The Malice King would be open to a deal... she has corruption, he has an egg. A trade makes sense."

Cursing, I swiped my hands through my hair. The

Malice Realm was bad enough. We weren't ready for Avalon. "What are we going to do?"

He slipped his fingers through mine, giving me a squeeze. "We're going to get it back."

Chewing my lip, I pondered how we were going to get to Avalon and steal the egg. "Do you know where the Dean is? I hate to say it, but we need her guidance."

And the Academy's resources.

"Hmm," Killian agreed, gazing toward the edge of campus. "She'd be on the frontlines, chasing our enemies back into the sea." He pressed his hand to the small of my back. "Come on."

Solstice and Topaz roamed the skies, keeping a lookout for any threat while we ventured out into the open. We found the Dean near the beach speaking with several of the professors and leaders of the Academy, beautiful on their prized dragons. They all nodded at something she said as they broke apart, fanning out in a beautiful display of colorful scales echoed by their wyverns' roars.

The Dean turned to us, nodding at our arrival.

"You should be resting," she chided at Killian.

I nudged him in the ribs, making him grunt in pain. "See!"

He waved me away, resting his hand on the hilt of his sword. "The healers fixed me up, Dean. I'm fine. Really."

She frowned, glancing down at the stolen blade. She'd never demanded its return, which meant she believed Killian needed the magical sword more than she did.

She could easily change her mind.

Her gaze flashed up to meet his. "You should rest after a healing to make sure it takes hold." She tilted her head. "May I assume there's a pressing reason you aren't? The battle is over, for now. Whatever they came here for, it wasn't to take control of the Academy."

"It was to take something else," I confirmed.

I explained everything about my mother and the Lost Queen, their plan to divert our attention and steal it back from us during the attack.

She carefully considered my words, then nodded. "She only has one of the Lost Queens. We have time before this escalates to the next stage."

I raised an eyebrow. "How many are there?"

The Dean glanced at the skies, dark magic glimmering from the remnants of so much corruption. "Only another queen can answer that question."

Solstice keened from the skies, reminding me that she was a queen, but she was also young. We had found one because the egg had called to us—to my mother. It would take time to find the others.

The Dean hummed in thought. "If this is the first Lost Queen she's recovered, and it was only because of you, that means we have time and we shouldn't take the bait."

"Take the bait?" I asked.

Killian caught onto what the Dean was saying. "She wants you to go to Avalon before you've finished your training as a Dragonrider. She waited, left you alone until you retrieved exactly what she was after."

I glowered. "So all this time... the Avalon Queen was waiting for me to find this egg."

The Dean nodded. "That's precisely what that means. And we're not ready to face her now. *You're* not ready, Vivienne."

I shared a glance with Killian as his jaw went hard. This wasn't the answer I had been hoping for. "What do you propose, then?"

"You complete this semester as planned," she said, her words sure. "Nothing has changed. We still plan to face the Dragon Queen, but only when we're ready and at our strongest."

"The graduation project will show we're ready?" Killian guessed.

It wasn't just about us. It was about all of the students at the Academy.

Something about that felt wrong. This felt like my fight.

"The graduation project is vital to the Academy's magical stores and our survival," she continued, "and only then will we be able to withstand another full-fledged attack."

I drew in a long breath. "So, I'm just supposed to go about my day while my mother withers into nothing again?"

"That will take time, time that you need to prepare," the Dean insisted. "Don't doubt the power of a Lost Queen. If she bonded to your mother, then that magic will be lasting as long as the Lost Queen lives."

"The Avalon Queen wants an army," Killian pointed out, glancing at me. "So she'll want the Lost Queens alive. She'll want their power on her side."

"I don't know if I can wait," I said honestly.

She held up a finger. "A compromise, then. Your graduation project will be to retrieve that egg—when you are ready." She swiveled her finger to Killian. "The both of you, but you must be prepared, and you must do this one by the books. Until graduation, neither of you are to engage the Avalon Queen under any circumstance outside of this campus. Am I understood?"

I clenched my fist.

Killian offered a short nod.

It felt like a betrayal against my mother not to leave this second, but I couldn't ignore the fear in the Dean's eyes.

Nothing frightened her.

Which meant she wanted us to do this the right way. If we failed by rushing, then it wasn't just my mother who would suffer the price. All of the realms would be in danger and the Avalon Queen would win.

It was why I had remained in my classes these past handful of years. I'd learned so much, grown with Solstice, Topaz, and Killian and become stronger than ever.

"Okay," I said, dipping my chin. "We'll do this your way, Dean."

I didn't envy the responsibility that weighed on her

shoulders. This was her call. If she was wrong, she would have to deal with the guilt of the aftermath.

It was why she was the Dean and why I was a student. It made me grateful for her.

"Get cleaned up," she said, rolling her shoulders back. "Rest. Recuperate. Attend the last few weeks of classes while we make a plan, together." She leaned in, giving me a faint smile, which from Dean Brynhilde was the equivalent of a bear hug. "This will be the mission of our lifetime. And from an immortal's perspective, that's saying a lot. Let's be smart." She squeezed my arm and then glanced at Killian. "I have faith in the two of you to see us through these dark days."

Killian bowed his head. "Thank you, Dean." He wove his arm through mine, pulling me away with a sympathetic look. I knew he didn't want to wait for the last few weeks of classes to face our enemies, but we needed a level head to do this right.

If he believed that going right now would be the right thing to do, he would defy the Dean, as would I, but we'd both matured during my time at the Academy.

Sighing, I turned back to the campus with a new thought in mind.

I had some studying to do, it seemed.

CHAPTER 3

JOUSTING

*L*uckily, studying wasn't just sitting down with a book.

Now that I was a fully-fledged dragonrider, it meant it was time to *fly*.

Holding tight to Solstice, I couldn't help but grin as we dove through the skies. My stomach flipped as the wind whipped against my face.

She threw her wings wide a second after feeding me the image. The move kept perfect synchronization with the rest of the formation, evening out her flight before she tucked her wings again and turned in a barrel roll that sent me squealing with delight. If I didn't have her warning in my mind, it would have been terrifying, but we were one entity in the skies.

Gratification filled our bond as the squad finally completed a series of maneuvers without a single mistake. We'd worked so hard for this moment, to practice in battle flight class for ultimate teamwork when we faced the real thing.

"Great job Squad D! Wonderful control!" the professor called from his hovering dragon. "Okay, everyone. Land and we'll start our next session. You've proved you're ready for it."

Squeals went up throughout the riders, excitement that we were one step closer to graduation.

And winning against the Avalon Queen.

All four squads landed together, nearly as one, like we had been taught.

I searched for Killian, sad that he was in another Squad, but frowned when I couldn't spot him in the mass of bodies and glittering scales.

Where did he go…?

The professor whistled, grabbing our attention as Jasmine and Vern landed beside him, the ground quaking under the full-grown wyverns' weight.

"All right, Riders, we're going to be practicing airborne lance training." He gestured towards a large pile of pointed sticks with handles at the end. "Each one of you will have a lance and we will spar one on one after Jasmine and Vern have demonstrated the basics for you. Graduated veterans, here, so pay attention."

Without any preamble, Jasmine and Vern dismounted and grabbed a practice lance before strapping back into their saddles. Jasmine threw me a confident grin before Jade shot into the sky, doing a flamboyant flip. After earning a few squeals from the squads, she settled into a hover a good distance across from Vern.

Show off, I thought.

The professor cleared his throat. "Proper lancing rules state you must have one hand positioned on the lance and one holding the front of your saddle." He continued with the technical rules for lancing while Jasmine and Vern demonstrated.

It reminded me of an airplane attendant showing everyone how to put the oxygen masks over their heads in the event of an emergency. It didn't seem hard to hold a lance, but Jas loved any chance to demonstrate how awesome she was. She held hers up proudly, running her lower hand underneath it as if it was a prize to be won.

Then, she anchored himself in the saddle that wrapped around Jade's middle and strong chest. She sprang when the professor shouted, "Go!"

Jasmine and Vern leaned into their dragons' necks to mitigate some of the wind resistance. They both held the lance straight out and slightly pointed toward the other armored chest. I tensed as they rapidly closed the gap.

At the last second, Jasmine and Jade jolted on a burst of speed and Jasmine braced herself as her lance made contact with her mate. Vern jerked back, caught only by the strap of his saddle as he gasped for air, clearly winded from the blunt force trauma of the practice lance that gave way under impact, but not entirely. The dragons wheeled past each other, everything going down in a fraction of a second.

The Squads cheered as Jas and Vern circled around

and landed in front of us once more, both grinning. Jasmine glowed with victory and Vern looked like he already wanted a rematch.

They were cute together, though. I had to admit.

"You've seen the basics now," the professor said. Grab a lance and a partner and let's spar." He clapped his hands and gestured toward the pile of lances.

I looked for Killian, even though he was part of another Squad. Before I could find my mate, a lance was thrown into my arms.

"Let's go, little goddess descendant. I want to see what you got," Jasmine said before turning on her heel and heading for her dragon, a replacement lance in her hand.

"Oh no no no," I called after her. "There's no way—"

She interrupted me with a wink. "I'll go easy on you."

I rolled my eyes in exasperation and finally found Killian across the field. He just grinned at me, sending his amusement through our bond.

The jerk had been hiding from me on purpose.

As my mate, he would go easy on me. That's likely why Jasmine had won against Vern. It was in our mates' natures to keep us safe.

Jasmine matched against me, though? Yeah. She wasn't going to hold back.

I made a face at him as I turned and scrambled into my saddle in resignation of my impending death by practice lance.

Solstice launched us into the sky and we took our

position. All around us, my classmates began rushing each other, clumsily angling their lances.

I found it surprisingly difficult to hold the lengthy weapon straight as Jasmine had. I tried to recall how she'd positioned her body. Leaning back, I anchored myself with my legs, holding the lance upright using my core instead of my arms.

Better, I decided.

Just when I was getting the hang of it, the professor whistled and Solstice launched herself without warning.

"Solstice!" I screamed. We needed to work as a team. When she provided me an image of what she was going to do in my head, that gave us an edge.

When she reacted on instinct, that's when we would fail.

In a panic as Jasmine's lance rushed toward my chest, I twisted, dropping my weapon as I avoided being slammed with the blunt end of the stick.

"Well, I didn't expect you to duck like a coward, little goddess!" Jasmine shouted from Jade's back, grinning widely at me. "And now you've lost your weapon. What'll you do?"

Glaring at her, I provided Solstice an image of a drop-dive. She obeyed in an instant, flattening her wings to the side of her body as we plummeted. She pulled them out at the last minute, sending us into a glide as I unhooked my belt—a move that made Killian's panic flare in our bond—as I leaned over and grabbed my lance from the ground.

Popping up again, I fastened myself with one hand, awkwardly holding the lance upright as Solstice repositioned us for the next round.

She whistled. "Now that's my kind of move."

The professor whistled and we rushed for each other again. This time I managed to hold the lance up as Solstice fed me last minute information, dipping down, allowing me to clip her shoulder.

Her lance slammed into the center of my chest at the same time, her angle deceptively on target. She'd taken the glancing blow on purpose just to throw me off.

I was thrown from my seat, the strap catching me with a tug.

Good thing I secured that again...

The air burst from my lungs as the practice lance buckled, giving way before it crushed me.

"Cheeky," I growled.

Jasmine gave me a smirk. "Try watching my lance next time. Again."

We continued like that for the rest of the exercise until sweat ran down my hairline, Jasmine giving me pointers and helping me refine my technique over the course of those two hours. By the end of class, I had finally managed to hit the center of her chest at least once. It was progress.

My arms and legs felt like jelly after the professor dismissed us. I dropped the lance to the ground, massaging my aching arm with a groan.

"Hey, Vivi." Jasmine strolled up to me looking as

though she had just been on a nice walk through a garden instead of jousting for hours. "You impressed me today. We're testing for new Valkyrie members. I think you'd be a perfect candidate to apply."

My eyes widened and excitement rushed through me. Me? A Valkyrie...

The image of them in battle flitted over my eyes, Valkyries flipping around their dragons like acrobats as they wielded their swords with masterful precision.

I wanted to be like that. Strong. Powerful. Feared.

If I could harness half of the ferocity of the Valkyrie, I might actually stand a chance against the Wild Dragons and the Avalon Queen.

"When's the test?" I asked.

"End of next week. You have some time." She offered me a reassuring smile.

I grimaced. It would take more time than that to prepare. A couple of hours jousting nearly put me out. No telling what kind of physical endurance I'd need to pass the Valkyries' test.

Killian caught my gaze from across the training yard, giving me a wink.

He'd probably known about this all along. That's why he'd forced me to joust with Jasmine to earn my invitation.

If Killian believed in me... then I knew I could do anything.

"I would be honored to be a Valkyrie," I told her with a grin. She returned my smile with one of her own and then she launched into an explanation of the test and requirements. She told me she would practice with me after my classes until the test.

"Thank you for your help, Jasmine. I really appreciate it," I said as gratitude filled my voice.

"No need to thank me. I just think that you're really the best candidate." She patted the rip on her uniform. "You actually hit me. Vern can't say the same."

Her mate, now talking with Killian, paused to give her a knowing smile.

One full of pride. Maybe I'd underestimated their relationship. He would never hold back with Jasmine, just like Killian would never hold back with me. Because if they didn't push us, we wouldn't be ready when our real challenge came.

I understood that now.

"See you there," she said with a wink and sauntered off, looping her arm through Vern's as they ventured onto their next class they'd assist as graduates. Their dragons soared the skies in a zig-zag pattern, glittering with a mixture of emerald and midnight tones, Vern's dragon a unique shade of black diamond.

"What was all that about?" Killian asked, he and Topaz walking over to us. Topaz and Solstice immediately began play fighting, rolling around on the ground, each trying to pin the other.

"Jasmine just invited me to apply for the Valkyries," I told him, excitement making my smile wider than usual.

"Seriously? That's amazing! I'm so proud of you!" He wanted to pretend as if he had nothing to do with this, and I let him have his moment. His grin made me feel like nothing else mattered. His pride shot through our bond, making me blush.

"Now I just have to pass the test," I countered, "while simultaneously planning a stealth mission into the enemy territory."

"You've got this." He pressed his hand to the small of my back as we took the long route to our next class.

Warmth filled me at his belief in me and I nodded.

I can do this.

CHAPTER 4

VALKYRIE TEST

*N*erves filled me as I stretched out my muscles in preparation for the test. The last week and a half had flown by in a blur of training for my test and planning. Though, admittedly, Killian had picked up a lot of my slack when it came to planning our little excursion.

While I had been doing push-ups, running like a crazy person back and forth on the beach, and practicing how many squats I could do before I passed out, Killian sat with my mother.

She was so proud of me. Patient, too. While she desperately wanted her dragon returned, she told us that she was safe, for now.

The Avalon Queen hadn't started corrupting the egg, not yet, which meant she wanted something before things became too serious. Perhaps she wanted all the Lost Queens in one place, or she needed my mother to crack the egg's shell and begin the hatching process, which meant, another attack would be coming if we sat around for too long.

For now, it was okay to focus on the task at hand. And sometimes, it was okay to relax, too.

Like I was doing right now with Lily on the training field before the hardest endurance test of my life began.

Lily stretched, reaching her hands up to the sky, then bending down, her body contorting in a distinctly reptilian way that made me jealous I wasn't as flexible.

"Are you anxious?" she asked, curling her fingers over her toes in an impressive stretch as she kept her knees locked.

"Yeah, a little. It is the Valkyries, after all. They're hardcore," I said with a laugh.

She nodded at that. "That's true. I have to admit that my stomach is doing cartwheels right now."

"You aren't alone," I assured her with a grin.

It was pretty cool that Lily had been invited to join, too. It would definitely be the first time that Valkyries accepted a dragon.

Or someone like me.

"Did you hear about their new diversity program?" Lily asked with a knowing grin. "They're trying to expand their supernatural acceptances from just angel hybrids and vikings."

I frowned. "Like... inviting a dragon shifter and a seer?"

She chuckled. "Something like that."

Great. I was just a box to be checked.

Feeling a little less secure of myself, I gazed around the isolated training field, noting roughly thirty students and their dragons ready to be tested.

Surrounding us waited armored Valkyries ready to judge if we would pass or fail.

One of the Valkyries broke from the group and looked as though she was about to say something when the familiar pressure drop of a portal opening interrupted her.

The rift ripped through the sky and the air whooshed in a vortex as a level seven tunnel opened.

"Is this the test?" I hissed at Lily.

She swallowed. "Seems so."

I gaped in shock as Wild Dragons poured from it, polluting the air with their corruption. Darkness covered the sky with a quickness that raised goosebumps on my arms.

The Valkyries didn't seem surprised at the tunnel's emergence. Normally, a tunnel of this magnitude would be all hands on deck, ordered by the Dean.

Which meant, the Dean had known about this and done this on purpose. The Wild Dragons were making their move, going after my mother. If we didn't stop them, there would be dire consequences to pay.

One heck of a test.

I ran for Solstice, jumping onto her back and strapping myself into the saddle in practiced movements. Suddenly I was grateful for all the boring drills the flight professor had made us do. Mounting and dismounting over and over had seemed like a waste of time, but the muscle memory was paying off in the heat of the battle.

Pulling out my sword, Solstice bunched her muscles, ready to launch when a battle cry caught my attention.

Lily ran, her body crystalizing with shimmering scales as she pushed off the ground, massive wings sprouting from her back until she changed into a beautiful dragon. While mesmerizing, we needed to keep a formation if we were going to fend off this surprise attack.

The Valkyries rallied behind Lily's call, letting us take the lead as I joined them with Solstice roaring into the skies.

And then Lily did something I didn't even know was possible in dragon form.

She spoke to them.

Her words rang out through the clouds, filtering into our minds.

Don't do this! She begged. *This isn't your fight. We can help you!*

Everything seemed to stop as if the Wild Dragons considered her request.

Then, with the roar of a single malevolent wyvern, they showed their teeth.

No! Lily's roar was deafening as she blocked their path to us.

I felt her pain, her grief, and her desire to save these dragons. Not harm them.

Closing my eyes, I locked myself onto Solstice, clenching my legs, and focused. That warm power inside of me had a use, a purpose, one that if perhaps channeled correctly, could do the impossible.

I reached out to Lily, providing her the power inside of myself as she drew in a deep breath and released fire.

Instead of flame, something new happened, something that kept all the Valkyries in place, locked in a state of surprise.

An opalescent stream released from Lily's maw, a mesmerizing flame of pure energy that swept across the Wild Dragon forces. They tried to wheel away, but the momentum of their flight pushed them all directly into her flames.

And then they changed.

As they passed through the flame, I was shocked to see they didn't burn up. They weren't injured by the flame. As the first dragon passed through the swirling colors, it was as if the black leached from its scales. The sludge was burned into vapor by the opalescent fire and the wyvern came out of the other side looking like a completely different dragon. Their scales were shinier, their flight steadier, and the menacing air that had always been a key distinction between the corrupted and the pure was gone.

Everyone around me cried out in a range of

shocked emotions. Even the Valkyrie leaders seemed to be at a loss as to what was happening.

The rest of the Wild Dragons all passed through Lily's miraculous flame in much the same way as the first. As they passed through, they all seemed to lose all aggression or urge to attack. So much so, that the Valkyries signaled us to land.

As we all touched down, the Wild Dragons landed with us in their own clump. One by one, to our astonishment, they all transformed into shaking, naked humans. They all huddled together, clearly unsure of their safety.

The Valkyries dismounted from their dragons and stepped toward the clump of naked humans, swords drawn in caution.

We couldn't be sure this wasn't a trick.

As they moved forward, Lily landed in front of them, still in her dragon form. She blocked their path and assumed a protective stance.

"What are you doing, trainee?" one of the Valkyries asked. "What exactly is happening here? This was supposed to be a test. Not a... conversion."

I have cleansed them from their corruption, she growled, her voice ringing in our minds. *They are of no threat to you now. Please, don't attack them.*

"What do you mean you've cleaned them? How is that possible?" another Valkyrie asked, her voice full of confusion.

Lily's dragon's gaze found mine, as if grateful for what I had helped her accomplish. *The corruption is a result of them giving up their emotion and capacity for empathy in exchange for power. The dragon shifters have been taken advantage of by the Avalon Queen. She convinced them all to give up their love and hope and compassion in exchange for more power. They've been manipulated. All I did was offer up some of my own love and empathy. Corruption can't exist where love does, so it cleansed their souls.*

The Valkyries nodded and looked at each other, seeming to share a conversation all their own with only a few glances.

"Very well, we need to get them to the infirmary. We'll see what the Dean has to say about this," one of them said, eyeing the clearly underfed group of dragon shifters.

With that, a runner was sent for med teams and the field soon swarmed with people all moving to their own orders.

"Okay candidates, these... people, are going to need lifts to the infirmary once the med teams have cleared them to be transported. Each of you will take someone with you back to campus," the Valkyrie leader said. Then she dismissed us and we lined up to wait for the med teams.

Taking a female by the hand, I smiled at her, encouraging her to hold onto Solstice as we mounted. She held on tight, her eyes wide, barely even breathing until Solstice and I landed in front of the infirmary.

It was almost as if she was a clean slate with no memory of who or what she was.

Dismounting, I turned back to help the weak female from my wyvern, catching her by her thin arm as she stumbled down. Two healers came and helped her onto one of the rolling beds before taking her into the infirmary. I was grateful I wasn't the one who had to explain this to the Dean.

Lily landed next to me, letting two of the newly cleansed shifters off her back before she transformed back into her human form, though the transition looked significantly less smooth this time. She fell to one knee as soon as she was fully human, her face haggard. Dark circles sank underneath her eyes and her form had thinned as if she'd lost weight.

"Are you okay, Lily?" I asked her, concern for my friend making my stomach clench.

"Yes, I'll be fine. I just expended a lot of energy to do that and I will need a while to recuperate," her voice was oddly void of emotion. Almost drained. The knot of worry in my stomach twisted further. "Thank you, for whatever you did for me back there."

I chewed my lip. "You're welcome. But… maybe you should let one of the healers check you over? Just to be sure."

"Sure," she replied flatly, her eyes empty as they stared back at me. She was like a brick wall, her exhaustion the only thing evident on her face.

She had said that corruption devoured emotion.

What emotion had she fed on to cleanse this group of Wild Dragons?

"That was amazing by the way. Like wow…" I told

her, admiration filling my voice, hoping some positivity might lighten the mood.

"It was a last resort..." Lily told me. "It has consequences."

I opened my mouth to ask her what she meant, only to be interrupted by James calling her name.

"What were you thinking!" he raged, making me frown. "You know what this takes out of you. You know the risks!" He threw his hands in the air emphatically as he spoke, clearly worked up by whatever risk Lily had taken to cleanse the corrupted souls of the Wild Dragons. He demanded, "You have to promise me you won't do it again. It's not worth it. Promise me Lily."

She stared at him for a moment before she shook her head and simply said, "I can't promise that. Not if they can be saved."

He paused in disbelief like he hadn't expected her to put up a resistance to his demand. "What do you mean you can't promise that? Yes, you can. You can't save everyone, Lily; it just isn't possible. You have a lot of love to give, but even your big beautiful heart can't fill this corrupted world with the amount of love it needs. You'll run out before you've barely even started."

She winced, tears springing to her eyes. I was almost relieved to see some sort of emotion from her. "I have to do something, James. I can't destroy them all like the Dean plans. I have to... that's why I applied for the Valkyries... There has to be another way!"

His voice softened and he wrapped his arms around

her. She fell into a fit of sobs, her body shaking as he held her tight. I hugged myself, tears rolling down my cheeks.

James sighed. "We'll get through this. I promise."

Killian rushed toward me then, panic on his face. He reached me and seemed to scan every inch of me looking for whatever injury he was expecting. Wiping away the tears, he pulled me towards him and captured my lips in a searing kiss.

I lost all sense of time and space as my world shrunk to include only Killian and I. My brain could only process the sensation of tingles racing down my spine as Killian wrapped his arms around my waist and dragged my body closer to his.

He pulled away, resting his forehead on mine to catch his breath.

"Don't ever do that to me again," he told me, breathless.

I grinned up at him. "I'm okay. It was hardly a battle, actually. Thanks to Lily we... saved them." I gestured around to all the blanket covered people around us on gurneys, people who had once been our enemies.

"Yeah, who are all these people?" he asked, confusion written all over his face as he studied the group filtering into the infirmary.

"They're Wild Dragons," I said mischievously. He narrowed his eyes at me and gave me an exasperated stare, knowing I was dragging out the information just to frustrate him.

As I was about to explain what had happened, a sharp command rang out over the campus. *"Vivienne, Killian, Lily, James, my office. Now."*

The Dean wanted a meeting, and she didn't sound pleased.

CHAPTER 5

STALL DUTY

The Dean stared us down, unimpressed as she narrowed her gaze on Lily. "You could have corrupted yourself, Lily. We've discussed this growing ability of yours." She tilted her head, glancing at me. "I'm going to guess how you gathered the energy to cleanse so many at once came with a little... help."

Lily huddled in the office chair staring emotionlessly at the Dean. James sat beside her, his expression sharing the Dean's concern.

"She was just trying to save—" I cut into the Dean's tirade.

Her sharp gaze silenced me before she continued on. "Neither of you can risk yourselves like that. You, Lily, are a Dragon Queen. And you, Vivienne, are a powerful Dragonrider. You are both too valuable to lose." She shoved a map of the realms at Lily. "You could serve us better using that power to find the Lost Queens. Those are innocents yet untouched by corruption worthy to be saved."

Lily shoved the map back at her. "What value do I have, if I can't help my people?" Lily asked, her voice finally regaining a little of her usual fire. "And I've already tried. The Lost Queens are *lost* for a reason."

The sting of her words wasn't lost on me. She viewed herself as a dragon first, and a member of Dragonrider Academy second.

The Dean straightened. "We will help your people by being smart and not taking any unnecessary risks. Such as risking the corruption of one of the only safe Dragon Queens," the Dean said, pointedly staring at her. "This was not the goal of facing the Wild Dragons I had in mind for your Valkyrie test. The goal was to hold them off and make them retreat back to their home realm until we are truly prepared for the final battle."

I furrowed my eyebrows at that. "Why wouldn't we save them if we can? They are obviously people too. I don't want to hurt anyone if I don't have to."

Dean Brynhilde met my gaze, her face full of disappointment. She shook her head at me. "I thought you were ready to go to Avalon and retrieve your artifact. I can see now, you are not. Naïveté will get you killed. War is no time for sentimentality." She leaned in, steepling her fingers. "We have a duty to protect the people counting on us, that means pushing back the Wild Dragons when they attack. Not risking everything to save a few who were already lost." She leaned back in her chair and sighed. "We won't know if they can even survive having the corruption purged from them like this. The healers have told me that their minds are weak and they have no memories to assist us either."

"But they're alive," Lily whispered.

I stared off with the Dean, not liking her view on this. I knew she was afraid, but if there was another opportunity to change the tide of war, then I would take it.

She spread her fingers out on her papers. "You both have stall duty for the rest of the semester. Maybe that will make you think twice before you let your feelings cloud your judgement again." As my mouth hung open, she directed her attention to Lily. "Lily, you are to stay in your bed for the next week. No arguments. We will be watching you closely for any signs of corruption. Let's hope we don't find any." She gave us all a short nod. "You're all dismissed."

I wanted to protest. How was it fair for me to be punished just for wanting to save as many people as I could instead of killing people who had obviously been tricked into giving up their souls? And Lily was a hero! She had saved those people. What was the Dean going to do if she did exhibit signs of corruption?

Killian seemed to sense that I was going to argue because he pulled me out of my chair and out of the door before I could say anything.

Well, seemed like I was going to be knee deep in dragon droppings for the rest of the semester then.

Fabulous.

CHAPTER 6

NO RULES

*M*y shoulders ached as I shoveled the bedding material into the clean stall. I had been cleaning the dragon stalls for the better part of two hours and my arms and back were throbbing from the strain of shoveling and scrubbing.

At least it made good practice to live up to my status as Valkyrie, assuming I was approved.

"Hey there, little goddess. Having fun in the dung?" Jasmine asked from behind me, amusement coating her tone.

Oh great, she was probably there to gloat about my punishment and fall from favor with the Dean.

I rolled my eyes and turned to her, leaned on my shovel and quipped dryly, "Oh it's a blast. You should try it sometime."

She threw her head back laughing. "Oh I've had my fair share of stall duty."

Killian came around the corner then, a bag hanging from his shoulder. He was fully outfitted in his flight armor and had a second pile of armor that had Valkyrie colors on it.

"You ready to go?" he grinned at me with a sense of mischief. "Or are you going to shovel crap all day?"

"Go where?" I asked him. I wasn't nearly done with stall duty for the night.

"To Avalon, of course. Where else?" Jasmine whispered, leaning in as she did. "As a Valkyrie," she added.

My eyes widened in shock and I gaped at Killian. "Wait, so. I passed?"

Jasmine laughed. "Of course you passed! You and Lily single-handedly wiped out an entire hoard of Wild Dragons without spilling any blood. That was incredible and even if the Dean is ticked off about it, the Valkyries unanimously approved your application. Lily's too."

My heart swelled at that.

"Did she approve a trip to Avalon, too?" I asked, raising an eyebrow.

Killian shrugged. "She approved a flight. We didn't specify *where*."

Both my eyebrows shot up this time.

This was so out of character for him. He generally wanted to do what we were supposed to. Follow the rules and do whatever possible to keep me and our wyverns safe.

And yet, perhaps following the rules wasn't going to work for us anymore, not now that we knew there was another way.

"Are you serious?" I asked, incredulous.

Killian straightened. "Listen. When those Wild Dragons never return to Avalon, what do you think is going to happen next? This *is* serious, Vivi."

I swallowed the lump in my throat. "She'll up the timetable if she thinks we're gaining the upper hand."

Jasmine nodded. "Which is why we can't play it safe anymore." She smiled. "You're ready for this, Vivienne. I know it. We don't have to take down all of Avalon. All we have to do is retrieve your mother's egg."

That sounded doable... right?

I held Killian's gaze for a moment, then glanced at Jasmine. She was staring at me with determination, a proud glint in her eye and a stubborn tilt to her chin. Killian looked just as defiant.

My smile grew slowly until it overtook my face.

"Tell me your plan."

It was time to ignore the rules and take matters into our own hands.

CHAPTER 7

TO AVALON

"We sneak out. That's your plan?" I asked them. I'd really been hoping for something more spectacular. "We can't exactly open a portal to Avalon right in the middle of campus. Everyone is on high alert," I said, pointing out the flaws in their plan as I put away the last of the tools I had used to clean up the dragon stalls. "Especially Dean Brynhilde. You know? The exact person who forbade the mission?"

"We have dragons, Vivi. Why do you act like we're tied to this campus and tiny stretch of beach?" Jasmine asked, giving me a sardonic smile to go with her dry tone.

Killian gave Jasmine a pointed disapproving look and then turned to me, explaining in a patient voice, "We're just going to have the wyverns take us to one of the farther training fields. We abandoned them once the attacks were too bad, but they're still out there. You can open the portal from there."

I hummed in thought. "Okay. But is it just us? That's not much of a squad. We were trained in units of four. What about Vern? Or Lily and James?"

Jasmine sighed. "My mate has no idea I'm joining you guys, and if you know what's good for you, you'll keep it that way until we've returned victorious."

I chewed my lower lip and nodded, not wanting to get on Jasmine's bad side. I'd gotten myself into trouble without Killian for the same reason, although I often regretted it. Her relationship with Vern was still relatively new, as was mine with Killian. I hoped we'd all progress and grow to a place where we were beyond secrets.

"Lily and James wanted to come," she added, seeming eager to get off the topic of her mate, "but Lily is still too weak from the cleansing. Instead, they're going to do their best to make sure that Dean Brynhilde is distracted long enough for us to make our getaway."

Killian winked at me. "Get dressed."

He tossed me the armor and riding gear. I grunted at the unexpected weight of it.

"All right. I'll be just a second," I told them then held up one finger in the universal signal for 'hold on' and darted into one of the empty stalls I had just finished cleaning.

I pulled the armor on over the riding gear and strapped my dagger and short sword to my belt. I took a moment to gather myself as I pulled my long hair into a single braid down my back.

I wished I had a mirror as I smoothed my fingers over the impressive armor.

A Valkyrie. Me.

We were about to head into the heart of enemy territory. Not only that, but we had no backup. This was officially an *off the books* mission. If we failed, we would die in Avalon, or live to be expelled from the Academy forever. If we succeeded, maybe we could justify defying the Dean.

We *would* succeed. I would make sure of it.

I stepped out of the stall and gave each of my co-conspirators a confident smirk, meeting each of their gazes directly.

"Call the dragons. It's time to go."

WE DUCKED LOW ON OUR DRAGONS' backs as they sped through the air, flying as close to the ground as they could to avoid any unnecessary attention. We had made it all the way out to the furthest training field.

How did I never know about this place? I wondered. Killian had taken me to other realms on adventures and romantic dates, but he's never really taken me to explore the Academy. Probably because the Dean was so tight about security, there was no reason for us to come out here.

Unless we were up to no good.

I hoped she couldn't somehow spot us. I peered over my shoulder, finding the Academy just a tiny dot on the horizon. As long as I kept the portal to a reasonable size, no one should see us leave.

As we landed I swiveled my head, making sure the field was as deserted as it had first appeared. No one appeared to be around, so I sighed, satisfied we were alone.

"Okay, we don't really know what to expect once I open the portal. Just follow the plan the Dean discussed with us." We'd already been through a few scenarios for Killian and I to retrieve my mother's egg as part of our graduation.

That plan involved a lot more dragonriders and multiple exit routes.

"The plan relies on stealth," Killian said, grinning. "It'll only be more effective with less people infiltrating.We get in, find the egg, take it, and get out."

"Hmm," I agreed.

"And, we try to stay out of trouble." Killian gave me a raised brow.

Jasmine eyed me as well.

"What? Why are you both looking at me like that?" I asked them, shifting uncomfortably on my feet. Solstice made a chuffing noise under me and I could feel her amusement through the bond. I nudged her side with my foot, disgruntled at the implication of that amusement.

"You're a magnet for trouble, Vivienne. It's a fact," Jasmine said, twirling one of her knives.

"Hey, that's not fair! I didn't—"

"Yes, yes, you don't ask for trouble blah blah," Jasmine interjected. "Don't we have an egg to save and a war to postpone? Let's get going."

I snapped my mouth shut as I realized she was right. There were more important things to focus on than my ego. Besides, I would never admit it to them, but they were right. Trouble did seem to follow me wherever I went. All I could do was hope that I could evade it long enough for this mission to go to plan.

I met their eyes and each of them nodded at me, indicating they were ready for me to open the portal.

I took a moment to gather myself again, placing my hand on Solstice's neck and taking comfort in the presence of my bonded dragon. Then I drew in the energy around me, pulling it into the amulet that hung around my neck. I focused on the Avalon Realm and then released the energy in front of me, letting it out slowly so that I could control the size of the portal. If the portal was too large, they would be able to see it from the Academy and we would be caught before we had even begun.

I let the portal grow until it was big enough for Jade to fit through.

I looked at my teammates one last time and gave them a reckless grin. "No going back now."

Then I nudged Solstice through our bond and she plunged through the portal. The familiar sensation of the ground dropping out from under me accompanied the usual static popping in my ears.

Then I was in Avalon.

The scent of saltwater and corruption made my nose wrinkle. Solstice crouched and shuffled away from the portal immediately.

We had already planned this part of the mission. By memorizing a map and crude drawing of Avalon, I had gotten a somewhat grainy picture of our destination. My portal was placed in an abandoned village a short distance from the Avalon Queen's stronghold. I grinned in triumph as I looked around and saw the cobbled building and short wall that surrounded the small territory. It looked like it had been beautiful, once. Now, shadowed buildings displayed empty gardens and overturned furniture.

Sadness overtook me as I absorbed the desolation.

There was a fountain the middle of a small-town center and cobbled streets stretched away from it in every direction. All the buildings and the streets had been overtaken by vines and thorny brambles. The air was heavy with corruption, a thick fog making the atmosphere murky and dark. Black veins ran over the ground and through all of the vegetation. It was like a disease, slowly devouring them.

The whole image was an echo of the sickness I had felt in the Malice Realm. Underneath it though, even through the creeping cold of disease, I could feel a warm inviting sensation.

An ancient presence called to me, though the connection seemed to be muddied by the corruption in the air. I had to save this place. I had to cleanse my ancestral home of this disease and bring back the life and love and beauty I could sense underneath it all.

Killian and Topaz came through the portal behind Solstice and I, followed quickly by Jasmine and Jade. We all crouched low, swiveling our heads to peer through the fog and straining our ears to hear any sign of enemies nearby.

The next part of the plan involved flying the rest of the distance to the stronghold. It was the riskiest part, aside from actually going into the castle, where we assumed the egg would be held. Anyone could see us from the ground, and we could run into any number of hazards in the sky. The hope was that dragons were very commonplace here, so no one would think twice about three more, as long as we kept our distance.

Grabbing some mud, I grinned at Solstice. "Come here, girl. It's time to get dirty."

She glowered at me, but lowered her head so I could smear the muck over her gorgeous scales.

A part of me feared that Avalon's dirt would contain corruption, and it might impact Solstice. There was a slight sizzle, but her playful mind brushed mine, seeming to tell me to stop worrying so much.

After we had successfully camouflaged our dragons, Killian mounted his wyvern and clicked his tongue. Then, he and Topaz were airborne, flying in the direction of the Avalon Queen and her hoard of corrupted dragons.

Jasmine and I locked gazes and then our wyverns were in the air and following him.

We were really doing this.

The view from the air was even more disheartening than the dilapidated village had been. The clouds hung over us, heavy and gray, obscuring us to the point that perhaps the mud-bath hadn't even been necessary.

Below us, the island of Avalon crested, nearly submerged in dark stormy water, the peaks of distant buildings poked out of the surface showcasing just how much of the island had been lost to the tumultuous sea.

Black veins spread through the earth, eating away at scenery that was once likely green and full and blooming with life. Some deep, distant part of my soul knew what this place was supposed to look like.

It wasn't this.

The lines of darkness all seemed to converge in the direction we were going. Of course, the Queen of Avalon was the source of this corruption, so it only made sense that all the paths of depravity led to her.

We wove in and out of treetops, staying low to avoid being seen. As we passed small camps of Wild Dragons, we saw something that chilled me. I sent a panicked wave through Killian, throwing my gaze to the encampment below when he met my eyes with concern.

Interspersed between the fire pits and tents, there were multitudes of humans, dark elves, and dragon shifters walking around preparing for battle. The vast majority of them carried dragon eggs. The thought of all of those dragons hatching into this sickness nearly made me sick myself.

What in all the realms could the Avalon Queen be planning to do with so many eggs?

I turned my attention back to the mission as we passed over the end of the camp. As much as I wanted to, we couldn't save all of those eggs yet. We were here for one specifically.

We continued on our way toward the Lost Queen we were seeking.

I felt her.

It wasn't exactly like the time she had called to me for help. Now she slept as if exhausted, but because she had bonded to my mother, I felt her energy, a reminiscent warmth that made me think of my mother guided us to where we needed to go.

"That way," I whispered, pointing as Solstice followed my direction.

We passed over more desolate and abandoned villages along the way, as well as more camps full of busy soldiers carrying dragon eggs.

Still, the pull was too faint. I wasn't sure where to go. The pull seemed to come from everywhere and nowhere. We couldn't infiltrate the castle without further recon, and we certainly couldn't invade the grounds only to find the egg had been hidden somewhere else.

Killian nudged me through our bond and threw his chin to the left when I looked at him. Looking down I recognized Evelyn and her Hovakim in a swampy area.

An unexpected detour, but perhaps exactly the edge we needed.

Killian and Topaz descended to land as Jasmine and I followed suit on our wyverns. Evelyn and her men looked up at us in shock and confusion as we landed beside them.

Max broke away from the group, grinning as he recognized me and Killian. We dismounted, and greeted them. A loud squelching noise drew my attention sharply back to our wyverns.

Solstice keened at a muddy swamp, claiming her "camouflage" needed to be refreshed.

I rolled my eyes. "Go on," I said with a wave.

She dove into it, Topaz joining her a moment later until they were both submerged in the thick sludge, rolling around as they playfully nipped at one another. Jade simply stood beside Jasmine, flicking her tail at the juvenile display.

I groaned and nudged Killian with my elbow. "We're never going to get all that mud out of their scales."

He sighed and nodded in resignation as he observed our wyverns slinging mud several feet in the air as they fought over a particularly long piece of seaweed.

"Definitely not," he agreed.

It seemed even fear of corruption couldn't pry away their adolescent sense of mischief and play. Maybe that's exactly what Avalon needed.

We turned back to meet Max and his companions.

"Hello, Max. How have you been?" I asked him as we came to a stop a few feet from each other.

"Vivi! I never expected to see you here. At least, not without there being a very large fight to accompany you…" Max said, the surprise still clearly written in his tone and expression. He glanced up as if expecting a squadron to descend at any moment. "How'd you get in undetected?"

"We have our ways," Killian said, his tone flat and down-to-business.

"We're here for an egg," I offered. "It was taken from the Academy a few weeks ago. It's a Lost Queen and my mother has bonded to it. So, obviously, it's important we find it," I explained to them, giving Evelyn and the rest of the Hovakim a strained smile as they gathered around Max.

"Oh yes, we know," Evelyn said. "Nera was not happy when you took it from the Malice Castle," Evelyn added, snorting in amusement.

"Nera?" Jasmine asked.

"Mmm," she replied with a nod. "The Avalon Queen."

"So, you know where it is?" I asked her hopeful that we might have some help.

She blinked at us. "Of course. It's our job to locate and log each Lost queen that's not in Avalon. Although, once they are here, only Nera's most trusted have access," she explained, a disgruntled look on her face.

I balked. Evelyn not only knew where my mother's

dragon was. She also knew the location of *all* the Dragon Queens!

And had she supplied us with that information? No.

Which meant she wasn't the ally I thought she was.

"Traitor," I hissed. "You can't give all the Lost Queens locations to Nera! She'll succeed in corrupting every realm if she attains that much raw power."

"Calm down, little goddess. We aren't planning on handing over the intel. We only have a few more to find and then we will be handing over the information to the Academy," Evelyn explained.

"Why can't you just give us the information now? Why wait when we could be going to retrieve the eggs before Nera even has the chance," Killian asked.

Marcus, one of Evelyn's Hovakim, rolled his shoulders back. "We can't blow our cover. If anyone tries to get the eggs before we are ready, then Nera will know that she's been betrayed. She would rather destroy them before she allowed anyone else to get their hands on the Lost Queens."

A roar from above us interrupted the conversation. My stomach dropped as I looked to the sky and saw Zelda in her half-transformed state. Panic took me and I froze as I took in how royally screwed we were.

So much for stealth.

Zelda flapped her powerful wings, gaining altitude, and then she shrieked, sounding the alert that intruders had been found.

The effect was paralyzing. My head immediately filled with glass. Each fraction of a second felt longer than it ever had and I covered my ears with my hands but it didn't help, the knives were still being driven straight through my eardrums and into my brain. The air vibrated with the high-pitched soundwaves of her call to battle and my knees shook with the strain of staying upright.

Finally, the noise stopped. My ears continued to ring, and disorientation made it hard to focus as Zelda dove down and swiped at me with her talon-like claws. I ducked, stumbling to my knees, crawling away as she swooped back up into the sky with a cackle.

"Viv!" Killian shouted, slashing with his blade, but he was just as disoriented as I was and missed.

Solstice and Topaz fought against the muck, their playful adventure turning into quicksand as they struggled to free themselves. Jade went to Jasmine, hissing to keep her safe.

"You're in my domain now," Zelda taunted us as she flew in a wide arc. "Thank you for luring them here, Evelyn. It was a brilliant move to earn their trust, however, I don't think the Queen would approve. If you let me kill them, I'll keep your little secret."

Evelyn just watched me with a dark gaze, backing away. "They're yours," she said, pain evident on her face.

Betrayal twisted in my gut, but I sensed she didn't want to comply. She had her Hovakim to worry about, and it wasn't just Zelda who threatened us. The alert had been sounded and the entire island knew we were here.

We were on our own, now.

Zelda shrieked, paralyzing us before she dove again.

Killian roared and held up his blade, catching her talons with his sword this time.

Seeing my mate in danger shot adrenaline through my body.

Brute force wasn't going to get us through this. If I had learned anything from the Valkyrie test, it was that the power of emotions would win our war.

Closing my eyes, I focused inward to that same place Lily had pulled my power from me. A cleansing power, one that she had only amplified.

It was the place where I kept my love, my love for Killian, my love for my mother, for Solstice and all my friends.

Unlike Lily, I wouldn't devour my love in exchange for a release of power.

The difference between us was I had goddess blood in my veins. I simply needed to be shown how the cleansing worked, and now I could do it myself—but only in Avalon where an ancient power rested. A power I was connected to because of my blood ties.

A trance fell over me as the battle cries echoed in the distance, as if far away.

My aches and pains faded into the background of my mind. Time slowed and I was able to pick out every detail of the scene. My heart rate evened out and I calmly stood and drew my weapon. I moved beside my mate, putting my hand on his arm to give him some of my energy.

Zelda pulled back then, cocking her head to the side as though she was listening intently.

Solstice, Topaz, and Jade all hissed at the same time, their heads swiveling in wide circles as they searched the sky.

Zelda's lips slid into a manic grin. "My reinforcements have arrived."

"Holy crap," Jasmine hissed as she mounted Jade. "That's... a lot of Wild Dragons."

Roars echoed and wings blotted out the dark sky. They came from everywhere, moving like a storm from every direction, swirling in a vortex.

Every Wild Dragon that had heard Zelda's call had answered it.

We all backed into the center of the clearing, instinctively forming a circle with our backs to each other. Killian stood on my left and Solstice took up a large space to my right, finally free of the muck. The tension ratcheted higher as the sky darkened underneath the cloud of corrupted dragons.

There were too many. Way, way too many. Even with Evelyn and her Hovakim should they defend us, there was no way we were going to survive this.

Panic made my blood buzz as it raced through my veins. I struggled to hold onto my goddess trance as the first dragons circled overhead and Zelda cackled at our terror.

Zelda raised a hand.

Everything paused for a millisecond and I braced myself.

"Kill," she hissed, letting it fall.

Killian braced himself, wielding his blade like a hero.

Jasmine readied her lance.

Solstice flared her wings, keeping one dipped to allow me to mount her for escape.

Although, there was nowhere to go.

Then they dove with synchronized monstrous roars. The buzz in my blood strengthened until I trembled all over.

I realized then that it wasn't panic that was making me shake like this.

It was something else entirely.

I focused all of my energy on the goddess trance, fully immersing myself in the calm. Then, as if I was being controlled by someone else, I knelt down and dropped my weapon to the ground.

"Vivi! What are you doing? Pick up your sword!" Killian's panicked shout was muffled to my ears as the buzzing grew until I was all but deaf.

I ignored him and pulled off my riding gloves. Then, I dug my hands into the muddy soil of the swamp.

I needed to be closer to the island.

The energy in my blood was matched by a much deeper, older energy in the island itself. I pushed my hands into the soil until I could feel enough of that ancient energy to call it into myself. I tore open the flood gates and let the wave of power rush into me like a roaring river. The vibrations were so strong now that

I registered pain somewhere in the back of my mind. I pulled until I was so full of energy that I felt like I would explode if I didn't let it out.

I looked up then to find Killian fending off talons and teeth, Solstice breathing fire to fight the flames coming our way.

They were all fighting off the Wild Dragons, their backs to me as they struggled to protect me.

A selfless act, one that filled my heart with love.

Going off of the same instinct as before, I pulled one hand out of the soil and threw it straight into the air. Teeth gritting in exertion, I directed all my gathered power into the mass of Wild Dragons pouring down from the sky.

The power shot out of my hand in a glowing, golden beam of light. It smoothly flowed into the air and then burst into a shockwave of power that spread out.

A golden dome covered the clearing, protecting us from the stragglers not caught in the stream of power I controlled.

I glanced at Solstice, knowing she was responsible for the dome. She met my eyes and sent encouragement and pride through our bond.

Killian and Jasmine stood beside me, with Evelyn and her Hovakim staring around them in slack jawed awe.

"Nice one," she murmured.

Zelda screeched, beating against the dome, her eyes blazing with rage. "I said Kill them!"

I continued to draw power from deep within the island and released it into the shockwave. The island seemed to give the power willingly. Almost like it was alive and understood that I was one of its own, come home to restore the balance it had lost.

No matter how much power the island had though, there was only so much that I could funnel out before I was out of energy myself. I didn't devour my emotions like Lily did. I was a conduit. I allowed the island to work through me. That's what I had been doing this whole time and it was amazing.

While the island's energy was endless, it shredded at me as it went, draining my own reserves in the process.

Despite my shockwave, the onslaught of dragons still seemed to pour from every direction, beating against the barrier and weakening my resolve.

"There's still too many of them! I'm not going to be able to hold them all off!" I gasped out between heaving breaths. The exertion of this whole ordeal was starting to wear on me.

"We need to retreat," Killian ground out.

Just then, the buzzing calmed. Like the end of a panic attack, I slowly stopped shaking and a strange peace overtook me.

"Look!" Max gasped, pointing into the sky.

We followed his gaze as each one of us gasped. From every direction, just as the Wild Dragons had, giant dragons approached.

Only these dragons weren't part of the corruption.

They were ancient and the sky took on a reverent

air. They glowed a soft blue and seemed ethereal, like spirits.

As they passed through the Wild Dragons, each one just fell out of the sky. There was no fight, no blood, no death. Just instant sleep for all of the corrupted dragons touched by the ancients.

The protective dragon spirits swept the sky above us until every last Wild Dragon had fallen to the ground in a deep slumber. They converged at the point of my beam then and flowed down through me, and into the island where I could feel they had come from.

I had awakened the spirit of the island itself.

As they passed through me, I could sense what, or who, they were. They were the ancient dragon spirits that had once been bonded to my ancestors.

Avalon inhabitants had been dragonriders, too!

It explained so much. Why I had come to the Academy. Why my mother had bonded to the Lost Queen.

It was in our blood.

When these dragons had died, they gave their soul to Avalon to protect future generations. I could sense their pride in me and their happiness that I was here to restore Avalon to its former glory. I opened my mind and let my own gratitude pass through the connection before it was gone.

A jarring shove pushed me back into reality and I fell back with a gasp, my hand pulling from the mud with a wet squelch. I landed on my back, staring up at the cloudy sky as I caught my breath.

"That was…. incredible!" Max shouted. "We almost

died and then Vivi with the glowy beam and the ghost dragons and the golden dome and—oh man we almost died!" Max paced back and forth as he rambled, clearly in shock.

I chuckled as Killian rested his hand on my shoulder.

Evelyn grabbed Max's arm and pulled him into a hug, the rest of her Hovakim following suit until they huddled together.

Solstice walked over to me and laid down beside me, putting her head over my stomach and humming in contentment at the moment of peace after the acute stress of the battle. Jasmine sat on my other side, a shellshocked expression on her face.

"We need to go home," Killian said. "This is way more than we planned for. They know we are here now. Zelda escaped when she spotted the spirit dragons. She's no doubt told Nera about us." Killian paced as he tried to work through what to do. "We have to retreat to the Academy."

His voice was strong and sure. He had no doubt that retreat was the right choice. Logically, I knew he was right. It was much smarter to go home, tell the Dean what had happened, and come up with a new plan.

Especially now that we knew we could fight them.

I knew I couldn't do that though. The image of those eggs being carried around by corrupted creatures passed through my mind. I couldn't endanger the Lost

Queens, or any other dragons for that matter, for a moment longer.

The island had helped me once, but would it really help me again? I couldn't be sure. The mass of the Dragon Queen's forces lay strewn around us, harmless and asleep—but not for long.

I had to go after Nera, and I had to do it now.

CHAPTER 8

THE FINAL BATTLE

*K*illian sat on Topaz looking down at me with resignation. "Let's go. We need to get out of here before more show up, or the magic from the spirit dragons wears off and all these Wild Dragons wake up."

I shook my head. "I have to stop her. I have to save those eggs."

Killian opened his mouth to protest but I held up my hand and shook my head with a decisive jolt. I walked over to Solstice and pulled myself up, strapping into the saddle.

"You didn't feel it," I said as he eyed me. "You didn't feel the island begging me to cleanse it. You don't have this feeling that you have to do something right now because you're home and your ancestors are being desecrated," I told him, passion making my words more forceful than I had originally intended. "I have to go now, Killian. Come with me, or get out of my way."

He stared at me for a moment before he nodded solemnly. "Okay, Viv. I'm with you. Always."

"I'm in too," Jasmine said, hiking her lance as she mounted Jade. "Let's show them what Dragonriders can do!"

Evelyn huffed. "Well don't count on us. I know a suicide mission when I see one. Good luck," Evelyn said, saluting sardonically. "Someone needs to tell the Academy what happened if you fail."

I chuckled. "Thanks for the vote of confidence." Most would have been offended by her words, but I knew Evelyn. She was practical, and I honestly appreciated knowing that no matter what happened, the Academy would still have an ally on the inside. I leaned in, my saddle creaking with my weight. "As long as you give me the locations of all of the Lost Queens when this is done."

She nodded with a wink. "You got it, Viv." And then she and her Hovakim melted into the forest. Max was the last to go and he waved sadly before turning and following his new family into the darkness.

"All right, time to get on with our suicide mission," I told the others, gritting my teeth in determination before I mentally nudged Solstice and we were airborne.

WE FLEW FAST NOW, gliding low to the ground, stealth out the window now that we had been discovered.

Scenery rushed underneath me and the sight made me want to cry. The closer we came to Nera, the thicker the dark veins in the soil became. The heavier the air.

Every once in a while, we encountered a cluster of Wild Dragons that we fought off before continuing on. These groups became more frequent the closer we came to the stronghold, and I knew there would be a point where we would just be fighting non-stop.

We weren't an army. We were a squadron of three, but because of that, we would be able to slip through the cracks.

The castle finally came into view and my stomach tightened in anticipation of the coming battle. The castle was huge, with five towers. Four towers anchored the corners of a square shape, each one built facing a cardinal direction. The fifth tower was the tallest and stood proudly in the center of the castle. The soft grey stone would have been beautiful if not for the cracks of rot and signs of neglect that spanned out everywhere.

As we approached, several groups of Wild Dragons took flight and made a beeline for us. We drew our weapons again and continued to move toward the castle.

Fighting the Wild Dragons was different for me now, after seeing what Lily had done. These were all just people that had been manipulated or forced into this life. They hadn't wanted this for themselves. Heck, when they had been cleansed, they didn't even remember their time as corrupted dragons. These were beings that weren't in their right minds It felt wrong on so many levels to hurt them now that I knew better.

I didn't have a choice though. It was either hurt them, or let them kill me. So, I swung my sword and stabbed my dagger as the Wild Dragons collided with us, claws and fangs swiping for vulnerable areas. Solstice tore her way through dragon after dragon, spewing fire at some of them and slicing through others.

I would call on the island again, when it was time. And those that were left I vowed to save.

We did our best to dodge and weave the majority of the sick wyverns, trying to engage as few dragons as possible. We crossed over the castle wall and then I felt it, the pull of the egg.

"I can feel it!" I called to Killian and Jasmine, already showing Solstice which direction to go.

A large squad of Wild Dragons rose over the wall and rushed toward us in response.

"Go!" Killian yelled back at me over the roar of the wind. "We'll hold them off!"

I nodded at him, opening the bond and sending as much love as I could through our connection. He put his hand over his heart and let me feel his love too. Then Solstice turned, flying in the direction of the egg and we were alone.

We moved toward the center of the castle, dodging and weaving around the Wild Dragons that we encountered along the way. The tallest tower loomed over us, oddly ominous despite the underlying beauty.

Then I saw her.

Nera.

It was surreal to have heard about the Wild Dragon Queen and finally meet her. I expected her to be in her dragon form, but she seemed to prefer her human one.

Not entirely human, I realized as we descended. Long graceful horns protruded from her head, framed by a black glittering crown. A tail swiped from underneath her long, golden dress, the color glimmering like Solstice's scales. Her back remained bare, two scars running down her shoulder blades.

She stood in what appeared to be the inner courtyard. There were remnants of a long dead garden around the perimeter. Dead vines and trees with no leaves sat amongst the brown grass and black-veined earth. Nera stood in the center of the courtyard, beside a fountain that spewed rusty water.

Solstice circled the courtyard apprehensively before I urged her to land. She slowly descended as far from Nera as she could possibly get.

Once on the ground, I could see the Queen of Avalon more clearly. She was tall, like most dragon shifters seemed to be. Her skin was pale, almost porcelain like. Her features were delicate and pointed giving her a sharp edge that said 'danger' despite the soft pout of her lips.

She had jet black hair and hollow black eyes. The thing that caught my attention the most though, was her wings. She released them from her body, those scars places where she could hide them.

They were the largest wings I had ever seen on a humanoid form. Inky black appendages that fluttered like silk when she moved, the mesmerizing color reminding me of light shining on an oil spill. The corruption had left its mark on her in much the same way as the island, with black veins that seemed to span the entirety of her body, concentrating around her heart. Her chest was almost completely black with the disease. Her eyes had a glazed madness to them that was at odds with the authoritative air with which she held herself with.

"I've been waiting for you," she said with a nasty grin. She gestured to the rusty fountain. "Zelda informed me of your little light display. I'm afraid it upset me."

Solstice keened as I dismounted, needing to see what she hid in the rusty waters.

She backed away, allowing me space as I covered my mouth with my hand in horror.

Zelda's lifeless body drifted in the water, slashes running down her body.

It wasn't rust turning the fountain red.

It was blood.

"I've been expecting you for weeks," Nera went on cheerfully, a tone of madness in her words. "That's why I've been working so hard to take the corruption into myself." She gestured to her chest with a confident grin. "Isn't it beautiful?"

Her expression abruptly turned flat and she stared at me, studying me for what felt like an eternity. She turned her attention on Solstice and I bristled, forcing myself in-between her and my bonded dragon. Whatever she was going to do, she would have to go through me first.

Solstice nudged my back with her snout, not liking that I was willing to sacrifice myself for her. I ignored her, keeping my eyes glued on the unhinged shifter in front of me.

"I have a proposition for you," she purred, her chest rumbling with every word. "I felt you earlier. You have power. Real power," Nera said, her voice like honey. "Join me! Get rid of all that wasteful, useless love, and take your rightful place as ruler of Avalon. You feel it don't you? That you're meant to be here. On this island."

She held my eyes the whole time, not even blinking. I paused to consider her words.

How did she know about my connection to the Avalon? How could she possibly know how I felt?

She took slow leisurely steps towards me and for some reason, I didn't step back.

"Come, I want to show you something," she smiled at me and turned, striding gracefully toward two double doors leading into the main tower of the castle. I followed her hesitantly, on high alert for when this became the trap I had been expecting.

She threw the doors open at the same time and I saw what she was heading for. It was the throne room, which explained why she preferred her humanoid form.

The room itself was massive, with vaulted ceilings and two giant chandeliers spaced evenly. Not one, but two thrones glittered against the far wall. They were both made from stone, intricately carved with images of water dragons and the lady of the lake as well as various allusions to magic.

The thrones were the only items in the room, or maybe in all of Avalon, that didn't look like they had been affected by the corruption. The stone was polished and gleamed in the light.

"This would be your throne room. Your seat of power." Nera's voice cut into my awe-struck silence and I whipped my head to face her. "Go on, sit in it," she told me, waving at me with a "shooing" motion.

I moved forward then, something in me unable to resist the urge to just test it. I walked the rest of the way and stepped up onto the platform.

I traced my finger along a particularly detailed wave, marveling at how warm the stone was underneath my fingertips. The warmth drew me in and I turned, sitting down on the throne with sigh of contentment. Despite knowing Nera was crazy, I couldn't help but consider her offer.

If only because it felt like I belonged there.

What's wrong with me? I wondered, my thoughts turning cloudy as Solstice's eyes went hooded, as if she'd grown sleepy.

"Yes, it feels nice, it's a good throne, yes?" Nera smiled at me, her fangs glinting in the light. "I have bigger ambitions, which is why I need you, dear.

Avalon was a stepping stone, one that will sink into the sea unless you decide to save it by ruling it."

She was right. The island was sinking.

So she needed me alive, and not just that. She needed me to rule.

"You would make a wonderful Queen of Avalon," she purred, clasping her hands against her corrupted chest, "just like I would make a wonderful queen in the other domains that we could rule together. Queen Vivienne of Avalon, servant of Queen Nera of All Realms."

She cackled at the end, a hint of madness leaking into her laughter and expression.

I shook my head then, lucidity finally seeming to come back to me.

"You killed my father, didn't you?"

Nera threw her head back and laughed as if that were the funniest thing anyone had ever said. I stared at her in bewilderment.

"Oh, do you still care about that? Means to an end, my dear. If you still experience grief, I have a fix for that." She spread her fingers, her eyes going wide, revealing pupils that overtook her irises. "Let them go. Let the corruption feast on them." Her voice rose in volume, echoing around the empty throne room. "What have your emotions really done for you? Think about it for a moment. Emotions only cause you pain."

Nera glided forward, moving toward me in an unnervingly calculating way that was at odds with her manic words.

"You will never see your father again," she hissed, "and no matter who actually killed him, the true reason for his death was your very existence. I was simply the carrier of an inevitable destiny set to play out regardless of which pawns are still in the game. To escape the endless pain that is life, there is only one solution. Throw it away. Get rid of all of your useless emotions, and join me. You and I could do marvelous things together," Nera said, her voice almost a whisper by the end, and held out her hand. Tension was thick in the air as she waited for my answer. "I can help you let go of that pain and finally step into your full power."

I held her black, depthless gaze. The temptation to get rid of my pain was strong. I wouldn't have to feel the grief over my dad. I would never have to risk losing anyone else. I would never stress over how to protect the world. I wouldn't even care about living up to my destiny.

Before I knew what was happening, my hand was reaching for hers.

I was weak. I wanted to get rid of it. I was tired of all these heavy emotions weighing me down.

"Vivi! Wait!" Killian burst into the chamber, the double doors hitting the walls with a bang that echoed through the room. I jumped in shock at the sudden noise.

The interruption brought me back to reality and I realized what I was about to agree to. I snatched my hand back and my frustration and anger at this entire mess just exploded out of me.

The throne I rested in was the heart of Avalon, and it was here I could resonate with it best.

I thought again not of my sorrow, but of my love, of everything I wanted to preserve and keep safe.

Killian.

My mother.

The Academy.

Earth.

My friends.

Solstice.

The world paused as a white light exploded from my chest, Solstice fanning her wings as she created a tether, a golden beam lighting up between us.

All the emotions I had been talking about giving up just seconds ago flooded to the surface and I felt the energy carry my emotions out into the island. I could feel it, as if the white light was an extension of myself. I felt it wash through the land, cleansing the darkness and corruption and bringing back the soft beauty I knew Avalon had underneath all the sickness.

The world stood still as I purified my ancestral home. Killian was next to me then, grabbing my face and kissing me all over. He repeated my name again and again, whispering it like a prayer that had been answered.

"Vivi, I thought I was going to lose you to the darkness." He brought my fingers to his lips, kissing each one. "If you throw away the pain, you'll throw away everything good, too. Grief is the cost of love, and I would pay that cost infinitely to have the privilege of loving you."

My heart nearly burst at his words, and then he kissed me and it raced. Everything faded. We weren't locked in a deadly battle anymore. We weren't drag-onriders or goddesses or half angels.

We were in love.

"No!" Nera shouted, and Killian jerked, throwing his head back as he gasped in a breath.

I couldn't comprehend the blood that trailed down his chest, Nera's tail having skewered him through his back.

"Killian!" I shouted as he slumped into me.

Rage filled me as I met her eyes.

"You could have avoided this pain, Vivienne. If only you have taken my offer," Nera said as she surveyed the scene.

The anger returned to me, just as Jasmine, Evelyn, Yosef, Jakob, Marcus, Liam, and Max came running through the doors.

"Topaz is flipping out and—" Jasmine cut herself off as she took in the state of us. Me and Killian on the floor, having slipped from the throne, covered in blood, and Nera standing over us.

I stood then, pulling myself out from under Killian carefully and moving forward so I was between him and Nera. I turned to half meet Jasmine's eye. "Get a healer, Jasmine. Take him home."

I held up a hand, blasting Nera with all the pain and love that Killian had given me over the years.

She screamed, covering her eyes. Jasmine took the opportunity and shoved past the Wild Dragon Queen. I opened a portal and she hesitated, looking between me and Nera as Solstice joined my side.

"Go," I told her firmly.

I would be staying.

I would finish this.

Killian would be okay. I had to believe that.

When Jasmine left with Killian, I hardened my heart.

The Avalon Queen eyed Evelyn and her Hovakim. "So, you're a traitor? I had my suspicions, but I could never be sure."

"I made my decision based on what was best for the realms," Evelyn said evenly, glancing at me. "I believe in the true Queen."

Fury rose in Nera's eyes and her face flushed in anger. She waved her hand and a swirling vortex appeared directly behind Evelyn. Nera waved her hand and sent all six of them hurling through the portal to some unknown realm. The portal snapped shut with a *pop* after another wave from Nera.

I stood there in shock for several seconds trying to process how quickly that happened. I had a sinking feeling I would never see them again. Which was bad for two reasons. One, Max had really grown on me, and two, they were the only people who knew where the majority of the Lost Queens were.

"Well, now that that unpleasantness is dealt with, it just leaves you and me," Nera said, almost simpering in her sugary sweet madness as she swiped at her eyes. "Sadly, I'm going to have to end you. If you aren't going to join me, then you will just be in the way. Better to be done with the whole sordid affair now."

As she finished the last word, she waved both of her hands in an abrupt backhanded motion. My body lifted and flew backward, slamming into the wall on the opposite side of the room with a thud. I gasped for air as the invisible force released me, then crumpled on the floor where I fell. She laughed, pealing high-pitched insanity leaked through the crazed mirth.

"Oh my, this is going to be much easier than antici-pated. I have to say, you are much more ferocious when protecting those you love." She brought her finger up to her lips as though she was thinking. "I know what will make this more interesting! I'll just kill your dragon and add her scales to my dress."

I gasped, her dress's glimmer making sense to me now.

She'd found other golden dragons, ones like Solstice, a rare color and made a garment out of their scales.

She said her decision so simply, as if she hadn't just threatened one of my only reasons for living. As if she hadn't just ended her own life with that one small statement. My pain suddenly didn't exist.

She was right. I was more ferocious when it came to protecting those I loved.

A red tint entered my vision as she turned on her heel, making for the door that would lead her to my wyvern still at the throne, bound by corruption tugging her down.

Nera turned her back on me so easily, like she truly didn't see me as a threat.

Underestimating me would be her end.

I shot out my hand, grabbing onto her life energy with a force I never had before. As soon as I made contact with her energy, I could tell that she had given up every ounce of goodness left in her.

There was nothing left to save in her.

I could cleanse her, but it would kill her.

So be it.

She hissed, pulling back on her life force, refusing to let me steal it from her without a fight. She had threatened my family though, she had threatened my very world. I couldn't let her get away with that.

I planted my feet and dug deep as my Valkyrie armor strained and cracked. I pulled every bit of strength from myself that I could. Then, I turned to Avalon, taking the energy from the island itself. Energy that was pure and warm now that I had cleaned the island of its corruption.

Nera and I struggled, tugging back and forth for several moments before I gathered enough energy to yank. It flowed after that initial sharp pull.

Nera's eyes went wide, as she struggled to take a step, fell to her knees and then clutched at her chest.

Her soul was black and sludge-like to me, moving slower and feeling much heavier than it should. An empty cavern filled with darkness.

She crumpled to the floor, her skin shriveling like a raisin as I cleansed the last of her energy.

"You could have ruled it all," she said, daring to have pity in her eyes as she grinned, madness following her to the end. Corruption bled from her chest, and once that was gone, she would have nothing left.

"The realms don't need a ruler," I glowered, closing my fist and twisting, making her gasp. "They need a savior."

As the light finally left her eyes, her skin cracked and flaked away. With a quiet whoosh, her body eroded into a pile of dust, leaving nothing behind.

A gentle tugging on my chest drew my attention. I turned towards the throne and crossed to it, feeling the pull from there.

A light thrumming sound drew me around the back of the throne. There, sitting on a red velvet cushion, was the Malice egg. A large crack ran from the top to the halfway point. Despite the crack, when I picked the egg up it was warm and I could feel the heartbeat of the tiny queen inside.

"There you are. Time to get you back to your rider," I told her in a whisper.

I cradled the egg to my chest and made my way to the exit. As I opened the door, several dragons landed. Valkyries leaped off their dragons, weapons drawn and ready to charge into battle.

It seemed that the Dean had responded to Jasmin and Killian after all, and in a way I didn't expect.

She wouldn't abandon me here. All of the Academy

had come out to support me, to fight a battle even if they weren't ready.

Only, there was no one to fight. All of the Wild Dragons seemed to have disappeared around the time Nera had been cleansed.

"Sorry guys, I had all the fun before you got here," I grinned at them all, shrugging.

Some of them snorted laughter that quickly cut off when Dean Brynhilde stepped forward with a glare.

"I hope you have enough fun to last you for a while, because it might be a long time before you have any more," she told me and then gestured roughly towards the open portal.

I knew better than to argue, and I was too exhausted to put up a whole lot of fight right then, so I quickly mounted Solstice and we took off through the portal.

Victorious, albeit in trouble.

EPILOGUE

*T*he hours after I returned from Avalon were a blur of being scolded for going rogue, people profusely thanking me, healers checking me over, and me asking to no avail to see my mate.

Apparently, he was going to be fine, but they still needed to do more work so I wasn't allowed to see him yet.

Hearing them say he was going to be fine, and actually seeing him were two very different things. I was going to be an anxious mess until I finally laid eyes on him.

The Lost Queen was the last matter I had to deal with before I could finally rest. So, I made my way to Central Hall, glad to walk calmly. I paused as I reached the door, and then gently pushed it open.

My mother was laying on her back, the covers tucked around her. She slept soundly, her breaths soft and easy.

She'd fallen into a coma again, so the Dean had warned me, but I wasn't concerned.

I knew how to wake her.

I walked over to the bed and tenderly placed the Malice egg on her chest, directly over her heart.

As soon as they touched, a cracking sound came from the egg. My mother's eyes snapped open and she sat up. Joy overtook her face and she watched in rapt fascination as the baby dragon pushed on its shell from the inside. Piece by piece the shell fell away to reveal a gleaming onyx dragon. The baby immediately made eye contact with my mother and I saw it as their bond fell into place and it keened in joy.

I couldn't help but smile at the beautiful sight.

"Oh, Vivi, how can I ever thank you? How will I ever repay you for this? It's supposed to be the other way around, you know. Mothers are supposed to take care of daughters," she told me, her eyes filling with tears as her emotions spilled over.

"I love you, Mom. Just care for her, that's more than enough repayment for me," I told her, leaning over to give her a hug.

The small black dragon gave me a curious look and shakily made her way across the bed to me. She nudged my hand and made a contented sound when I scratched her head.

Finally, the Lost Queen that had called to me for months wasn't so lost anymore.

THE SMELL of food permeated every inch of The Great Hall. Conversation hummed through the room as every resident of the Academy, and many who weren't, celebrated our victory over the Wild Dragons and Queen Nera.

I shifted uncomfortably in my seat of honor at the head table. They had insisted on making me a spectacle for the whole celebration, when all I had really wanted was to sit with my mate and friends who were all laughing at something two tables down.

Killian was okay, which meant that all of this was going to work out.

I studied my people as they continued to converse, their tone merry and joyful. The hum of excitement that came with victory and the knowledge that the realms were safe.

Jasmine and Vern were on the end, across from my mother and Ivar, the King of the Knights of the Silver Order. Lily and James were next to Ivar, and James was clearly annoying his older brother on purpose if the sour expression on Ivar's face and the grin on James's said anything.

Then there was Killian.

He gazed at me as if I was the only person in the room.

I smiled and winked playfully, making him grin. James elbowed him then and said something that made them all laugh again.

As I watched my mate, mother, and friends laugh,

carefree and happy, a deep feeling of contentment welled up.

This is why the pain and grief were worth it.

That thought made my dad come to my mind. He would have loved this celebration. He would have been the life of the party.

I stood up then, wanting a moment alone. It had been a long time since I'd just talked to him, wondering if he could hear me.

Knowing what I knew now, he probably could.

I slipped away, trying my best to be discreet as I stepped out into the garden. Killian had caught my eye, but the unspoken assurance in our bond told him I needed this.

I walked alone, looking up at the stars and thinking about what my dad would be saying if he were here.

Out of nowhere, a whooshing sound came from behind me. A bright swirling portal opened up into the night, the light almost blinding.

A Level Seven Light Tunnel.

My stomach dropped as a man stepped through and smiled at me with adoration.

Dad.

He looked exactly the same as the last time I had seen him. Right down to the smile that said he loved me more than anything else in the world.

"Dad!" I couldn't help the girlish scream that came from my mouth as I rushed forward, afraid that he would disappear if I didn't grab onto him.

"Oh, baby girl." His deep baritone rumbled against

my head as I buried my face in his chest. He wrapped his arms around me, clutching me fiercely. "I couldn't be any prouder of you, my Vivi. You have come such a long way to achieving your destiny."

Tears sprung to my eyes, because as much overflowing love I had for my father, the pain was there, too. "I did this to remove my grief," I told him, knowing that to be true. I hugged him tighter, knowing he wouldn't be staying long. Already golden light leaked from his skin, as if he bled onto the ground, his form unable to be sustained in this realm. "How am I supposed to go on knowing that grief will always remain?"

He kissed the crown of my head and pulled me away. "Because there is love, Vivi. That is what you must focus on, and there are so many more who need your help."

I blinked at him, then swiped away the tears. "The Lost Queens?" I ventured.

He nodded. "They're in danger, sweetheart. That's the only reason I was permitted to come to you to deliver the message. When Nera died, she sent out a wave of corruption to all the Lost Dragon Queen eggs. She made sure that they would be just like her, born into madness. They will have the sole mission in life to bring Nera back from the dead."

"Wait…They can do that…?" I asked him, dread filling me.

"Yes, they can, and they will, unless the corruption is cleansed. You must find them." He squeezed my hands, smiling at me. "Don't look so upset, sweetheart. You have time. For now, live your life, and most importantly, love as hard as you can. That's what this world is really all about." He pulled away as he finished talking and began to walk back toward the portal again. "I have to go now, my sweet girl, just know I'm always with you." He blew me a kiss. "I love you, Vivi."

With that, he backed into the portal and it collapsed with a *pop*.

A mixture of emotions threatened to overwhelm me.

Happiness at seeing him and earning his pride. Sadness at having to watch him leave again, at having to lose him again. Anxiety at the new information he gave me.

Most of all though, I felt an overwhelming sense of love. For my dad, for Killian, for my mom and Solstice and all of my friends.

He was right. That's all the world was really about.
Love.

To be continued in Dragonrider Academy
Season Two...

A Note from the Author

Thank you for reading the entire first season of Dragonrider Academy!

All of my stories come from my heart, but Dragonrider comes from a special place. The beach described in the prologue is inspired by a place I would go with my family, and dreams I would have. Nothing tragic took place, luckily, but dreams of riding dragons into the sky were very real. It's pretty fun to live out those dreams as an adult in the stories I write.

When I was in school, I devoured books, especially anything with fantasy or dragons in them. I had read every fantasy book in my middle school library before I went to high school. While that sounds impressive, I lived on an island, so I'm not sure how big the library really was, but it felt big to me! And in high school, I had some good friends, but they loved to read just as much as I did and we often would lose ourselves in a good book during lunch or breaks. I had the choice to hang out with the cheerleaders, or the "nerds," and I chose the latter without a second thought. That was a choice I never regretted, and I hope all my childhood friends and everyone I went to school with are living happy, fulfilling lives right now.

I know I am fulfilled by these stories, and I thank you for joining me on this journey. It brings me joy, and I hope my stories have brought you joy as well.

Thank you as always for being a loyal reader! Be sure to leave a review and share a post on social media about what you enjoyed. As an indie author, I am my own publisher and it is only by the grace of readers that I continue to make a living writing my fantastical stories. I'm grateful for it every day.

Thank you for allowing me to share my stories with you.

See you next time!

A.J. FLOWERS
ANGELS, SHIFTERS AND FANTASY ROMANCE

Read Crown Princess Academy!

Did you know that the Malice Realm is a cross-over into the next series in the Magical Realms Universe? Learn more about the Malice King and the characters of a fabulous and twisted fairytale that'll have you questioning everything you thought you knew about darkness and light!

This is one crown you don't want.

Born and raised in the Dregs, the last thing I expected was the "honor" of being recruited to Crown Princess Academy.
And by honor, I mean fighting for my life against the fae that rule our world.

Our first exam is in three weeks and not every student will make it out alive… don't these bimbos realize that? I'm not fooled. I know how ruthless the fae can be.

All the princess initiates are captivated by Lucas, the sexy fae Crown Prince who, in turn, seems fixated on *me*. He can't know that I'm actually the most powerful Malice Caster in the Dregs. I'm sure my talents for the Criminal Guild won't earn me any extra credit in my princess classes.

All my life I've stayed one step ahead of the two-faced fae and their Malice, the out of control black magic that has nearly wiped out all of humanity. This is my chance to do more than survive—this is my chance to fight back.

I'll play the Crown Prince's game.

I'll wear the tiny initiate crown, dance in my glittering pink dress, survive the deadly exams, and ultimately graduate as the Crown Princess all while he thinks I'm playing right into his plans.

He's in for a surprise when I reveal who I am and wipe that sexy, smug grin off his face… I just hope my heart doesn't forget he's the enemy.

Be sure to head to Amazon and grab your copy of Princess Academy!

Read James and Lily's Story!

Did you know that Lily and James have their own novel? Be sure to read Daughter of Dragons, a standalone tale complete at 62,000 words!

Ever get that sense you just don't belong?
I should be happy. It's my sixteenth birthday and my best friend and boyfriend are pulling out all the stops. No parents, plenty of friends, and a wild party that'll test my relationship with Nimrock Ohio's local small-town police.
Nothing exciting ever happens at Nimrock.
At least, not before James arrived.
He came blazing in on his motorcycle with entirely inappropriate leatherwear for the hot climate, but

when he takes off his jacket those tattoos would make any good girl question her life choices.

There's something about James that I can't shake.

I'll soon find out James is my knight in shining armor... and I'm the dragon he's meant to slay.

Find Daughter of Dragons at any retailer, or your local library!

ALSO BY A.J. FLOWERS

YA Fantasy Romance

Valkyrie Allegiance (A Complete Series)

Valkyrie Landing (Book 1)
Valkyrie Rebellion (Book 2)
Valkyrie Uprising (Book 3)

The Magical Realms Universe

Daughter of Dragons (Standalone)

Dragonrider Academy (Episode 1)

Dragonrider Academy (Episode 2)

Dragonrider Academy (Episode 3)

Dragonrider Academy (Episode 4)

Dragonrider Academy (Episode 5)

Dragonrider Academy (Episode 6)

Dragonrider Academy (Episode 7)

Season 2

Dragonrider Academy (Episode 8)

Crown Princess Academy (Book 1)

Crown Princess Academy (Book 2)

Celestial Downfall: Twisted Angelic Realms (Complete Series)

Fallen to Grace (Book 1)

Rise to Hope (Book 2)

Stand for Justice (Book 3)

Manor Saffron (Book 4)

Epic Fantasy

Soul Legacy: The Dweller Saga Duet

Soul Bound (Book 1)

Soul Child (Book 2)

The Ancient Realms Collection: Books 1-6

Grimdark Fantasy

GameLit

Reborn Online Book 1: Dungeon Worlds

Reborn Online Book 2: Dungeon Seeker

Reborn Online Book 3: Dungeon Master

Post Apocalypse

40 Days: Book 1 in the Atomic Fall Series

40 Weeks: Book 2 in the Atomic Fall Series

CPSIA information can be obtained
at www.ICGtesting.com
Printed in the USA
LVHW081413200522
719342LV00021B/559/J